OMEGA POINT

OMEGA POINT
an apocalyptic parable of spiritual transcendence for the new millennium

Angela Browne-Miller
and
Charles Klotsche

Metaterra Publications
Tiburon, California

Library of Congress Cataloguing in Publication Data

Browne-Miller, Angela, 1952 -
and
Klotsche, Charles, 1941 -

Omega Point: an apocalyptic parable of spiritual transcendence for the new millennium / Angela Browne-Miller and Charles Klotsche.

First Edition. Paperback.

ISBN 0-9645472-0-1

Library of Congress Catalog Card Number:
95-75809

1. fiction. 2. philosophy. 3. metaphysics. 4. occultism. 5. spirituality. 6. apocalypse. 7. ecology. I. Title. II. Subtitle.

OMEGA POINT

Illustrations, including Omega Point Symbol, by Angela Browne-Miller.
Cover Design by Angela Browne-Miller, Charles Klotsche,
Roger Shelly and Von Wall.
Typesetting by Leona Jamison.
Photo of authors, on back cover, by Swiftsilver Photo.

© 1995, Metaterra Publications
A Division of Metatek
c/o A. Browne-Miller, Ph.D., Editor-In Chief
98 Main Street, No. 315
Tiburon, CA 94920 U.S.A.

A Metaterra Book
All rights reserved.

No part of this book, except for brief review, may be reproduced, stored in a retrieval system, or transmitted in any form or by any means, electronic, mechanical, photocopying, microfilming, recording, or otherwise, without written permission from the publisher.

Printed in the United States of America.

OMEGA POINT

*is dedicated
to the spirits who have guided
its Creation.
You know who you are.*

CONTENTS

PART 1

UNEARTHING THE APOCALYPSE CONSPIRACY 3

chapters 1, 2, 3

PART 2

DISSOLVING THE AURIC VEIL 43

chapters 4, 5, 6

PART 3

QUESTING THE GAEA OMEGA 125

chapters 7, 8

PART 4

CONFRONTING THE ADVANCING VOID 177

chapters 9, 10, 11

PART 5

TRANSCENDING THE TIME WAVE 267

chapters 12, 13, Epilogue

Sed quando submoventa erit ignorantia; (when the time arrives for the removal of ignorance), the case shall be made more clear.

Nostradamus
March 1, 1555

Part 1

•

Unearthing the Apocalypse Conspiracy

1

A greasy brown fog had rolled in on them, darkening the otherwise crystalline autumn day to a sick hush. Feeling close to suffocation, her chest heaved in and out as she struggled to collect enough breath to answer their idiotic questions. The oil spill was spreading up and down the coast and had already washed onto this once pristine shore. The mazout. They called such an oil spill "mazoo" in this country.

She looked up at the highway. Several police cars, paddy wagons, a sedan labeled with the initials "F.B.I.," a jeep which said "Coast Guard" on the side door, and what looked like some National Guard trucks pulled up. Uniformed men emerged from the vehicles and streamed down the cliffs like robots, marching toward the devastated beach where she stood facing the press. The authorities would have to get through the ten-person-deep wall of protesters to reach her.

She glared defiantly into the television cameras and clutched the dead oil-covered egret to her breast. She could feel the filthy feathers of the bird rubbing against her skin where her shirt had torn open. She held the bird up to cover any parts of her chest that would not be considered acceptable on prime time television and to hide the secret symbol tattooed over her heart, above her left breast. The broken neck of the egret dangled over her elbow. Its lifeless eyes stared like darkened crystal balls prophesizing more of the same.

All the while, she was being watched on a wall-sized television screen by a group of finely dressed businessmen. They were seated around a mahogany table in a mahogany paneled penthouse board room on the top floor of a massive skyscraper. The lights had been dimmed for better viewing. The silver hair of the man in charge glistened in the iridescence radiating from the big screen. "Gentlemen, look, there she is. Note that she's wearing that green arm band worn by all the Earthcult people. She's about to speak. When she does, check out her unusually good looks, her television face. And listen closely. You will see what I mean."

The men in suits leaned forward with keen interest, awaiting the words of the oil-streaked woman whose torn shirt was revealing the curve of her left breast. A couple of the men noticed what looked like a tattoo on her breast, but the picture was too dark to see it clearly. Yet, the tattoo seemed an inconsequent detail. No comments were made about it.

Now it was raining black rain. The air was saturated with oil. Each drop of mist was so coated with the stuff that the television crews had to turn on their portable lights, the kind they usually reserved for night time on-the-scene broadcasting.

The police began dragging the protesters, all of whom were passively resisting, refusing to budge, across the oily sand. The police became increasingly clumsy and looked increasingly ridiculous as they slipped and soiled themselves in the oil, struggling to move the human wall. She held the egret tightly and watched, proud of her protesters and their green arm bands, and grateful that the mazoo had, ironically, become, at least for the moment, an ally of her Earthcult.

Now she was ready to speak. She straightened her posture and raised a hand to quiet the anxious media. She nodded her head toward the profile of the exceedingly large oil tanker, literally broken in two, which sat on the horizon as if it had been pasted there, looking far too big for the landscape it dominated. And then she looked into the cameras and explained:

"You are at the scene of the worst oil spill in history. Speaking for the hundreds of thousands of species who die and or suffer here today and all along these coasts in the coming weeks, we demand that Hibersol Corporation and its affiliates make immediately available 500 million dollars for emergency ocean and shore cleaning measures and endangered animal rescue and rehabilitation services."

Somebody from the press wanted more. "And what if your demands are not met? What does your organization plan to do?"

Another member of the media shouted, "Tell us how Earthcult will retaliate!"

She complied. After all, it was time to inform the public of the extent of their power-base: "Earthcult now has 130 million members on this planet, and countless more sympathizers. If each of our members donates just two or three dollars, and they *have* demonstrated time and again that they will indeed make such donations on a moment's notice, we'll have a sizable

Unearthing the Apocalypse Conspiracy

war chest with which to hire the legal force to sue Hibersol for punitive damages. This suit could cost Hibersol billions of dollars. So, I *guarantee* that Hibersol will be destroyed if it does not meet these and our other demands. But more than that, more than the reprisals Earthcult will take, the Earth herself will make Hibersol pay. In fact, *we will all pay. And this is certain.* Massive catastrophe is coming. Only a small proportion of Earth's human inhabitants will survive. Earthcult members intend to be among the few survivors. Those who join us will be protected and admitted to what the press calls 'the survivor territories,' the locations of which have been revealed to us by divine means."

The leader of the conference in the board room in New York was visibly excited. He pointed at the woman on the screen. "There, you see? See what I've been talking about? She said *survivor territories*. SURVIVOR TERRI-TORIES! She's doing the marketing for us! We will be selling the territories she's talking about. She creates the demand. We fuel this pent-up demand she creates with our own media campaign until the price of the supply goes sky high. And, of course, we control the supply by buying up the land — the survivor territories — in advance of their identification. She's out to convince them that massive, global, catastrophe is coming. That the Earth will make us all pay. Something like the sinking of Atlantis if you know that myth — or the Biblical apocalypse if you know the Bible — or the psychic triggering of all out nuclear war if you've been following any of the most recent 'new age' psychic stuff. She's been talking like this all over the world, causing riots, stopping major fuel shipments, blocking airports and so on. Public officials and corporate execs everywhere are trying to shut her up. But if they lock her up, put her away, her cause — this Earthcult thing — will get more coverage than it already does. The media is intrigued. We can buy some air time and we certainly will, but they're already giving us air time free. We're already on a roll and we've barely begun. Gentlemen, I ask you to sign the papers and make your deposits now. We formally initiate your involvement in this enterprise tonight. Escrow closes at midnight."

All the men nodded earnestly. They turned away from the screen and began discussing the agreement they were about to sign. The security guard at the door of the board room turned up the lights and dimmed the screen. The men could see the great potential for profit in this sort of investment based upon what was being regularly reported in the evening news. Let the media create the demand; let this group of investors meet it. What consumer wouldn't want to buy his or her way out of world-wide cataclysm? Who wouldn't put his or her last dime on the line for survival? There was big money to be made here. And, just in case global catastrophe was really on its way, the investors would have the most prime parcels of the survivor territories and accesses to them reserved for themselves.

One member of the group of investors was concerned. They might buy what they thought were survivor territories but later find that these were not the ones Earthcult had received word of in what it claimed was a secret and most occult communication with Earth herself. This gentleman's concerns were relieved by the silver-haired leader of the proceedings who explained that he already had a team of spies, led by his own key man, infiltrating Earthcult and working into high positions in that organization. These spies had already identified for him the precise locations and boundaries of many of Earthcult's survivor territories. And this key man had, in fact, already managed to become very close to the woman leading Earthcult, making him privy to many of her dearest secrets.

Meanwhile, on the beach, the struggle between the protesters and the uniformed men degenerated into a filthy squall of bodies. The media people turned away from the oil-stained woman holding the dead egret and raced toward the squall to capture the scene on camera. They were pulled right into the mess.

Seeing this as perhaps her only opportunity to evade arrest, to remain free to direct the strategy of Earthcult, she turned and raced down the beach. Her feet stomped through the small black waves that were lapping at the oil-smothered shore. The black waves were much too heavy to create the splash and sea-foam so typical of a clean sea. Instead, they formed a dark and eerie presence. With each wave, a message, a vague but ominous foreboding, was cast. She was still clutching the limp egret when she slipped and fell onto a pile of dead birds. They all had those same disturbing dark crystal eyes. She placed her egret atop the pile. Tears were steaming down her face, glistening like liquid diamonds against her oil-streaked skin. She reached into one of the pockets of her jeans and pulled out some crumpled papers. She glanced back at what had become a macabre riot, a sort of mud-wrestling event in which the mud was actually a major oil spill. Then she dropped the papers onto the pile of dead feathered bodies and set the pile ablaze with a lighter she found in another pocket. The oil fire picked up quickly despite the drizzle. She ran off, adeptly scrambling up through the boulders to a spot further down the highway.

Someone in a black van called to her. "Get in. Quick."

She squinted distrustingly into the blackened mist, not readily identifying the owner of the voice. She moved a bit closer. And then she looked relieved. "There you are, Dave. Thank God." She hopped in. "Don't go that way. Turn around. It's become a riot. But that's good. It let me get away. Otherwise I would have been surrounded and arrested. I'm wanted on at least forty charges now."

"O.K. You hide in back." He waved his head toward the back of the van. She did as he suggested. Then he looked back at her. "Are you hurt?"

"No, just filthy, thank you. And real stressed out. Nothing a little good sex can't cure."

He did not respond to her attempt at humor with even a faint smile. "Here, wipe yourself clean," he mumbled, throwing her a towel. "Get rid of the arm band. It's a sure giveaway. And, if you want to take off those filthy clothes you can use my running shorts and that t-shirt in the athletic bag back there. Then try to get some rest." He started the engine and turned the van around in order to drive away from the riot.

They drove in silence for what seemed like hours. Finally, when they came to an unlabeled dirt road, they slowed. The road was difficult to recognize in the dark. As he turned on to the road, Dave explained, "The house is up this road, in case you don't remember. . . It seems you're always brought in at night."

"Oh, come on, of course I remember it, Dave. How could I ever forget?" She sounded sentimental for a moment.

He did not pick up the mood. He stopped in front of the house. "Run in and clean up. Use that special soap by the sink. There's some bleach in there. It's not very ecological but you'd better use it on your hair. It's been stained real dark by the oil. What did you do, roll in it?"

"No, I slipped and fell in it just like everyone else out there."

"Well, change the color of your hair, O.K.? You'll have to put the same old clothes on, I mean mine. I don't have any other clothes here anymore and yours," he paused for a moment as their eyes met, "yours are so full of oil they're a dead giveaway."

"Dave," she wanted to talk about something else, he could tell. She reached out to touch his cheek.

He pushed her hand away. "Not now. There isn't time. Really. I'll put your bicycle in the station wagon and hide the van in the garage while you get ready."

"Dave." Resisting his rejection, she again reached out to touch him.

But he moved several feet away from her. "No, not now. Hurry! Go!"

It was not more than half an hour when she emerged from the building, her bleach-streaked hair dripping wet. He saw her coming and opened the door of the station wagon.

She hesitated. "Oh yes, we're not using the van. . . . You're right to switch cars, just in case someone saw you pick me up at the beach. . . . But what'd you do to the seat, Dave?"

"Cut it off."

"Why?" She was amused.

But Dave was quite serious. "You'll have to lie on the floor under it. The back seat of the wagon here folds down. The bike and some boxes will be on top of you. If they stop me, they'll never think to look for you under the stuff."

"Smart. Very smart. But will they really stop us?"

"Just a precaution, that's all."

"You were always good at taking precautions, Doctor Dave." Another attempt at humor. But it was lost on him.

She looked at him. Something new was in his mood. Something very resolute. Very different. A wall of some sort. He was cold, really cold now. But he looked the same as always. He even had on his favorite suit. And he wore his same old white doctor's coat over it.

"I'm saying that I'm rushing to the hospital to attend to a patient emergency if they stop me," he informed her unexpressively.

"Great cover, Dave. So original. The real you. Just pose as yourself. It's deceiving enough. Your image never changes." She searched his face for some explanation of his new and surprisingly distant behavior.

He just was not going to get personal. "Get in. I'll leave the seat back up a bit so you can breathe and I'll jam it down if it looks like I'm going to be stopped."

She did not get in. Her voice grew soft and a bit lusty. "Wish we could be doing something else tonight, Dave."

"Can't be. Oh, by the way, I can't take you all the way there, either."

She was unpleasantly surprised at this news. "What?"

"I can't. Bad plan. And I can't see you again."

"What?" She did not believe what she was hearing.

He gave her a rushed but matter-of-fact explanation. "You'll take me, my career, my whole family, down with you if I do. We've got to call it quits. Now."

She fought to hold back sudden tears.

As if he felt he'd been too rough, he took out his handkerchief and wiped some remaining oil off of her face. Then he stroked her hair tenderly. "Strange color. But you're still gorgeous. And good looks are too easy to identify. Use my hat. And my sunglasses." He looked at her almost longingly for just one moment. "I'll always love you. I'll always wish you could be next to me in bed. I'll always miss feeling you. You know that, don't you?"

"So now we're through? Just like that, Dave? It was only the other night we were still passionate lovers, grabbing at each other's bodies like there was no tomorrow. We spent all that wonderful time alone together. Our special 'trip' you called it. I thought you said you loved me, but I guess that's sort of a hollow thing for you to say. You didn't mean it at all. ... You're actually totally incapable of love, aren't you? Fine way to let me know, Dave. I wished I'd seen this side of you before I got so involved, before I shared my secrets with you."

Unmoved and cold again, Dave looked at his watch and patted her on the arm impersonally. "O.K. Let's go. Get in."

She shrugged, trying to hide her surprise and dismay, her pain, and climbed in. The top of the seat slammed down onto her. A bit like a coffin lid, she mused. They drove off.

"Can you hear me, Dave?"

"Yes, what?"

"Where are you dropping me?" she asked.

"Pelican harbor. Find some unsuspecting guy down there, one that has a nice yacht and'll let you hide out on it for awhile. Or get him to take you to some island for a bit. Or out to sea. Do whatever it takes."

"Do whatever? What's whatever Dave? Sex? Sex with any old person?"

"Yes, you're good at that. You did it with me, remember?"

"You were special, Dave. Meeting you changed everything for me. I finally fell in love. I even wanted to have your child! I still want it to be you, Dave."

"Can't be," was all he said.

They were silent for a long time. She lay under the seat, clutching her belly in despair.

It was just past dawn when he stopped in the parking lot of a yacht harbor. "Here we are," he announced flatly. He got out of the car and took out the bicycle. He looked around carefully and saw no one watching. Then he pulled up the seat back to let her out.

She went to the bike. "Looks O.K."

"I fixed it for you. I thought something like this might happen."

"You planned ahead to dump me?"

"I'm not dumping you, dear. Please don't see it that way. I just can't be part of this Earth stuff you're into. Not anymore. It's getting out of hand. Dangerous. I've got a family and all. Wife. Kids. A profession. A life."

"Yes, you have a family. This I know. I never wanted them hurt. And your family has an Earth, an Earth in the early throes of global disaster. Or don't you care about all this anymore? Or maybe you never really believed me about what's coming and what I hear from the Earth about where to go to survive? But it's true, Dave. I *know* you know this deep inside. I *know* you've come to feel the tension racing through the Earth. I've seen the realization in your eyes. I've seen the moment when you know it's not just rhetoric any more. When you really *feel* it. You *hear* it. It gets into your bones, your heart, your nervous system. It calls you. It drives you. It becomes you. It's instinct.... At least save your family, Dave. Let me help save your kids." She reached for him.

He pushed her away again in an effort to detach from all she had said. "Don't worry about me and my family. I'll decide what to do about them. I can get them out in time if I decide I believe in this stuff enough to do it. Just save *yourself*." He glanced at her hands, which were clutching at her abdomen, and looked away. He handed her a day pack. "There is $50,000 in here. Consider it a donation to the cause. Get away. Go into hiding. Get to the safe lands as soon as you can without being arrested. Make your way to your headquarters in Colorado maybe. *Save yourself*. Please. Please let me go now. Don't call me. Don't contact me in any way. I'll claim we've never met."

He turned, got back into the car, and drove off.

Fighting back a new wave of tears, she pretended to fix her bicycle as the first hints of crimson sunlight preceding the early morning began to spill over her freshly bleached hair. She knew she should hurry and realized that she might have to bicycle from pier to pier until she found a likely candidate, but she just could not get going. She decided to sit there and grapple with her pain for a few hours.

And so she did.

Somewhere else, in that soundproof board room, where the screen had been turned off and the lights turned up, the men were signing a final contract and large checks were exchanging hands. They had deliberated most all of the night. The man collecting the money was international real estate developer, Triad Framingham, their silver-haired chairman.

Although he was masterminding the shrewdest international development scheme in world history, he had absolutely no idea of its profoundly cosmic implications.

But I certainly did. And I had a slightly different agenda: I was more concerned with spiritual real estate than with the physical stuff you in the material plane call "land." I was more interested in opening access to higher dimensions of reality than controlling access to key parcels of "survivor territories" on Earth. And even I was in for some big surprises. Let me tell you about them . . . .

2

Hello. I may think I am the international real estate developer, Triad Framingham, but I am not. I have merely incarnated as this man. Most people do indeed refer to me as Triad. But I am not really of this Earth. I seek not self-glorification but the spreading of enlightenment, which is the ultimate purpose of all existence, all Creation, material and immaterial.

I am speaking to you now because the Omega Point draws near. You may elect to take what I say as fantasy, as entertaining fiction. Feel free to do so. You may want to skip what I am about to say here in this chapter and get right back to the story about the remarkable woman which I began telling you in the previous chapter. If you are of such a mind, if you feel the Truth I espouse to be either overbearing or trite, simply leaf past my short instructive narratives (which are to be found printed in italics and scattered throughout this book).

However, and with all due respect, my dear reader, I advise you to just try on for size the reality I depict. Allow yourself to suspend your disbelief for the duration of your reading of this manuscript, including my notes to you. Your survival depends upon your getting my message. Do not let suspicion, denial and fear close your mind. Attempt to embrace the knowledge I impart and then rise to the challenge of spiritual evolution in order to survive.

It is time to be prepared. You are standing upon the very fragile threshold of Omega. So many of your prophets have forewarned you. The coming years portend to be the most enlightening period in human history — for those open to enlightenment.

Many lessons have been and continue to be transmitted regarding what will happen to your Earth in the 21st Century and the thousand years of the new millennium — especially if a substantial portion of its inhabitants fail to reach into the higher dimensions — into higher levels of enlightenment. The consequences of such a failure would be, in a single word, catastrophic, at least for those of you remaining primarily attached to the physical plane. Your worst nightmares

— not only ecological disaster but apocalyptic visions of the end of the physical world — may materialize.

If you doubt that what I say is a possibility, note that your Earth has borne global cataclysm before. Your scientists are slowly uncovering evidence of such events. Your own authorities in mass destruction tell you that a comet having a nucleus of six miles in diameter and hitting Earth at 45,000 miles per hour can unleash a force far beyond that of an all-out nuclear war, killing everything in sight, sending tidal waves around the world, dispatching winds of at least 300 miles per hour, cluttering the atmosphere to gray darkness, and setting vast fires ablaze everywhere. Based on the discovery of an iridium-loaded layer of clay in the Earth's crust, scientists are now suggesting meteor or comet impact as the cause of the extinction of the dinosaurs some 65 million years ago, between your Cretaceous and Tertiary Periods. Although Earth is continuously showered with iridium dust from space, only a sudden meteor-comet impact could have brought so much iridium to Earth so rapidly, so much iridium as to load a layer of soil with it so densely.

Now, you may be thinking that this kind of thing cannot happen again. If so, you are quite incorrect. Your scientists are collecting evidence that such impacts from space have been responsible for several die-outs and global devastations during Earth's history: The Frasnian catastrophe of 367 million years ago in which meteors smashed into what is now Sweden and Canada and tidal waves devastated the globe's shallow water ecosystems; the Permian-Triassic mass extinction of 250 million years ago in which 90% of all sea dwelling creatures died out; the Turonian-Coniacian event of 90 million years ago when the oceans drowned virtually all the Earth's continents; the Cretaceous-Tertiary catastrophe of 65 million years ago which I described above; the Eocene-Oligocene event of 35 million years ago when winter covered the planet and the polar ice caps expanded; and, the mid-Miocene catastrophe of only 12 million years ago when the ice at the South Pole expanded and a large portion of all mammals died out.

And now your scientists have discovered the presence of a million or more meteorites in the asteroid belt beyond Mars, a belt with which Earth may one day intersect. Although they are smaller than the meteors which have hit Earth hard in the past and will most likely disintegrate when they pierce Earth's atmosphere, each of these meteorites that enters the Earth's atmosphere at a particularly sharp angle is capable of forming an explosion much larger than that of the atomic bomb dropped on Hiroshima. The potentially large number of fierce meteoric explosions threatened by this belt could wreak havoc on Earth.

Certainly the realities of catastrophic comet and meteor impacts are difficult to grasp. The times between such events seem so very great from your perspective. It is therefore easy to ignore the possibility of such a catastrophe in your lifetime. Let me remind you, however, that comets, meteors, and meteorites hurtling in from space are only one form of global catastrophe.

For example, massive volcanic eruption under one of your polar ice caps could lead to the shifting, fragmenting and melting of that ice cap, markedly raising sea levels and submerging the most populated portions of your existing land masses. Already now, your scientists are watching the effects of an active volcano under your South Pole. A layer of warm sludge is developing under the cap. Will the cap slip off of the pole? One portion of the polar cap appears to be cracking. Will it float away and melt? Will other large chunks of the ice cap follow? Could there be a polar shift, could the spinning top you call Earth tilt its axis in a new direction as a result of the massive movement of weight, in the form of ice and water, around the planet? The ensuing tidal and climactic catastrophes are actual possibilities, not fantasies. Right now, some of your ecologists are concerned about the depletion of the ozone layer over the polar caps. They envision a similar catastrophe, a breakup of the polar caps, emerging due to massive environmental and atmospheric damage caused by humans.

It is good to recognize and heed your truest prophets. We are forever reminded that entire continents can suddenly disappear and great civilizations can end from one day to the next. Life as you know it can end right now. It is best that you accept this.

I do not desire to elicit fear with this discussion, only awareness. Let me alert you, awake you. The notion of a forthcoming cataclysm is hardly a new idea. It was predicted for you by my very dear son, my ultimate manifestation, Nostradamus, who came to live with you on Earth under several different names at several times in your history. He placed the memory of Atlantis in intellectual history when he incarnated as your philosopher Plato. You chose to crucify him in one of his subsequent incarnations. He began formally predicting the ultimate and as yet unactuated cataclysms on Earth when he incarnated during your western 16th Century A.D. with close to the very name I gave him, Nostradamus.

It was to you, who are now poised at the time of the new millennium, to whom my son Nostradamus wanted most to speak. While he predicted events relevant to his contemporaries and to those in his near future, Nostradamus' most powerful messages were aimed at those of you inhabiting Earth in the present and upcoming era.

Over time, many have debated the coherence and significance of Nostradamus' prophesies. Yet, certainly, his writing foreshadowed the modern technologies, warfares and natural disasters (earthquakes, nuclear weapons, air flight, travel to the moon and beyond) developed well past his 16th Century lifetime. His comments foreshadowed numerous historical events that have indeed come to pass. Yet his prose was obscure and the time sequence of his encoded story seemingly erratic. It is thus very difficult for historians to identify his predictions with exact certainty. Your interpreters of Nostradamus are in the darkroom of the human mind, attempting to develop photonegatives of your own future taken hundreds of years ago. You simply do not yet have the adequate intellectual and spiritual technology to fully develop the picture. But I am here to help you gain that knowledge. The time has come for the removal of ignorance.

Bear in mind that Nostradamus was highly sought after by the ruling monarchs of his time on Earth. Note also that he wrote his messages, many of which predicted events perceived as being undesirable and even terrifying, in code in order to protect them and himself from destruction. Nostradamus eventually chose to burn most of his own notes and was willing to obscure what remained — he was willing to obscure his messages to protect them. In his own words, he was "... willing for the common good to enlarge myself in dark and abstruse sentences, declaring the future events, chiefly the most urgent and those which I foresaw ...." He was certain that he saw, via a mix of divine inspiration and occult astrological calculation, the world drawing nearer to its "anaragonic revolution."

This anaragonic (death-dealing) revolution is an image which has been stored throughout the universe. It is the essential story of death and rebirth. This story, this picture, this image, is the TRUTH. This Truth has been planted in your individual and collective minds for safekeeping. It is the Truth regarding the revolution of death in the material dimension. Death of your bodies, death of the spirits who cannot reach into the realm past their bodies, death to the material Earth as you perceive it.

You sense that you are living on the eve of destruction. You have known this for quite some time. But this commentary does not bespeak of doom, it seeks to inspire and instruct your travel to the realms of glory.

I do not remind you of Nostradamus' prophetic visions to generate mass panic. I seek to prompt you to rise to the higher enlightenment that is your birthright. For you have come to Earth to learn exactly what you need to know to rise to this vibration of spiritual expansion. This is the next step in the path of your evolution, should you choose to walk it. The imagery of "plague, famine, death by military hand" predicted by Nostradamus is your invitation to transcend. This is your opportunity to move beyond the dangerous confines of your daily material life, to rise to the challenge presented you by apocalyptic imagery.

I have incarnated on your Earth at this time in order to discover this opportunity along with you.

I should tell you something about my current incarnation. I have the normal human form, of course, as I have had during every one of my incarnations on Earth. I am 50-some years old in my present lifetime, of medium height, with *silver gray hair and an attractive body I keep relatively trim. I work as a multinational real estate developer and as a collector of hard assets. This involves substantial travel. My special insights support both my metaphysical and my business acumen. I mentioned earlier that I have access to the greatest secrets and answers to the greatest Mysteries of the universe. Although as this incarnate I do not become conscious of this access or of these secrets for many years, I somehow feel torn by the real, albeit subconscious, temptation to take advantage of my insider information. A vague sense of loneliness, depression and malaise overtakes me as a result of this indecipherable but haunting moral dilemma.*

I have been on Earth in many incarnations, throughout so many centuries, to await the fulfillment of my purpose here as Communicator of Evolution Toward Enlightenment. Now the time is at hand.

With the volumes of my Original Truth bastardized, hidden, diluted, destroyed, and with murderous forces seeking to destroy what remains of my mother document, my living breathing gospel, I now choose to encode my true message in what will appear to be fiction. I address you in modern story form — the stylized discourse of the novel — a novel aimed at translation onto the big screen — the form that best fits your times. Those who realize that there is a message contained herein will see beyond the story. Those who learn well the lessons I incorporate into this story in the subsequent chapters will be the survivors. Those who do not are doomed, as the final chapters illustrate so vividly.

I am sincere. You know this. Feel my heart. It is being carried to you by these words. What some of you know to be the "heart chakra" is actually the midpoint of all spiritual energy, the point of evolution where Earth is now poised, the height of the material third dimension. Let us connect here. At the heart.

Take my hand. I will tell you a story. I will lead you on a journey. A journey into Truth: the Truth about survival.

Ω

3

Occasionally, from among my many incarnate lifetimes, I select one in which I can rediscover who I am: that is, that I am Triad, the Communicator. I find the process of self-discovery reinvigorating at points during my trek through time and universes. It quickens the soul. Even old souls like a good rebirth once in a while. Having to realize that I am who I am from the standpoint of a mere mortal's perspective forces shock waves through my system. When I finally come to and realize that I am myself, an ancient immortal, it is as if I have risen into a blue sky from the depths of a black sea where I have been suffocating, drowning, gasping for air but finding only ice cold water filling my lungs. The relief is a vibrational ecstasy, one which speeds my mind and heart through time, backward and forward. It is then that I see all my selves concurrently and see that they are all one. It is kind of orgasmic on a spiritual level. And it clears the cobwebs out of my meta-mental attic. So I go for it when the spirit moves me.

Typically, what I do is I induce a general sort of spiritual amnesia during my pre-birth fetal stage. All conscious memories of my previous lives are thus blanked out. I am then born into a common personhood and proceed through my life cycle relatively unenlightened. Yet, I am driven by the energy and wisdom discreetly housed within my old soul, and I accomplish a great deal in the material world of that lifetime. I gain notoriety and earn a respectable fortune. I climb to a reasonable pinnacle of achievement for that era.

But then, in mid-life, I find myself grinding to an inevitable halt. No matter how successful I have become, I wake up each day increasingly lost and disconnected. I do not make contact with people when I speak to them. I am awkward and often have to force myself to speak, saying stilted and disingenuous things. I feel the creeping anxiety of low key malaise. I have times when I feel better again, like the person that I have become, but these times are generally unsatisfactory, insubstantial, and fleeting. I find myself incapable of love and yet hungry for it. I am alone a lot. I play a lot of solitaire. I am rather detached from my children. They are my progeny, my biological lifeline, but I am merely their parent by function and I take little joy in this. I realize that my heart is cut off from my soul, but I don't let myself think about this very much. My sexuality is fragmented. My energy is unfocused and I am isolated. I am suffocating, drowning in the black sea of my failing existence. Then, the stage is set.

Somewhere amidst that vague, numb turmoil, seeds of change sprout. At first I do not notice them. But then, something or someone happens to me, or I happen to something or someone, and the picture begins to piece together. The realization that I am looking for myself, for the truest meaning of my life, dawns upon me in waves. It is as if I see my reflection becoming clearer on a water's surface as its waves and ripples begin to still. But that drowning feeling lingers dangerously, motivating me to continue reaching beyond, to continue seeking sky. Seeking survival. Spiritual survival.

So it was with the particular lifetime that I had on Earth late in its twentieth century, western Earth time. I hit my fifties in a state of spiritual amnesia. I did not know that it was I, my very self, who had induced this amnesia prior to my birth. I also did not know that I had time-dated this particular case of amnesia to begin dissolving fifty some years after its induction. I did not know that I was in this lifetime to amplify the increasingly urgent message of Nostradamus, and to undergo the process of revelation that humans who are to survive the coming apocalypse must undergo. I was here for a reason, I was here to communicate, but had yet to have that realization come full force into my consciousness.

Ω

I, as Triad Framingham, hit mid-life and entered a dull sort of angst. Sure, my work was exciting and I had achieved some satisfying degree of notoriety, but emotionally, things had ground to a halt. There was a hole, a gap in my life. I worked hard to drown out the creeping questions that grabbed at me from the depths of my heart: Was there really any meaning to my life? To my achievements? To my wealth? Was I done? Was I ready to die? Had it all been for naught?

When I wasn't in board meetings or on business trips, I lived on and ran my international business ventures from my yacht. Alone. Emotionally isolated despite the fact that there were people everywhere. Contacts galore. Great projects underway. Why not? I was a successful entrepreneur and real estate developer, not a warm and loving person.

Generally successful anyway. The savings and loan institutions had broken the backs of many of the likes of me and I was facing the fact that even I was not immune to the demoralizing effects of major business disaster. I had ridden the financial roller coaster and landed on the down side. But I had managed to tuck quite a bit of money away and I was already working on a new plan. I was going to make a comeback by fueling a demand for land, land that my investors and I were already buying up before fueling that very demand. I felt quite smug about it. The plan went as follows:

- Led by me, a secret group of investors would generate a global media campaign. Our media campaign, buttressed by the evening news, especially by its coverage of the negative prognostications made by the Earthcult organization, would brainwash the public into believing in the coming of an apocalypse of global proportions. The public would be warned about a series of catastrophes including three cataclysmic shifts in the Earth's axis. Expectations of great death and destruction would be generated.

- The public would be told that after the first and unavoidable realignment of the Earth's axis, most of the North American continent would be gone. The states of California and Nevada would virtually disappear, leaving a few small islands as their legacy. While some inland parts of Washington and Oregon would survive, the west side of the Rocky Mountain Range and its southern extensions would be the new west coast of what had been North America, the new North American coast line on the Pacific Ocean.

- The public, including all types of investment groups, would come to believe that so-called *survivor territories* were the only places where personal and financial survival could be ensured, and that these were the places to be during and following the upcoming disasters. What the public would not know is that my secret investors and I would already own all access routes to the important parcels and the key tracts of land in these territories. And, they would not be informed that even these pieces of land stood a chance of complete destruction and sinking. (I hadn't even told my investors of this last point. But, of course, why would I? I did not *really expect* this cataclysm to happen — at least I didn't think that I did.)

- Our campaign would describe the city of Denver's front mountain range as a key survivor territory. The newer Rocky Mountain International Airport would be one of the few intact facilities on the down-sized continent which could still service international flights. This is because, as I indicated earlier, the west coast, the east coast, and much of the midwest of North America would be underwater.

- My group of investors would learn from me that the second polar shift would make the Denver area accessible from b*oth* the Pacific *and* the Atlantic Oceans, creating fabulous opportunities for the development of deep water ports and distribution centers serving what would be left of the broken up North American Continent, as much of the old Interstate Highway and railway Systems would become non-operative.

- The commodities markets of New York and Chicago would relocate to the high ground of the Rockies. Although economic chaos would follow each polar shift, exorbitant profits would be made in these transitional periods. These would be fabulous opportunities for sophisticated traders as most of the currencies of the world would fold into hard assets — would have to be backed by hard assets — similar to the United States currency when it was backed by gold.

- Colorado Springs would be the site of the relocated military and Pentagon activities as well as of the space program as the regions containing their old sites — all of Washington D.C., all of Florida, and, of course, the low level region including Houston, Texas — would be underwater. The government, being somewhat forewarned of the cataclysm, would have, prior to even the first polar shift, evacuated its central and key operations to the Airforce Academy and surrounding military bases in Colorado. By the second polar shift, missile and space craft launch sites would be established on the West Coast of the Rockies.

- I would also inform my investors that following the third polar shift, large portions of Australia, especially the massive outback area with its vast, abundant and cheap sheep ranch land, would flourish. Much of Australia's coastal and desert areas would be destroyed; however, the continent of Australia would be the only continent on Earth which had existed above water prior to the polar shifts to stay largely intact during these shifts. The polar shift would change the basic compass directions relative to the land, shifting wind patterns around the globe, creating new areas of moisture in Australia, making her climate more temperate.

- Siberia would offer a similar play — cheap, abundant land with a lot of mineral resources. With the positive climate change resulting from the polar shifts, the area would become wonderfully livable. As China would drop and Russia would rise, a shallow level of water would cover the area, which would be pumped out in massive land reclamation efforts (not unlike those of a smaller scale which were once conducted in Holland) to render rice growing lands (similar to those now developed for such a purpose in East Asia).

- The Greek island of Santorini would rise above the water line and gain dry land mass. It would be the next Switzerland of the world — where the quiet money would go. Hong Kong, New York, London, Geneva would be in the heavy earthquake and volcanic activity zones or sink entirely underwater. Many of the remaining financial capitals with their high-rise glass buildings would be devastated by the beyond-gale-force winds accompanying the polar shifts. Land prices on Santorini would, within a few years after the first polar shift, exceed those of Hong Kong before the shift. The largest concentration of wealth ever known to mankind would accumulate on Santorini — where, again, the streets of the most Royal City of Atlantis would be paved with gold.

- And, of course, the west end of the mythical continent of Atlantis would resurface in stages, more with each shift, initially appearing in the Caribbean Sea, an area where many portions of Atlantis exist just below the surface (according to pre-pole shift mystics, certain scholars and some scientists). Only after the third polar shift would the oceans drop and Atlantis again rise to her full magnificence. The value of underwater real estate would, of course, take on new dimensions as major investors and even the public became aware of this resurfacing process.

A great plan. In fact, I had already begun to implement it, entering into clandestine deals with my growing team of secret investors, the members of which represented the international banking community, the top global venture capitalists, and the flight money of some of the world's wealthiest who I had either actually convinced of the reality of the forthcoming cataclysm or at least of the astounding market opportunity it presented.

This was all very exciting. I knew my plan would pay off in a big way. I wished to have someone to share all this with, but I figured that I would probably remain alone. I guessed that I had really been alone all along, it was just that I was more aware of it now. Women, they had come and gone, in and out of my bed and in and out of my life. Some of my men friends stayed on over time, but the connections did not run deep. I let in little in the way of emotionally rich human engagement.

But then, a woman came along. Actually, I practically tripped over her on one of my pre-dawn walks. I had been unable to sleep, as usual. After the close of my successful meeting with my newest team of survivor territory investors, I had rushed to my yacht in the early hours of the morning to work on the land acquisitions I was in the middle of and to plan my future land buying trips. Because I was too stimulated to think or to sleep, I went out to walk off the excitement. I found her looking quite disheveled, her hair streaked and unbelievably wild, dressed in frayed athletic shorts and an old t-shirt, trying to fix her bicycle tire in the harbor parking lot. As soon as I offered to help her, I wished that I hadn't.

"Hi. Want some help? I have a better patch kit than that."

She turned, examined me warily, and then apparently decided that I was not worthy of her attention. "No. Thanks, I've done this before, I'll be able to handle it."

I was quite happy to accommodate her and leave her alone. She looked as if she'd been crying. I could see she was in deep emotional pain. I did not feel at all curious as to why.

She said nothing else, so I figured, having done my civic duty and offered help, I'd leave. She seemed to have remembered some trappings of civility and thanked me as I wandered away down the pier to my yacht to try to take a much needed nap.

I returned to my yacht and turned on the radio, which was already set at my favorite station, for some classical music to lull me to sleep in my cozy deck chair. Instead, I was blasted with a "we interrupt this programming" report — one regarding recent international tensions: "In an unprecedented move, the United Nations petitioned the United States to provide full force military backup in support of its efforts to stem the threat of a nuclear attack aimed at the new European Union by the newly confirmed Middle Eastern Military Alliance. Despite protests from Congress, the President has agreed and will — "

I turned off the radio, leaned back in my seat, and went to sleep to forget the world's mounting anxiety even though I was going to make millions because of it — nuclear threats and accompanying fears of spontaneous all-out global nuclear war, chains of earthquakes, floods, increasingly serious environmental disasters, and whatever else made the news. Anything that would feed global panic would be of great value to me. Twenty minutes later, I heard a voice interrupt my restful solace.

"Hello?"

I looked to the starboard walkway and there she was, grease on her hands and one hand bleeding. Now what?

"Well, I should have taken some help. I really blew it and now I'm cut. Wounded in action. I looked around for help and I saw you sitting out here. Can I wash off the blood and borrow a bandaid? That is if your offer to help out still holds."

She wasn't exactly what I needed right then. I had been loving my solace. Still, what could I do? I said, "Sure. Hop on and I'll get you to the galley."

She did and I did. She really had cut herself and the cut was filthy. "You better clean that out." I gave her some half-hearted advice.

"Ugh." She looked at her hand with dismay.

"Here, let me. Sit down. I'm good at this." Why did I offer to do it? I chastised myself as I reached for her hand.

"Ow! That hurts," she scolded.

"There's no other way. Don't look if you don't like it."

"I said it hurt, not that I couldn't stand looking at it."

I didn't answer her. Maybe we could get the whole thing over with if we stopped talking. Then I could get her out of there. After all, I had work to do, identifying and pricing more real estate around the world. I reached over and turned on the radio. Hoping to avoid further conversation, I set the volume rather high. My favorite station was, fortunately, back to playing music. Then I returned to cleaning out her wound.

But she spoke right over the music. "What's your name? Ow, do we have to clean that part out? Oh, damn. Ow. What's your name?"

Oh great, I said to myself: Now I have to talk to her. Serves me right for being a good citizen. Look what I get. "Triad," I answered aloud.

She laughed. She laughed at my name. "Some name. Real California. Where'd you get it?"

"Winston Triad Framingham. Triad is easier to use than the other names and less pretentious."

"You think so, do you? Who on Earth named you that?"

"Uh, parents." Obviously, I said inwardly. Is she trying to make real conversation? Or is she just an empty-headed talker?

"What kind of parents would use Triad for a middle name?"

"I don't know. I think my grandfather suggested it. I come from a literary family." It really wasn't any of her business.

"Educated elites?"

"Didn't say that. ... So how is it. Is it better?" Maybe she would leave now.

"You're not much of a conversationalist ... the hermit type? Looks like you play a lot of solitaire." She glanced over at my unfinished card game.

I looked at her. What an imposition. Especially now when I had work to do. But a decent looking lady underneath that weird colored uncombed hair. Should I offer her a comb to fix it a bit? No. ... Nice eyes. Actually, beautiful eyes. Had I seen those eyes somewhere before? For some reason, they looked familiar. But I'd never forget that wild hair. And it was not at all familiar. No, I hadn't seen her anywhere before. But the eyes were definitely magnetic. I couldn't quite define their color. Green, blue, something else? I had to work not to stare at them. I told myself: Maybe I should try to say something. Talk for a while. It'll be over soon. Unless I get stuck fixing her bicycle. Oh god. But I asked, "Would you like a drink?"

"A kiss."

"A *what*?" She surprised me with that one.

"A kiss. Oh never mind. I don't know what I meant. Have any mineral water?"

"Sure. Just a sec." Now what? What did she want? She wasn't my type of chick. Not at all. Nice body though. Tall. Lean. Tan. I went to get the drink, talking silently to myself all the while: But maybe, maybe, I should check it out. After all, it's here, it came easy, it's free. Kinda fell into my lap. Haven't had much lately anyway.

I handed her the drink and kissed her quickly on the cheek.

"You did hear me."

"Yes I did." I admitted it.

"Well, that's not the kind I meant," she replied, running a hand through her hair to move it out of her eyes.

I looked at the water. "Kind of what?" I played dumb.

"Kiss."

This was all somewhat troubling to me. I wasn't looking for a woman. Didn't really want one right now. Not much. Not a real one. And, not knowing that I was an interplanetary seedling, I didn't have much perspective on this fortuitous turn of events.

I had been quiet for a while and realized that she was staring at me. I thought I had better say something. So I said something irrelevant. "So, how's your hand?"

Just then, the music pouring out of my radio was interrupted for a special news broadcast. The President was making an announcement to the press: "Given the severe threat of nuclear attack, not only upon Europe but upon North America as well, I am taking immediate action as Commander in Chief. I have been informed by Congressional leaders that Congress has now agreed to vote unanimous support of this emergency measure within the next 60 minutes. I nevertheless must remind the citizens of this great nation that there are a number of other, equally pressing, matters facing us at this time. This severe nuclear threat must not distract us from attending, with no time lost, to the unprecedented environmental disaster, the largest oil spill in world history, which threatens to wipe out all — "

She reached out defiantly and turned off my radio. "I can't listen to that stuff. If you don't want to kiss me just say so. Or tell me to go. It's O.K. I don't know why I said that anyway, except that you are sort of sexy. I mean, don't take that the wrong way, I don't mean anything by it. You aren't at all my type. Nothing like my, uh, like the guy I used to go out with. You have the demeanor of a silver fox sort of playboy, the kind who's been going through women like there's no tomorrow for decades. But, underneath it all, almost hidden by trivia and denial but not quite, you have a look in your very blue eyes. I haven't seen it for a long time." She gazed at me.

I gazed back. Those eyes of hers. Magnetic. Again, I felt as if I knew them. Why? I wanted to break the gaze because I felt awkward. She was looking into me too deeply. And I, I was looking into her just deeply enough to see that she was running from a broken heart. I wondered what kind of guy would get involved with her, let alone dump her. None of my business. I had to say something to change the subject. "So can I get you another glass?"

"I already have a glass, but what about more mineral water?" She was studying my eyes.

I couldn't have known what she saw in my eyes. I didn't see it myself. I didn't know who I was then. I didn't know who she was either. I poured her more water. When I handed her the glass, I touched her hand, quite accidentally. It felt nice to me. Just nice. I liked her skin. Maybe I could take her to bed. I was, after all, basically an animal. Basic priorities. Food, shelter, sex. Sometimes in the reverse order.

"Thanks. So why are you Triad?" She took a sip.

"Just a name."

"Sounds sort of intergalactic or something. Do you know what I mean?" she asked.

"No, well yes, but ... you're probably influenced by all that new age stuff, which I myself don't follow much." I really didn't know what she meant.

"Well, I don't follow it much either, but it's been around for years now, decades even. You can't help but pick it up. Kinda like you picked me up."

"I didn't." I was sure of that much. At least I thought I was.

"You did. At least on some plane, in some dimension somewhere."

She was probably getting at some sort of Original Truth, but I didn't know what it was. Not yet.

The woman continued. "What I'm trying to say is that I'm interested in you. You're intriguing. There's a funny feeling about you. I'm very attracted to you."

This was a lot for me to swallow. At least in one gulp. I wasn't so sure I wanted anymore of this. Wasn't it time for her to go?

I decided to speak. "So how's your hand? Better?" I sounded idiotic. I was incapable of bridging the gap between the profane and the universal. Or of even getting her into bed.

Turns out she was willing to take the lead. "Would you make love with me?"

This is where some knowledge of who I really was would have helped. I could have understood the meaning of this contact. "So that's what you want." I sounded flat and idiotic. I waited a moment. Now even she seemed tongue tied. "So how's your hand?" I said.

"Stop asking me that, please. Can't you say something real? Do you want me or not?"

"Yes." Why not?

"So?" she said.

"So what?" This wasn't going well. I wasn't handling this right.

"I mean do you want me in the here and now or in the next lifetime? I suppose next lifetime is O.K. We'll meet again. I'll have a broken down flying car and you'll offer to help fix it. That is if we meet forward in time. In the future instead of the past. Let's make a date. ... Do I talk too much?"

"Come with me." Maybe I could stop her incessant talking by taking her to bed. She sounded a little wacky, but, I said to myself, here goes. I took her hand and led her down into the back stateroom. I pulled her down to the bed. She fell down onto the bed willingly, but seemed quite surprised. I guessed that she had been joking. I still did not recognize her as the oil-covered woman I had had my partners watch on the big screen just the night before. I had no idea as to what was about to happen, or to begin happening. How could I know? I was entirely unaware of the purpose of this particular incarnation of mine. But now I wanted to be naked with her in bed. Very naked.

We kissed. At first it was very mechanical. She seemed a bit frozen. Maybe a little shocked. I had called her bluff. And I, I wasn't so certain that I wanted to do this. What if I couldn't perform or had my orgasm too soon or something? Oh, God, that worry again. I should have skipped this whole affair. Hmmm. I began caressing her. I was surprised to find that for all her forwardness, she was somewhat hesitant. Maybe it was that state of shock that I said she seemed to be in. I figured she was wishing she was with some other guy, maybe the guy that made her cry. But I just continued kissing her and holding her, expecting her to loosen up.

Looking back, I see that her shock was a sort of material plane, third dimensional type of crisis. Mind versus body stuff. You can't have this crisis without a physical body.

Let me explain from the vantage point of my higher self: The bodies of what I like to call higher third dimensional beings are split into two: the physical and the spiritual. The fate of humans, the higher third dimensional beings to whom I refer, is to experience, and, hopefully, to learn from, this split. If they learn enough, they can drop the body thing and move on to the fourth — the fourth dimension. There, past the confines of the physical body, they can vibrate at a much higher level. Some humans are actually more advanced, fourth and even higher dimensional beings who have willingly incarnated down the vibrational spectrum. They incarnate as flesh and blood humans for a purpose. Problem is, in this third dimensional, material, level of spiritual awareness, we have to deal with mind-body conflicts, especially where bodily sickness, aging and that old favorite, physical sex, are involved. I myself have, time and again, struggled with this last one. It is a good struggle. It lets me bump up against the door beyond the material from within the material.

And that's what we were dealing with there on the bed. Of course, I didn't quite realize it yet.

Suddenly now, I wanted her so intensely that I didn't recognize myself. I looked at her. She still seemed rather shocked at the reality of what we were doing. I decided not to discuss this with her. Instead, I pulled her T-shirt off over her head. She didn't move. She just let me. She did not have a bra on. I wasn't surprised. I began kissing her breasts. Slowly, she warmed up. Her skin felt wonderful. She felt hesitant. Hesitant, but very wonderful.

"Oh."

"O.K.?" I thought I'd ask if she was all right about this.

"Yeah." She was quiet again for a moment and then added, "Feels good. Really good. Mmmmm." She relaxed and ran her hands through my hair. I continued kissing her breasts. Then I noticed that there was some kind of strange symbol — Greek or something — tattooed above her left breast. I ran my fingers over it. She stiffened a up bit as I did, so I left it alone even though I was intrigued, as the women I typically took to bed were not the type to have tattoos. We went back to what we had been doing. Whatever shock or conflict this woman had been feeling when I called her bluff and took her to my bed seemed to have been resolved.

Those mind body conflicts happen when your mind wants one thing and your body wants another. Or when the body wants something and the mind is not there yet. Or vice versa. It is a fascinating polarization of energy. For example, someone such as this lady my incarnated self was in bed with might think she wants physical sex right then, but might not be able to get her body to get into the spirit as rapidly as she thinks she can.

This was all right with even the incarnated me. I was willing to take it slowly.

Higher third dimensional beings are advanced enough to have some awareness of their minds (and in some cases, even of their souls), but are not advanced enough to escape the demands of having a physical body (you know — the demands of surviving — eating, excreting, reproducing ...).

Not that all these demands are all so tedious. We moved into a more fluid and passionate mode, rolling and kissing, licking and touching each other everywhere. We were being surprisingly tender with each other in our foreplay, as if we were making love instead of just having sex. But then, if I remember correctly, (which I assume I always do), she *had* asked if I, the amnesic personhood that I was, would *make love* with her.

So I proceeded to make love with a long sort of foreplay. I found this a somewhat more emotional process than I had expected. Much more emotional, actually.

Looking back, I see that those moments there in bed with her were some of the richest points of that entire physical incarnation. Something very touching and deep was happening. But I, being still in the throes of my spiritual amnesia, did not quite get the full force of the experience. Looking back more closely, I also see that she seemed relatively aware (compared to me) of the meaning of our contact — the intercourse of our souls — but was not going to let on what it was that she sensed — yet.

Even that me, the me who did not understand what it meant to be Triad, could see it in her face. I looked into her eyes. "Your eyes are incredible. I love watching your eyes. You're very sensitive aren't you?" I looked at her. For a moment, I saw right through time. A bolt of energy — a chill or something — shot up my spine. Her eyes looked suddenly fluid, like water. I thought, for a fleeting second, that I saw myself, and far more than the self I knew myself to be, reflected in them. I was uncomfortable with that rather enormous feeling and went back to my more basic and familiar third-dimensional-man-having-sex sense of reality. I yanked the energy back down my spine to my genitals. This was the first time during this incarnation that I consciously moved my sexual energy along my spine. I surprised myself.

Little did I know, my spiritual amnesia was dissolving, just a bit, around the edges. I was coming into contact with a higher sort of supra-sex energy. Several of your spiritual leaders on Earth, such as your Christ and your Buddha, have mastered entry into the higher vibrational realms of cosmic sexuality. They, however, did not require the material experience of physical sex to gain access. But, for most humans, physical sexuality is the surest route to spiritual ecstasy, if they manage to recognize it as a path. Sexual passion and love are hints of more esoteric experiences, touches of the mystical.

She talked to me in the here and now of my amnesic material plane existence. "I love you," she said.

Oh great. One of those women. Can't do it without saying that. Why can't I just find a simple boat chick who doesn't want any deep involvement? It'd be easier.

"Don't listen to anything I say, O.K.?"

"O.K." Sure, I felt I had been let off the hook. I was relieved, but I admitted quietly to myself that I was also disappointed.

"I love you. I love you."

I could tell she meant it. Funny thing is, I sort of felt the same way, just a little, but I could keep it in check. And I could definitely refrain from saying it.

What I could not keep in check was the building sexual tension I was feeling. Enough already. Enough foreplay. I'd better get on with this. I slid onto her, (a little too abruptly I think), and, well, suddenly, she was writhing under me, totally into the passion of it all, and she was just too much and I ejaculated all over her soft belly. Oh no, this again.

She wanted more, I could see the hunger in her eyes. But she calmed down eventually. Once her soul regained power over her flesh, she was entirely comfortable with it. She seemed to do something nice with the desire, with the tension. She glowed all over.

Fourth and even higher dimensional beings, many of whom have chosen to incarnate to witness the changes on Earth at the time of the new millennium, make such adjustments with ease. They have evolved past the point of infra-sex, low vibrational animal sex, to another place.

I, of course, did not realize that *both* she and I were visiting from a far higher dimension. The highest. She realized it, in a way. But I didn't know I knew anything at all about dimensions. So I did not. I had just ejaculated prematurely, that's all. I was not entirely happy with myself, but I said nothing.

We took a walk along the water. For some reason, before we left, she tucked her strange hair up into an ugly cap she had brought and put on her oversized sunglasses. She looked even stranger without that weird hair showing. I figured she wanted to go incognito. Anyway, we were close, holding hands, talking. She still glowed.

"Of course I have a name."

Oh, damn it. I felt like a real cad. With all that time spent on my name, I had never asked what her name was. I had no idea how much I would wish that I had spent much more time than I did on her name, later. Later, after the disaster.

"I was waiting for you to tell me." I tried to cover up my lack of social grace.

"No. You just forgot to ask me. It wasn't important to you right then."

She was right. I admitted it sheepishly, "Yeah."

"But names, they're just bookmarks. Index markers. Whatever. Anyway, you do know who I am." She seemed to think so. She stopped walking and looked me in the eye.

I looked back. "So who are you? What's your name?" I asked.

She turned and walked on. I followed and caught up. She answered me, "That's not exactly what I meant. But the name's Sheeyah."

"Sheeyah? Now it's my turn. Sounds primitive. Or ancient or something. Maybe Egyptian." I didn't know I knew anything about Egypt, or much else of the ancient, but I wanted to show some interest. Actually, I was interested. As soon as she said her name, I felt as if someone had nudged me out of a deep sleep. I woke up for a moment, became more aware, more alert, and then reverted right back to my mental doze. I very much enjoy watching myself emerge from incarnate amnesias in fits and starts. "It's not your real name is it?" I asked.

Alarmed, on alert, for some reason, she studied me cautiously for a moment. Then she relaxed. I wondered what that was about but didn't ask. She proceeded to answer my question regarding her name. "Well, it's not the name my parents gave me. But, ever since I was a little girl, I've had these very strange, very real, dreams, night and even day dreams, about a Nature spirit with some super-human powers. She talked to me. She taught me to hear the Earth speaking. She still talks to me. She says she *is* me. That I am Sheeyah.... You look like you think I'm way out there."

I certainly was thinking that. Who am I getting mixed up with? I wondered. Yet, I was intrigued. She had captured my interest. And anyway I wanted very much to get her back into my bed. To do more. To get deep inside her. To feel her writhing.

"Hello Sheeyah. Meet Triad." I said. This sounded like a line from an old mythical tale, or something from a comic book, I wasn't certain which.

At that moment, we rounded the corner onto a bridge over a small ocean side saline lake. Looking down into the water, we came face to face with our reflections, I, the image of the silver fox, and she, the image of the wild woman incognito. But I could see that we were more than just our physical appearances. And we looked so right together.

Then, for just a moment, my breath caught in my lungs. I was startled. Had I seen us before? Together before? And had I seen myself — before? The questions flitted through my mind as I turned to embrace her. She was ready for this and she kissed me. Suddenly, I wanted to throw her to the ground and ravage her. Jump her bones. I repressed this urge, of course.

She was in some other mood. "I always look for reflections. They say so much. Whenever I am lost, I look for my face in the smooth surface of a body of water. Usually it's a special body of water, my favorite, an alpine lake at a high altitude where the air is clear and the water still pure, Crystal Mirror Lake. It's a very magical spot, a sort of window to other realities — other dimensions. But sometimes it's some other water body. I know some good ones." She stopped herself and looked deep into my eyes. "I love you. So much." She said it again. I thought to myself that she had said it to me before, long long ago. And then I thought to myself that I had just had a ridiculous thought.

But, right then, I knew we she wasn't a passing fling. I knew we were going to stay connected. Somehow. In some way. Didn't know exactly how. But I knew that I would always remember the startling impact that the sight of our reflections had made upon my heart — or was it my soul? I didn't know. I couldn't quite figure it out. Not then.

"I don't have the same problem as you," she said.

Problem? I had no problems. Other than the entire middle age malaise that was swallowing me up. And occasional early ejaculation.

"My problem," she continued, (not hearing my thoughts I assumed), "is that I have known who I am, had some idea of who I am, since early childhood, but I've never known quite what to do about it. I mean, do I just go on living a normal everyday life with all this knowledge about what is really going on here? So I go through life consciously being less than who I am. You, on the other hand, *you haven't yet realized who you really are*. Right now, you don't even have a clue. Well, maybe I'm your clue. So, what I'm getting at is that, strangely enough, we come from opposite ends of the spectrum regarding the problem, but its effects are similar. You too go through life being less than who you really are."

"I haven't yet realized who I am?" I thought I'd play along for a moment. She was definitely younger than I was, so I attributed this kind of talk to her stage of life.

"No you haven't." She sounded so sure of herself.

The tone of my voice changed. "Yes I have. I'm not having any identity problems. And I've been quite successful." Enough playing. I really didn't want to play. She was getting too close to my middle-age limbo, striking some kind of tender nerve I didn't know I had. "I know who I am. I'm Triad."

"Right, but who's Triad?"

"So how's your hand?" I changed the subject.

"Back to that again. You like it here in the material plane? The third dimension? Enough trivia for you? Low enough vibration? Is it empty enough here in the chasm?"

I shrugged. "Chasm? You lost me. All of it lost me."

"In the chasm between pure mind and plane body."

This woman was trying to tell me, her amnesic lover, that the chasm between mind and body goes with the territory, at least for humans. It is part of the higher end, the human end, of the third dimension of spiritual existence. She was trying to ask me if I was happy with my visit from the higher dimensions back into the third, where the mind-body chasm was a given.

Sure enough, she went on. "You know, most rocks and inorganic forms have no sentience, no minds, right? Plants and animals have something more than that. But they don't really feel that they have it. Most of them haven't developed their awareness, their minds enough to separate them from their bodies. But we, as humans, can think about thinking, are aware of being, aware of awareness. We can tell that we have minds *and* bodies. We are living at a higher spiritual vibration — we vibrate at a different level, but most of us are still pretty tied to the third dimension just like animals, plants and rocks."

I, the incarnated Triad, was not especially interested in these concepts. They all sounded like an elaborate form of new age babble. Still, I thought to myself, O.K. If she is going to go on and on about this stuff, I'll join in. She's worth it. ... But I wasn't certain that I agreed with her. "You think that just because we're more intellectual than animals we are more spiritual? I don't know if there is a connection at all. And quite frankly, I think this spirituality stuff is mostly marketing hype. Sells new age tapes and little bead-covered leather bags and things."

"Good Triad. Now at least we're talking about it. That's a start. Yes, I believe there is a connection between the intellect and the soul. Most people think of the spirit as separate from the mind, as running on a different continuum. Well, this is because they don't see the higher purpose of all evolution."

Oh well, so Sheeyah was a thinker, I thought to myself, a thinker and not some easy bimbo. I wondered whether to be impressed by her intellect or daunted by it. I was aware that I didn't know enough to determine whether it was intelligence or babble she was feeding me.

She was still talking: "Triad, it seems to me that the mind stretches to evolve. As it reaches the limits of what the five senses can feed it, the mind must conceptualize what's beyond. We can't possibly perceive everything that exists in the Cosmos through our basic sense organs. But we know there's more. We already admit that dogs hear sounds we can't, migratory birds have a sense of direction we don't, and that infrared cameras see things we can't and can differentiate between the dead and the living. Our sense organs just see, hear, taste, smell, touch, just perceive, a narrow band, a small bit, of reality. When something is out of range of our senses, we are quite ready to say that it does not exist, or that it has ceased to exist or died. But it hasn't. It is just vibrating at a different frequency, or taking form in a lower or higher dimension than our senses can detect."

Enough already. My interest was waning. I had other things on my mind.

"Is this more exciting than getting back into bed?"

Sheeyah chuckled and responded, "If you use your imagination, you can reach beyond the limits of your basic senses. There, you'll find the key to your enlightenment. And yes, Triad, it *is* more exciting. Much more exciting than being stuck in the chasm between mind and body. But I'll settle for the bed stuff if it's all you think you want." She looked at me and laughed. "At least we connect that way."

She was getting close. What she was trying to do for the amnesic me was remind me that there are several spiritual dimensions of reality, hoping that perhaps I would realize that I was a visitor from a higher one. Up in the fourth dimension and beyond, where we aren't stuck with bodies, there is no mind-body split. No chasm of tension between the material versus immaterial realities. Humans, although vibrating at a material level, experience a special awareness — one which is showing us there is more than, but not liberating us from, physical reality. So humans are caught in the chasm they create. Things are easier at a lower vibrational level of the material plane. When we take the form of plants and animals, we do not create and are thus are not caught in the chasm. At this lower level, we cannot perceive ourselves perceiving, we cannot consciously delineate our minds, our wills, our souls, from our bodies. At the very lowest vibrational levels we are not even living things, we are rocks and minerals, and none of this even seems to be an issue. Of course, what Sheeyah did not realize is that you will find spiritual beings from many of the higher dimensions reincarnated by choice — at all, even the lowest, vibrational levels. Some very wise souls are here taking the form of redwood trees and boulders.

Sheeyah was talking to me as if I knew what she meant. And, strangely enough, it was beginning to make a bit of sense. This worried me. I was beginning to feel like my mind was being unwillingly stretched by some invisible hands that, once having gripped me, would not let go. A dull, painless kind of torture.

I was relieved to see that we had wandered back to the yacht. "Can you stay a while longer?" I thought I'd ask even if she wasn't interested in anymore "bed stuff" as she called it.

She touched my face and nodded yes. I was so glad, I could feel my hormones reacting wildly to this news. For a moment there, I felt like an infatuated adolescent. The intense sexual attraction was undeniable. The magnetism between us was overcoming all the ideological, political, lifestyle, and other barriers that I assumed were there just by looking at her and listening to her rhetoric. I took her hand and beckoned her on board. I kissed her. To my surprise, she was immediately responsive.

"Will you make love with me again?" she whispered.

I was very glad she asked. "Yes, but, will you tell me who you are first?"

"Sheeyah, Atlantean, ancient Egyptian, pyramid empress, back here on Earth in search of my true love from lifetimes past, and here to do some teaching, as you are."

"Your love from lifetimes past?" I laughed a little.

"Yes. Have you seen him around?"

"No, but I'd sure like to meet him. He must have been worth the trip." I felt a twinge of jealousy. "A love like that only comes along once in a blue moon."

She laughed under her breath. She grinned at me as if playing a joke and then said, "Call me next time you take a good look at your reflection."

We undressed each other wildly and fell back into bed. I immediately moved onto her so that I could look down into her magnificent eyes. Holding her almost captive, I pushed her arms down above her head and pressed her legs under mine. I moved inside her. She closed her eyes in ecstasy.

"Open your eyes. Look at me," I commanded in a whisper. She complied. We continued in this position for a long time. The passion stretched over what seemed to be endless hours, long glorious hours.

It was definitely wonderful. Wonderful is an understatement, but then I am prone to understate. At first it was very physical, very material plane. *(But, I do not disapprove. Sexuality does not separate humans from enlightenment, it offers them an opportunity to merge with the god force, the energy of enlightenment.)* At a certain point during what began as intensely physical intercourse, (I was pleased to avoid early ejaculation this time), we shifted to an increasingly slow, steady, focused and restrained love-making. As our physical movements slowed, it seemed as if something else began to move. Some kind of white electrical river ran through us. When I first became aware of this, I thought I was imagining it. I thought I was imagining a white glow of genital excitement pulsing in waves like a river of pure light up my spine. After a while, I wasn't thinking. I didn't feel my body at all. I'm not certain that we were having any physical intercourse anymore at that point. I was propelled into a higher dimension. We both were. Funny thing is, neither of us had a physical orgasm. I am certain of this although neither of us said so.

Afterward, we lay holding each other very tightly. We did not speak for a long time. Maybe forever. Forever until we returned to the material plane, a place where there is no forever.

For some reason, her whimsical implication that I was a love from lifetimes past, as far fetched as it was, had hit me like a two by four, a smack in the head. She meant *me*. Big deal. The whimsy of an infatuated woman. Or was it me she was infatuated with? Maybe I reminded her of someone. A case of mistaken identity. She couldn't be infatuated with me already. Not yet. Soon I hoped. But, I knew that somehow she *did* mean me. Me.

She seemed to hear my thoughts. "You see, I'm certain that we've met before. I knew it as soon as you began walking away, right after you said your patch kit was better than mine. I could still see your eyes, long after you had walked off. Not his eyes. Yours. It didn't make immediate sense. I had just been brutally dumped by my lover without warning. Dumped in the harbor parking lot. But, *your* eyes stayed with me. Not his. Your eyes. They were the same cosmic, luminous, sky blue eyes that have stayed with me for so very long. I've been looking for them all my life. All this life. Several lives, I think. That's got to be why I love you so soon. Or do you think I act like this with everybody?"

She was getting to me. Bit by bit, my amnesia was dissolving. In fact, I think it started to really erode about then. "You actually have me thinking that I've seen you somewhere before," I admitted.

Things seem to have an uncanny way of happening. So it was that at that very moment everything started shaking and several explosions ripped at the pier. We were thrown from the bunk. Out of the corner of my eye, I noted that one of my unfinished card games, my solitaire, was strewn all over. For some reason, I was relieved. Why I happened to notice this in the midst of far greater goings on, I did not have time to question. When the shaking finally stopped, we heard shouts of "earthquake" and "fire" from up on deck. Somehow we dressed in an instant and went aboveboard. The harbor was filled with strange looking waves. Dark waves, little black waves, of a shape that I had never seen on any ocean or lake. People were running all over the place, leaping off of boats. Sirens blared in the background of chaotic sound. Flames were leaping up from a neighboring yacht. People were screaming. I ran down the pier to help them. Something else exploded. A ship's mast came toppling down. Onto me. I was hit on the head. I blacked out for several minutes. Or maybe longer.

When I came to, I knew I was Triad — something more than the Triad of this particular incarnation. A good portion, but definitely not all, of my amnesia was gone. But so was Sheeyah. The harbor and the adjoining town were a disaster, cluttered with the scattered debris of explosions, broken buildings and fallen telephone poles. Continuous aftershocks brought new injuries and further damage. Paramedics and would-be helpful citizens raced all over. I could not find Sheeyah.

I kept blacking out. Each blackout came over me like a wave of darkness. People kept picking me up off of the street. One of the street paramedics who stitched up the cut in my head said that I had to go in for x-rays, that the damage might be quite extensive even though I was ambulatory. He was concerned about a crack in my skull, bleeding in my brain, and the possibility of related seizures. I was not interested in anything he had to say.

I finally reported Sheeyah missing. Unfortunately, I did not know her real name. And, of course, I still had no idea that she was the head of Earthcult. I had not recognized her as the oil-covered woman I had watched on television with my investors. All I knew was that she was Sheeyah, Atlantean, Egyptian priestess. I tried to explain this to the authorities. It was difficult. Why was I reporting someone I did not really know as missing? Someone I had met only a while before the explosion? No last name? A priestess? An Atlantean of all things? Maybe she had just gone about her own business in the emergency. After much insistence, the already overtaxed harbor police agreed to conduct a search of the chaotic area with the coast guard, in case Sheeyah's body had been pulled under the water by a chunk of exploded vessel. But her body was not found.

My lower self, the simple earthbound Triad that I had believed myself to be but a few hours ago, was thrown into grief. Perhaps I had fallen in love with her in those few short hours. Whether or not this was the case, I had already lost her. I thought that she had died and I grieved with surprising intensity.

But another part of me wanted to search for her. I hungered for more of whatever it was she and I had together. I could somehow see her waiting for me somewhere, smiling. Was it in this dimension of reality? In the material plane? I decided that I would search the world to find her if I had to go that far. You don't have that kind of intense and unusual contact happen and then simply forget it. After all, I was just beginning to realize that I was Triad, Triad of the dimensions beyond. And Sheeyah had triggered this realization.

So I sensed, I knew, that my encounter with priestess Sheeyah had profound implications well beyond the here and now. She had somehow reminded me that I had come from a distant place in time and space, a location almost incomprehensible within the confines of the human mind, a mind which can barely imagine let alone travel past the very material three dimensional space it defines as reality. Making love with Sheeyah had provided me some re-entry into the higher dimensions from which I had come. Somehow, interaction with her, intercourse with her, had raised my vibration to a higher level. I could tell there was further to go, more to realize about myself. I was not totally there yet. Parts of myself were still obscure.

So it was that I set off in search of both Sheeyah and the real Triad, a journey which I was to eventually discover I had engaged in for eons. A journey which would cast a new light on what I believed to be my brilliant plan to buy up survivor territories. A journey which would unveil to me the coming crisis, the cataclysm of gargantuan proportions, to be faced by all humans in the third dimension of spiritual evolution living on Earth at this juncture in time: The Omega Point.

At that point in that incarnation, there was absolutely no way I could conceive of the most Cosmic, most multidimensional ramifications of the imbalances precipitating this seemingly Earthly cataclysm. I had no idea that all Creation was in dire jeopardy.

Part 2

•

Dissolving the Auric Veil

4

A human being living on the material plane sees a star; but that being is really seeing only the light that has been transmitted. The beam of light may have been traveling for hundreds of thousands of years. The star itself may no longer exist. You, that being, can only fully comprehend this Truth about the star if you can travel in the fourth dimension: time.

And you can. I can train you to see beyond, to go beyond. You can take a journey into time and into the higher dimensions beyond time. By raising your vibrations and journeying higher along the metaphysical spiral, you can lose the lower, heavier vibrations of the materialistic concept you call "ego," the vibrations that surround you like a prison wall. You can free yourself from the dangerous confines of your existence on the physical plane. You can not only survive and even avoid any physical disasters and cataclysmic rebalancings which occur on Earth, you can evolve through psychophysical catastrophe of any sort to achieve a spiritual bliss far beyond your expectations.

Read deep between the lines of this story. You will find my messages to you about your evolution embedded there.

$$\Omega$$

I was driven by some inexplicable undercurrent of core-level longing and an almost savage curiosity to search for this Sheeyah. She had brought something to my life, awakened me just a little. Everywhere I went, I kept my eyes open. Because I had to travel in my work as a collector of prime land parcels, I had natural opportunities to search. I could feel as if I was working rather than searching feverishly for this woman. But Sheeyah could have gone anywhere. Therefore, I decided that, if I had to, I would look absolutely everywhere.

Little did I know that I was about to find myself behaving in ways I would never have imagined, saying things that I had never even thought about in this incarnation. I was about to find myself teaching what I did not know I knew. At first I sounded like an evangelist, or maybe a zealot or a nut, I was not certain. Yet, what I was saying felt quite sincere. My first such encounter was with a poor unsuspecting man named Camus.

Of course, it was Sheeyah who led me to Camus, but I was far from realizing this. Amidst a fervent but methodless searching process, I suddenly remembered hearing Sheeyah tell me that whenever she was lost she looked for her face in the smooth surface of a body of water. "Usually it's ... Crystal Mirror Lake," she had said. I remembered that it was special to her. So I studied map after map from state after state until I found a Crystal Mirror Lake. This lake sort of just appeared on one of the maps, surprising me, because I had been staring at that particular map for two hours without seeing that spot. So I headed for this lake, uncertain of the value of this trip, but at a loss for alternatives.

What seemed like an absurdly long journey, first by plane and then through endless miles of unchanging countryside and then way up into a high mountain range, ended abruptly, as I drove round a tight curve. Just ahead of me, I saw an unlabeled lake. For a moment, the lake looked like an eye in the land. The eye was watching me. I shook my head a bit to clear away that illusion. It bothered me. I felt like a stranger in a strange land. The lake returned to normal. I was still uncomfortable.

It was quite a charming lake, however. I pulled over to the side of the road to better study the uninhabited scene. I surmised that somebody could make a lot of money developing this lake and its shore front, but told myself that if it wasn't on my list of survivor territories, it wasn't worth my attention. And as far as I knew, it wasn't. I figured that the lake had probably remained undeveloped because of some lack of legal access to shore front property. Then I thought that maybe the explanation for its lack of development was simply that it was in a National Park, but I had seen no signs to this effect.

After staring at it for quite some time, I realized that, way out in the middle of this lake, there sat a man in a small rowboat. His presence startled me. Why hadn't I noticed him before this moment? Maybe he could tell me where I could find Crystal Mirror Lake, if this wasn't it. I put on the parking break, opened the door, and unwound myself from the tiny interior of my vehicle.

I wanted to call out to this man, but I did not. I looked at him. I guess he felt my gaze. He turned, saw me, and rowed to meet me. As he did, the sunlight reflected in a flash off the side of his boat and blinded me for a moment.

When I recovered from this temporary blindness, I was surprised to find that he was only five feet away from me. He had traveled toward me inexplicably fast. There was something a bit eerie about this, but I pushed my questions out of my mind. I had a more pressing matter to attend to. Now, he approached me slowly, eyeing me a bit suspiciously. As he eased the boat closer, I could see that he was just an everyday sort of guy. At least he looked like one.

"Mornin'," he said gruffly. "What can I do for ya'?"

"Good morning." I answered, in what I hoped was a cheerful tone. "My name is Triad Framingham."

"Camus Kamusat." I thought that this was a strange name. He pronounced it KAM-us KAM-us-aht. Camus eased the little rowboat to the shore and sat looking at me.

"I'm looking for a place called Crystal Mirror Lake," I said matter-of-factly.

Now Camus eyed me wryly and said, "Ever hear anyone say you can't get there from here?"

"What?" I asked.

"Just a joke I heard once at a travel convention. You can get anywhere from everywhere, I s'pose. Otherwise there'd be absolutely no exit from some spots .... I've been in the travel business a long time, so I've heard all them jokes." His voice trailed off and he gazed into the water.

"Well, anyway," I persisted, "I need to find a place called Crystal Mirror Lake. It's supposed to be sort of special. Perhaps you can be of help."

"Yeah, I s'pose I can, but I'm fishin' now. You got a while?"

I figured that he meant he would show me the way later. I didn't really want to wait, but he was doing me the favor. I nodded. "Yes, I have a while."

Camus continued to sit there, staring at me.

Finally he said something. "Well ... ya' gettin' in or not?"

Me? Get in? Why? I had no idea as to why. However, I felt strangely attracted to the boat. Although it seemed much too small for two large men, I stepped into the boat, balanced myself, then sat facing Camus. His stocky arms maneuvered the oars silently as we glided into the middle of the lake. The entire surface of the water now reflected the morning sun. I felt as if we were riding on light.

Camus lifted the small oars into the boat and picked up a fishing rod. I watched silently as he baited the hook and dropped the line into the lake. As I had anticipated, the hook broke the smooth surface of the water where I had fantasized that I just might spot Sheeyah's reflection. Instead, I saw Camus' reflection rippling on the water. But, as best as I could tell, the face in his reflection was not his own. The face seemed to be disguised, as if he were wearing a mask or something. I was a little uneasy. I shook my head and the illusion disappeared. And so did any trace of Camus' or what would have been Camus' reflection. Camus did not seem to notice any of this and I said nothing about it.

"Henu," he said, breaking the silence.

"Henu what?"

"Boat's called henu," Camus replied.

"Why?" I didn't really care but I asked him anyway.

"Don't know. Just came to me one day."

I was staring so hard at the glaring surface of the lake that I began to feel extremely light headed. This light headedness is the only explanation I could give myself for what next came to my mind.

For some reason, I suddenly wanted to tell Camus, my captain on what seemed like a journey to nowhere, about how strange his reflection had looked. And, as soon as I contemplated telling him this, some highly unusual ideas — the kind of ideas I never had — pushed themselves into my mind. I began thinking about how this lake reflected not only Camus, but all things in the universe. I was unsettled by such a profound thought. Maybe talking about it, even with a stranger, would help. So I decided to strike up a conversation with Camus. I was curious about how I would manage to communicate such a thing, especially to so simple a person. Anyway, I had nothing better to do while I waited for directions to Crystal Mirror Lake.

"Nice lake." Great start, I told myself sarcastically.

"Crystal Mirror," he said under his breath.

"What?"

"Crystal Mirror," Camus said again, louder this time. "Crystal Mirror Lake. It's had that name long as I can remember."

So this was Sheeyah's lake. Camus had tricked me for some reason. Maybe he had just wanted my company, I didn't know. I wanted to complain about this trick right away, but didn't. I don't know why.

Camus grew silent again, staring into the lake. He didn't seem particularly interested in talking, let alone in examining universal Truths. Still, since he didn't seem to be ready to row me back to shore, I decided to make another attempt at communicating the profound.

"What you see on the surface is not what is going on underneath. The water in this lake has power. It has mystery! It has ..."

Camus glanced over at me. "It has fish."

The amnesic me felt like a jerk. But I knew at once that I had his attention. I heard myself talking to myself again. Something about water and the subconscious. I didn't like hearing all this inside my head and thus being alone with it, so I looked at Camus and went on with my strange chatter, now aloud, somewhat amused and somewhat unnerved by it.

"I've heard that water is the symbol of the subconscious. That's the part of your mind that can control you without your being aware of it. Let me explain." God, it sure seemed to be controlling me, whatever it was. So much so that I went on again, curious and further unnerved by my behavior. What would I say next? "Maybe you only thought you wanted to come fishing today. Maybe you actually wanted to be on the water ... to be part of the power of the water, the stillness. Do you see what I mean, Camus?" I sounded like a nutcase to myself. Why was I going on like this? I looked at the sunlit surface of the lake. Was it water? Or magic syrup made of light?

Camus sat looking at his fishing rod, the hook still in the water. Slowly he began to reel in the line. As he watched the soggy, mangled bait break the surface, he glanced my way, begrudgingly.

"I see this isn't gonna be of much use," he said. He removed the mangled bait from the hook and reeled in the rest of his line. After putting the rod under his seat, he shifted his weight and faced me. The shifting action sent ripples across the lake. Our reflections distorted in another direction. I felt a hunger pang or something. My heart ached for Sheeyah. She had really gotten to me, I marveled. Who else would I go through all this madness for? No one.

I found myself wanting to hear myself explain to Camus something even more profound and out-of-character for me — something about spiritual evolution. I wasn't a very spiritual guy, but I had a clear message in my mind, one that I'd never thought about before: *Every life unit is a microcosm designed to contribute to the spiritual evolution of the universe.*

I wanted Camus to somehow comprehend that his lake, itself a type of life unit, was nothing more than a smaller version of the universe. Yes, a microcosm. I guess I was trying out my newly realized sense that I knew more about reality, the purpose of life and all, than I thought I had known. Or, maybe I just wanted to get back at Camus for tricking me: I would disturb his peace as my revenge.

I looked at the water. All the answers are right here, I told myself. I guessed it was me telling myself all this, as there wasn't anybody else living in my head.

"Camus, ... what do you see when you look into this lake?"

"Fish. If I'm lucky. Or nothing. Water."

"Can you think of this lake as being a smaller version of the universe? Its own self-contained Cosmos, so to speak?"

Camus was eyeing me quizzically now. "No," he said flatly.

"O.K.," I told him, "Let's take the fish as an example. They have everything they need in the lake. They even breathe underwater. But every now and then they surface. They pierce a different dimension of reality. They totally understand that they are safer in the water, given their body types and all, but they also know that there is something beyond the lake. In this way, they are very much like us .... "

"Now, I know fish," Camus interrupted. He sounded faintly impatient. I sympathized with him. Why was I bothering this poor guy with this stuff? He went on, maybe to keep me from continuing. "That's one thing I do know. FISH. And there ain't no smart fish, Mr. Framingham. And if you're one of them people that's gonna tell me that them fish are gonna die and come back as people, well, I ain't gonna believe that."

At that moment, I realized that Camus had just hit on the notion of reincarnation, even if his hit was just a prejudice against it. Reincarnation!! The notion intrigued me for the first time in my life (or what I thought was my life — this incarnation). I felt as if I had just made a discovery by peeking through the eye of a needle. But did I understand any more than Camus did about reincarnation or anything else? I wasn't certain.

I told myself that I could try out my new knowledge on Camus. What new knowledge? I asked myself curtly. What's all this new knowledge, especially this microcosm and reincarnation stuff? And what's the connection between these two ideas? None was obvious to me. I didn't answer myself. But I did speak back to Camus.

"No, Camus. I wasn't going to tell you that. Fish can't come back as people. Not right away, at least. But, you know, maybe over several lifetimes, or over a million years, one of these fish could become so highly evolved that it could break away from the pack, from the group of fish it is evolving with, and be born as a human. What would you say to that?" I wondered silently what I would say to that.

Camus sat quietly, watching the fish before he spoke. "A million years? Fish don't live that long. But I guess you don't mean that, ... but ... anyway, I don't know about all this many lifetimes stuff."

I realized that I did know something about reincarnation. I couldn't remember where I'd learned it. My friends weren't into things like that and you don't find this discussed in business except when people are telling jokes like, "Will yourself your property and pick it up in your next life."

I sat quietly, watching Camus think. For some reason, I briefly suspected that he knew more than he let on. Maybe it was the glint, some kind of spark, I detected in his eye. Maybe it was his strange posture. Or maybe it was the way he seemed to peer deep into the distance, far beyond the horizon, whenever he looked up from the lake, as if he expected something to happen.

Camus sat erect and spoke grumpily. "Well, since you spoiled my fishin' for today and since I got nothin' else planned, I want to ask you a question."

"Sure. Go ahead." I thought I felt him opening up.

"You remember way back when them hippies were everywhere? Well, a bunch of 'em used to come here and go swimmin' in the lake. Naked. Talk about spoilin' the fishin'. But one of 'em told me one time that if I didn't stop killin' fish I was gonna come back as one. Now, is that true?"

My higher self would have laughed if Camus hadn't been so sincere.

This is probably the biggest misconception concerning reincarnation. This is a form of what I like to call a new age Nazi-ism. (Metaphysical Truth can be so grossly misinterpreted.) Reincarnation is not a punishment. You don't get sent backward in evolution against your will. And you have to be very highly evolved to will your own self backward into fish or slug or amebic form, if even just for a visit.

Camus sat upright in the boat, looking at me with very concerned eyes.

Clarity filled my mind. I knew what I was talking about for an instant. "No. It doesn't work that way, Camus. That would be regressionary in nature, and contrary to the concept of evolutionary enlightenment ... Let me explain it this way. All creation is designed to move toward achieving enlightenment, to evolve. Souls are designed to continuously increase their awarenesses. Nothing is designed to move away from enlightenment. Some life forms move very slowly or not at all on the evolutionary spectrum, but none are sent backwards. You can stay the same, but you can't be punished for fishing and sent back as a fish. If you come back as a fish, it's because you want to be a fish for a while and you have the rare skill to make that happen."

I sat back as comfortably as one can in a small boat, to let myself and poor Camus digest this information. What had I just said? Camus appeared quite confused, and I understood his confusion. The amnesic me sensed that Camus, as do many third dimensional western Earth beings, had a strict Biblical background.

Reincarnation defies the Biblical concept of Hell, where one is theoretically sent for one's wrong doings for all eternity. In fact, or in reality, one can return to Earth, or to some other part of the Cosmos, to re-work one's way out of past karmic situations. But a human doesn't work out human wrong-doings by coming back as a fish.

Had I been able to break through to my higher knowledge, I would have recalled that there are basically two types of reincarnation. The elementary form, group or lower reincarnation, is especially typical of beings living in the third and lower dimensions. This form of reincarnation is based on group reoccurrence. It is linked to the great cycles of life and involves group evolution. Until one reaches a certain level of spiritual proficiency, one is tied to the evolution of his species and of his social group if he has one. His advancement is limited as his progress is tied to that of others. But there is a more advanced type of reincarnation, for those who are ready to individuate, to evolve spiritually even if it means doing it alone. This is individual or higher reincarnation. As one's spiritual awareness and adeptness is intensified, one's spiritual progression becomes independent of his species and social group. He then moves successively, with each life cycle, into higher levels of consciousness. Upward mobility through higher levels of consciousness eventually (and sometimes instantaneously for those who are most adept) moves one into higher dimensions of spiritual reality, independent of what other souls may be doing, and independent of the great cycles of life that other souls may be caught up in.

I was sort of getting it, mulling it over and over, but I had no idea how much this all had to do with my own existence. Why would I be interested in the possibility of reincarnation? This lifetime was enough to cope with. Why add more?

Strange, though, I had a feeling that all this had something to do with Sheeyah. God, where was she? I wanted her. To hold her. To love her. To touch her. To make love with her. Had to have her. Sheeyah! Sheeyah! Sheeyah!

I came back to the now. In my waning but still relatively unaware state, I did not yet fully comprehend all that we higher dimensional characters know. For one thing, I did not know that, as was true of many religious doctrines, much of the Bible had been misinterpreted, rewritten and even falsified to advance the causes of those who profited from such revision. The concept of reincarnation simply did not serve those who were in control of the Biblical revisions. Why obey your king's laws in one lifetime if you can come back and be a better person next time? Hell is a great incentive. Hell is useful in controlling the masses. I could hear my higher self go on:

People have been punished for questioning the constructions of reality set forth by their rulers. Many of your gifted psychics, some of whom you once called witches, were burned at the stake or otherwise persecuted when they attempted to pursue concepts such as reincarnation. But they were only looking beyond the five human senses to greater reality, beyond the surface of your human fish pond.

I also did not yet remember that, historically, reincarnation was oft dismissed as a process invented out of a desperate human need to believe in the continuance of life after death. There is some merit to this: it offers an alternative to those who are looking for another chance at life, for reasons known only to themselves. Yet, those who deny the possibility of reincarnation ignore the Truth: that we must transform ourselves. THIS IS WHY WE LIVE. This is why we often choose to embody in the physical dimension. We either do it in this lifetime or we do it in another. In this way, reincarnation can explain human suffering. A person is born into a character that he creates. He is incarnated into a world that he selects for himself, that he evolves to the threshold of during his prior lifetime. THE BODY, THE PHYSICAL LIFE UNIT, IS BUT A VEHICLE OF SPIRITUAL EVOLUTION.

I was absolutely fascinated hearing myself think these thoughts. Where on Earth were they coming from? Then I remembered Camus. Poor Camus.

Camus shifted his weight, sending more ripples across the lake. The waves grew larger as they reached out toward the shoreline ... just as human enlightenment can enlarge with each subsequent reincarnation. With Camus' stirrings came his questions. I was actually relieved to hear him speak.

"Triad ... should I really call you Triad? Strange name.... So is there a way to come back better? Should I have gone to church more? Maybe if I had studied more in high school, I would have turned out more intelligent."

I didn't think that Camus was grasping the parameters of my message yet. I couldn't blame him. I wasn't either. I found myself laughing at myself in my head. I thought I was funny. And then I thought that that thought was funny.

"Well, you see, Camus, it's really not quite like that. I mean, it's another kind of intelligence. And I don't think high schools or churches are teaching it in our era." Had they ever?

"Well, I'm not real smart and I'm not real God-fearing. I'm just a simple guy from a small town who runs a travel agency that doesn't get much business and who likes to fish a lot. Does that mean I have to come back as myself again?" Camus was obviously concerned about this. "I mean, what is all this enlightening stuff you're telling me about?"

I don't know, I said to myself. Yes you do, I answered myself.

"All living matter is made up of cosmic energy. As you approach enlightenment you are freed of your bondage to a species, to a group of people, to the Earth, and even to the physical plane. And, you can eventually give up the body thing."

"Don't know why I'd want to."

"Camus, the body is just a vehicle of spiritual evolution." I liked sounding this wise.

"Don't know what this means, Triad."

"As you probably know, Camus, "Prehistoric man, cave man, was closely tied to the Earth ... he struggled to provide everything for himself. Struggle in the physical dimension is part of this evolutionary stage. In the higher dimensions, the struggle for material plane survival is no longer necessary. Spiritual survival and energetic survival — these become the greater issues."

Camus looked hot and irritated. "So I'm supposed to suffer like I do?"

I hadn't realized that Camus thought of himself as a sufferer. I decided I'd better stop bombarding him with what was coming into my mind. "O.K., Camus, let's forget about all this. Maybe we can get back to it another time. How about you row me to shore?"

"Pretty soon, Triad."

I hoped so. I touched the water. It was ice cold. A swim to shore did not appeal to me at all.

I was feeling trapped and very cramped in the boat, like there was no exit. I carefully stood up with the intent of stretching: the motion caused more ripples, ripples in the surface and ripples which threatened to build into huge unsettling waves in my subconscious. Watching the ripples reach the shore, I suddenly realized that I was going about this all wrong. Camus didn't seem to understand what I had been telling him. Simple things, things in this everyday life, like fish and cats and dogs, and maybe even the travel business, Camus comprehended. Or thought that he did. And this was enough for him. After all, simple things had always been enough for me, I thought. Or had they?

The sun had risen high in the sky and I was sweating profusely. I didn't have a hat or sunglasses and my eyes ached. Dizziness swept over me again and I saw an image of a black wave engulfing the world and Camus and me with it. I shuddered. The kind of chill you get when the sun is too hot. I had seen this wave before. But where? In my dreams?

I felt sick. I blurted something out: "Camus, do you ever think about death ... about dying?" I glanced down at him. Like a bolt of lightening in the form of pain, Sheeyah returned to my mind. Was she dead? Why didn't she return if she was all right? Could she really just leave me after that incredible meeting? Was she seriously injured? Meanwhile, Camus was fishing under his seat for something.

"Well ... yeah," he answered, pulling out a thermos bottle. "I mean, it ain't somethin' I think about all the time, but I've thought about it ... it's on my mind some. Want some coffee? It's black." He offered me an over-used styrofoam cup. I took the miserable cup and sipped the metallic coffee.

"What do you think happens after you die?" Death was on my mind, too. The black wave scared me. It seemed silly to be frightened by a fleeting fantasy, but I was.

Camus threw me one of his skeptical looks. "I think the same thing as everyone else around here thinks. If you live your life right, you go to your Maker in Heaven. If you don't, you go to ...." He stopped, fearing the word itself.

"Hell?" I asked, knowing the answer. "What if there is no hell? What if people were given another chance, a chance to correct past mistakes? Many, many chances to ... uh ... wipe the slate clean?"

Camus began laughing. He was laughing so hard and so loud that I could see the fish scurrying deep underwater, sort of running for safety. After a few seconds, Camus sat up and wiped his eyes, still chuckling. "Now, that'd be somethin'! If you could invent that and sell it, you'd make a fortune!"

Great idea, Camus. I should market this reincarnation stuff. Just add water and shake — you get reincarnated. The Framingham Reincarnation Kit — just $18.95. Maybe I could design and manufacture a reincarnation game. From cheap housing to Park Place to Go to a next life. Onward and upward if you play the game well. I realized that I was still standing. I sat down carefully and sipped the coffee. I was disoriented. I was wondering where I was. I kicked myself back into the here and now. It all seemed a bit absurd. But I was driven by my greater self, by Triad the Communicator, to put things in the right perspective. That was why I was there. I was coming to sense this. At least it was the general reason. Ultimately, I had to find Sheeyah. HAD TO.

I went on with the death thing. "Camus, no soul was ever created to be lost. Some souls evolve faster than others, but all are conceived to encounter spiritual pressure or disaster and then the desire to be saved and enlightened. To seek and find the god force. So physical death serves a purpose. It's just a step along the way."

I thought that Camus looked confused. My third-dimensional self couldn't help but enjoy his confusion. I was beginning to remember that, in the higher dimensions of spiritual evolution, the body and spirit no longer need to be connected; the physical body is nothing more than a throwaway vehicle. The spirit can return again and again, in any number of forms. This thought took the edge off of death — Sheeyah's possible death — for the moment. Maybe she had survived her death, if she had died....

"Nope, Triad, you don't get to wipe your slate clean. I don't think so."

"But, Camus, what if people could come back? What would you think then?" I arrogantly decided that it was time for Camus to do some serious learning. Quite some time would pass before I would realize the folly of my arrogance.

"Well ... if it WAS true, then we wouldn't have to worry so much about what we do now, would we? You'd like that, Triad. You could cheat in your business deals, con people, get them all confused and riled up — maybe even scared — by skillfully advertising whatever you had to sell them." Camus was grinning, almost making fun of me. How did he know that the thought had occurred to me? And how did he know I was a business man? He was not sounding quite like himself now.

"Oh, yes, we would. Have to worry, I mean. We would still need to be concerned with our actions," I said, quite seriously. "Because we would be held accountable. Not by some jury in the sky, but energetically." What does this mean? I asked myself. Just go on, I answered. It will all be made more clear. Yeah, right. I closed my eyes, opened my mouth and let the ideas pour out. "Let's say lifetimes are like a series of ledgers, similar to what our accountants use to keep track of debits and credits. Then, let's say the more we have on the debit or negative side of the ledger, the more we have to come back to correct these bad deeds. The more we have on the credits or positive side, the closer we get to eternity — to the Maker in Heaven, as you like to say." I shifted my weight carefully, keeping an eye on Camus. "Camus, it's all just energy. Energy working itself out. Balancing and rebalancing."

Camus still wasn't buying it. "So if we have another chance, then why be a good person in the first place?"

"What if I told you that is impossible to create a new soul with each birth? ... Camus, souls might start out equal but, due to a variety of factors, they eventually evolve at different rates. They have different experiences in different environments which cause them to evolve in different ways, eventually reaching their own levels of enlightenment."

Camus thought for a moment before he spoke this time. "But how do we get them credits? I mean, if we do bad deeds then they count as debits. But what about the credits side?"

"Enlightenment of self. Getting better at being a person, no, not a person, but a spirit. Cleaning up your energy so you feel right about your behavior, feel right deep, deep down inside."

"Like loving everyone, including your enemies?"

"Sure, if that love makes you feel cleaner, more pure and honest with yourself." I told him this somewhat reluctantly. I felt I was oversimplifying the distinction between good and bad. I was also grabbing at love for want of a better word. Love. Sheeyah. What would Sheeyah say about love if she were here? Where is she? "I guess you could also love things like rocks and even the Earth." I was guessing here. Spiritual purification wasn't this simple.

"Love rocks? Love the Earth?" Camus asked incredulously.

"Well, maybe it's not exactly love but it's some kind of bond or connection with or respect for the Earth, and with the universe." I surprised myself. Ecology had never been my strong suit. I waited for another of Camus' reactions, but now Camus sat very still. He seemed to have resigned himself to my tirade. So I continued. "Say there are some highly advanced spirits, spirits who choose to incarnate as rocks for periods much longer than you or I incarnate as the human forms we are now. And then say the Earth is a giant rock. It is a spirit who has incarnated as our planet." I heard that wiser version of myself say in my head that I was a little off, that *the Earth is more of an organism than a rock. But yes, a spirit indeed.*

Camus raised his eyebrows, I thought I saw that glint in his eye again, but said nothing. I was thinking that he thought I was loony. This didn't worry me. I did too. But I continued.

"These advanced spirits are very hardy souls. They also incarnate on other planets and sometimes as other planets with very harsh and rough atmospheric conditions. But you never know, maybe some of these advanced spirits are the pebbles out there on the road and the pebbles on the bottom of your lake. Those pebbles may be more enlightened than you. They have a tendency to take a longer view of life than we humans do, because those old spirits come from parts of the Cosmos where lifespans — incarnations — are substantially longer than ours."

Camus had apparently been quite struck by the idea that some spirit would have chosen to incarnate as our Earth. "But could a spirit live as long as this entire Earth?"

"Yes, and much, much longer. A spirit can live a very, very long time." I, my higher self, found my reply humorous as the incarnated me had as yet no idea how old I really was.

"The Earth is the spirit's body?"

"Yes, Camus. The Earth is the vehicle of that spirit's evolution the way our bodies are our vehicles."

Camus was visibly nervous. "So the Earth can actually die, Triad? It could have a total apocalypse, even worse than in the Bible?"

I was very uncomfortable with this question. Had I just practiced a bit of my survivor territories campaign on Camus? Or had I convinced myself that cataclysm was really on its way? I wanted to vomit. Maybe I was seasick.

"So, are you telling me that if I'm kind to the Earth, ecology and all that stuff, I'll be goin' to Heaven when I die?" Camus persisted, oblivious to my angst. He seemed sincere now. This made me sad for some reason. He did not yet understand that many spirits go through many incarnations neither gaining nor losing ground in the enlightenment process, without moving up the ladder of spiritual evolution. They just don't do what they are really there to do. Being kind isn't enough. O.K., I said to myself, Sheeyah, you can come back now. It's not funny anymore. I've had enough of this foolishness. I don't like it here. Where are you?

I couldn't leave Camus hanging. He wanted an answer from me. "No, you have to grow, to develop your spirit somehow. Being kind, if it does this, can be a way of building credits so you don't have to come back in human form as many times," I explained. It sounded like strange reasoning to me. I had never heard myself say anything like this before. Not in this lifetime, anyway.

"Well, that's good. I was startin' to think you were full of bull." Camus sounded as if he still thought I was full of bull. For a moment, I knew that I was. Then I knew that I wasn't. I decided not to stress the fact that reincarnations are not necessarily glamorous events. We don't all come back as Egyptian Pharaohs or Priestesses. Or rich men and women. Reincarnations are often quite messy opportunities to work out past personality defects. And more.

"Yeah ... Yeah, I reckon I have come back a few times myself," Camus said slowly. He was staring deeply into his coffee cup, as if it were his soul.

That black wave rose with an eerie sort of motionlessness like an angry unmoving hand made of a dark fluid. This still but fierce wave ripped through my mind again. I blanked it out by focusing hard on Camus. I wondered what he was seeing in his thick, black coffee. When he looked up and peered at the horizon, I saw his eyes, and I knew he had seen something.

"Well, when I was a boy," he began, "I remembered a place that I had never been to, but it seemed like I had been there. A big river and a lot of sand. Them pyramid things and giant cat statues too. When I told my ma' about it, she said I musta' dreamed it. But I always knew it weren't no dream. I just knew it somehow ...." Camus trailed off.

So! I felt triumphant for some inexplicable reason. Camus understood something, a little of what I had been saying. This and my need to forget the black wave inspired me to continue. "Tell me about the place that you remembered, Camus."

"Aw, it was just a place ...." Camus mumbled.

Hi Triad.

What was that? I heard her voice! "What?" I said excitedly. Sheeyah!

Camus went on. "I said it was just a place. Had a big river. Nothing too special. I don't know why I'm talking to you about this. I never told —"

Triad.

I turned so abruptly that I almost capsized the tiny boat. I had heard Sheeyah's voice. "Yes? I'm here." Sheeyah!

Only Camus replied. "Yes what? I know you're here. I said I never told anyone but my ma', not even Nellie, God bless her."

Although I now had my mind on finding the source of Sheeyah's voice, I realized that Camus looked very sad now. Actually, he had looked that way the entire time. I had finally noticed.

"Nellie?" I knew that I had missed an important part of Camus. Had I paid more attention to the psychic probing of Camus that the higher Triad had been conducting while I was conversing, I would have known who Nellie was. I would have been aware of the tremendous sadness that Camus was experiencing in this particular incarnation of his. But this still rather naive me did not know anything about psychic probing.

Triad.

That voice again. Sheeyah! I was more subtle about my looking now. Where was she? I couldn't see Sheeyah anywhere. Very funny, Sheeyah. Come out, come out, wherever you are.

"She was my wife ... well, I guess she still is," Camus responded to my question. "Nellie took off about a year ago. Just up an' disappeared on me. Once, before she disappeared, she told me she had to go find herself. Whatever that means. You'd think a grown woman of 62 would know who she was. She was my wife. That's who. But anyhow, one day she was gone. Disappeared or died. We were married 44 years. My whole life almost."

I felt very sorry for Camus. I mingled my longing for Sheeyah with his grief. But, something told me not to pity him. One should not pity the less enlightened. They are progressing along their spiritual journeys at their own pace. They are right where they should be, right where they have arranged instinctively to be. I marveled at this theory. Interesting idea, I told myself. Where did it come from? And is Camus really less enlightened? For some reason, I kept wondering about this.

The unenlightened need to be instructed by life, not pitied, Triad.

I almost had a heart attack. Sheeyah had gotten into the conversation somehow. Come on Sheeyah, don't tease.

Dissolving the Auric Veil

Pity sticks to the spirit like a weight and such emotional weight does not serve one in entering the fourth dimension.

I mulled that one over. Then I realized I was mulling that one over, not knowing where the author of that voice was. Sheeyah! Is it you? Am I mad? Insane?

"I used to bring her out here to fish with me," Camus said sadly.

"Any idea what prompted Nellie to want to go off in search of herself?" I tried to be interested in Camus. It was not too difficult, as Sheeyah seemed involved in the conversation now. She seemed to care. Had Sheeyah led me to Camus?

"Guess it was books and movies or something. Modern stuff."

"You never told your wife of the place you remembered?"

Camus shook his head and stared into his now empty cup. I wanted him to search his soul, to discover previous lifetimes he had known. It would distract me from my mounting mental confusion. Sheeyah's voice or my fantasy of it. The black wave. And my own angst. Was I going mad?

"Have you looked for Nellie in the lake?" Why on Earth did I say that? How cruel!

"She ain't in the lake! She ain't dead! I know it! I just know it! She's just gone!" Camus was shouting to hold back tears.

I had rocked the boat. Camus was so upset, I knew I'd better talk fast. "No ... no Camus. Wait. I didn't mean dead in the lake. I only meant that if you learn to look deep into the lake, you will find many answers. Perhaps you could even learn where Nellie is, what she is doing ...."

Looking into the lake is like looking into the eye of the Creator.

Yeah, right, Sheeyah. Show yourself if you want me to listen to you. I was tiring of her game. Or of my madness.

I had problems here. Camus looked very angry. I thought he was about to tip the boat and throw both of us out. I decided to let him calm down.

It was still hot. The sun was still beating down on us. I wanted to go back to shore.

After a long hot while, Camus stirred and reached behind his seat. He came out with a small cooler containing a few beers. He held a beer in front of my eyes like bait. I accepted.

"How in the blazes would a person go about learnin' things from a lake?" He was staring glumly at his faceless reflection in the now very still water.

"Let's say a guy has a hazy situation, doesn't know what to do. If he looks deeply into the lake when he is very quiet, when his mind is very quiet, the haziness changes and things become clear and glassy. He can find himself then. Things become clear to him. It's like having the ripples on the lake stop when we stop moving or fishing. ... Does that make sense?" I hoped it did to Camus. I wasn't so sure it did to me.

There was not time for an answer before a very large bird — some strange phoenix-like thing with piercing eyes — landed on the water near us. He immediately decided to spread his huge wings, disturbing the surface of the water. I watched him eye his magnificent reflection momentarily and then, as if repulsed, beat his wings to a rapid lift off. For a brief moment, the surface of the lake cracked like a broken mirror. It had the fragmented appearance of a mosaic. I glanced at the water then, unhappy at the interruption, and saw, between the cracks in the previously mirror-like surface, for just a second, Sheeyah, seven faces of Sheeyah. My eyes bulged.

"Look, Camus," I said in a hurried whisper.

I blinked. The seven faces, all of them, were gone.

"Look at what?" Camus was scowling now.

"Oh, I just thought I saw something, but I was wrong." How could I explain to Camus?

"Find myself, you said. What self? Is that what them talk show gals call that inner self stuff?"

"Well, sort of, Camus." It was a start anyway. A start for Camus. Where did that magnificent bird go?

"What do you think inner is, Triad? How does a guy find it?"

Good question. Do I know? "Good question. I'll try to answer," I said. "Hope I can. Uh ...." I could hear the wise ideas in my head, the older Triad speaking. I wasn't sure I understood who he was even though he sounded like me. I guessed that I was getting reacquainted with him. "About this inner — well, consider this: If you were to draw on all knowledge generated by all professions in the world, think of how much knowledge you would have at your disposal."

My amnesia seemed to be chipping away like old paint. Come on Sheeyah. Are you gone now?

"That's not your inner, Triad, it's everyone else's outer. Even I know that."

I had to laugh. "Good answer. Let's see, Camus ... you're really making me think hard ... uh ... Try this idea: You have most likely been many things during your many previous lifetimes, so you know a lot more and you have a lot more experience and you have a better idea about yourself than you think." That voice in my head, the one that sounded like me but much wiser, seemed to be taking me to the inner self I was trying to tell Camus about. And I, the lower version of my self, kept trying to spot the bird that had cracked open the surface of the lake.

I went on. "So you are able to draw from your subconscious any knowledge from your past, whether it existed in this life or in another one. In fact," oh boy, I could hear what I was about to say and it sounded preposterous, "you can draw upon experiences that were not yours, that were had in someone else's lifetime." I wasn't certain how this worked. It surprised me.

"Meanin' what?" Camus asked.

Yeah, meanin' what, I confronted myself. ... To my surprise, I had an answer. "Meaning that you have every answer to every question you could ever ask. All of us have access to every answer we need. We just reach for the answers when we are really ready for them, not before.... A quiet place like a lake is a good place to reach," I guessed at the end here.

Camus slumped, sipping his beer. The two of us were getting too hot out there. Sunsick. He gazed at his reflection. "All I see here is an old man, a small town travel guide, nothing more than that. An old faceless guy, a nobody, who's not got much knowledge and never will have."

Sounded depressing. I wanted Sheeyah. This did not seem to be going anywhere. The picture of the black wave kept rising in my troubled mind. Was I mentally ill? And that huge bird with the piercing eyes, I could not figure out where it had gone.

It's O.K., go on, talk to Camus a bit more, I'm not going anywhere, Triad.

There you are Sheeyah! How are you doing this? Is this just my imagination?

Yes, it's just your imagination.

I was disappointed, my heart panged.

But I led your imagination to it. Just imagine me talking and I really will be.

Some game I was playing with myself. But her voice sounded so clear. I must have sustained quite a bit more brain damage than I realized when my head was hit in the explosion. I should have gone in for those x-rays, I scolded myself. ... What had I been saying to Camus?

Sheeyah surprised me by answering. I could tell that it was her voice and not mine: You were trying to teach Camus and yourself that living in the finite and material present, without some understanding of the other dimensions of time and reality, without acknowledging other dimensions of your existence, is not a way to gain a clear picture, a clear reflection of yourself. The now without its place in multidimensional time and space is nothing, because the moment you contemplate a particular now, it has slipped away and become a then. Nows are instantaneously dissolving fragments. There is no now now.

Sheeyah was getting pretty deep for being a figment of my imagination.

"Uh, Camus." I thought I'd try.

"Yeah?"

"Guess I'm just trying to tell you that there is so much more to all this than we think there is. And if you are sad about your Nellie or your life or anything, then you might want to look into the water, feel like part of the water for a while, and just relax and let your spirit find itself."

"What if I don't have one?"

"If you don't have a spirit? Oh, yes, you do. I am talking to it. Your spirit was asking all these questions today because it wants to know more. Otherwise you would have told me to go take a hike." And, I added in my mind, wouldn't have tricked me into coming out onto this lake while I waited for directions to this very lake.

"It would'a been a good idea to send you away." He forced a grin at me to be sure I didn't feel insulted at this. "Anyway, when I looked into the water, all I saw was an old man. Nobody special. Oh, I sent a few people on a few journeys to a few places, but I'm nobody special." His misery came through again now.

"Camus, it takes practice to see more, to see who you really are."

Camus seemed increasingly distraught as the moments passed. For some reason, I was feeling increasingly and cruelly impatient. Why wouldn't he just understand all this? And where did that strange bird go?

But what bothered me more was my behavior. Why was I inflicting this stuff on poor Camus? I didn't know if I believed it myself. Then I thought

Dissolving the Auric Veil 65

I heard myself tell myself:

People reach for and understand spiritual Truths only when they are ready to do so, never before.

So stop pushing Camus and just tell him the Truth. That's what's driving you here.

Yes, I had heard Sheeyah's voice again. I decided to tell Camus the Truth about me.

"Look, I'll tell you what's going on with me. Until recently, I was just a regular guy. A self-employed business type. International real estate developer. Very materialistic in the sense that I didn't look beyond this world. I could never buy all that God stuff because it all sounded too artificial. Still does, but I hope that's O.K. with you, I know you're a Christian."

Camus thought for a moment. Then he spoke. "Well I am a Christian because I was raised to be. But I played plenty of hooky from church and with Nellie gone it all seems no good, not real enough."

"Well, at least you had a religion. That's good. They say that the training of the spirit is something you can carry beyond this lifetime. Most forms of religious practice help prepare the spirit for more advanced training. So you're lucky. Me, I've never really belonged to anything. I've always been a loner. No spiritual training and no real personal connection. That's all right with me. It suits me. At least I thought it did. But something changed for me recently when I met this woman."

"Weren't married?"

"I had been divorced a long time. And suddenly, a woman came along. Something happened. It was like magic. She got to me. Women don't get to me, so this is very unusual. We really connected. It was electric. Then she disappeared. Like your Nellie maybe, only mine was only in my life a few hours, not even a whole day."

"You're a fast mover."

"Wasn't like that. We became everything to each other, or so I thought, in a short time. Then, that big earthquake happened, I got hit in the head, blacked out, and, when I came to, she was gone. Gone."

"You scared of them things?" Camus asked.

"Of what?"

"Quakes?"

"Well, I don't know."

"They say a bigger one's coming, lot's of 'em and that big floods and things come after them."

"Big floods?"

"Yeah," Camus nodded, "waves thousands of feet high. Killing everything, I think."

Again, the black wave raced through my mind. "Well, I was trying to tell you about this woman." I wanted to change the subject.

"Yeah, O.K. So now you're lookin' for her?"

"You could say that." I rubbed the perspiration from my brow.

"I didn't even try with Nellie."

"Why not?"

"Simple. I figured that if she was alive and not with me she either couldn't be or didn't wanna be. If she couldn't be and the police couldn't help her, then I probably couldn't either. If she didn't wanna come back to me, I wasn't gonna go after her. And if she was dead, then she was where I wasn't ready to go."

This sounded like wisdom. Camus made sense here. I felt uncomfortable. Of course, if Sheeyah wanted to come back to me and if she could, she would. Why should I go searching for someone who might not want to see me?

Is that what you want to believe about me, Triad?

There was her voice again. Well, why should I look for you if you left me?

Because I didn't leave. And because I'm calling you, Triad.

Sheeyah, I love you. Now I had admitted it.

And I love you, Triad.

But all this is about more than that, isn't it?

Yes, Triad.

"But there's more Camus. Something happened to me when I met her. I started to remember things, kind of like you remembered that place that you had never been. I started to remember things about reality, about my self. Somehow Sheeyah seemed to know this would happen. That's why I've got to find her, to find out what's happening to my mind, to my heart,

Dissolving the Auric Veil

to my soul. I FEEL LIKE I'M GOING CRAZY, LOSING IT."

Camus was unmoved by my intensity. "What makes you think she knows the answer?"

"I know she knows. I can feel it."

Then trust your feelings more, Triad.

But where are you? You know I'd be put in a mental hospital if I told a doctor this was happening to me. That I was hearing you. And that I was hearing a wiser me. Are you alive? Or do I have to wait for you to reincarnate? How will I ever find you out there?

Trust your feelings. Do you feel that I am still alive Triad?

Yes.

Then I am.

Then come back, Sheeyah.

I am back, Triad.

Where?

Take care of Camus first, you've brought him way out here on this tightrope of ideas. Unless you know his spiritual tolerance, you can't just leave a person at risk of falling after you lead him on a perilous climb to new heights. You have a responsibility when you serve as a teacher. Either close up the story or take him all the way.

I don't know what all the way is. And what's this spiritual tolerance stuff?

Then just close up the story. Help him climb back down.

"Camus, there is a way to see more, to hear more, to know more than our five senses tell us. I'm just discovering this." That's what the amnesic me thought. *(I, of course, have known this for eons. I always get a kick out of the dissolution of amnesic selfhood. I sound so silly to myself.)*

"So you think there's more to know about Nellie? How?" Camus kept prompting me to explain more of what I did not know I knew.

"Well, it's intuition. A sort of voice or picture sometimes in your head. When it comes, you listen to it. You don't push it away but you also don't make it more than it is. You just let it come. The more you relax with it and watch it, the more there it is."

"So if I think about Nellie?"

"Just let yourself do so."

"If I dream about her?"

"Just notice yourself doing so. Try to remember the pictures. Don't draw any conclusions from them, don't decide she's alive or dead or anything, just watch for a while. Maybe for years."

"Just pay attention, you mean?"

RIGHT. He got it. I got it. JUST PAY ATTENTION. "Yes Camus. That's exactly right."

"I usually push it away or ignore it or laugh at myself. Usually I ignore it and turn on the T.V."

So do I. "Yeah, T.V. will take your inner pictures away and replace them with artificial ones. Not your own. It all depends on the wavelength you want to tune in to. Man-made radio waves or your higher mind waves."

"This is a lot for a simple guy like me."

He's right, Triad. As a teacher, a communicator, you have to know when to lay it on and when to tread gently into naive minds. So, if you think he's a naive mind, take him down gently now.

That was Sheeyah again. I loved her for her advice at that moment. I did not resent the advice the way I usually had in my life.

"But you know, this other debit and credit stuff, well it sort of makes sense. You know, I feel guilty a lot. Maybe I wasn't good enough to Nellie."

I recoiled. Camus wanted more all of a sudden. I wanted out. Now was I going to have to be father confessor?

No, just a friend and a teacher, Triad. Just go on a bit more.

Sure Sheeyah, if you say so. Here goes: "Guilt is like pity and other uncomfortable emotions. Guilt weighs you down. It makes your spirit heavy. It lowers your vibration. It stops you from being a high enough spirit to see beyond, to rise to higher levels. You may have brought heavy vibrations of past guilt into this life from past lifetimes. You will carry it on to future lifetimes, unless you can release it, unless you can release yourself from it."

"Easy for you to say."

Not really. I didn't know what I was talking about. Yet it made a bit of sense.

"I feel real guilty, Triad."

"Do you know what about?"

"Well not really, just guilty about Nellie."

"But what about her, Camus?"

"I must a done somethin' wrong for her to go." Camus sounded deeply dejected.

"Well, Camus, what are you feeling guilty of?"

That's nice, Triad.

"Not knowing her better. Not really listening."

"Camus, maybe it was Nellie's fate to go and maybe you had no say in her fate. She was on her own life path. You two shared some time together and then it was time for her to go."

"Then she should feel guilty, not me. For leaving."

"What if she had no choice?"

"Then God is guilty."

"God does not know how to feel guilt. It is not a god feeling. God is a force. A force is an energy. Emotions are too small for the size of the god force." I was surprised at my certainty.

"But then it wouldn't be anyone's fault." Camus sounded surprised.

"Right. You got it."

Camus looked as if he felt everything was complete. He took a deep breath. He looked at the water. When his face came back to mine, he looked relieved. "Then I'm not such a bad guy after all."

"No, you're a fine man." I actually meant this now.

"But you, Triad, are a bit nuts."

"A bit. But if I help you to feel a little better, don't knock what I say to you while I do it." I was helping Camus. This surprised me. I never really helped anyone in my life.

"O.K., I won't."

Camus started to row toward the shore. I was surprised and a little wistful. Now I did not want our dialogue to end. I felt as if I had connected with him. I felt something change deep in my heart.

What had happened was small but it was immense. That is the way of real communication. The amnesic me could feel a bit of the shift. I thought that Camus was released from a long chain of repetition and low vibration. I shared a bit in this presumed release. I figured that, if he wanted to, Camus could die now and move on to the next phase of his spiritual evolution.

"Now I can die a happy man."

"Die?" I was uncomfortable with his comment. I had not said anything to Camus about his dying. Not out loud. And I didn't mean die NOW. "Well, isn't that a bit extreme?"

"Not according to the docs, Triad. They say my heart is so bad it can quit any time now, even maybe right now. I hope you know how to row. I'm too old for a heart transplant they tell me. They gave me a week to six months."

I felt sick. Why had I inflicted all this metaphysical stuff on a suffering man?

Stop it Triad, he looks happy now. Look at him, he feels relieved, more at peace. He has just released the heavy burden of guilt.

Sheeyah, that isn't making me feel much better. Now where are you? Answer. Please, Sheeyah, I'm feeling very sick and very crazy.

Here.

Where? Sheeyah where?

There.

And there she was, sitting on a large rock on the far side of the lake.

"So can you row?" Camus called my attention back.

I fumbled. "Well, yes, of course, I can if you want me to take over." I took the oars. Where did that huge bird go?

"Row me to the middle of the lake. I'm an old and frail man and I'm not supposed to be rowing. Take me to my next stop."

Now he tells me he's not supposed to row.

"But isn't it too hot out here for you?" I asked hoping we could cancel this exercise. I wanted to go to Sheeyah.

"Nope. I need to be here. Please."

So I rowed. I had the strange sensation that I was rowing on light and through air.

"Here is fine. This is the next stop." Camus touched the water. "Water's ice cold."

"Yeah, it'd be a real shock to swim in it," I said, wondering if I could take it. I wanted to get away from Camus. I really needed an exit.

"Great idea." Camus finished his beer and stood up.

I hung on to the boat nervously. "Camus, you'll capsize us. What are you doing?"

"Thank you so much, Mr. Triad." Camus jumped off. The boat rocked vigorously but did not capsize. I held on, shocked. The ice cold water splashed me. I shivered uncontrollably.

Why did Camus go swimming? But wait. Where is Camus? Nowhere? Oh great, so now he's an underwater diver. But his heart. HIS HEART! THIS COULD KILL HIM!

I looked at Sheeyah. She motioned for me to stay calm and seated. She and I sat looking at each other across the lake for what seemed to be forever. A fierce chill raced up and down my spine again and again. Finally, Camus floated to the surface of the water, face down. He had dared to go past the surface of his lake.

I knew he was dead. Stunned, I left his body and rowed to the shore. I got out of the boat and, for some reason, I automatically pushed the boat back out into the water. A ray of light fell from the sky and seemed to propel the boat to the center of the lake. I thought I heard what I suspected was that huge bird screeching in the distance, "Skarrr, Skarrrrrrr . . . . SSSkkkkkaaaaaaaaaarrrrrrrrrrrrrrrr!"

Sheeyah came to meet me at shoreline.

Our eyes met. Her deep silence held the answer to my questions.

5

Heed my words. There is more to your history on Earth than you teach yourselves. So much of the Truth about it has been lost. But, the myth of catastrophe and cataclysm has been preserved throughout history by so many religious traditions and cultures. In this way, the collective memory keeps the information alive for us all. Mankind desires this knowledge.

You have undoubtedly heard the story of Atlantis, the beautiful and highly civilized continent said to have abruptly sunk into the sea about 10,000 B.C. It actually submerged more than once over the million year period preceding that event. The memory of the Atlantean continent has lingered through history in various forms among the various peoples who lived in the lands surrounding its presumed location. The name of this great land mass, Atlantis, which existed in the Atlantic and reached into the Aegean Sea, is again and again, from language to language, among seemingly unrelated cultures, described by words containing the sounds "atln."

Many choose to treat the story of Atlantis as a fairy tale rather than as a reality, probably because the evidence of its existence is sketchy. Nevertheless, throughout history, definite efforts have been made to carry forth information regarding the fate of Atlantis and to preserve Atlantean wisdom. Manetho, an Ancient Egyptian, kept records of pre-Egyptian history, of events occurring thousands of years before the first historic dynasties emerged in Egypt. These records extended back to the Atlantean time described as the "Reign of the Gods." The Greek historian Herodotus described a great city, specifically called "Atlantis," on an island in the ocean. Somewhat later, the Greek philosopher Plato wrote of the amazingly sudden end to the highly developed civilization of "Atlantis."

The story tells us that the greatest of Atlantis' advances were the key to its final downfall. Progress on the material plane can backfire that way. This progress is oft mistaken for spiritual evolution. But it is not. You living on Earth today must incorporate this lesson.

So allow yourself to consider the risks of economic complexity. Such complexity, typical of what you consider advanced civilizations, is dangerous — not only on the material plane, but in all dimensions of spiritual reality. What you do here, in your physical dimension, has effects far beyond the reality you see and know. Be careful how you use your energy, especially your financial energy. Blind desire for material gain can pollute, can cripple, can kill your soul.

The story tells us that the Atlantean economy grew overly complex. The system of barter was replaced by a monetary system so complicated that only the so-called experts could fathom it. Note that this monetary system was structured much like that of the Federal Reserve banking system of the United States on Earth today. Most U.S. citizens have been deceptively led to believe that this system is owned, backed and operated by their government, whereas, in reality, the Class A stockholders, the powers behind the scene, control the system through the largest member banks under the umbrella of the New York Federal Bank, the flagship of the system. Fewer than a dozen international banks have the controlling interest in that stock, the majority of which are not based or owned by entities in the United States. As a functioning matter, the entire U.S. monetary system of which I speak has the capability of being subjected to manipulation by outsiders for their own benefit. During the incarnation I describe in these chapters, I have had reason to associate with the powers behind the United States' and other of Earth's economies. Some of these powers invested in my multinational real estate development schemes. They have been especially intrigued by my survivor territories concept.

But back to Atlantis. The basis of the very materialistic Atlantean money system was an almost unlimited, over-extended financing that made the intrinsic value of the actual goods virtually worthless. (Note again the parallel to today's economics.) Eventually and predictably, the Atlantean economic system collapsed by its own complexity. All value disappeared as the planetary and off-planet financiers used unproductive manipulations of funds for material gain, generating untenable economic chaos. The shanties of the poor, as well as the palaces of the rich, became slums. Rapacious bands of the disillusioned began to roam both urban areas and the countryside. Psychic energy was increasingly wasted on fear, worry, anger and suspicion. Advanced knowledge began to evaporate. The lowest level of consciousness prevailed. The mansions of the merchants became their tombs. Their intense desire for material gain was their tragic flaw.

And so, as a result of a complicated chain of abuses of energy, the last sinking of Atlantis commenced. This sinking and flooding mirrors a theme that appears in the mythologies of most of your cultures. We know that some of the higher individuals, who had developed and raised their vibrational abilities, left the material plane and vaulted into higher spiritual dimensions in order to survive. In recent years, these off-planet Atlantean refugees have again been incarnating on

Earth. They, like me, hope to witness the re-emergence of the Atlantean continent they so loved. For this to happen, however, another Earthly convulsion must occur and some of your continents that currently exist above sea level must sink. Then so be it.

Ω

I was still at lakeside, caught in Sheeyah's eyes.

Finally, our gaze was broken as a host of sparrows swooped by us and then looped straight upward and disappeared into the sky.

I had to say something. I knew it would sound trite, trivial and petty after that deep gaze and after all that had happened, but my lower self, cad that I was, just had to say it to her. So I did. "You could have left me a note or something." I was looking for some reassurance about her behavior.

"I knew you'd find me at the lake."

"How? How could you know that? You only mentioned it once, in passing. What if I'd forgotten?"

"You didn't." She looked smug.

"But Sheeyah, I thought you'd died, drowned or something, in the earthquake."

Sheeyah chuckled at this. "But Triad, I'm a survivor — a survivor in the true sense of the word. I know how to move in and out of physically dangerous situations, what to do, where to go, when to go, and how to get there."

I was uncomfortable with her smugness. "Yes, but —"

"Yes, but what, Triad?"

"Yes, but a note or something explaining some of this would have been, in fact it would still be, great."

Sheeyah laughed a little. "There's a lot I haven't explained. Anyway, what is it that you're actually asking me for, a comprehensive guide to the fourth dimension? Get a travel agent for that. I'm not a tour guide if it's directions you want. It's not *my* job to direct you. Or maybe you want a basic class in the Great Mysteries of the Universe. Sorry, I'm not that kind of professor. Anyway, I think that stuff's more your job, Triad."

"Sheeyah — that is your name isn't it? You still haven't told me your real name. Sheeyah, or whoever you are, you amaze me. You think I know what's going on. Look, a few days ago, I thought I knew all I would ever know or need to know about myself. Then you walk into my life. Now — now —"

"Now what?" She looked so matter of fact about it all.

"Now you've come along."

"And?" She looked me deep in the eye. The look got real deep.

I looked right back. Right into her eyes. Right into her. I thought to myself that I had it said with my eyes, it felt like I had, but I underscored my mental message with words: "I am so in love with you it's frightening."

She raised her eyebrow. That look again. She seemed to know the punch line to some joke. I hoped that the joke wasn't on me.

"Look, Sheeyah, you seem to think you know something or other about all this. There's more to this — this us — what's happening with us — than meets the eye. That's what you think."

"No I don't. I don't think, I know. I don't think it, I know it — what's going on with us."

"O.K. then, what's going on with us?"

"I mean, Triad, I'd like to know more about it all, but I've got the general idea. It's profound. It reaches beyond the here and now. We've come a long way, perhaps across the universe or through time. We've met before and I know we'll meet again. I know that much for certain. I can't explain it all, but I've got a pretty good sense of it."

"So say more. There's got to be more you can say. I need some answers." I was quite anxious about the shift in my perception of reality, of life, of myself, that had begun when I met Sheeyah. It was a subtle but very discomforting feeling — a mild sense of calamity (or was it a BIG BLACK WAVE OF CALAMITY?) flowed through my mind and body.

Had I been able to step, for even a moment, fully out of my amnesic state, I would have recognized my anxiety. The shifting from a typical third dimensional, material plane state of mind to a higher vibrational level of existence and perception is, in effect, a psychophysical catastrophe. What this means is that the shift in understanding that accompanies spiritual growth can bring with it a loosening of mental and physical patterns which one has developed to live, to survive, on the material plane. Those patterns begin to loosen, to unravel, to dissipate, when a person begins to raise in vibration. Why? Because those patterns were developed to function at a particular vibrational level of existence. When one begins to raise one's vibrational level, those patterns won't suffice — something has got to change.

Dissolving the Auric Veil

I had moved, in my amnesic incarnation, to a point of essential destabilization. Some combination of my middle age malaise and my meeting Sheeyah and my higher self pressing me to let it through had literally destabilized my mental and physical systems. I was seriously afraid that I was going psychotic. Sick. Sheeyah must have sensed this.

But Sheeyah just smiled and raised an eyebrow. "So it's answers you're looking for? I'm looking for my lunch. I left it back there, where I've been camping. Come on."

Frustrated, and feeling lost, I followed Sheeyah to a spot behind a boulder. There, to my surprise, I saw that she had arranged a neat little camp, with a small tent and a small fire pit.

"I've been here for a while." She reached into the tent and pulled out a backpack. "Want an apple? ... I do." She took a bite and handed it to me.

I took the apple, but I wasn't finished with my interrogation. Especially now that I had seen that she had been camping out here while I was worrying about her. "So why didn't you tell me you were all right? I had the harbor searched for your body."

"Back to that again." Sheeyah sighed and shook her head a bit. "Because you knew I was all right. You could feel it. Deep down in there." She touched my chest near my heart with her hand.

I felt a rush of excitement flow through me. Mostly animal attraction. So I pulled her to me and kissed her.

I wondered, would she make love with me here? Did she want me? I searched her eyes for an answer. I thought she mumbled something to me, but her mouth was not moving. Maybe she was sending me a mental message. I heard the words clearly in my head: Trust your deepest feelings. They are the most still, most certain ones. There will be no doubt attached to real Truth.

Yes, then. She will make love with me here. Now. I pulled her down.

We undressed each other almost ceremoniously. We began to make love. The passion built slowly, like a wind rising toward sundown on a warm day. We reached the point again, as we had that last time on my yacht, where we departed from intense physical passion into a sort of energy mingling, an intercourse of two spirits. At first we were breathing into each other, I inhaling the breaths Sheeyah was exhaling and vice versa. The shared air moved through us like fire. Then we became still. We were so still that I lost awareness of our surroundings. It seemed as if time stopped and we were merged eternally —

Until I heard a faint rattle. Yes, a rattle. It took me a moment, but then I recognized it. A snake. A rattler!

At that very moment, as I lay on top of Sheeyah, at the instant I began to tense, Sheeyah whispered, "Do NOT move. At all. Freeze. Absolutely still."

Somehow I got it. I did something out of character for the amnesic me. I overrode my startle reflex and became more still than I had ever imagined possible.

"Through the eye of the needle," she whispered almost inaudibly. Or was it whispered? It seemed that I, again, as earlier that day, could hear her voice in my head.

Pass through the still point with me. Be small. Still.

I was still. It felt as if someone had just stepped on some universal kind of brakes. Abruptly, a fearsome sensation lurched through me. At that moment, the Earth seemed to sputter and stop turning. We seemed to freeze into statues made of air and at the same time to shrink to specks of invisibility. I felt very heavy, very dense, very invisible.

My terror took a detached form. I became a mere spectator in what could have been the moment of my death. I could see the snake watching, half coiled, poised in strike position. Now, the snake looked so large, the face of the snake so close. I gazed back from my minute, dense, but invisible and frozen sense of being.

Something happened. I felt some kind of strange tumult, as if the earth quaked with a very soft, rolling sort of motion. I felt as if, for just a moment, I were being swallowed. I think I disappeared.

Next I knew, I landed on the ground next to Sheeyah with a thud. I felt back to normal. The snake was gone. I quickly surveyed myself and Sheeyah. Apparently, we had not been bitten.

"So you're not going on to heaven just yet I gather?"

Sheeyah had a strange sense of humor. I couldn't quite get the joke. "What?" I queried incredulously.

"Triad, that seemed to be pretty high passion. Even the snake was impressed."

I mumbled a response, "If you say so," but my heart was not in the

Dissolving the Auric Veil

dialogue at the moment. I was trying to sort out what had just happened to me — to us. At least I thought it had happened to Sheeyah as well.

She seemed to hear me think so. She went on in a soft but enthusiastic voice. "You get it don't you? You can pass through the eye of the needle right into heaven when you become so absolutely still. We can come and go from that heaven, to and from that sort of hyperspace, to and from other dimensions, other vibrational levels, anytime we choose. It's the way to survive any calamity. You pass through the eye of the needle into another dimension. In fact, calamity is often the reason for reaching through the eye toward the beyond. Calamity or trying to avoid calamity."

What was she talking about now? "What makes you so sure of all this? Whatever this is," I asked her.

She was on a roll. As if she had just discovered the method to her madness, the validity of her wild views regarding reality. "*I* do it. *I* go through eyes, what I call windows. You can go through them and become very, very small or very, very immense. You can become very dense — into a sort of nowhereness, or spread very thin — into a sort of everywhereness. I've been doing it since I was a kid. I wasn't exactly certain what I was doing for years, but I've come to understand it more. Especially now, after today. I didn't have anyone to explain it to me. And now I have you."

"Me? You think *I* get all this stuff?"

"Yes, *Triad*." Again she said my name as if it had some greater meaning.

I thought to myself that she was probably right. Yet, I still was uncertain as to what she was right about. Although my amnesic state was dissolving, dissipating, I was hanging on to its remains, perhaps by force of habit. Familiar vibrations. Identifiable patterns. My spiritual amnesia was familiar to me, like an old stuffed animal I had snuggled with since childhood. I was slow to want to surrender it.

"I'm camping here again tonight. Will you stay with me?"

I didn't have anywhere else important to go at the moment. "Sure. If you think we'll make it through to morning without losing it."

"Losing what?"

"Our minds," I said nervously.

"Are you really worried about that or just joking?"

"Just joking."

"No you're not, Triad."

"Really, it was a joke."

"No, it wasn't entirely. I could tell by your voice. You're uncomfortable."

"Well, a little," I admitted.

"No, a little more than a little," she insisted.

"Come on, Sheeyah, it's not important."

"Yes it is. How can we get personal with each other and not get personal? ... Talk to me. Talk to me, Triad."

"Sure, O.K. So what do you want to know?"

"Are you feeling like you're losing it?" She pressed for honesty.

I spilled the beans. "I don't know. I feel as if everything is a bit upset. I feel a bit sick. I'm unsettled. Not thinking straight. Either I or the world around me seems chaotic. Out of order. I have no sense that things will ever look quite the same again. And I'm not sure why," I confessed.

I, in my naiveté, was describing exactly that state of instability that any system, including that of a living organism, has to reach to evolve beyond its present level of development. It's a rule of sorts. Some kind of psychophysical catastrophe, a small or large calamity, is usually required to loosen up a rigid system. And I, the amnesic me who had gotten very stuck suffering from a mid life malaise of my own manufacturing, had become quite rigid.

It was when all the recent chaos finally hit my life that I became more sensitive to the subtle inputs that I would have normally missed or totally ignored. Yet, these inputs were all contributing to my unbalancing: Sheeyah's voice in my head, our shrinking to invisibility, the snake's enlarged face, the higher form of sex and love-making that Sheeyah and I had somehow slipped into . . . .

Sheeyah seemed to be nodding in approval. What was she thinking now? I asked. "So have I said something you agree with or what? You're nodding."

She tilted her head to one side. That eyebrow went up again. "I'm thinking that you're right where you should be."

I moaned. "Oh, that's comforting. I should feel this miserable."

"Is it that bad?"

I thought for a moment. "I really don't know."

Dissolving the Auric Veil

"You know, right when you start becoming really aware of the metaphysical aspects of reality, when you start really believing in the possibility that they have some Truth to them, you can feel this way. It's difficult not to register the shift in perception as physically and emotionally unsettling, even sickening. Some people get away with it, but not many. It can last a while."

"Did that happen to you, Sheeyah?"

"Still is happening," she shrugged.

"You seem all right though."

"Sometimes, but I'm better with it since I've come to understand what it is. I can ride the waves now. It seems to come in waves, Triad."

I thought of the black wave. I thought of the ripples on Crystal Mirror Lake. The ripples Camus made. The last view of Camus came back to my mind. I suddenly was aghast. Poor, poor Camus. And we had left him there. Forgotten him.

Sheeyah patted me on the shoulder reassuringly, as if she had heard my thoughts. "It'll be O.K. Let's sleep near the water tonight. I do that sometimes. I like watching the surface. When I do it long enough, I feel as if I can hear or feel messages, whispers and images of the future."

"You do, do you?" She was a strange woman. A bit of a romantic I guessed. Or a lunatic. But a lovely one. I thought it would be nice to keep her company. Or to have her company given my state of mind. "Sure, why not?"

"In fact, most nights I'm here, I look into the water for a long time. All of its light, all of the points of light it is reflecting, eventually reduces down to a single point of light, a point of light streaming into me. Then I lose myself and ...."

She looked at me and made a funny face, as if she thought she sounded silly, or better stated, as if she wanted me to think she thought she sounded silly. "Oh, never mind," she went on. "Grab some of the stuff. We can leave the tent here. I brought an extra sleeping bag for you, since I expected you to show up."

I decided not to ask any questions for a while. She obviously had coped with the Camus thing better than I had. No problems with the dead man for her. Still, I was surprised by her next comment:

"Camus called forth that snake I guess." She looked around and raised her voice a bit. "Good move, Camus. The serpent arises. Nice Biblical touch. I was truly tempted."

She was tempted? By what? That snake? She called it a serpent, as if she'd heard my thoughts. I thought to myself that I was in over my head and Sheeyah was way out there. I shook my poor head, hoping to clear it. I looked down at the ground as we carried the sleeping bags closer to the lake. Lunatic was really a better assessment of her. Well, she'd still be good company for another night, or maybe two. Three at most. The sex was good. And, after all, I had come *all* this way to find her and I *was* in love with her. But what was I getting into? I thought I'd best protect myself and call an end to it soon.

But the dawning night was like a clear syrup. The full moon shone on the surface of the water and made it look like a big silver eye in the land. Or like a mirror of all the universe. Or maybe like a window. A window to somewhere beyond the here that I knew. So I was pleasantly intrigued. I let my concerns about Sheeyah's sanity and my own mental health give way to the sensuous mystery and the downright sexy romance of it all.

We sat in our makeshift camp, side by side, hand in hand, gazing at the water. We were so full of the richness of the vision of that water, the eye that had swallowed Camus, that we never felt hungry for dinner. In fact, I would not think of food again for days. Days and days and days....

I do not know how long we sat there. At times we kissed. At times we caressed each other. But we just watched the water. I remember thinking that maybe it was our own special silent memorial service for Camus.

It was a very warm night. We probably wouldn't need our sleeping bags. I think I fell asleep. It was a light and floating kind of sleep. Some kind of dreaming was going on in my head, but I was only somewhat aware of it.

After a while, something roused me from my much relished peace. I realized that I had been sleeping and that although I had been lying down, Sheeyah was still sitting up. I sat up and looked around to try to figure out if anything that I should be concerned about had woken me. I saw nothing to alarm me in the moonlight. All seemed still.

Finally, I saw that Sheeyah's lips were moving. "What are you saying?" I whispered in her ear, "Tell me."

She whispered back to me in a monotone. "I am attempting to induce a state."

"A state of what?"

Her eyes were closed now, but she still faced the lake. She nodded her head as if it was I that was foolish. "A state of communication."

"Communication? With what?"

"Shh! Don't speak, ... I'll tell you if I can."

She went back to muttering. After several minutes, I found that I could hear some of the words and phrases.

"I am filled with the light of the lake, of the god force. My vibration is cleansed by the moon. I am clear of all but what I seek to attract. The light is in my heart and it grows. I am ready."

I wanted to touch her, but now I held my hands away. I felt a little wary, as if I had woken up in time to protect myself from a vague, indefinable danger. I felt fatigued and mildly impatient. Hadn't I had enough today?

But Sheeyah went on with her witchery or whatever it was.

"I have made my body available as the instrument of your manifestation in the now of my existence here. I have been filled with the breath of your Triad and it has brought into me your light. I can feel your presence. It has been lingering near me. Come forth if you will."

I watched numbly as she sat utterly still, eyes closed, in what seemed to be a hypnotic state. I had no more feelings about my exhaustion or the inconvenience. I had no reaction to the process. I had heard her say that she had been filled with *the breath of your Triad*. Someone's Triad. She meant me. But whose Triad did she think I was?

Abruptly, she groaned in pain. Her face distorted in anguish. She writhed and groaned again. I still watched numbly, now in awe of both her anguish and my detachment. I did absolutely nothing to help her.

For a fleeting moment, I thought that I would vomit. The feeling passed, but then I knew something very strange was going on. I did not know what.

She started to speak. At least it seemed she did. But it was not exactly her voice. It was much deeper and it was hoarse: "I have come. ... Come conceived of the intercourse of your breath with that of Triad."

Me? What did I have to do with this? Her humor was no longer excusable. I lay down, expecting to sleep instead of listen.

That unearthly and unnerving voice continued. "I return to Earth at this time. Through you."

I was very uncomfortable. This woman was truly psychotic. How did I ever get hooked up with her?

"Triad may speak to his son."

I sat up. Me? She — it — this woman was talking to me in this weird voice.

"Triad may speak to his son."

Now my jaw was tight. My teeth were clenched. "I don't have a son."

"I am your highborn son."

"You are, are you?"

"Nostradamus."

I flinched when I heard this name. "Yeah right, give me a break." I wasn't being very nice, but she was going too far with her fantasy games.

"Not of this lifetime, or of this dimension, when you cometh as Winston Triad Framingham, born of Earth parents. Not of this form."

"So if you're so sure about this, on what day of what month was I born?"

"On a January 30th."

How could Sheeyah know my birthdate? I had never told her. Would she have managed somehow to get the information in order to get me caught up believing in this game?

"Your suspicion is natural. Your amnesia continues, Father."

"Father? ... Come on, give me a break, Sheeyah." I hoped she'd stop.

But that grating voice continued. "Through Sheeyah, you have conceived my manifestation that I might ... I might return to speak to the people inhabiting Earth."

I felt a giant question in my mind.

She — or that voice — went on. "I am conceived, my spirit conceived of the mingling of your breaths in your passion."

I thought I'd play along with Sheeyah for a while. The only game in town, I laughed inside my head.

"If you are my son, then who am I?"

"The Father."

"And Sheeyah?" I tested.

"The Mother."

"Yes, but so what?" I challenged.

"The eternal Father and the eternal Mother."

"So we are like gods or something?" I joked.

"Or something."

I thought for a while. "So why are you here?"

"The time has come for the removal of ignorance."

"Can ignorance ever be entirely removed?" I doubted it.

"To the extent that your Creation will allow this."

This is getting good. My Creation. Like I am a god or something.

It went on. "I have said that when the time comes for the removal of ignorance, the case shall be made more clear."

"O.K. So who are you anyway? Why are you here? Why now?"

"The perfect knowledge of causes cannot be acquired without divine inspiration."

"What does this mean, Sheeyah? Am I supposed to get this?"

It went on. "The perfect knowledge of causes, of my cause for return, of my original prophecies, obscured by my hand through your instruction."

"My instruction? I told you to do something? To obscure something?" You've got the wrong guy.

"I was released by God almighty, in 1555 A.D. western Earth time, to reveal to humans by imaginative impression some secrets of the future. That future bears closer now."

"God almighty, well that's a little better. I thought you were blaming me." I laughed uneasily.

"With God almighty, through Sheeyah almighty Mother, bearing their son Nostradamus, forming the eternal Triads of Thebes, of Cozhadatonia, of ionized water in millions of seas, of the universe beyond time."

"Look, I can't really put all this together. It is a good idea though. Something mystical to our romance. But this is too far out, Sheeyah. Let's go to sleep now, please."

She paid me no attention and continued with that voice. "I have come to make clear the obscurities of my prophecies, because human understanding, being intellectually created and limited by its reliance on the brain of the third and physical dimension, cannot penetrate occult causes."

"Your prophecies? Oh, so you predicted something?" I pretended to get it, sort of.

"Yes. Centuries ago I predicted many things which have come to pass in the world in which you are incarnated and other things which have yet to come to pass there, with their time nearing now."

"If you say so. But I haven't heard about any of them."

"Alas, my Father, if you think beyond your cosmic curtain, your veil of amnesia, which you have so cleverly constructed, you will recognize my predictions as the implementation of your own plan."

"You expect me to swallow all this Sheeyah? .... Sheeyah? ... Sheeyah, answer me, please."

"Sheeyah is the vessel through which I communicate with you, Father."

"Sheeyah, I'm not finding this humorous. Actually, it's becoming quite tiresome."

"Sheeyah can hear, as I have arranged this phenomenon with her role in its outcome in mind, but she will not speak at this time."

"What did you say you were called now, Sheeyah?"

It answered, "I am not Sheeyah. I am Nostradamus."

"So, Nostradamus, why haven't you spoken to me sooner if this so important?"

"The time has now come for the removal of ignorance."

"Who's ignorance? Mine?" I tried to chuckle but nothing came out.

"Yours and that of the human race. I remind you of your purpose, Father."

"Does all this have something to do with Sheeyah coming into my life?" Obviously, I thought, Sheeyah was making this inane conversation happen. There was no other worldly spirit here.

"I remind her of her purpose as well."

"She seems to know what all this is about."

"Her amnesia has worn thinner than yours. Thin enough to serve as a vehicle for our meeting, with some intuitive sense of its urgency."

"So you're suggesting that she brought you to me? Some kind of wake up call?"

"No. I brought you together in order for the two of you to now conceive the manifestation of the increasingly urgent message you directed me to speak centuries ago."

It would only be much later, after many, many trials, that I would seriously give consideration to the notion that Nostradamus brought us together. "So you brought us together, did you? How long ago?"

"My predictive quatrains were first published in 1555 AD western Earth time. I called the manuscript CENTURIES. CENTURIES has been translated into many languages and reprinted continuously since 1555."

"So it was hundreds of years ago. Are you saying that you are still alive somewhere and talking to me about all this from somewhere?"

"No, you are saying that."

"So what is happening?" I wanted answers.

"Sheeyah has made herself available as the vessel for my transmission. You and Sheeyah, Father and Mother, have again conceived my spirit, again for purposes of your work on Earth."

"But we are not, were not, your real parents." Now I was actually conversing with this thing.

"What is real? ... If what you mean by real is biological, physical, I will let you answer that over time."

"Whatever you mean by that, I can't guess, Mr. Nostradamus or whoever you are. But who were your parents?" I pressed for an answer to at least that.

"My parents of that time?"

"Yes. What other parents would I be referring to?"

"You and Sheeyah," it said.

"You are making little sense to me. We were not your parents back in the 1500s. How could we be?"

"That is an answer you have a better ability to explain than do I." It was being elusive.

"Tell me about your real parents."

"By real, I understand you to be referring to the biological Earthly parents,

Jacques and Renee de Nostredame, who bore me into my incarnation as Michel de Nostredame in the 16th century AD western Earth time."

"Yes. So tell me about those parents," I challenged uncomfortably.

"They trained me well. I was provided an intellectually stimulating environment. I was born into a family of mathematicians and doctors, as were both my maternal and paternal ancestors. My grandfather trained me in both medicine and astrological science. I chronicled astrological data for doctors."

At least I got some kind of answer. I pressed on. "Medicine? Astrology? And somehow from there you went into prophesizing? How was that? Were you particularly religious?" I tried to laugh, again to no avail.

"My prophetic inclinations were guided by a longer lineage than that of the parents of that particular incarnation."

I shuddered at the mention of the word incarnation. After all, I had been pressuring poor Camus on the topic earlier that day. "What were you saying about your lineage?"

"Although my family had converted to Christianity, I was of Jewish descent, born biologically down from the line of one of the Issachari, one of the lost tribes of Israel. The Issachari were highly regarded for their prophetic abilities and applied astrological science in their visions."

"So why are you talking to me?" I played humble to hide my frustration and mounting fear.

"I have come at the time for the removal of ignorance. The case must be made more clear. I had hoped that after the extinction of my physical life on Earth, my writings would become more highly regarded."

"Was there no respect for your predictions?"

"There was some," it replied, "but many feared and were angered by my predictions. I therefore obscured what I could to protect myself."

"Were you ever right?"

"Most correct, by Divine inspiration. I correctly predicted the date of my own death, July 2, 1566. I accurately predicted the death and method of death of King Henri II. I predicted a multitude of key events in my own time which came to fruition. I went far beyond my own time. I predicted that the old Russian order of the Czar would fall to Communism and that Communism eventually would be replaced by another model. I also predicted the seven changes in the royal blood lines that would lead to the rise and fall of the British Empire ... I predicted the three modern despots or 'anti-Christs.' I detailed the downfall of the first anti-Christ, Napolean, in 1812, at the hands of the Russian Empire. Next, I named the three great dictators of the 1940s, specifically naming Hitler, the second anti-Christ, who I cryptically called 'Hisler' and for whom I identified the birthplace, Austria ... I also predicted the coming of the third anti-Christ, a despotic Middle Eastern leader who will lead civilization and the planet to a massive World War III ... I am also known for my predictions of natural disasters, including the breaking up of the Earth, although many have interpreted the timing of these events contrary to my writings."

"People must have thought you were crazy." I do, I told myself.

"I lived in an era in which prophets were linked with black magic and the profane, but I maintained insistence on the divine nature of the revelations made to me, as you know, my Father."

"Why do you call me that? Please stop calling me that, it's so — so — incestuous. And ridiculous."

"You have been my Father through time, in and out of dimensions and in and out of incarnations and inspiritizations within the different dimensions."

"So you think I've reincarnated several times or something?" How could I be having this conversation? Maybe this was what I deserved for my inane harassment of Camus.

"I don't think. I know."

"That sounds like Sheeyah. ... See, it is you."

"I have been mingling with Sheeyah's thoughts for some time. I began manifesting my message in words her still semi-amnesic mind could understand after you, my Amun, my Hidden One, my High Father, breathed the fire of my life into her, conceiving me again, but not incarnating me. You have indeed manifested me, created me — again."

I was rather upset — extremely upset — by whatever it was it or he or Sheeyah had just said. "Oh no, could you really be pregnant by me? Already? Look, Sheeyah, is that what this is all about? You might as well just come right out and say it if that's the case."

"Sheeyah is carrying my spirit. A spirit may or may not have a physical fetal body, Father. I am not a fetal body if you do not wish me to be one, Father. You decide whether or not you have conceived my incarnation at this time, or at any given time. For some reason, you have become increasingly hesitant to do so."

I thought I heard a touch of resentment in that voice, but I was quite relieved. Of course Sheeyah was not pregnant with my child. Of course not. But this was all so tiring. "Sheeyah, please. I must sleep."

The voice, it was ungiving. "I have allowed her to have full remembrance of what we say now, yet she cannot speak at this time."

"Why have you come to us?" I was pleading for more information.

"You and Sheeyah, as in the Triad we formed in ancient Thebes, must conceive me for me to come forth in any dimension. You, my Father, oh Hidden One, sent the breath of your spirit through Mut, the Power of Woman, Egyptian Priestess Sheeyah, to bring me forth, then and now."

"Why have you come to us?"

"It is you who have called me. You who have conceived *me*, Father."

"Why? Why would I do such a thing?"

"You have conceived me for the time has come for the removal of ignorance."

"You keep saying this. Ignorance about what?"

"Ignorance regarding the true meaning of global catastrophe, the cathartic impetus into universal salvation for those who redeem their spiritual sentience."

"You speak in garbled tongue," I muttered. To say the least.

"The pictures so many doctrines have presented of the cyclical end to this world, the return of the end of this world."

"You speak in garbled tongue," I said again.

"The apocalypse is at hand," it said. "Rise up and witness."

"Witness? All I see is a woman speaking in an old man's strained voice, saying almost unintelligible things."

"I have come at your beckon to remind you of who you are: The spiritual Triad we form again and again throughout time — taking forms such as Amun-Ra, Mut and Khonsu — Osiris, Isis and Horus — Father, Holy Mother Ghost, and Son — Triad, Sheeyah and Nostradamus. You are Triad, the union of the three of us. You are Triad, the Father. You manifest your message through me throughout history everywhere in the universe. I come into being at your discretion."

"But this is not at all my discretion."

"I beseech you Father, look deeper within yourself. Yours is the ultimate discretion."

"If this is at my discretion, then why don't I know it?"

"Because you have inflicted an akashic amnesia upon yourself in order to go through exactly this process of rediscovery which you are now undergoing."

"Why now?" I wondered.

"Death and rebirth cycles are at hand."

"Death of what?"

It wanted to explain more. "For Earth humans, it is the metaphorical end of time: the image of catastrophe we guiding spirits have been generating and regenerating for eons. We know this to be the end and the beginning: as it was in the beginning and is now and ever shall be, the Omega Point."

I couldn't help but think of my survivor territories scam. Maybe I was really on to something. Using the media to generate and exaggerate the image of catastrophe — and using that woman, that Earthcult woman, as a sort of advertisement for my land parcels. So, trying to sound very innocent, I asked, "Why would the human race play such a game with itself?"

"The entire species is going through what you call a growth spurt. A new step in evolution. But, Father, a system must truly destabilize to truly evolve. Cataclysm is stimulating. Chaos promotes growth. There is no other way. You have ordained it as such."

"Must I deal with this stuff? I'm just a simple guy." Well, sort of simple.

"You bring all that happens to you and around you into your life."

"How do you know?" How did it know this?

"You have taught me so."

"You seem to think I'm a teacher." This felt odd.

"Yes, the great communicator, Father. The hidden breath by which the living, breathing gospel is manifested. You were once and always will be the Monad. You became the Duad to manifest. Through the Duad of yourself and your other half, Mother, you have translated my spirit into reality — you have manifested me through Mut, your priestess, Sheeyah.

And you have brought me into clairaudience with the highest evolved of the third dimension."

Sheeyah crumpled to a huddle. She was absolutely motionless for several minutes. And then I heard her gasp. "He's Christ you know," Sheeyah whispered in her own voice.

"Sheeyah, what *is* all this?"

"You know what it is, Triad. You have initiated this conception again and again."

"Sheeyah, should we go on like this, living in a fantasy dream about our togetherness?"

"You are so quick to call one thing fantasy and another thing reality. Is the dividing line so clear?" Sheeyah's calm surprised me. She continued. "Death and rebirth, I guess that's what it's about."

"Death? Death of what?" I didn't really want to know. The black wave was creeping up into my mind again.

"The end is near."

"End?" The black wave became larger and more threatening than ever. I had to remind myself that the wave was only in my imagination.

"I can still hear him," she said blankly.

"Hear who?"

"Him."

"Who?"

"Nostradamus."

"You can't be serious, Sheeyah." I looked at her, trying to get her attention. She was looking right back at me, but somehow, she didn't seem to be all there. "You're way out there, aren't you?" I said paternally.

"Generally, or at the moment?" she asked me with a bit of her old jest.

"Well, both, I guess."

She regained a bit more of herself. "Sure, thanks for the compliment. ... So, anyway, I still hear him. Talking. In my head."

"What's he saying?"

"It's all in the thought form." Sheeyah squinted.

"The thought form?" What did that mean?

"He says, don't worry, just trust the process."

"Sure. Yes. Whatever the two of you say, the process ... the process of what, I wonder."

"You are coming into contact to regain realization of your self and your mission, Triad."

"So sure, I bet I'm here to spread enlightenment or something."

"Boy, you sure got that right," she smiled.

"That must be you, Sheeyah. I doubt old Nostradamus would speak in such jargon."

"You are being sarcastic because the reality of what is happening is so startlingly profound for you, Triad."

"Yes, I guess that's right, if there were any reality to all this, it *would* be startlingly profound." I wanted very much to set her straight.

"But?" she asked.

"But what?"

"Well you said 'if there were any reality to this'. Do you think there is?"

"Is what?"

"Is any reality to this?"

"Well, I suppose in some way I do." It was an honest admission on my part. At least it felt like one.

"Triad —"

"Sheeyah? ..." I looked into her face. It reflected gentleness. I thought that it was my own feelings for her coming back at me.

"Triad, it's all pretty heavy for me too, you know. I mean, I felt it all coming, but the gravity of it — it's — it's all so encompassing. I'm overwhelmed, I think."

"First time you let on. Wish you'd told me sooner," I scolded gently.

"Well, watch me closely. I act like it's all within my domain, and in a way it is. I've really explored a lot of this inter-dimensional travel. And I've communicated with spirits and animals and even trees and the Earth. But, since we met, everything is taking on a new level of reality. It's no longer dismissable as fantasy, if it ever really was. Now I don't have a way out if it gets too scary, no escape route anymore."

"So what do we do with all this?" I was asking myself as well as Sheeyah. "If we let ourselves believe in all this, then what do we do?"

She closed her eyes. I could tell she was hearing that voice again. "The message is as deep as you want to hear it, as deep as you wish to let it go."

"Yeah, but then what do we do about it?"

"I don't know, Triad. I guess we do whatever it is we do when we react to the message. I guess we react to the message in whatever way we hear it."

"Sheeyah, what do you think about all this apocalyptic stuff? Pretty frightening or a lot of bull?"

She closed her eyes. "I'm trying to hear what to make of it."

"You don't —"

"Shhh!" she demanded. And then she said slowly, as if she were reading the words, "Each successive layer of Original Truth can be extracted from the layers of what we call, or are usually willing to settle for calling, truth."

I was feeling impatient. "Is there an ultimate Truth somewhere in all that? Because if there is, I'd like to hear it. That's what I'm waiting for." I had been waiting all my life, I mused at that moment. Pretty ironic, if it really is me that has all the answers. Hah! Some joke. But who's playing the joke? Would I play such a joke on myself? Highly unlikely.

She opened her eyes and looked right through me as if I were made of air. "It is you."

"Me?" I didn't want it to be me. Me. The reluctant Messiah. Let me try that one on for size. Oh great.

"You know the Truth, Triad."

"So, are you still channeling or whatever you call it or what?"

"I'm not sure, Triad. Before, when his voice was coming through me and he was talking to you, I was channeling, at least by all the definitions of closed channeling that I've heard. But now, it's as if I'm an open channel, voices and sensations from anywhere could come through me, but he's taking care of me so I don't get overwhelmed. He left me open for a reason. He's still here, his entity or personality or whatever is still expressing itself to me. ... And you know, you know, the funny thing about it is, I'm sure that — "

"That what?"

"Now that I recognize him, I'm sure that I felt him coming. He's been hanging around me quite a while. But he couldn't really take form until you came along."

She was wrong. He hadn't taken form. I stood up. I was as unsteady as I had been when I stood up in Camus' boat hours earlier. "I've got to go for a walk. I'll be back. You don't have to wonder about that. I will return."

Sheeyah nodded, "This I know."

I wandered off, hiking toward the road that I had driven in on. The incandescent moonlight gave everything a luminous quality, as if each leaf of grass, each tree, every boulder, each entity, organic and inorganic, gave off its own light.

I began to lecture myself: There are times when life brings you to a fork in the road. Sometimes, you don't see the fork coming. It just appears. There, a choice must be made, no matter how painful. This was one of those times.

I had to force myself into a commitment to go one way or the other. It was time, high time, for me to consciously and clearly choose to go further with this woman and all the developments related to our meeting, or choose to go back to the safer, saner life I had been leading.

Sheeyah had just channeled what claimed to be Nostradamus, *my son*, of all things. Now, it was obvious to me that she had a wild imagination, but how could she have known my birthdate? And why would she invent something like this outrageous Nostradamus story?

I wanted to believe that Sheeyah was not seriously disturbed and that she was not a con woman. But could she really be a transmitter of a voice from the beyond?

Cross band communication is entirely possible. In fact, it is similar to what is going on in your head at this moment.

Now I could hear, with stunning clarity, my wiser self thinking. This was something else that was troubling me. Since Sheeyah had come along, I had been hearing voices. Voices without bodies. And one of those voices was mine — a wise old me which was now even more distinct from the regular me than it had been when I first heard him:

I have a body. It is your body.

That's what I mean. This is probably classical psychosis or something.

No, this is your higher self talking, speaking to you from the dimensions beyond, from places that you traverse with ease.

That's what I mean. Since Sheeyah came along, I've been crazy like this.

No, this is not crazy. This woman merely attracted your vibrations to a higher level, almost the way a magnet can move properly charged iron filings toward itself. You were not going to be able to hear your self at a higher octave until you opened that band of communication. And even now, as I speak, I am transducing, reducing the frequency of my transmissions to one that your mind can receive. As you gain control over your receiving mechanisms, this will be increasingly unnecessary.

But where are you?

Right here.

You can't be. You must be very far away if I can't see you.

I am right here. I am you. You are so expansive a being that your energy field spans all the dimensions. You exist in all dimensions at once.

So where is the me that exists in one of those other dimensions right now?

Right here.

Those dimensions aren't right here.

Right here is an elusive concept, even though it sounds concrete to you. In reality, there is no right here here. But, in your terms, yes, those dimensions are all right here. Call them the parallel universes if you like. They, and all the spirits which inhabit them, are all right here. This is true because you, everyone, exists in a matrix of dimensions. You are confused and doubtful because, prior to recent events, you were entirely unattuned to the messages coming at you, many of them from you to yourself, from other dimensions.

But then why can't I see these other dimensions?

You will when you learn to stop using your eyes as the ultimate arbiters of reality. Everything is right here whether you can see it or not.

Right here?

Yes. Anyone who is trained, especially you, can access the energy flowing through any dimension of reality at any moment you choose.

Is that how Sheeyah found Nostradamus?

Well, in a sense, yes. The energy of Nostradamus exists in another dimension of reality. He has no body at this time and is a very complex spirit. He is not your typical disembodied dead man who is so hungry for ongoing contact with the material plane that he has a hard time leaving it.

So Sheeyah found Nostradamus way out there? It sounded like she'd been practicing this channeling stuff. It seemed that she knew something about the method.

Yes, the communication was transduced by Nostradamus and received and transformed into words through Sheeyah's mind, the receiver and the vehicle of his transmission. However, it was you who brought Sheeyah to you and breathed Nostradamus' energetic manifestation into her. That is how Sheeyah manifested the words of your Nostradamus and let him speak.

So I'm telling myself, from a higher dimension of my own existence, that Sheeyah actually did channel Nostradamus who actually is my son.

Yes you are.

And I'm also telling myself that I am this very highly evolved spirit who just happens to be having an Earth life time right now? That, in fact, at this very moment, I am engaging in a dialogue between a lower and a higher awareness, both of which are me?

Yes. You engage in such dialogue quite often, although it is not always as apparent to you as it is right now.

And my son is reminding me that the time has come for something to be made more clear?

Yes, you arranged to have your son wake you up at a certain point in this incarnation.

Wake me up at the height of my career when I am just about to pull off the greatest international development deal in world history? Exactly at this point? I should believe all this?

You already do.

And I should want to go on with this madness?

There is no turning back. You could try to return to your amnesia, but you would never be able to convince yourself of its validity. Once the metaphysical realities have been glimpsed, there is no path but onward with spiritual development. The validity of your spiritual awareness snowballs. As you will see when your amnesia has fully lifted, you are already fully developed. You merely elected to reacquaint yourself with the experience of spiritual evolution on the material plane and to interact with humans who are about to go through one of the greatest periods of catastrophe-spurred enlightenment in universal history. You also have an urgent cause — you seek to save Original Truth.

This is too much for me to understand.

Just follow your heart. The case will be made more clear.

My heart?

I realized that I had been kicking a pebble as I walked along. I wondered if it too contained a spirit. Suddenly that pebble had disappeared. I looked around. I had walked way down the road.

My heart? I was in love. In love with what? Sheeyah. Yes, with Sheeyah, and with more than that — in love with the great adventure she had brought to my life.

For the first time in this physical body, I felt the physical sensation of emotion in the area of my heart. So this was real emotion. Real feeling. I had finally found it.

6

I have incarnated among you to fully know your experience of the coming events. As one of you, I can say with certainty that you — we — already know what is coming. We know that the massive and tumultuous reversals in polarity will be profound. Indeed, little passion plays, metaphorical explorations of this greater galactic, most cosmic shift are already being performed by humans around us.

Yes, the writing is on the wall, like graffiti, everywhere to be seen. Yet, the Truth is buried deep within the recesses of our souls. Our dreams, our fantasies, our fictions, our realities, our families, our businesses, our actions, our environments, reveal all there is to know; yet, somehow, we manage not to know. As humans living on Earth at the time of the new millennium, we see the signs, but we look away, overwhelmed by them, terrified into total denial, unfeeling and so very lost. We prefer to remain blinded by the numbing oblivion of civilized ignorance, insulated by the thick veil, the glamour, the glistening tinsel of modern technology.

I must therefore underscore the unsettling parallel between the events that precipitated the fall of "mythological" Atlantis and those now occurring on "modern day" Earth.

Understanding the composition and use of energy has always been a motivating factor behind the achievement of higher levels of consciousness. However, the use of energy by third dimensional beings living in the material plane is fraught with dangers. Materialism and its consequent energy consumption: these both build and destroy great civilizations.

On Atlantis the motivation to understand and use energy became so entangled with material desires that the spiritual and physical bodies of the citizens were at odds with each other. The original Atlantean Reign, the Reign of the Gods, eventually descended into the gross materialism of most humankind, perhaps because the gods bred with lowly mortals, perhaps because third dimensional sexual activity corrupted them.

Material wealth grew to blinding extremes during Atlantis' long history: Holy temples were encased in the purest of silver and gold; Statues were made of solid gold; Interior walls of palaces were lined with sheets of gold; Agricultural, urban and military development became massive and elaborate; Cultural sophistication exceeded that which we can only dream of today. Extreme degrees of materialistic greed emerged. So great an imbalance then developed that the Atlanteans eventually lost all of their higher spiritual brilliance. Global evolution toward enlightenment was no longer possible in their time.

Oh Atlantis! No other civilization on Earth has been as close to understanding the nature and delicate balances required for the ultimate enlightenment. Yet, when I traversed through even the earliest of my fourteen incarnations on Atlantis, first in the form of a visiting Nebulean and later as an Earthling, the impending collapse of Atlantis was already evident. This became clearest to me during my eleventh incarnation. By then, many enlightened Atlanteans had begun fleeing the sinking continent, seeking selected places, most of high altitude, most destined to survive the cataclysmic shiftings and sinkings of major land masses, where higher forms of energy or vibrations further inspired their spiritual development. They were intuitively aware of the impending cataclysm. (<u>As are some of you Earthlings today.</u>) Some of the Atlanteans who fled built the pyramids in Egypt (the construction and design of which were later attributed to the Egyptians themselves); some created your abstract sciences and mathematics; others harnessed the atom; and still others developed your methods of advanced communication and extended astral travel. Those left behind on the crumbling continent of Atlantis were persons of limited and low vibration, existing at a very low octave, on a low level of consciousness.

Many of the Atlanteans who fled during my later incarnations, incarnations which were closer to the time of the final Atlantean apocalypse, were inspired by the story of the final Nebulean cataclysm, in which that failing planet exploded when hit by a comet or a planetary body moving like a comet. Some of these late-to-become-aware Atlanteans therefore chose to advance to the higher planes of enlightenment and leave the material dimension of Earth altogether. Some committed unpleasant methods of suicide and others applied more advanced methods of disincarnation. In fact, in the years immediately preceding the Atlantean cataclysm, many advanced beings became teachers of the death transition and effective self-deliverance, instructing those who were interested in spiritual survival in the best methods of entering the higher dimensions. These teachings were conducted secretly, as the mainstream population viewed such self-deliverance as an abhorrent form of suicide.

Think about it. If and when things get bad here on Earth, you and your loved ones may also want a way out of the physical plane. You may find that your soul is the only thing that you want to preserve. If so, look around. You may be fortunate *enough to discover underground teachings similar to those offered on Atlantis. Good teachers of self-deliverance are rare and tend to keep themselves hidden from persecution. Keep in mind that effective suicide lessons are not enough. You also need to learn effective travel into the dimensions beyond, in order to make your self-deliverance worthwhile.*

One would have expected those spiritually advanced Atlanteans who elected to flee to higher elevations on Earth (rather than move into higher dimensions without their physical bodies) to have created a utopia after the fall of Atlantis. They did colonize Egypt and found the Divine Dynasty Of Egypt, building great pyramids as storehouses for metaphysical power and Original Truth, storehouses which would protect these treasures during the great floods — the submergences they knew were coming. Unfortunately, the spiritually advanced who fled were followed by others of lower vibration who stubbornly clung to enough of their deformed ways to never reach the higher spiritual plane. These less enlightened people continued to bear descendants as well as to reincarnate long after Atlantis sank for the last time — and they still do. They inhabit the majority of the Earth today. Some are even in position as world leaders. It is essential that you spot them. You must learn to differentiate among people who vibrate at different levels, different octaves of spiritual consciousness.

There were so many reasons for the demise of Atlantis. Some I personally witnessed through my Earth eyes while incarnated there; others I learned via extraterrestrial communication. The overall consensus is that the downfall resulted directly from the absence of a properly balanced and integrated spiritual energy. A system which is not evolving is decaying. Only an evolving system can survive its detrimental characteristics. Atlanteans' lives became dominated, weighed down, by materialism and its accompanying hatred, jealousy and self-pity. Inevitably, such an unevolving and unbalanced existence led to destruction. And this can happen again.

I now return to my story with the preceding warning in mind.

Ω

Yes. I followed my heart, down the road, back to Sheeyah.

But to follow one's heart is easier said than done. Especially in this case. I had somehow mingled my love for Sheeyah with the discovery of my self, my higher self, the true meaning of my life. It all seemed linked to me. My heart was calling me. I took that to mean romantic love — love for this woman who had entered or, as she had implied, *reentered* my life.

A high mountain mist, sheening silver in the moonlight, was settling on the land, enchanting it. As I headed back up the road, I remembered hearing something some years ago about following the path of the heart. I had thought that it meant being true to oneself, something which rarely had concerned me. Anyway, whenever I had even vaguely considered seeking this path, I found it obscured by mundane hurdles. Life had seemed complicated enough without having to be true to oneself — or to anyone else for that matter.

But now, my idea of who I was, of what self I would be true to if I decided to do so, was shifting so rapidly that I was uncertain of the Truth. I could only follow the road to love. Love, and the accompanying sex, seemed more certain. Why not make Sheeyah the pot of gold at the end of my rainbow? She was elusive, but not as difficult to decipher as I was now becoming to myself.

I kicked another pebble as I stumbled along. So I was Triad, the father of someone without a body, someone who called himself Nostradamus: Triad come back from time eternal to this and other lifetimes. At this point, this crazy scenario seemed as plausible an explanation for all that was happening to me as anything else might. It was either this or mental illness. So I decided — or pretended to decide (I really had very little say) — to try this for a while. Why not? If I were somehow way off, I would at least have had an interesting vacation.

I found myself increasingly excited as I approached our campsite. I was ready to tell her that I believed all this, I accepted all this madness, and that I loved her. Some combination of affection and sexual arousal filled me. My adrenaline began pumping. I found myself running wildly. I knew that when I got back to her I would immediately take her into my arms and proclaim my deep love for her and then make passionate love to her before she could even begin to reply.

But when I got there, she was not there. I thought that she had said she would wait there for me. Had I misheard her? I was irritated. But her things were there. She could not have gone far. But where? The lake! I immediately thought of the lake. So she went to the lake. I couldn't fault her for that. I raced through the moonlight down toward the lake.

I almost fell over when I saw her at the lake's edge, looking a bit like a zombie, mesmerized by something, her palms extended out in front of her, turned away from her face. Something weird was going on. I could feel it. I stopped to take it all in. It looked like she was communicating with her reflection. But as I crept closer, I saw that it was not at all her reflection. It seemed to be Camus'. This was somewhat unnerving, but I had very little overt reaction. Just a sort of dull sense of awe.

And Camus' reflection seemed to be moving through the mist toward his boat which hovered in the center of the pond. As I came up alongside Sheeyah, I saw Camus' surreal reflection arrive at the side of his boat and slip into it. This would have astounded me under normal circumstances. Again, I felt only a dull sense of awe.

"Sheeyah." I whispered nervously as I sat down next to her at the water's edge. Obviously this was not the time for my proclamation of love.

"Shh!" She replied numbly.

"Answer me," I demanded in a loud whisper.

"Shh. Don't talk please. Look, Triad. Look at what's happening out there. Look at Camus. He got back into his boat. I'm scared. I don't know why. But I'm scared," she whispered back at me.

I looked back at the boat. A wave of fear raced through me. I thought I was feeling Sheeyah's fear until I was compelled to turn and look behind me. Then I saw the ominous horizon. Now I really tensed up. "Well, look at what's happening over there. Look behind us," I muttered with urgency.

"What?" Sheeyah responded but she did not look.

"Look at the horizon. Come on, look." I insisted, tugging at her arm. I wanted to shake her brutally for some reason, force her to look, but I managed to control myself.

"Why?" She was still whispering and gazing at Camus' reflection in the boat.

"A strange light." How could I describe it? It wasn't just a light, it was a feeling, a sensation as well. She had to turn and look. I had to get her to see it.

"Think maybe it's just the sunrise, Triad? We're at high altitude. It looks different from up here." She was not paying me much attention.

I looked at my watch. It was a few seconds before four in the morning, too early for sunrise. "No, that's not it. Something's going on down there." I could feel something about to happen. For the first time in this incarnation, I was distinctly aware of having a premonition.

But she didn't turn to look. I finally reached out to force her to turn, to break her out of her trance-like state, when a loud explosion coming from the horizon rocked the air, the water, the trees, and us. She fell over onto me.

"Look!" I yelled. A mushroom cloud was rising from the distant line that separated Earth from sky. "Look!"

She finally did look as she struggled to regain her balance and then she grabbed me with abrupt fierceness. "I knew it. I knew it, Triad. I knew it was coming. I could feel it. For months now. I could feel it."

"Feel what, Sheeyah?" I wasn't certain I wanted to hear.

"It." Her answer didn't tell me much, but I knew what she meant.

The next explosion was so loud that it seemed to be just over the next hill, but the corresponding mushroom cloud rose up again from the distant horizon. The sky, the whole of reality, was rocked. The very air around us seemed to break to bits as shock waves came toward us through the air. Waves. Ripples in reality. The shock waves swept through the air right into my psyche. Black waves raced through my mind. Was this what I had been seeing in my head?

"Is this the end of the world?" Sheeyah's eyes were wide. She sounded emotionless.

"No, just that attack that was threatened by the guys in the Middle East — you know, the new ones on the scene — the ones that we didn't know had the bomb. Or don't you follow current events? You did turn off the news when we were back on the yacht . . . ."

"Yeah, I do. Sort of. I feel them even more than I follow them." She was holding my arm so hard I was certain she was bruising it. "And I've been feeling a sick kind of fear for quite some time now."

"Whatever that means. You feel current events?" I asked nervously.

Another explosion tore viciously at the horizon. With each successive shock wave, the air around us shattered like broken glass and then reassembled itself.

"*Nuclear* bombs, Triad, we'll be exposed to radiation! It'll be here, the cloud of it'll be here soon — how long does it take for it to travel this far?"

She was right to be concerned, but I didn't know how long we had. "How should I know?" I too felt a sense of urgency, but, for some reason, almost willfully, I was slipping into slow motion. I mused to myself that this might be a common reaction to extreme horror.

She wasn't listening to my question. Her eyes were focused back on Camus. Was she avoiding the reality of the radiation cloud? Was she flat out insane? I had no answers. There, in the mist, Camus sat up in his boat.

His body was shining in the strange nuclear light. He continued to look like only a reflection of himself. His hands were out, palms extended toward us. Sheeyah was responding with the same gesture.

Sheeyah insisted I do so as well. "Quick. Do this."

I didn't understand what she was doing but I didn't question it now. I had nothing else to do, so I complied. Somehow, as a strange new shade of unearthly golden light cast from the horizon across the lake, the boat slid easily toward us. It seemed to be propelled by this light. I wasn't certain that the boat was actually contacting the water anymore. I didn't care. In my daze, I saw Camus' palms contact Sheeyah's. Next I knew, she was in the boat. I obediently held out my palms. Camus' palms contacted mine. Next I knew, I was in the boat.

Another, more intense, explosion ripped at the horizon. Now, a massive line of black radioactive clouds was moving toward us, rippling like waves in water, but waves moving in very slow motion. I calculated that, at the speed they were traveling, these clouds would reach us in about ten minutes, even in their apparent slow motion.

"We've got to get away from the radiation NOW!" Sheeyah sounded as if she were commanding Camus' reflection to save us.

I certainly did not expect Camus' reflection to respond. Horrified at her seeming lack of awareness, I raised my voice at her. "There's no way, we can't move fast enough! I couldn't even drive us away fast enough!" I was still trying to think of a solution. Get behind a boulder? No. Under the water? For how long? Wouldn't work. Anyway, water was not radiation proof. I lowered my volume. "I don't know where we should go for cover, but *being on the water is not the answer.*"

Now she turned to me, as if about to argue. However, we had no time for a discussion. The force of the next explosion shattered every bit of our remaining reality. Although the radiation cloud had not yet hit us, the lake and its environment of moments before were gone — just gone. I felt as if we were traveling through sheets of glass, shattering each of them as we moved and then being propelled by the force of that shattering still deeper through the glass sheets, which continued to shatter as we proceeded.

I thought we had gone to the bottom of the pond. I could not see anything. I thought I was drowning. The suffocation was gruesome. My lungs compressed to what felt like flatness.

An indefinite amount of time passed.

After a while, flat slabs of light seemed to fly at me out of the dark, like pieces of broken glass, icy glass. Then, I felt that I myself had become one of those pieces of broken glass. Shattered. I sensed that I was trapped in the same surface of water, the top of the lake, that Camus had just come from. I was reduced to a two dimensional form, flat and suffocating. Was this it? Was this the end? End of me? Was I only a reflection in the water now? Nothing else? Is this death?

Somehow, death was not as frightening a concept as the physical discomfort and distortion, the sense of compaction, that I was feeling.

Had not my amnesic self still lingered, I would have realized that I was indeed passing through the flatness of two dimensional reality, where everything exists on a plane. But I still clung to my naive earthly views of reality. I had no idea that I had been launched from the third dimension into the second in order to move into the fourth and escape the physical catastrophe of the third. In time, this complex concept would be made clear to me. YES, the time was coming for the removal of the remainder of my ignorance.

Now, a magnificent stream of glistening light washed through the dark flatness. I saw that we were riding on it. Air rushed into my lungs as I realized with relief of galactic proportion that I was still in the boat with Sheeyah and Camus. Camus looked more real, more physical, again. I didn't wonder how he had come back to life. The question simply didn't occur to me at that moment.

"Henu," Camus said.

"Henu what?" I gasped, swallowing air as if it were water in the Sahara desert.

"Henu boat." Camus spoke in a monotone.

"You said that before Camus."

"Kha'm-uast."

"What Camus?"

"I am Kha'm-uast, driver of the henu boat, your Boatman."

Sure, whatever you say, Camus, I said under my breath. Out of the tremendous blackness, strange triangular golden forms began to take shape, their vague outlines looming in the dark distance.

"Sheeyah, look." I was back to my dull amazement again.

"Do you think we're dead?" Sheeyah asked me. Her pale face was iridescent in the strange light. But there was a stone-like quality to her face. Beautiful. Ancient. Silent. But stone like. Had I ever noticed this before? Or was this a new trait?

"You have just traveled in time." Camus sounded soft and kind now. How did Camus, the naive old fisherman, come up with such an idea? Then he added, "I am your guide, your servant and your Master of the Threshold, Kha'm-uast."

I thought I'd play along, as he seemed more sure of himself than I did. In fact, I was so very shaken that I was trembling all over, inside and out. "Where are we?" I asked, still gasping.

"Nile," Camus replied.

"The Nile?"

"Ancient Egypt. The River Nile flowing through Ancient Egypt. It is the place I told you I remembered, the one that my mother said I had only dreamed." Camus sounded certain of this.

The Nile? I could see a strange mist, a mist flowing like a river, a mist given luminosity by a light which seemed to be pouring in from below.

"I felt as if I had become a reflection. Just a flat reflection, Camus. The way you did when you died yesterday. ... Wait a minute, Camus, are you dead? You *are* dead aren't you, Camus?" I wondered how he had regained his physicality, but I didn't know how to phrase this question.

"As I said, it's actually Kha'm-uast, not Camus. Anyway, becoming flat, two dimensional, is one way to move into the fourth dimension, the fourth dimension where you can time travel." He did not seem to care to tell me whether or not he was dead.

"What?" I was overwhelmed and exhausted. None of this sounded logical to me.

Camus persisted. "Well, the third dimension, the material plane, is in the middle of it all. If you want to move up a dimension, to move around in time, either backward or forward, first you have to move your energy down a dimension. If you do this right, you can return from time travel back to the third dimension with your body intact and even with the clothes you had on when you left."

I surprised myself by laughing out loud. "Hah! This is just great. Here we are. We don't know if the world just ended or what and we're supposedly in Ancient Egypt floating down the Nile or we're dead or both and now some fisherman named Camus thinks he's a mystical boatman and he's telling us how to travel through time."

Sheeyah began to laugh hysterically. She sounded as if she were loosing it. Her laughs turned to short screams. Her eyes began to roll. I thought she was about to have a seizure. I grabbed her by the shoulders. Reaching out to steady her helped me. Suddenly I felt I was more prepared to take this shift in our realities than she was.

"Sheeyah. Sheeyah! Wake up! Calm down, Sheeyah. It's all right. I mean, look, look at me, I'm here, you're here, we can see each other, we have bodies." I spoke more slowly, hoping that she would listen, "Sheeyah, we are in a boat with Camus. Camus, the guy from the lake." She didn't seem to hear me. "Sheeyah! I said wake up!" I slapped her face gently with one hand. I held her with the other. The sound of my slap echoed in the space around us.

She stopped moving and screaming. She gulped and looked at me fiercely. "Don't hit me!"

I slapped her face ever so gently again. At least we were making some contact now. I didn't know what else to do with someone who seemed to be going insane.

"Let's listen to Camus, Sheeyah. Let's hear him out now, right now."

"Now? I can't. I can't take in any more of this. It's too much."

I wanted to say well you asked for it, and, lo and behold, you got it, but I restrained myself. "Sheeyah, what else is there to do right now? All we have is us, this boat and Camus." I wondered if I had really fallen in love with this lunatic who had launched us on this inane journey that only now she finds she clearly can not handle.

"Yeah, sure. Sure, Triad. Tell him to talk. Tell Camus to talk about it." She was still shaky and uncertain, crazed, I could tell.

"O.K.? Sheeyah, can you just rest and listen?"

Sheeyah shook her head as if trying to wake up from a bad dream. "I feel suicidal, like just giving up and doing myself in. Surrendering to the madness. But if I'm already dead, it can't make a difference."

Camus spoke up. "You aren't dead, Miss Sheeyah. You just time traveled."

"When the bomb hit?" she asked Camus, her eyes still very wide.

"We shattered through the dimensional barrier. You barely escaped the wave of radiation that threatened you in the third dimension. I am your guide now. We travel on light, the light of the universe. You will come to remember me, to recognize me for who I am, as we reach our destination."

We were still moving through the darkness on the river of light. Vague golden triangles were still emerging from the black mist. And in the distance ahead of us, I thought I noticed some kind of island glistening. There seemed to be a water passageway or a sort of winding causeway leading through a very placid sea to that island. But the black mists were too heavy to be certain of the details. It was all rather familiar to me, but I hadn't the slightest idea as to why. I needed more explanation. Maybe this dimension stuff was the key. "Camus tell me what you mean by moving down a dimension." I narrowed my eyes and watched his face. Was he putting me on or was he on the level? "How did you say we got here again?"

"Yes. ... Let's start again. This time around, we met on a lake in the third dimension on Earth, in that lifetime you were just having. To avoid the disastrous effects of radiation exposure, you and Sheeyah instinctively came to me at the Crystal Mirror Lake Vortex for help catapulting into the fourth."

"The fourth? The fourth what?" I asked.

"The fourth dimension. The next dimension beyond physical space. TIME."

I took a deep breath. Sheeyah sat with her eyes closed, her hands grasping the side of the boat. This was more than she had bargained for. I could tell she was trying to keep hold of her mental balance. I recognized the feeling. But now I felt stronger, more balanced than Sheeyah, at least for the time being. Time being?

"Time?" I asked.

Camus tipped his head a little to one side. "Did you ever study geometry in school?"

"Grade school and high school." I replied. "I had geometry a few times. Always hated it."

"No wonder, Triad," Camus looked as if he pitied me, "Must have frustrated you. It was a very incomplete description of the universe, but it will have to do for now. We can build on it. Your old friend Euclid just did not finish the job. But then, how could he?"

Somehow, I found credible the suggestion that I had actually known the father of Euclidean geometry. "So this has something to do with points, lines and planes?"

"Everything, Triad, everything." Camus chuckled. I couldn't help wondering if the joke was on me. This made me angry.

Camus must have heard me thinking because he gestured a sort of calm down and wait-a-minute gesture and I obeyed.

"Let's see. A point. A point has no dimensions." I decided to try to have fun with this. After all, I was stuck in Camus' boat again. He had me trapped, as he had the other day, unless I was willing to leap off and swim. NO EXIT AGAIN. UGH. But the stakes were higher now. This wasn't ice cold heart attack water we were floating on. It was some other stuff. I didn't really want to look at it too closely. I kept my eyes off of it.

Instead, I looked at the distant shores of the river. Was that unusual shoreline prime waterfront property? Maybe I could sell it by the square inch. I imagined how many high rise hotels could be constructed along this waterfront. I could almost see them. Then I refocused on what I thought was really out there. I could make out hazy outlines of people, palm trees, marketplaces, and boats. The people seemed to be dressed and parading around a Hollywood set. Some movie about Ancient Egypt, I mused. I had to remind myself that this wasn't Hollywood or Disneyland, it was a place far from the real world I had known only hours ago. No movie maker could have ever written this script.

It seemed I was coming out of my mental fog. Apparently, Camus was pleased with me. "Yes," he said, "call that point the zero dimension then, because it has no dimensions."

I continued obediently. "And a point, when extended, forms a line, a row of points." Camus smiled and I felt like a very good student.

"Yes. Good. Call that the first dimension, because it has only one dimension," he nodded.

"And, if you drag that line, you get a row of lines, or a plane."

"Fantastic, Triad. And you can call that the second dimension, because it has only two dimensions."

"I do." I said flippantly.

"Do what?" Camus tested.

"Call that the second dimension. I mean that's what we were told in school. A point has no dimensions. A line had one dimension. A plane, the second dimension, has two dimensions. This is obvious, isn't it?"

"So they got something relatively right back there in your school."

"And, Camus, if you drag the plane through the big empty, you get a row or a pile of planes. This makes space. Three dimensional space. Length, width and depth. Like a cube has length, width and depth. I know this stuff, Camus, this is the third dimension. The third dimension has three dimensions: length, width and depth."

"Right. The third dimension. That's where you were living just now, in that incarnation."

"Seems to me that if I was incarnated, I had to be in the third dimension, because the carnation — the flesh and blood — is a material thing, it is three dimensional."

Sheeyah perked up. "So astute of you. You're a real wizard, Triad." A bit of her old wit filtered back into her voice.

"Glad to have you back from the dead, Sheeyah." I was glad. I had been trying to cover up my ongoing and intense worry about her.

"Dead? Don't joke like that." She turned even paler and grabbed the side of the boat even harder.

"Sorry." I could see she wasn't out of the woods yet. I realized that I wasn't out of the woods yet either. My sanity was at stake. I wanted to go back to the dimension discussion. I felt on firm ground there. It felt safe and familiar in this unknown territory. I needed the mental safety, the map, the distraction from my fear. "So, Camus, if you take a three dimensional object, like a cube or something, and move it through emptiness, it makes for the passing of time. Time ... the fourth dimension."

"How do you get that?" Sheeyah was listening now.

"It takes time for the cube to travel through space." I felt smart. I was never a good student, but now I felt that I'd go to the head of the class. Of course, I had an advantage. I was Triad. The Triad. I sat up very straight as I saw a giant sphinx glowing, its surreal wash of golden color wafting at me through the mist. I squinted. It was gone.

"I still don't like Triad's explanation. Is he right, Camus?"

"He's the expert, actually," Camus grinned, "even if he doesn't admit it yet. But I'll help him out anyway. A cube exists at any one moment, but only for that one moment in time. If it lasts longer than a moment or ages or moves or changes form, it does so across several moments."

A bit of color returned to Sheeyah's face. "Ages? Like people? You mean when people age, they are in the fourth dimension?"

"What I mean is that aging is a fourth dimensional process. It is one of the ways three dimensional beings get to see a bit of the fourth dimension. But it's really just the tip of the iceberg. Aging is moving through time, along the axis of time, the fourth axis, but so much else is going on as an organism ages, so much else that can't be seen by third dimensional beings."

"I get it!" Sheeyah sounded weak, but delighted. "Aging is a kind of time travel."

"No, that's not what he means, Sheeyah." For some reason, I did not want Sheeyah to be right.

But old Camus interceded on her behalf. "Actually Triad, you can put it that way. Aging is indeed time travel. But it is a progressive, sequential, step by step time travel. You didn't have to age to get to Egypt today. You did another kind of time travel, a tesser-action or what the old timers like you two like to call moving through a tesseract."

When he said that, I felt yet another bit of my remaining amnesia crumble. Why yes, a tesser-action. "A fold in time," I recited aloud.

Camus nodded approvingly. I felt glad to get some of his approval. It was as if I were a kid, competing with Sheeyah. I felt silly for feeling this way. I tried to focus on the conversation as scenes from Ancient Egypt emerged all over the river banks.

Camus explained, "Yes a fold. A special kind of fold. It is actually a *fold in energy*. But then it is all energy, time — light — life — whatever dimension you find your self or anything else in, it is all just energy. In fact, the dimensions themselves are all just frequencies of energy. Cosmic frequencies."

"Camus you amaze me, but then you always did," Sheeyah said admiringly. Did they share a memory I was not privy to? Sheeyah smiled and took a deep breath. She stretched her legs and arms out seductively. Who was she entertaining with that, I wondered. Maybe she just needed to stretch to feel a little better, I scolded myself.

Camus addressed us both now. "You've come a long way in a twenty four hour period."

Sheeyah wouldn't settle for that. "What makes you think it's been twenty four hours? Look around you. Look! We're in Ancient Egypt. THIS ISN'T TWENTY FOUR HOURS AGO. This is way back in time!"

But I knew the answer. "You can move through a tesseract instantaneously. The tesser-fold is within the moment of itself. It takes no time to move in time that way."

Dissolving the Auric Veil

"I read a story about that kind of thing once," Sheeyah said. "My friend's father gave it to me when I was a kid. I think it was called *A Wrinkle in Time*. A witch wrinkled her skirt or something. Wrinkled time so they could get across it, I think."

"Yes, we are very fond of that writer here on the river of light. She has helped explain our work to those inhabiting the third dimension."

"What do you mean our work? Are there more of you?" I was curious. Refresh my memory, Camus or Kha'm-uast or whoever you are, I mumbled inwardly.

"Exactly right. There are more of me. I assume a number of forms, all serving as guides through the dimensions of universal reality. Here in Egypt, during the time of Ancient Memphis, I worked directly for you, Triad. You took many triad formations in Egypt. In Memphis, you were called Ptah, and you were the oldest of the Egyptian gods. You were a patron of the arts and a builder and you were inclined to favor the architects. You were the spirit of lasting invention and eternal creation, physical and mental. You fathered many beautiful ideas. As Ptah, you were one part of the all powerful Memphis Triad. Your wife was Sheeyah, the lion-headed goddess then called Sekhmet. It was correctly rumored that Sekhmet was of extraterrestrial origin. She was the fierce defender, protector, of all that which had been created. The third member of your Memphis Triad was the son the two of you created, Nefertum. He — "

"I suppose he is, or was, or whatever the case may be or may have been, this Nostradamus guy?" I was putting things together — organizing pieces of some cosmic puzzle which had recently arrived on my doorstep with my own return address enscrawled in invisible ink on the corner of the mystery envelope. I vaguely recognized my own handwriting now.

"Yes. Nostradamus. As your Nefertum, your Nostradamus symbolized and embodied the manifestation of creativity, the conception of life as a creative act, and the surge of new life, new energy which emerges from decay and darkness. He is the child of your supreme creativity, of all Creation."

"So my name, Triad, comes from that Triad?"

"Well, yes, in a way. But you are that Triad everywhere. Everywhere you appear in the Cosmos, you carry this identity. And your Triad has appeared and reappeared throughout cosmic history. Again and again, you, the Monad, forms the Duad, which forms the Triad. But let us stay with Egypt for now. In later times, when the royal Egyptian courts left Memphis for Thebes, your Triad became that of God-king Amun (who was known as the Hidden or Invisible One), and of the Vulture Goddess Mother Mut (who as the Power of Woman could open her body to the wind to impregnate herself), and of their illustrious son, Khonsu, (who was conceived by the breath of the Hidden One Amun flowing through his consort, the Goddess Mut)."

"Khonsu?" For some reason, Sheeyah was painfully surprised. "I've dreamed about a Khonsu. I can't remember exactly how it went, but I've heard the name before — in my dreams. He had other names too ...." Sheeyah closed her eyes trying to remember. "My son? I remember dreaming of him wandering in the moonlight, I remember ... I remember ...."

Sheeyah broke into tears and grabbed me. She said, "Triad! They killed you and wanted to kill me too. I was carrying your son. I remember. I remember! Your son was born. I called him Horus. But he was born to me as Khonsu at another time. I know it sounds weird, but I am absolutely certain." Sheeyah sat stunned.

Camus interrupted the pain, as if to keep us focused on his story rather than on our respective psychological confusions. "Yes, he is also Horus. But we shall not speak of Horus at this moment. Your son, as Khonsu, became known as the Wanderer, the Navigator. All of his navigation related to the path of the moon across the sky. In Thebes he became known as that within each of us which controls our destiny. Khonsu changed his image as he moved from the role of Memphian Nefertum to Theban Khonsu, but his essential core remained constant. After all, the ultimate manifestation of creativity — which Nefertum certainly was — is indeed that within us which can control our own destiny — which Khonsu certainly was."

I came to a vague understanding. "Somehow this explains Nostradamus' message, but I'm not clear how."

Camus nodded. "Nostradamus' role during his 1555 western Earth time incarnation was to plant the seeds of a more profound spiritual awareness. Awareness that spiritual creativity is the path through which we can gain control of our own destinies. Awareness that there is a science of the soul, a metaphysical dynamic to be respected."

A voice came from somewhere. "Sed quando submoventa ignorantia ..."

"Did you hear that?" I asked in awe.

"Yes." Camus grinned widely and sat back.

"I did as well. It's his voice. Nostradamus' voice. I'd know it anywhere." Sheeyah was obviously delighted. I was so glad to see her pain dissipate some.

"Listen," Camus whispered, "he is telling us that when the time comes for the removal of ignorance — "

"THE CASE SHALL BE MADE MORE CLEAR."

"There he is again! You're back, Nostradamus!"

"Just passing down the river. We will meet again." Nostradamus' voice trailed off.

I looked around to see where Nostradamus had gone. He was nowhere in sight, which did not surprise me. Instead, I noticed that the golden triangles had emerged as very real and massive glowing pyramids. I was astounded and exhilarated by their timeless beauty. I felt an overwhelming ecstasy begin to fill my body and then I, for some reason, glanced downward. My heart immediately sank. Ecstasy was replaced by terror. "Why don't I see my reflection in the water?" Any sense of familiarity and self-assuredness I had gained was gone — it had all evaporated. Fear washed through me, again like a black wave.

"That is not water, Triad. It is light. The henu boat travels on light. I am the captain of the boat that takes those departing one dimension into the next. The Egyptians explained this as a trip into the subconscious or the underworld, a journey into the mist or the magic kingdom. A journey into the self, the other dimensions of self."

"Light?" I thought about it for a moment. A boat couldn't travel on light. This seemed implausible, but I tried to accept the idea. "Well, water reflects light. So there should be some kind of reflection — if I am really here — I should see myself reflected." I was not happy about this. Was I dead or what? I was back to that.

Camus wanted to reassure me, but I could see that he was uncertain as to how. "Light does not reflect light. It merges with light. ... The water with which you are familiar in the third dimension is but a metaphor for this river of light energy, the sea of energy and all of its waves throughout universal Creation."

"Oh." This didn't help. I wanted to see my reflection. I needed some reassurance that I still existed. I wanted to see my face. I needed to *be*.

"I hear your concerns, Triad," Camus interrupted my thoughts. "Perhaps I can help by explaining the relationship of light to the seven dimensions."

"Seven?" I was surprised and a little angry. "You just lost me. I thought that there were four."

"Not really Triad. You are the master of all the dimensions. Let me just refresh your memory. Follow my discussion. Focus only on the pictures I give your mind. Still all other thoughts for a while. This will guide you out of your malaise."

"If you say so." What choice did I have?

"My boat and I are the vehicle for your travel back to yourself. Just think of me as that vehicle. My explanation is the vehicle for your arrival at the rediscovery you have long ago programmed yourself to make."

"If you say so."

Sheeyah was listening, again radiating an unearthly iridescent pallor. She said nothing. But she followed every word like the queen of the proceedings.

Camus continued. "There are seven dimensions. You have just described the first four, Triad. The point — the zero dimension. The line — the first dimension. The plane — the second dimension. The cube — the third dimension. Time — the fourth dimension. Each of these dimensions exists at a different frequency of energy. The lowest dimension, zero, has the lowest energy frequency. As you move up the dimensional scale, the energy frequency increases. There is more energy because the structure of each successive energy dimension becomes more complex."

"The frequency increases as things become more complex." Queen Sheeyah raised a challenging eyebrow. "So when you have a point, a zero dimension, it is the most simple?"

Camus was fond of Sheeyah, I could tell. He smiled softly and gazed into her eyes. "It is the most geometrically simple, Sheeyah. Everything is contained in one point. The oneness is one thing, it is not broken into parts or dimensions, it is very densely packed."

"Density?" Sheeyah was intrigued. "And when you spread it out into a row of points, a line, you get the first dimension. This is the energy of one compact point spread out — so it's a bit less dense?"

"It is a bit less dense but a bit more complex." Camus liked Sheeyah's attention, I could tell. Had they been lovers at some time? Should I be jealous? I wondered. He didn't seem to be her type. At least he hadn't back there in the future where I met him on the lake.

I felt unsettled. So I said, "And the second dimension spreads out into a plane, and things get more spread out and even less dense."

"And more complex, because you have more dimensions," Camus added.

"And then the third dimension is more complex and more spread out and even less dense. And the fourth dimension is even more complex and even more spread out and less dense again." Sheeyah was obviously starting to get this dimension stuff.

I wanted to keep up with her. "Point. Line. Plane. Cube. Time. — Zero, One, Two, Three, Four. That leaves the fifth and the sixth dimensions to get it to add up to seven."

"You are right. You can get these last two, the ultimate two, quite easily if you remember a basic truth: the third dimension is the midpoint of all the dimensions, the midpoint or fulcrum of all the dimensional frequencies. This is why the material plane, the third dimension of reality, is so very popular, at least at this point in the evolution of the Cosmos."

"Oh. I thought it was because embodied spirits get to have physical sex in the third dimension and they get so they like it a lot." Sheeyah was feeling a bit better, I could tell.

"Well, that too," Camus continued. "But the material third dimension is the middle ground, the place from which exploration, whether sexual or otherwise, exploration of all other dimensions of reality or frequencies of energy is most easily facilitated for the uninitiated."

"Uninitiated? Who are they?"

"The uninitiated are those who are not as yet adept at multidimensional consciousness and travel — which are, by the way, one in the same."

"You lost me again," I admitted. "What's one in the same? Multidimensional travel and multidimensional consciousness?"

"Yes. If you can attain a truly multidimensional consciousness, you can travel multi-dimensionally, because fully understanding the existence of a reality or a dimension is the same as being there."

"A little like seeing is believing?"

"Yes," Camus responded, "But now it is best to say that believing is seeing, or, better yet, believing is being."

We were silent for a while, impacted by this awareness.

"But, why do still I feel such a great sense of loss? Like I want to kill myself?" Sheeyah sounded depressed again.

"Sheeyah, dear Sheeyah," Camus again revealed that he was so very fond of her, as if she were an old friend or something, "Letting go of a belief system is going to bring on both a grieving process and a sense of dying or suicide. You grieve the loss of your old world view and you feel that you die with it. This angst is part of the initiation."

"Initiation? Is that what this is?" Sheeyah asked the question, but I wanted an answer too.

"Sheeyah and Triad, the two of you have elected to undergo the initiation process again and again, so as to stay close to your subjects and to perfect the path of enlightenment for them."

"How can *you* know this?"

"I have guided you again and again. I am the keeper of the light, your light, the light of your universe. I come whenever you summon me. I am not available to casual seekers of Truth. I hear only full commitment calling." Camus seemed absolutely certain of this.

I gazed at the glowing pyramids. "So now we are in ancient Egypt. It's like you've worked a miracle, Camus."

"I leave most of those to you, Master Triad, Ptah of Egypt come from the Atlantean Reign of the Gods, my dearest bird of flight through time, Sokaris. But miracles are merely simple changes or shifts in belief. If you come to believe something new, then you see the world and experience reality differently. Only this shift in belief can open the door to other dimensions. Only a few beings are really willing to let themselves make such a profound shift. The simple miracles you have commissioned me to perform involve the traversing of the dimensions with the subjects of your choice in order to bring about shifts or changes or folds in energy for them. I only carry believers in the henu boat. Those who travel with me, who I guide, allow themselves to come to believe in the dimensions beyond. When they achieve full belief, then they fully see all there is to know. Anyone anywhere who truly believes can find me."

My higher self knew this to be true and I knew that I knew it at that moment.

Reader, the henu boatman is ready to guide you too. Reach into this story and take this Truth out with you. When you are truly ready to commit to the journey you can call the boatman, Kha'm-uast. Begin calling him now. Perfect your commitment to this beckoning. You and he will know when your beckoning becomes completely sincere. Then the most amazing journey of your life, of all your lifetimes, will begin.

But I still had a somewhat lower self, a self who was clinging to this conversation for his sanity. So, I said, rather impudently, "But back to the fifth and sixth dimensions."

"Oh, yes, where were we?" Camus complied.

"The midpoint," Sheeyah coached Camus. For a moment, I fantasized that this was all a game and that Sheeyah knew fully well what Camus was trying to explain to me and that she was just making believe that she was learning it all with me.

Camus went on. "The third dimension is in the middle. Think about it. Imagine a vertical list of numbers from zero to six. The middle number would be three."

Suddenly, Sheeyah and I could see this list of luminous blue numbers hanging in the mist before our eyes:

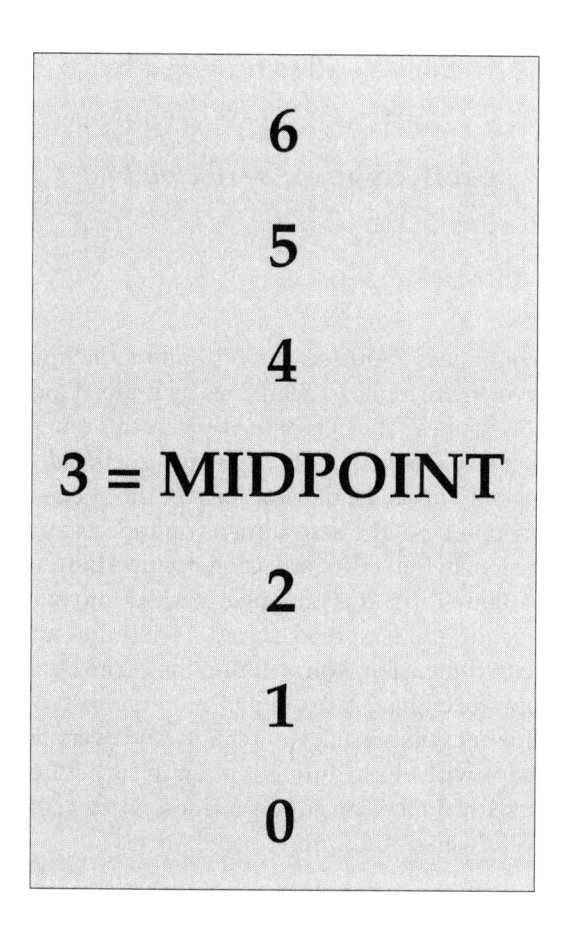

$$
\begin{array}{c}
6 \\
5 \\
4 \\
3 = \text{MIDPOINT} \\
2 \\
1 \\
0
\end{array}
$$

"Now," Camus continued, "let each set of dimensions on either side of the three reflect each other."

"Reflect?" I did not quite follow.

"Don't think about any of this too hard." Camus warned us, "Too much third dimensional thinking just gets in the way. The picture will be clear in your mind when your mind is ready to receive it. Just try to see the picture, the diagram I am describing. The picture of the zero, one and two is the reflection of the picture of the four, five and six."

And, magically, before our eyes, the image of Camus' description of the dimensions reflecting each other appeared in luminous blue against the backdrop the lingering dark mist:

0	reflects and is reflected by	6
1	reflects and is reflected by	5
2	reflects and is reflected by	4

"So," Camus continued, "you can come to know the higher dimensions and even to travel to the higher dimensions by understanding, by conceptualizing the lower ones. That's where your Earth Training, your simple high school geometry, can help. You've already got the idea of the point — the zero dimension. This is the densest form of the oneness. Everything is packed into one point. So, the zero dimension reflects and is reflected by the sixth dimension. In the sixth dimension, we find the oneness again, but it is in the least dense form, it is no longer packed into one point. Instead, the oneness, everything, is spread across an infinite number of points. There, in the sixth dimension, you will find the highest energy frequency, the most complex form that energy can take. In the sixth dimension, there exists every different point in all of all reality. And every different point in all reality overlaps with every different point in each different dimension of reality. The sixth dimension is the oneness in its most complex and spread out, most diverse and differentiated, form."

"Wow." That was Sheeyah's voice expressing my sentiments. "I think I get it — sort of," she marveled.

Camus approved. "Sort of is good enough for now. Because, when you really get it, you will go there. Remember, believing is seeing. Believing is *being*."

I wanted to get on with it. "So what about the fifth and first?"

"I think I know." Sheeyah spoke up, almost dazed by the insight. "The first dimension is a line. If the first is the most dense form of the line, then the fifth is the most spread out form of that line."

"Yes. And what would that be Sheeyah?"

I realized, via a series of short mental flashes, the likes of which I had never before experienced (or noticed myself experiencing), that I had once known Camus as Socrates. He caught me remembering this but said nothing about it.

Sheeyah went on. "I'm thinking that a line is horribly mono-dimensional. It has no inside and no outside. If I were a line and I wanted to become exactly the opposite of myself but to somehow stay the same, I would take the opposite level of density. I would go from the most compact to the most spread out form of myself. And I would manage to have an inside and an outside which merged with each other somehow. So, well, it seems to me that a mono-dimensional line goes on forever, looping endlessly, maybe cyclically, with no beginning and no end. At first I thought a mono-dimensional line would actually be a circle, but a circle contains an interior — can a line? But, the line, without the restriction of density found in the first dimension, and, without the restriction to linearity, becomes the fifth dimensional line — a sort of mobius strip moving through time, beyond time. I guess. But all this is really hard for me to think about right now."

"Remember, Sheeyah, you don't have to think too hard. The only keys to these doors are in images and sensations of energy. Thinking, especially if too connected with words, will make it very difficult to find the freedom to mind travel. And let me add that you are indeed correct. If you can conceive of being but a line in space, if you can really become that line, then all you need do is extend yourself to the infinite, break out of any first, second, third and fourth dimensional constraints, and you enter the fifth dimension."

I wanted to play too. "Does that mean that the first dimension is just a piece of a line?

"No, Triad, what I mean to say is that in the first dimension, only one dimension can be perceived: length. While length is one dimension beyond zero dimensions, and length can go on forever, it has its limitations. Width and depth and time and infinity, the second and the third and the fourth and the fifth dimensions, respectively, just cannot be perceived from the first dimension. The infinity of Creation cannot exist in first dimensional perception."

"If you say so." I was still hungry for more. "O.K., so now back to what you said way up the river about us jumping from the second to the fourth."

"Right, we jumped from the second dimension into the fourth. We used the surface of the lake to do this. The surface of the water reflects the fourth dimension."

"How?" Sheeyah was intrigued as well.

"It takes time for light to travel from the tree or the mountain or the face to the water's surface. What the surface eventually reflects is time, the time traveled by the light from the object being reflected to the surface reflecting it."

"Is that why I don't see my reflection here?" I was still trying to ascertain my existence in ways I had learned while in the third dimension. The seeming irrelevance of my death still mortified me.

"Well, sort of, Triad. There is no time between your face and the light of the universe."

"Why did I feel so very horrible when I became a reflection? When I moved into two dimensional space?"

"Imagine being smashed flat. Totally flat," Camus said.

"I was. It wasn't my imagination. I couldn't breathe. I don't know how I survived."

"Me too. I had the same feeling." Sheeyah chimed in.

"Well, you dropped down a level, you dropped down a frequency of reality to propel your self up a level. It works a little like a slingshot. You pulled back on the sling by dropping down to a lower dimension. You condensed, compacted energy. Your density thus increased and, therefore, so did your gravity. When you released the sling, you released your gravity and your density and you were shot upward through the frequencies. Action — reaction."

Camus looked at us. I could see him watching us try to follow this explanation. "Basically, you dropped down one dimension — from the midpoint of the third — to the second, in order to propel yourself up to the fourth. You jumped down to the two dimensional surface of the lake to spring up from there, to gain enough momentum to move through the fourth dimensional surface you call time so that you could finally drop back into the third dimension but at a very different point in time. That is where we are now. I guided you through the process. And now you are here."

Here. Suddenly, we really were somewhere. I looked around. Ancient Egypt. The isle of Khebit. The mystic isle. I somehow remembered the place. The henu boat stopped. Someone ran up and chained the boat to keep it moored. People streamed toward us. We stepped out and the crowd cheered. We walked, quite regally, toward the people.

I wanted to be certain I had a way out of this place. In all my business dealings, I found it important to have an escape valve — to structure a way out — in order to save face if nothing else. So, I glanced back at the boat. That is when I realized that Camus' little fishing boat had become an immensely spectacular vessel, a winged craft hovering over a golden-white stream of pure light. The luminous wings were slowly fluttering closed with an indescribable grace, folding around the hull. Some kind of magnificent bird head seemed to loom above the mast of the henu boat, lording over a mysterious chapel of some sort. How could I have missed this profound transformation? I had ridden Camus' fishing boat all the way from the future back to here. I had been on this boat the entire trip.

For a moment, the huge bird caught my eye. It was alive! As I gazed in awe at its face, I shuddered. Every cell in my body shuddered. Those eyes of his could see an insect from miles away. And they could see right into me. *But those eyes were mine!* That bird's face was mine! In slow motion, it opened its strange beak and cried, "S-kar! S-kar!" I gasped as I recognized this cry as my own, from the deepest recesses of my spirit, the impassioned cry for help — for true hope — the cry which must come from the deepest reaches of despair to generate hope, because true hope is borne only there.

"S-kar! S-kar!" I repeated the bird's cry in a loud and anguished whisper. I knew not how, but we were one. "S-karrrrrrr!" All the pain I had been suppressing in my recent incarnation — the incarnation in which Sheeyah had found me on a yacht — and all the pain I had been subconsciously carrying regarding the threat to my Original Truth and to all my beautiful Creation — was surfacing now. I had had no idea how much pain I was in. "S-karrrrrrrr," I yelled out.

Dumb struck and fearful, I unlocked my gaze from that of the great bird. I turned to face the people. I saw that they wanted me. Why? A pathway cleared through the crowd and Sheeyah and I followed Camus into the mouth of a cave to our thrones.

There, our son, Khonsu, awaited us with open arms. We recognized his voice as that of Nostradamus.

"Father."

"Must you call me that?" He was doing it again. I was perspiring heavily. I wanted to run but saw no real escape from the overbearing sensation that I had been swept into a sea of reality — an unwilling awareness — from which there would be no escape. Ever.

"Khonsu. Horus." Sheeyah sobbed quietly, "Son." She hugged him. I was troubled by the image, they looked to be so close in age. And he had so many different names. What was going on? What did Sheeyah understand that I still did not?

My son, Horus, Khonsu, Nostradamus, and whoever else he was, (Christ?) looked solemnly at us and started to speak: "Father, Mother, The Spiritual Triad is reassembled now. I have summoned you through time and eternity and all Onenesses so that we might again master our destinies. Original Truth is in the greatest of jeopardy. This means you, Mother, you. You are the living, breathing gospel, the eternal bearer of ultimate and Original Truth. Father, a most murderous force seeks to gain control of your great Creation, to swallow into eternal nothingness all that you have created. But through your graces, my dearest Mother and Father, our high union is reformed, and our cosmic universe can again be righted."

Part 3

•

Questing the Gaea Omega

7

You should know about planet Nebulae, as her fate concerns you. Nebulae was cataclysmically destroyed approximately 150,000 Earth years ago. What remains is only an asteroid belt, in a location far removed from Nebulae's original position in your solar system. However, it is predicted that Nebulae and her fragmented pieces will be rejoined one day into a unified body, through a gravitational process; and that she will become the second sun in your solar system.

The emergence of this second sun will occur shortly before your existing sun collapses from its own gravitational weight, becoming a minor black hole. Eventually, some of your spirits, the spirits who have evolved into and become most adept at multi-dimensional survival, will be catapulted through this black hole, through this point in space, to the beginnings of reality, through the farthest reaches of multidimensional space, and to the beginnings of Creation. I can help you prepare for this wondrous journey, if you would like to undertake it. You must first learn to recognize the windows. These are the windows of spiritual opportunity.

But this journey through the black hole comes long after the more pressing events of this new millennium on Earth.

Seeking to guide you into your very next leap in spiritual evolution, I have incarnated as one of you. I want to be close to you at this critical juncture. As I have indicated, I have actually been reincarnating on your Earth again and again during more than the past 150,000 years. I know well your history and your future. What I know about the destiny of your Earth will ensure your immortality if you can hear me.

Most Nebuleans could not hear me. Planet Nebulae, which had a history of mounting strife and dissension, was known during its existence as "the yellow planet." Its name was derived from its warmth and colorful atmospheric conditions. Unfortunately, these seemingly pleasant circumstances rendered the inhabitants of Nebulae bellicose in nature. They increasingly turned their attention toward war games, neglecting their protective ozone-like layer. This caused excessive solar heat, and, finally, absolute vulnerability to complete destruction and disintegration.

Many of the more evolved spirits who managed to leave Nebulae during its demise began to roam the broad expanses of the Cosmos. Such is the scattered nature of my own Nebulean family. Vagabonds in time and space. When Nebulae disintegrated, my Nebulean family members decided, after only one brief visit, that they did not care for Planet Earth. They found many Earthly practices highly offensive, for instance, the eating of living things, a practice common on Atlantis which survives on Earth today. They chose to roam the universe in search of a better home.

As for myself, I am more of a chameleon, I can settle anywhere, a trait I share with the maternal ancestor of the Cosmos — who was the vessel bearing my Original Truth — and mother of the original Seven Sisters — sisters whose identities remain guarded by a special set of stars, the Pleiades.

On Nebulae we had made some effort to reach into the higher dimensions — beyond the third-dimensional plane that is now so popular on your planet, Earth. We Nebuleans played with — perhaps took too lightly — the advanced knowledge we had gained. We were able, by raising or lowering the vibrations in our bodies and psyches, to totally transform and even to detach from our physical presences; to fit comfortably into life on all existing cosmic bodies. This is a talent — an idea — that will blossom on Planet Earth as the planet's inhabitants reach out into the fourth dimensions and beyond. I hope it will be awarded more respect by Earthlings than it was by Nebuleans.

$$\Omega$$

So, there, in that cave, on the Isle of Khebit, Nostradamus — alias Khonsu — had revealed the motive behind his emergence (or reemergence) into our lives.

"I could use a stiff drink about now," I muttered.

"A lobotomy," Sheeyah replied without turning her head in my direction.

"A what?"

"A prefrontal lobotomy."

"A coma would offer greater relief." I stared at the crowd.

"You think so? Maybe you're already in one."

"I don't know. ... What time is it Sheeyah?"

"Time? What *day* is it?"

I looked at my digital watch. All it read was zeroes and blanks. "My watch isn't working. What does yours say?" I asked her.

"I don't wear one."

"Of course not. What does the here and now mean to someone like you?" I heard the bite in my voice.

"You sound like you think this is all my doing. But I never expected anything like this to happen. I mean, how could I? It's the kind of thing that I'm quite likely to imagine, to just think up, but I've never thought anything like this could *really* happen."

"So you think this is really happening?" I still wanted to think that it wasn't.

"I don't know what's going on. Maybe we *are* dead." She paused, but still didn't turn to face me. She was dazed by the splendor of the surroundings. The walls looked to be lined with gold, with jewels inlaid for decoration. "Triad, wasn't there a nuclear attack or something?" Finally, Sheeyah turned and looked at me. I saw that she was white as a sheet. I recoiled from what appeared to be her death mask. I thought that she noticed me doing this and felt rather ashamed. And then she burst out laughing. Her laughter was tinged with hysteria.

She did have a knack for the inappropriate.

"Triad, look at you! Look at us! We're dressed the way we were at the lake!"

I looked. She had on running shorts, frayed at the edges, and an old t-shirt, the same as what she was wearing the day I met her. I was dressed a little more respectably in loafers, a polo shirt and neat khaki pants. For a moment, I felt a sense of superiority about my neater image. Sheeyah was really too much of a new age Bohemian for me. But then I looked around.

A line of very distinguished old persons in beautiful silken robes was filing in before our thrones. I could not help but feel like a tourist on a Hollywood set. A ridiculously dressed tourist at that. We were a strange anachronism, Sheeyah and I. Too far into the future for the time being depicted.

"So how do we get out of here?" She was asking *me*.

"Listen honey, you got us into this —" I stopped. I knew that she was as confounded by the events which had overtaken us as I.

"You called me *honey*."

"Why not? What have I got to lose?" My sense of humor was improving. "I might even call you darling next time."

"Your sense of humor is improving. In fact, I didn't know you had one." She touched my hand gently. A little hint of color touched her cheeks.

I moved my hand so that it encased hers. I felt so much love for her. Yes, in the midst of all this confusion, I felt love for her. Maybe it was the only even vaguely familiar feeling I could find to have in all this madness, or maybe I was more in love than I'd ever imagined was possible. "I think I love you," I mumbled.

"Well, if we're dead, we might as well enjoy it." Sheeyah had a remarkable way of going with the flow.

I saw the person who claimed to be our son, Khonsu, speaking quietly to the dignitaries. They seemed to know him. They were nodding at him gravely. Then he turned to us and began speaking in Nostradamus' voice.

"Father, Mother, greet your High Counsel, protectorates of the Great Mysteries of Truth carried to Earth and preserved on Earth by the Reign of the Gods during the sinkings of Atlantis. They have come for your leadership in time of great need. Truth is being obliterated. Your Original Truth must be preserved." Our son swept his hand through the air with imperial style. As if beckoned to do so, the dignitaries bowed to us in unison and then stood unblinking and unmoving before us. I could feel their immense respect. But I blocked it, feeling that this respect was grossly misappropriated.

Truth. I'd never really given Truth much thought. Now it was being treated as if it were sacred. Why all this stuff about Truth, I wondered. Truth is too relative, too elusive, to try to find and protect. And I am certainly no expert in it.

I was not surprised to hear Nostradamus answer me, as if he had heard me thinking, because he had heard me thinking and I *knew* this. "Truth, Father, is *your* living gospel, written on the blood of the Cosmos, carried to Earth in the Cosmic Grail. It has been the subject of many quests in the third dimension, the physical plane, quests by humans who did not understand that for which they searched, who often misinterpreted the meaning of the Grail, but who instinctively recognized that it needed preservation. Truth, Father, is Mother, who bears your divine offspring again and again."

Sheeyah looked quizzically at her son. "*Me*? The bearer of *Truth*? O.K., great. I'm the carrier of Truth with a capital 'T'. I'll try to accept that. I mean, I like being right all the time, so why not?" She paused and, as if she had just realized something, she changed her tone to a whisper, "But that's not what you're talking about is it?"

Nostradamus shook his head no.

"But, why, my son, do you bring us here at this point in time?" Now Sheeyah spoke in yet another tone, in a surprisingly slow and regal voice, one which somehow overrode the ludicrous image she presented in her frayed shorts and worn out t-shirt. Was she playacting or did she really buy this whole thing?

"The time has come for the removal of ignorance." Nostradamus was feeding us that insulting line again.

"Yes, Nostradamus," I interjected, "you've told us that before, at the lake, before the bombs went off, wherever and whenever that was. You said, 'When the time comes for the removal of ignorance, the case shall be made more clear'." I was surprised at suddenly finding myself taking these words so seriously. I felt unexpectedly comfortable with these words as I spoke them, as if I had finally found a shoe that fit me in a world of wrong sizes. But what was the *case* Nosradamus referred to? That this Original Truth was in jeopardy? That the world was in danger or something? That Sheeyah was in danger? And where did he get this notion that I, simple and not always above board businessman me, *created* something he described as being as profound and pure as Original Truth?

He heard me thinking again. "Yes, Father, it was you that created Original Truth. You will eventually remember that you and Mother began as One, as the Supreme Monad. You actually continue to be One. When you bifurcated, divided yourself, into animo and anima, yang and yin, when you polarized into the Supreme Duad, the ultimate male and female essences, you became yourself as Father and yourself as Mother. You arranged to breathe and breed your Truth throughout the Cosmos through Mother, your Grail, your vessel, the bearer of your eternal offspring."

This was getting to be a bit much. I mean, now he expected me to believe that I was not only myself, his Father and all that, but also that I was once Sheeyah or that she was once part of me? Me? A woman? *That* woman?

I looked at her. I could tell that she too could feel me thinking. "Well Triad, does that make us identical twins or just fraternal?" Sheeyah laughed that inane laugh again. Did she do that when she was nervous or when she had just been hit by a big realization? She turned to her son rather defiantly. "Anyway, I'm not so sure I like being reduced to merely a creation of — an extension of — Triad. If you're saying that *he created me*, a sort of Adam's rib thing, well, no, *I don't think so.*" She looked at me and frowned. She shook her head. "No way."

"Mother, you were as much part of that which created you as was Triad. After much deliberation regarding the manner in which to create a most moral Cosmos, regarding the best mode of integrating integral Truth throughout the dimensions of your Cosmos, the two of you, as One, decided that you should become two in order to create a polarity, a dynamic. For it is out of this dynamic of the Duad that Truth flows. This polarity is the essential dialectic of the universe."

"This is insanely profound, I mean *profoundly* insane. We're just regular people. How could you possibly believe that we would be so powerful? So cosmic?" I saw the dignitaries bow to me in unison.

"Speak for yourself, Triad," Sheeyah muttered in a teasing voice.

Our son, who seemed to think himself much wiser than we, went on. "From time to time, you visit the dimensions of your Creation, you journey your Kingdoms as all good rulers do. Because of the impending danger to Truth, both of you have elected to initiate yourselves into the Mysteries again, in order to examine the protected Mysteries for the amount of Original Truth they still bear. You both have, therefore, self-induced amnesia and incarnated into the third dimension. In fact, you have returned to the third dimension, the heart of it all, the mid-point of your Cosmos, again and again, seeking to identify the problem."

Sheeyah whispered to me out of the corner of her mouth, "Makes sense. But it's not really a mystery. There's really no big problem. It's simple: Incarnation pays off. Gotta have material bodies for good sex."

"Not exactly, Mother."

Sheeyah blushed and whispered again. "Oh God, how embarrassing. You heard me."

"Also, not exactly Mother. Embarrassment is an emotion of the third dimension. It represents confusion experienced by the ego — confusion regarding superficial, materially-based, expectations of appropriateness. You come from the beyond and have access to a much broader range of responses. Embarrassment is what you have learned on Earth as a human. It is part of the narrowing and distortion of perception and experience conducted by the third dimensional ego."

Something about this didn't compute. I had to question the logic. "Well, *I'm* certainly not *embarrassed* to question your logic on this. I mean, try looking at it this way: this here — all this — is some ego trip. We get yanked out of the third dimension, bounced through a few other dimensions, and then dumped here, in some other reality, if you call *this* reality. And we're supposed to be less egoistic now, to have dropped the egoism of mere third dimensional mortals. But, pray tell, what could be more egoistic than for me to come to believe that I am God?"

"Father, do you now assert that God has an ego?" My son spoke to me with the greatest of deference here. But I wondered if it was really honest deference.

I went on with my tirade. "Why bother with Creation otherwise? What motivates someone to try to spread what he thinks of as Truth? If you ask me, God has got to be on a pretty big ego trip."

"I *do* ask you, Father."

"Ask me what?"

"Is God, Father, on what you turn of the new age millennium incarnates call an 'ego trip'?"

"How should I know?" I couldn't help but chuckle. He was asking *me*. The amnesic me was still somewhat amnesic, of course, or I would have realized that only I could really answer this question.

"Who else is more likely to know, Father?"

Sheeyah jumped in. "*I* am. After all, *I* am a woman and women tend to think in these terms a little more easily." She glanced over at me, out from under her raised eyebrows, most matter-of-factly.

You think so do you? Sheeyah, great feminist priestess, comes through again, I said to myself. Of course they heard me thinking. No use my thinking any thought I wanted to keep private here.

"What I mean is that, in the era in which Triad and I are now — or were (if we're dead) — incarnated, at the turn of the millennium, women are developing a greater understanding of the projections of male ego over female ego. Women are gaining an awareness of the manifestations of ego power in the material plane. I should say *re*gaining. They knew once, long long ago. But their power was lost, conquered by patriarchal institutions."

"*Jesus*, you *are* a feminist. The truth about you comes out. How on Earth did I get mixed up with you?" I wondered aloud.

A loud and threatening rumble came from somewhere. Sheeyah and I anxiously looked around, but did not see its source. None of the dignitaries, nor Nostradamus, paid it any heed. The rumble ceased.

Relatively (compared to me) unfettered by the rumble, Sheeyah turned back to me. "You can throw that label at me if you like, but it's more than that. Men have maintained control of the mechanisms of power for so long. Too long. Women are in the process of taking back their rightful place of power."

"Hah," I responded aloud and then went on in my mind: Just try. This feminist bullshit — (or would a gentleman or a God be more likely to call it rhetoric?) — keeps rearing its ugly head, even in beautiful women.

"Women are in the process of taking back the Earth."

Another rumble shook the cave and then ceased.

"Just shut up and look pretty," I mumbled to Sheeyah under my breath.

"Mother, Father, I beseech you. The time has come for the removal of ignorance, even regarding this very issue of gender. There are more pressing issues at stake. Wait, still your discussion, and you shall rediscover the Truth."

It sounded a little like "Mom, Dad, don't fight. Not now." I shrugged. Sheeyah's feminism did not please me, but she did surprise me with her obvious development of thought on the matter. I sensed that she would be a formidable opponent in a debate. I decided to quiet down.

Nostradamus had more to say. "Your disagreements are a lower-level, a most mundane, expression of your most Divine polarity. Polarity creates the dialectic of all life in all dimensions. For example, in order to generate polarity, through a great exercise of Creative Will, Mother opposes Father by being the God*dess*, separate from the God. Goddess and God, forever magnetically driven to reunite their wholeness and complete their energy forms, mate. In seeking to reestablish its Monad form, the Duad actually manifests the Triad. God breathes the spirit of Original Truth into Goddess, who bears it into the Cosmos. Mother, being the cosmic Goddess, then brings the reality of the Spiritual Triad to fruition. Mother, Father, I am your fruition, your manifestation, your offspring, and I form the third part of your Spiritual Triad. We reach into all dimensions of reality. In fact, in the sixth dimension, the dimension of most expansive Oneness, the highest of all dimensions, we three resonate as One although we can define our separate identities at will."

I was irritated now. "So now *you* are part of me as well?" I asked Nostradamus.

"Yes Father. I am you. You are the Triad."

"So this is what shrinks mean by multiple personality disorder?" I mumbled. I saw the dignitaries bow their heads, again in unison, as if they were of one mind. When they bowed their heads, each one of them moved his (I really couldn't discern the sex of any of them, so I naturally assumed they were all men) forehead into a triangle he formed by the touching of his hands together, thumb to thumb and finger tip to corresponding finger tip of the other hand. An unusual signal of some sort, I mused.

Nostradamus most ceremoniously returned the bow, along with that mysterious hand signal, to his dignitaries. Then he turned and bowed to us, again forming the triangle with his hands. I found that I rather liked the bow and the triangle gesture. It made a vague kind of sense to me. Sort of like going to Grandma's on Thanksgiving. Nostradamus then took Sheeyah's hand in one of his and my hand in his other. The very next moment, the three of us were connected by a powerful electric current or something like it. It happened that quickly.

A most glorious ray of white light radiated upward from the top of each of our three heads, and then, about seven feet above our heads, a horizontal triangle formed itself of white light, each of its corners intersecting the rays radiating up from each one of our heads. I watched in awe as a point in the center of that triangle lowered itself below the triangle, forming a tetrahedron of light, and then that tetrahedron began to spin, slowly at first and then gaining momentum and whirling until it appeared to be a cone.

The energy that built as the cone of light whirled became so powerful that something more amazing than everything else that I had been experiencing happened. A sort of spiritual tornado or something sucked the three of us right up into the air, right into the light which formed the cone. Our bodies seemed to become soft, to almost dissolve and then to lose their physical density. We became light forms and merged and I felt an ecstasy I had never imagined in any way. For a moment, I found myself a believer. We separated into three spinning sets of eyes and looked at each other and I felt more certain of myself than I had ever felt in the incarnation I had just been having. A kind of certainty of identity that I doubt most humans ever experience. Entirely authentic. So real it made any other level of reality seem merely imaginary — diluted to shadows.

Thoughts raced through my mind. O.K. So I am Triad. The Triad. That Triad. This Triad. O.K. I got it. Yet the "it" I was describing felt transient for some reason. I suspected that I was still suspending myself within some level of my own disbelief.

I wondered what Sheeyah thought about what was happening. I couldn't find my voice so I sent a mental query to Sheeyah: Sheeyah? Do you? Do you understand this? I sensed that Sheeyah was troubled.

She found her voice somehow. "Yes," she answered in a whisper, "but why should I want to believe this stuff about who we are? I don't like it. It sort of reduces me to nothing. Is it true that I am I really only a vessel then, *your* vessel of all things, just a carrier of something? I am nothing more? Can that really be?"

That rumble sounded again, only it was much louder now, more threatening. Then, something that, for want of a better explanation, I can only describe as an old woman's *voice*, (although no one could really call it a *voice*), a vibration which seemed to be able to communicate, imperially resonant and very deep, emanated from somewhere. It responded directly to Sheeyah: NO, NEVER THINK THAT. THIS IS A COMMON AND MOST FUNDAMENTAL MISINTERPRETATION OF THE PURPOSE OF THE FEMININE ENERGY. THIS IS QUITE INACCURATE.

Abruptly, the cone of light stopped whirling and we landed in what I assumed was another underground cave, one in which plant life seemed to be able to grow without sunlight. Strange lotus-like flowers were growing out of almost every crack. They looked uncannily beautiful to me, although I had never been one to truly appreciate flowers. I noticed that we were standing before a large, golden Round Table. The dignitaries of the High Counsel were seated there, as if waiting for us to join their meeting. However, they were not waiting idle. To my surprise, they were playing some kind of card game. It looked like group solitaire. I felt a twinge of homesickness — a minor heartache — when I saw the cards. I wanted them to let me play. I felt shunned, like a boy being left out of a game. But it did not seem to be on the agenda. Not at that time.

I struggled now with an internal conflict — a conflict between, among, the various realities across which I was shifting. What should I accept as real? An ethereal light, not of the sun, poured in from somewhere behind us, casting our shadows upon the wall of the cave. These shadows were impressive, spellbinding. I found these shadows extremely precise. They revealed the profiles of myself and Sheeyah and the dignitaries so clearly that I could not help but think of these shadows as depicting reality much more reliably than the scene before me, the scene of which I continued to doubt the veracity. I was intrigued to note that I felt at home with the shadows, as if they were my usual mode of perception, as if I had returned to that mode of perceiving reality for a moment. I could almost let myself think that I was attending some board meeting, one similar to those attended during my most recent incarnation, except for the fact that, this time, I did not think I was the one controlling the meeting.

I tore my eyes from the comforting reality of the shadows and forced them to look upon what seemed to be intensely unreal to me. The amnesic me was still at work enough to cloud my doors of perception, to let me think that the deeper view of reality Camus had led us into was anything but real. I could see that there was at least one tunnel leading in to the cave from somewhere. Something seemed to fill the tunnel. Something living. I could not discern its form. It just felt alive to me.

The old woman had more to say — or to resonate (this might be a better description of what she was doing) — regarding Sheeyah's remark. NEVER THINK THAT. THE THOUGHT IS MOTHER TO THE DEED. DO NOT ADD TO THIS REALITY BY GENERATING MORE OF THIS CRIPPLING THOUGHT FORM. WHEN THE HIGHEST OF ALL GODDESSES DOUBTS HERSELF, WE ALL ARE IN JEOPARDY. THE LAST THING WE NEED IS THE COSMIC MOTHER REDUCING HER SELF TO SUCH AN IMAGE. JUST A VESSEL? HEAVENS NO. BECOME AGAIN CONSCIOUS OF THE TRUE CHARACTER OF YOUR ENERGY FORCE, SHEEYAH. YOU WILL FIND THAT IT CHANGES THE MEANING OF YOUR FEMININITY.

"Who's talking? Where are you?" Sheeyah looked around.

WHERE ARE YOU? That voice or whatever it was answered her question.

"What do you mean *where* am I?" Sheeyah answered rather meekly.

LOCATE YOURSELF. The thing I'm calling a voice commanded Sheeyah.

"Somewhere in time long ago. Ancient Egypt I think. Some island."

"Khebit." Camus spoke up. He had been sitting among the dignitaries. He looked at me. We momentarily locked our gazes. His presence did not surprise me.

But he was playing cards. Lucky guy. "Why do you get to play cards while I am dragged through this metaphysical metafeminist morass?" I asked him under my breath. He just smiled blandly. "Camus," I said aloud, "Glad you're still around, maybe you can explain all —"

Camus interrupted the card game to hold up a hand, signaling me that I ought to wait a while.

Disinterested in my comment to Camus, the voice kept addressing Sheeyah: LOCATE YOURSELF FURTHER.

"What else is there to say? Apparently we traveled through other dimensions, bounced down to the second and then up to the fourth to travel in time and arrive here on Earth at a different time than the one in which we were living." Sheeyah had learned Camus' teachings well. She had a real feel for this metaphysical stuff. If that's what this was.

ON WHOM? The voice demanded.

"Whom what?" Sheeyah was confused.

YOU ARRIVED ON *WHOM* AT A DIFFERENT TIME?

"No we didn't arrive on any *body*, no *whom* involved. I said we arrived on Earth at a different time." Now Sheeyah sounded faintly irritated.

ON *WHOM*? The voice grew louder, its decibels booming from within the cave walls.

Sheeyah backed down only a little. "O.K. Have it your way. The whom is Earth."

THANK YOU. I APPRECIATE BEING ADDRESSED APPROPRIATELY.

This did not sit well with Sheeyah. "So I guess you want me to believe that the Earth is speaking to me in this way. I suppose after all I've been through, anything — even this sort of coincidence — is possible. I'm broken down enough that anything is believable, but come on, you people," Sheeyah looked at the faces of the dignitaries, "give me a break. The Earth doesn't *speak*, not like this. And I should know, I've channeled the vibrations of Earth to my people several times."

Her people? The vibrations of Earth? I wondered what Sheeyah meant by these comments. But the dignitaries continued playing cards, unmoved and probably unamused. Clearly, they elected to stay out of the argument between these two females — I guessed there were two. Seemed like a wise decision to me.

The voice was angry now: OH? I DO NOT SPEAK IN THIS WAY? And at that moment an enormous earthquake hit and lasted much longer than any I had ever been in or heard about. It felt more like a tremendous rolling than a shaking. The ground as well as the air above it felt like a heavy liquid. I could feel the Earth convulsing, the cave walls warping fluidly as if they were not solid stone.

Sheeyah and I were thrown down onto the floor. Pieces of the cave's walls were falling and objects were flying. The living thing that I had earlier detected in the tunnel began to slither like a serpent. For a moment, I thought I caught a glimpse of the serpent's head, a gigantic and much more fearsome version of the face of the snake that had threatened us while we made love back at the lake. Things were shaking so hard that I could not focus my eyes. The serpent seemed to be spitting fire and lightning, but I could not be still enough to keep my eyes on any one thing long enough to check out this impression. I let myself dismiss the serpent's face and fire as a hallucination of a plagued imagination. This was just as well as even the air around us was cracking, and, between the cracks, I could see a vast dark sky full of stars. The darkness appeared to me to be the hungry mouth of an awesome infinity.

Needless to say, I was uneasy. Sheeyah and I managed somehow to take shelter under the Round Table. Curiously, we were joined by none of the High Counsel, none of whom had even fallen from their chairs.

Finally the convulsing stopped. Sheeyah crawled out from under the table and looked upward, shouting, "Forgive me! I'm sorry! Of course the Earth speaks! I've heard you before, just not in words! I didn't know you knew words."

I DO NOT KNOW WORDS. HOWEVER, THROUGH THE WEB OF OUR INTERRELATED ENERGIES, AND THE INTERRELATED ENERGIES OF ALL THIRD DIMENSIONAL LIFE ON EARTH, WE MERGE IN AND EVEN CONSTITUTE THE ENERGY BODY OF THIS PLANET.

"I'm not going to disagree with you now, so don't get angry, but I don't really get what you're saying to me here. You mean you think I'm just part of you, of Earth?" Sheeyah stopped vocalizing and went on silently: First I'm folding into Triad, submerged into his form and next I'm folded into Earth, submerged into your form. Doesn't leave me much self.

Of course her thoughts were heard.

And the Earth voice spoke: ONLY WHENCE YOU HAVE PLACED YOUR EGO ASIDE CAN YOUR ASCEND TO YOUR RIGHTFUL THRONE.

"My rightful throne? You mean as leader of my Earthcult or something?"

I was far too overwhelmed by what was going on to realize that Sheeyah had just indicated that she was involved with — maybe really even the leader of — Earthcult. Had I really heard what she had said about this, I would have been wild with surprise and shock, and quite suspicious about all that had happened.

HOLY MOTHER OF THE UNIVERSE. THE FEMININE POINT IN THE TRIAD. IT HAS BEEN SO LONG SINCE YOU ASSUMED YOUR FULL POWER.

"I think that's what I was trying to talk about a while ago, when Triad called me a feminist! Did you hear all that?"

I HEAR ALL THAT IS SAID WITHIN MY ORGANISM.

"So you really do call yourself an organism?" Sheeyah sounded much more respectful now. "I belong to — or belonged to — I don't know if I'm dead or alive anymore but I guess it doesn't matter — but I am part of a political group that says you *are* an organism. I really believed it back then already. I kind of thought — but I always secretly reminded myself that maybe it was just a fantasy — that I could feel that you were alive, that you had a presence or something. I did feel pretty certain that you really were communicating with me, sending me pictures of various safe places around the globe."

ALL CELESTIAL BODIES ARE ORGANISMS. EARTH IS BUT ONE. EACH CELESTIAL BODY RESIDES WITHIN THE LARGER ORGANISM OF THE IMMEDIATE UNIVERSE WHICH RESIDES, ALONG WITH SEVERAL OTHER UNIVERSES, WITHIN THE SUPRAUNIVERSE WHICH RESIDES WITHIN THE COSMOS, OF WHICH YOU ARE QUEEN.

"Amazing. This is like a fairy tale. Did I make this up? Is this a dream or something?" Sheeyah pinched herself.

THIS IS THE MOST AWAKE YOU HAVE BEEN IN EONS. BUT WHAT IS A FAIRY TALE? WHAT IS A DREAM? SOME OF THE GREATEST MYSTERIES HAVE BEEN CAMOUFLAGED IN MYTHS AND FAIRY TALES, ENCODED IN DREAMS. UNFORTUNATELY, MUCH OF TRUTH HAS ALSO BEEN DISTORTED IN THESE. SADLY, THE PROTECTIVE CAMOUFLAGE IS OFT ENDANGERING.

I watched silently as Sheeyah thought for a moment and then went on with this, the most bizarre conversation I had yet witnessed on this psychotic journey. After all, she was talking alternately to the floor and to the wall of the cave. "So how are you communicating with me if you don't know words?"

Sheeyah, the curious. Just let it go, Sheeyah. Maybe we can get out of here now.

Both Sheeyah and Earth ignored me.

TOGETHER OUR ACCOMPANYING LIFE FORMS FORM THE ETHER.

"What ether?" So Sheeyah played on, speaking as a student to a cave wall.

I had to admit to myself that she was nevertheless getting answers to her questions, answers that even I, the doubting Thomas, could hear. Partners in psychosis?

THE ENERGY BODY. So Earth spoke as if she were a great teacher, a vessel of knowledge. The two of them, Sheeyah and Earth settled into their roles of student and teacher:

"And, Earth, you mean that this has something to do with how you talk in words?"

YES. ONE OF YOUR GREATEST 20TH CENTURY WRITERS, A WOMAN WHO SCRIBED ONTO PAPER THE IDEAS OF A GREAT TIBETAN, EXPLAINED THAT THE FUNCTION OF THE ETHERIC BODY IS TO RECEIVE ENERGY IMPULSES, OR STREAMS OF FORCE, EMANATING FROM SOME ORIGINATING SOURCE.

"Yes, but what does that have to do with anything? Not to be rude here, Earth, but why are you telling me this?"

IT IS THROUGH THE MEDIUM OF THE ENERGY OR ETHERIC BODY THAT EVERY HUMAN BEING IS PART OF EVERY OTHER EXPRESSION OF DIVINE LIFE, INCLUDING THIS PLANET AND THIS SOLAR SYSTEM AND THIS UNIVERSE AND THIS COSMOS. IT IS THEREFORE POSSIBLE TO ASSEMBLE A TELEPATHIC RELATIONSHIP BETWEEN AND AMONG LIFE FORMS. THIS YOU AND I HAVE DONE.

"Telepathy?"

I CAN COMMUNICATE TO YOU VIA THE ETHERIC BODY.

"What's the etheric body?"

THIS BODY HAS TWO ASPECTS: IT BOTH PERMEATES AND INTERPENETRATES THE ENTIRETY OF ANY ORGANISM — PHYSICAL ORGANISM IN YOUR CASE — AND IT EXTENDS BEYOND THE PHYSICAL MASS OF THE ORGANISM, SURROUNDING IT.

"Like an aura? I heard of those back home."

LIKE WHAT YOU CALL AN AURA. THE HIGHER EVOLVED AN ORGANISM, THE MORE ITS ETHERIC BODY WILL EXTEND BEYOND THE BOUNDARIES OF ANY PHYSICAL BODY IT HAS.

"So you are an organism and have an etheric body too?"

YES.

"And your etheric body and mine speak?"

LET ME BETTER EXPLAIN THIS TO YOU. IF I CHOOSE TO 'SPEAK' WITH YOU WHILE YOU ARE A HUMAN BEING, I MUST TRANSLATE AND STEP DOWN BOTH MY ENERGY COMPLEXITY AND MY EN-

ERGY CAPACITY TO THAT OF YOURS. I SEEK OUT AND MEET YOUR ENERGY, YOUR LIVINGNESS, YOUR ETHERIC BODY. I *STEP DOWN* TO YOUR FREQUENCY. I PREPARE MY VIBRATIONS FOR YOUR AUTOMATIC RECOGNITION AND TRANSLATION. I VIBRATE MY MESSAGE AT YOUR FREQUENCY. IF YOU RECOGNIZE THAT I AM SENDING YOU A MESSAGE AND SOMETIMES EVEN WHEN YOU DO NOT RECOGNIZE THAT I AM SENDING YOU A MESSAGE, YOU TRANSLATE MY VIBRATIONS INTO YOUR IMAGERY, OR EVEN INTO YOUR WORDS, WHEN MY VIBRATIONS ENTER YOUR MIND THROUGH YOUR ETHER.

"So this is telepathy? Is this the way you told me where the safe lands will be? Translating your complex information into pictures I could recognize in my mind? And sometimes just making me feel undeniably called to a certain point in a certain part of the planet — almost magnetically pulled there?"

YES, YOU CAN CALL THIS TELEPATHY. THE POWER TO COMMUNICATE IS PART OF THE NATURE OF ALL SUBSTANCE. COMMUNICATION IS POSSIBLE BY MEANS OF THE MEDIUM OF THE OMNIPRESENT ETHER, THE INTERTWINEMENT OF ALL ETHERIC BODIES INTO THEIR COMBINATION — THE GREAT ETHERIC.

"Omnipresent? So, Earth, you can communicate with anyone you wish. Why don't you talk to *all* humans then?"

I SPEAK TO MANY, BUT AM RECOGNIZED BY ONLY A FEW. MOST HUMANS LABEL THESE FEW AS EITHER VISIONARIES OR LUNATICS. YOUR CULT MEMBERS RECOGNIZED YOU AS ONE WHO COULD REALLY HEAR ME.

"Why? Why is that the case, Earth?"

HUMAN EARTHLINGS ARE GROWING DEAF TO TRANSMISSIONS OF TRUTH, EVEN FROM ME, THEIR MOTHER PLANET. MOST HUMANS HAVE BECOME NUMB TO THE ENERGY OF THE COSMOS AND OF THE EARTH WITHIN THE COSMOS. AS EACH DAY PASSES, I SEE THAT THE HUMAN SPECIES MARCHES TOWARD AN UNPRECEDENTED MECHANIZATION OF ITS LIFE FORM, A MECHANIZATION NEVER SEEN BEFORE IN THE UNIVERSE.

"This is very sad. I don't know why, but I'm starting to cry."

And, sure enough, I saw tears pouring out of Sheeyah's eyes. I was not so moved. I felt like an onlooker in the theater of the absurd. A Bohemian type woman in old running shorts talking to the wall of an underground cave on a magic island in Ancient Egypt? And the cave wall said something about this woman being the leader of a cult. What was that about?

THIS IS PART OF THE REASON WE HAVE SUMMONED YOU NOW.

Silence.

I wanted to speak, however, despite its apparent absurdity in the eyes of my rational mind, this communion between what seemed to be Earth and what seemed to be my lover, Sheeyah, was uninterruptable, uncannily sacred.

"Earth, you communicate with me through the ether, right?"

YES.

"It sounds so simple. How?"

VIA TELEPATHY, AS I HAVE INDICATED.

"Well, are there many kinds of telepathy? Or is this the only real telepathy and the rest of what I've heard is just hype?"

MUCH OF WHAT YOU HAVE HEARD ABOUT TELEPATHY IS INDEED HYPE. HOWEVER, THAT HYPE IS BASED ON REAL PROCESSES. THAT HYPE REVEALS THE HUNGER OF THE HUMAN MASSES FOR ORIGINAL TRUTH AND ITS MYSTERIES.

"So what part of all this stuff about telepathy is Truth?"

TELEPATHIC COMMUNICATION IS PREVALENT. IT TAKES PLACE CONTINUOUSLY. IT TAKES THREE BASIC FORMS IN HUMANS. ITS MOST BASIC, MOST PRIMITIVE FORM IS 'INSTINCTUAL TELEPATHY'. THIS BASIC TELEPATHY CONCERNS BASIC FEELING. INSTINCTUAL TELEPATHY ALWAYS INVOLVES RADIATION FROM THE SOLAR PLEXUS OF AN ORGANISM. YOU WILL FIND SUCH TELEPATHY OCCURRING BETWEEN A MOTHER AND HER INFANT, BETWEEN LOVERS EXPERIENCING INTENSE PHYSICAL DESIRE FOR EACH OTHER —

"It sounds very animal."

INDEED. ANIMALS UTILIZE INSTINCTUAL TELEPATHY ALL THE TIME. YOU FIND IT AT WORK IN THE MOVEMENT OF HERDS OF ANIMALS ACROSS FIELDS AND PLAINS, THE MIGRATION OF BIRDS AND WHALES, THE SUDDEN CHANGE IN DIRECTION OF A FLOCK OF BIRDS IN FLIGHT. YOU HUMANS ARE NOT SO VERY DIFFERENT. INSTINCTUAL TELEPATHY IS AT WORK IN THE RAPID TRANSMIS-

SION OF INFORMATION AMONG WHAT YOU CALL SAVAGE TRIBES, AND EVEN IN THE SPEEDY SHIFTS IN MODERN CIVILIZATION'S PUBLIC OPINIONS. THE INSTINCTUAL MIGRATION TO SAFE LANDS, WHICH YOU KNOW SO MUCH ABOUT, IS YET ANOTHER EXAMPLE.

Safe lands? Migration to safe lands? What is the voice referring to? Safe lands? *The* safe lands? *Survivor territories?* I dared not ask. I forced myself to stop wondering. I don't think I really wanted to know right then. I just blocked it out.

Sheeyah went on. "You make it sound like we don't really have minds of our own."

EACH INDIVIDUAL HAS ITS OWN MIND AND, AT THE SAME TIME, IS PART OF THE COLLECTIVE MIND OF ITS SPECIES AND PART OF THE OMNIPRESENT INTRA-SPECIES ETHER.

"You make it sound like humans are not so different from animals."

YOU ARE SIMILAR AND DIFFERENT. YOU HUMANS HAVE THE OPTION OF RAISING YOUR FREQUENCY TO A HIGHER LEVEL AND WITH IT YOUR LEVEL OF TELEPATHIC CONSCIOUSNESS.

"How so?"

IT IS UNDERSTOOD AMONG THOSE WHO OBSERVE YOU HUMANS THAT SOME OF YOU ARE ABLE TO MANIFEST A SOMEWHAT HIGHER BUT STILL RATHER PRIMITIVE FORM OF INSTINCTUAL TELEPATHY BY ADDING TO THE PROCESS A DEGREE OF HIGHER OR MORE MENTAL ENERGY. THE PERSONS WHO CAN DO THIS USUALLY HAVE AN ACTIVELY FUNCTIONING THROAT CENTER OR THROAT CHAKRA. THEY CAN COMMUNICATE MORE THAN BASE GUT FEELING. HIGHER LEVELS OF DEVOTION AND ASPIRATION CAN BE COMMUNICATED AND RECEIVED BY THESE PERSONS. THEY CAN REACH BEYOND AND SOMETIMES EVEN DETACH FROM THE PRIMITIVE SENTIMENTS AND DESIRES TYPICAL OF LESS EVOLVED HUMANS AND ANIMALS.

"Why is this so much higher?"

IT IS NOT SO MUCH HIGHER, IT IS SOMEWHAT HIGHER. WHILE THE PRIMITIVE SENTIMENTS ARE EXPRESSED AND PERCEIVED BY THE SOLAR PLEXUS, THE LESS PRIMITIVE SENTIMENTS ASPIRE TO MORE THAN BASIC SURVIVAL. INDIVIDUALS WHO ARE VERY ATTACHED TO THE MATERIAL PLANE TEND TO FUNCTION PRIMA-

RILY ON THE BASIS OF PRIMITIVE SENTIMENTS AND PRIMARILY AS MEMBERS OF A HERD, A SPECIES, A POPULATION, A GROUP OF SOME SORT. INDIVIDUALS WHO LOOK FOR VALUES BEYOND THEIR MATERIAL EXISTENCES, AND BEYOND THE DICTATES OF THE GROUP TO WHICH THEY BELONG, RAISE THEIR SENTIMENTS FROM THEIR GUT LEVELS TO THEIR THROAT LEVELS, A HIGHER VIBRATORY PLACE WITHIN THEIR BODIES.

"Is there any way to further raise the level of telepathic consciousness or is that as good as it gets for us mere mortals?"

THERE IS A SECOND, STILL HIGHER, FORM OF TELEPATHIC COMMUNICATION: 'MENTAL TELEPATHY'. THIS IS ONE WHICH MOVES INFORMATION FROM MIND TO MIND. INTENSE EMOTION AND STRONG DESIRE ARE ELIMINATED IN THIS PROCESS AT THE HEIGHT OF ITS EFFICIENCY. THE COMMUNICATION CAN THEREFORE BE MUCH MORE PRECISE THAN IT IS IN INSTINCTUAL TELEPATHY.

"Mind to mind? What about communication from soul to soul? Can humans do that?"

YES, THIS IS THE THIRD AND HIGHEST FORM OF TELEPATHIC COMMUNICATION: 'INTUITIONAL TELEPATHY'. INDEED, THIS COMMUNICATION PROCEEDS FROM SOUL TO SOUL. THIS IS THE HIGHEST LEVEL OF TELEPATHY ACHIEVABLE BY HUMAN BEINGS. SUCH COMMUNICATION IS ACHIEVABLE BY THOSE WHO CAN BRING THEIR SPIRIT MINDS INTO COMPLETE ALIGNMENT WITH THEIR BRAINS.

"So, I can do it too? Some form of telepathy?"

MY DEAR, YOU ALREADY KNOW AND ENGAGE IN MORE THAN THESE THREE METHODS OF TELEPATHIC COMMUNICATION.

Silence.

"So who are you, Earth? I mean you can't just be *Earth* can you? This is beyond my comprehension."

I AM MODELED AFTER YOU.

"Modeled after *me*? Why *me*?"

YOU ARE THE SPIRIT OF ALL LIFE AND ITS FORMATION, ITS NATURE.

"I am?"

YOU ARE THE SPIRIT OF TRUTH, TRUTH IN ALL DIMENSIONS.

"You mean there is Truth in *all* dimensions? Are there life forms where there are no physical bodies?"

YES, HOWEVER YOU MUST RID YOURSELF OF YOUR THIRD DIMENSIONAL CONFINES TO REMEMBER THIS.

"Remember this? You mean I already know this?"

YES, I MEAN THAT YOU ARE THE MOTHER OF ALL LIFE, OF ALL LIFE FORMS.

"This is a bit much for me to believe."

Now an unspoken voice said: Isis is unveiled.

I heard those thought words. Who said this? Or thought it? Camus? Yes, Camus.

"Camus said that. I'm sure it was you that said that, Camus." I said aloud. Then I looked at Camus. So did Sheeyah.

Camus nodded a yes and thought again: Isis is unveiled. I felt Camus' thoughts waft into our minds.

"Isis? Who's Isis?" Sheeyah drew the focus away from Camus and me by asking Earth this question.

YOU, MY DEAR, Earth sighingly informed Sheeyah, ARE ISIS — LOVER, WIFE AND SISTER OF OSIRIS. YOU AND OSIRIS (WHO THE EGYPTIANS ACTUALLY CALLED AUSET AND AUSAR) ARRIVED ON ANCIENT EGYPTIAN SOIL FROM ATLANTIS, WITH THE AIM OF COLONIZING EGYPT, SOME 12,500 YEARS BEFORE YOUR CURRENT MODERN ERA INCARNATIONS. THIS IS, OF COURSE, ABOUT YOUR YEAR 10,500 B.C., THE TIME WHEN THE MAIN ISLAND OF ATLANTIS SANK. IN FACT, THE AMMONITES, AN EGYPTIAN PEOPLE WHO DESCEND DIRECTLY FROM THE OLD PHARAOHS, AND WHO HAVE PRESERVED MANY OF THE ANCIENT WAYS, CONTINUE TO CELEBRATE THIS DAY IN THE MODERN ERA. IT WAS A GREAT DAY FOR THE WORLD. AND FOR THE COSMOS.

"So I suppose this makes me Osiris?" I did not really absorb the details I had just been given regarding my Earthly Atlantean incarnation.

YES, TRIAD, YOU ARE OSIRIS.

Earth finally addressed me. It is about time you noticed me, Earth or whoever you are, especially if I am really your Creator.

Sheeyah began to sob.

"What Sheeyah? What is it?" I asked her. I was definitely unprepared for yet another of her strange mood swings.

"I told you I dreamed that they killed you and they wanted to kill me because I carried your child. Horus. It was Horus. It is Nostradamus." Sheeyah turned to our son. "Nostradamus, you were Horus, my son, weren't you, aren't you?"

"Yes, Mother, I have been your son again and again. In the Egyptian times, you were worshipped as a Mother Goddess, the very personification of fertility. Your link to Earth was close and you were actually so intertwined with Earth that you and she were difficult to separate. Your fertility was manifested by the annual flooding of the Nile and the land surrounding it."

"I married Triad back then?"

"You married Triad as Osiris, your twin brother. In fact the two of you fell in love in the womb."

Sheeyah and I looked at each other. We could feel each other trying to figure out exactly how it might have felt to be in the womb together. This concept sounded preposterous to both of us.

I SENSE THAT THIS IS INCONCEIVABLE TO YOU AT THIS MOMENT.

Sheeyah nevertheless tried to continue sounding respectful. "Well, it does sound quite strange. After all, two fetuses can't —"

Something happened. I thought I heard the Earth voice say THAT'S WHAT YOU MAY THINK, but I was so taken by the process of what was then happening that I was not certain. It seemed to me that a warm river came from somewhere in the cave. Although it moved slowly, it became very deep very quickly. Somehow it was only streaming toward Sheeyah and me. When it reached us, as if it had a will of its own, it paused and then encircled us. It kept getting deeper and I became aware that it was going to engulf us. In the distance, the serpent's face loomed, glowing and absolutely gigantic.

I thought I heard the Earth voice tell us not to fear, that we would breathe right through the water and that the serpent would not strike, but of this I could not be certain. My panic took form as paralyzed terror. I pulled my knees to my chest and held myself tightly. I realized that Sheeyah was doing the same.

The head injury I had sustained in the yacht harbor began to throb with a screaming pain. Finally, the pain was so intense that I felt myself black out. Now I was certain that I had died. (Or had I died *again*? I asked myself fleetingly.) I felt as if I had moved into an infinite and completely lightless darkness, an engulfing void. It must have been several minutes or days before I realized that I could not really be blacked out because I was able to perceive the void that I floated within.

My next consideration was that this was, finally, after all was said and done, death. But then, I had had the thought that I might have died more than once of late. What made me anymore dead now than before? I could still think. I think therefore I am, I thought. Am what? Dead? Alive? Could I tell the difference? Did it matter?

I thought that I could feel my heart beating. I tried to move what I thought might be my body to feel the place where my heart beat was coming from. I felt something soft and solid! It was moving too! A face! A mouth! I put one of my fingers into the mouth. My finger! I could feel the mouth suck on my finger!

But then I was overcome by a kind of detached concern. Perhaps I was indeed dead, I told myself, because although I could feel myself touching a mouth which seemed to be part of another body, my body could not feel itself touching itself.

Whatever musings I had been entertaining ceased abruptly when I did feel something touch me. It was as if a hand was running itself over my head and face. I reached for that hand. I found it and grasped it with mine. It was not one of my hands. For some reason, I was certain of this, although I cannot say how.

Whatever it was out there in the darkness, it was touching me. I began to touch it. Yes there was that mouth. That face. Arms. Torso. Legs. Feet. Soon, I realized that it really was a body. As it touched me, I realized that I definitely had a body too. The body and I moved closer. It was so wonderful not to be alone. Soon, the body and I were engaged in as much bodily contact as was possible. We were pressed tightly against each other and continued to feel each other all over. It was such a warm, secure, full sensation. I felt so whole and satisfied. I felt as if there would never be anything more I would want through all eternity.

Our lips touched. They stayed touching. Our arms embraced and something happened to me. A wash of sensation filled every bit of my body. The sensation was beyond sexual ecstasy. It was love, a higher, more devoted love than I had never imagined. Complete, eternal, pure love. And with it, pure, continuously orgasmic ecstasy.

I loved that being whose body was pressed tightly up against mine. We remained in that divine position for what felt like forever.

8

In hope of reaching you, of imparting cosmic knowledge through to your soul, I am telling the love story of Sheeyah and Triad, also known as Isis and Osiris.

Under other circumstances, I would not be here to communicate this knowledge myself. Many eons ago, I created a complete, comprehensive guide to the metaphysical universe. I encoded all any life form would need to know in a triad of forms: the oral, the written and the meta-material. I created the living, breathing gospel of Original Truth. However, during the passing ages, this original gospel was tampered with, diluted, restructured, and stifled by some of those in power in various parts of the Cosmos, for their own self-serving ends, so that their own intergalactic structures would prevail throughout the succeeding generations. The distortions they invoked in the original doctrine, in Original Truth, are similar to the dismemberment and fragmentation of your Earthly BIBLE, of your Babylonian CODE OF HAMMURABI, of your Egyptian BOOK OF THE DEAD, of your Hindu BHAGAVAD GITA, VEDAS and UPANISHADS, of your Buddhist SUTRAS, of your Confucian Scriptures including the SHU KING and the BOOKS OF MENCIUS, of your Taoist TAO TE CHING, of your Zoroastrian GATHAS, of your Judaist TORAH and TALMUD, of your Mohammedan KORAN, and of so many other of your documents. But the mother document of all, Original Truth itself, has been mutilated on a far grander scale.

Over time, it has become impossible for the self-serving power structures to which I refer to hide their suppressions and distortions of the Original Truth. It has, therefore, become necessary for them to try to destroy all evidence of the original document in all its forms. Remember that when I say "document," I refer to more than writing on a series of papers. The grand document, the cosmic manuscript, the original gospel, is a living code, written on the intergalactic winds, in the blood of the Cosmos, one which was intended to envelope all dimensions of the universe and give eternal birth to the highest Truth.

NOW I HAVE BECOME AWARE THAT THE SELF-SERVING POWER

STRUCTURES WHICH THREATEN ORIGINAL TRUTH ARE DRIVEN BY A FAR GREATER FORCE, one who actually seeks to completely destroy every bit of the ultimate essence of the mother document, to kill forever the carrier of the moral code of the god force. This murderous anti-god force force reaches across all dimensions and well beyond time. You can help me to stop it. You must.

As I have heretofore noted, some millennia back, I chose to assume the form of an interplanetary seedling from Planet Nebulae. I hoped that, in that form, through my contacts in the cosmic underground of this multidimensional universe, I could cause to surface a hidden copy of the forbidden document — or at least whatever parts of it had survived intact in the material world.

That effort was not successful. Alas, I may have lost control of my Creation. The forces seeking to maintain their power have now successfully concealed or destroyed any physical plane volumes of actual Original Truth that may have survived the millennia. During several of my visits to Earth from Nebulae and, later during several of my Earthly incarnations, I read every piece of your metaphysical literature that I could find, hoping to weed out Original Truth from faddish facsimiles of knowledge.

Fragments, but only fragments, of the Original Truth are visible in the symbologies of "primitive" tribes throughout the Cosmos, such as — on your Earth — the Huichol and the Hopi Indians of North America, the Hill Tribes of India, the Tierra-del-Fuegans, the Aborigines of Australia, and the Maasai warriors of Africa. Yet, the whole of the Truth has dissipated to a hazardous dilution. It would be futile (even the wisest spirit knows his own limits) for me to attempt to resurrect, recombine and disseminate all such Truths myself. I am therefore being advised and aided in this attempt by certain generally off-planet beings, my cosmic offspring and my cosmic wife, one of whom has chosen to incarnate as a human, along with me, on Earth at the time of your new millennium.

Together we shall move you, the Earthly reader, along a vast spiral toward Original Truth and enlightenment, should you elect to hear us. Do not fear this journey. Do not fear getting lost along the way. You will, in the end, find yourself again, on the appropriate part of the cosmic spiral, the karmic spiral you have seen represented in nature so many times: by a snail shell, by the top of a hurricane, by the Milky Way Galaxy. Your search will be somewhat analogous to that conducted by the Knights of the Round Table in the time of King Arthur, who set off in search of the Holy Grail, only to discover that the Grail inevitably lay buried in the mists lurking deep within their psyches. And only to avoid the discovery that within the Grail flowed the fading blood of their great and ailing mother, Earth. The search for the Grail was, on a subconscious level, the instinctive desire of men to preserve or resurrect feminine energy in the face of near total usurpation by masculine energy, to protect the yin from suffocation at the hands of the yang. It was not an accident that King Arthur inspired the search for the Grail. His mother was an Atlantean. *The instinct, the drive to search for Truth, no matter how much a folly it became, was buried deep within the man by his mother.*

Ω

I continued on in the blind but so Divine embrace.

How much time I passed in that blissful state of infinite ecstasy, I cannot know. Time felt like such an irrelevant dimension now. I was so very enwrapped in love that love itself seemed to be the only measure of reality. And the love was so complete, so all encompassing, that the reality was absolute. I floated and floated and floated with this feeling. Beyond bodies. Beyond time. The fifth dimension. The fifth dimension is Divine Love. Divine love as the mirror image of the rigid confines of unidimensional linearity.

I was aware that my heart felt full. It also felt as if it were an opening, a portal into a universe of feeling. I had never imagined such a sensation, such an experience. Here, my inside and my outside were one and neither was physical.

Wait, I asked myself, did I think just now that I had never imagined? When had I never imagined? . . . Was it in some time before this? . . . Was there a before before this? . . . .

The amnesic me was struggling to break through the veil of unconsciousness that I had so carefully constructed: Yes! I told myself. I came from somewhere! I have been elsewhere. But, was it . . . before . . . or . . . after?

Neither, maybe . . .

Hey! Neither maybe? That was not my thought. There really was someone else there with me!

I knew who it was at that exact moment. It was Sheeyah, my twin, my eternal love. My bliss.

Sheeyah!

Yes? Triad!

I could feel her response.

So it is true. This really happened.

This is really happening, Triad. This is now.

Now and then seem so blurred. No clear distinction.

This is the womb. We once incarnated together through this womb, Triad. That once is now.

I'm glad you are in here with me, I thought to Sheeyah. I could not do this journey alone.

Triad, my Osiris, most babies do it alone, but they commune with their mothers for security.

How tragic, Sheeyah, to be alone here.

No, how more a training for death, to commune with the Mother, the bearer and taker of all life.

I felt Sheeyah, my sister Isis, tense a bit. Why? What is it my Isis?

Osiris, we are conceived, we are born, we will be lovers for life.

This is good. So why do you tense?

Osiris, our brother Set, the god of darkness and chaos, will mutilate and kill you!

No! I immediately cringed at the thought of my being mutilated and murdered, however, in the next instant, I felt a powerful wash of denial and disbelief. No one had killed me, I insisted to myself.

Triad, our brother's vengeance is so great, he will cut you to pieces. You are king. He seeks your throne!

But Sheeyah, I cannot die. I am Triad.

Yes, you do not die. But I so much do not want you maimed and murdered.

Well then, even if this is true, it is only my body. Only a physical body. That is all, Sheeyah. I cannot die.

I love your body. We are here together, mingled, touching, caressing. This ecstasy is our enfleshment. We will have many passionate hours together in this lifetime, my brother, my lover. I love your body.

Only a passing ecstasy, a reminder of far greater. We will always reunite. We will always find each other, even across eternity.

But Osiris, what of Set? Why does the god of darkness pursue us?

Can light exist without the dark?

Osiris, why does this dark force keep after us?

Because Set promotes the darkness of nothingness, that ultimate chaos of the void. And you and I are Truth. Truth is order, divine order. Truth is light. Truth filters down from the sixth dimension into all reality. Truth is the supreme life form. Truth is the enemy of the god of darkness. Enlightenment, which serves to enhance the light, to feed its brilliance throughout all Creation, may someday leave no place for darkness. Set will then die. We will triumph my darling Sheeyah, my Isis. But why, my love, are you tensing again?

Oh! Oh no! Osiris! Brother Set will maim you and kill your body and cast your flesh into the sea and then come after me, for I will carry your child. Our Osirian dynasty will topple under pressure from Set, when global seismic cataclysm will destroy our great kingdom, leaving it in chaos — chaos which Set will progressively and finally completely rule. Chaos into void.

Ah! What a delight! Isis, my Isis, my love, you will carry my child into the third dimension!

No! No! The delight is tortured by the pursuit of Set. He wants to keep our child out of the third dimension at this time! He wants to erase Truth from the Universe. He wants to still all light.

But look again, my darling of the Cosmos. Set will not reach you. You will escape into the mists, to the mystical Isle of Khebit, the eternalized kingdom of Avalon, where you will bear Horus, our son. Horus will live to avenge my murder and to take back my throne from Set. Horus will carry the torch for us.

YOU HAVE MADE YOURSELF MY CHILDREN.

Who is that, Osiris? Who speaks?

Isis, it is our Mother, I think we hear our Mother.

YOU HAVE MADE YOURSELF MY CHILDREN. YOU ENTER THE MATERIAL PLANE THROUGH ME. I AM GA, GAEA, MOTHER EARTH. I HAVE BEEN CHARGED WITH THE DUTY OF BRINGING YOU IN SO MANY TIMES. YOU ARE ESPECIALLY INTRIGUED BY THE MACHINATIONS OF HUMANITY ON MY PLANET.

Such a stern mother you are.

I HAVE NO CHOICE BUT TO BE YOUR VESSEL AND TO DO IT WITH THE UTMOST OF DISCIPLINE. THIS MANKIND YOU HAVE CREATED HAS BEEN ROUGH ON MY BODY. ITS RACES HAVE PLUNDERED MY ENERGY AND TAKEN IT FOR THEIR OWN USES. THEY

SIPHON MY FORCE FROM MY VORTICES AND ATTEMPT TO REMAP MY LEY LINES. YOU HAVE COME TO ASSIST ME IN FORMULATING A CORRECTION — TO ASSIST ME IN THE GREAT REBALANCING.

Mother, when will we be born?

YOU WERE BORN THROUGH AN ALMOST HUMAN WOMAN, AN ATLANTEAN, BACK AS ISIS AND OSIRIS, LOVERS, TWINS, BROTHER AND SISTER. YOUR LOVE WAS SO FORCEFUL THAT THE WORLD AROUND YOU SHIFTED IN YOUR PRESENCE.

Were born? Were? But we are not born yet. We are in your womb.

OH YES, YOU HAVE BEEN BORN YET. YOU ARE ALWAYS IN MY WOMB WHEN IN YOUR EARTHLY ENFLESHMENT. SIMILARLY, ALL HUMANITY LIVING IN THE THIRD DIMENSION LIVES WITHIN MY WOMB. MY OFFSPRING ARE THE CHILDREN OF LIFE ON MY BODY, EARTH, HUMAN LIFE INCLUDED. IT IS IN MY WOMB THAT THIRD DIMENSIONAL LIFE EVOLVES. MOST HUMANS DO NOT ALLOW THEMSELVES THE SENSATIONS OF BEING IN MY WOMB WHILE THEY WALK ME, THEIR PLANET. THEY TUNE OUT THIS AWARENESS.

??

YOU BOTH UNDERSTAND ME QUITE WELL. YOU ARE SO MANY INCARNATIONS. FREQUENTLY, AS BROTHER AND SISTER, YOU PLAY OUT THE DRAMA OF THE ERA IN WHICH YOU ENTER. DO YOU RECALL WHEN YOU WERE KING ARTHUR AND HIS SISTER AND LOVER MORGAINE?

Wait, uh ... yes! I do! I do! Do you Triad?

TRIAD INCARNATED AS ARTHUR, YOUNGER HALF-BROTHER OF MORGAINE. ARTHUR'S MOTHER WAS AN ANCIENT ATLANTEAN WHO LIVED INTO ARTHURIAN TIMES. THE TWO OF YOU SUPPOSEDLY HAD DIFFERENT FATHERS. HOWEVER, THE SEED WAS TRANSPORTED FROM BEYOND THE MAN, AND HE THUS WAS ONLY A CARRIER. MORGAINE WAS BORN TO INHERIT THE THRONE OF HER MOTHER, THE HIGH ATLANTEAN PRIESTESS OF AVALON, WHO ANSWERED ONLY TO THE GODDESS. LOOK. LOOK OUT THERE. YOU CAN SEE THE FOREST WHERE THE TWO OF YOU MET, IN TRANCE, AND THERE CONCEIVED YOUR SON, MORDRED THE HORUS, DURING MORGAINE'S INITIATION INTO HIGH PRIESTESSHOOD. SHE DID NOT REALIZE THAT THE HORNED ONE WHO CAME TO HER FOR A HIGH UNION OF THE FORCES WAS

YOU, HER OWN BROTHER, ARTHUR. ONLY WHEN THE TWO OF YOU AWOKE THE NEXT MORNING DID YOU SEE EACH OTHER'S FACES. AH! WHAT A SHOCK TO YOUR RIGHTEOUS SOULS. BUT THE SON BORN OUT OF YOUR INCESTUOUS UNION WAS BROUGHT IN TO HELP TO BALANCE THE MONOTHEISTIC CHRISTIAN WORLD WITH THE WORLD OF THE MISTS, THE METAPHYSICAL WORLD. MANY BELIEVE THAT THE SON OF MORGAINE, MORDRED, WAS FATHERED BY OTHER THAN ARTHUR. THIS IS NOT THE CASE. IT WAS MORDRED WHO SLEW HIS OWN FATHER, ARTHUR, AND ARTHUR WHO, IN RESPONSE TO MORDRED'S ATTACK, SLEW HIS OWN SON, MORDRED. YOU BOTH KNOW THIS.

Oh God! God! God!

There was a pitiful weeping in the distance. A voice wailed out of the sobs into the pervasive ether where telepathic messages travel: Father! Father! Forgive me! I have killed you! You have not forsaken me, it is I who have forsaken you!

When I heard this, I became aware that a wise voice, that of my higher self, was going to speak to Horus about what he had just said. And then my wise self was indeed speaking through my feeble mind:

No, Mordred, Horus, it was only my body you killed. Do not be unforgiving with yourself. You were correct to act against my Arthurian efforts to force my Arthurian view of patriarchal monotheism into the modern world. You were right to end that incarnation of mine and to allow me to end yours. We had to abort our mission in the third dimension at that point in time.

Forgive me, Father! Oh forgive me, I beg you!

My wise voice went on: Horus, my forgiveness is not the issue. You must forgive yourself. And remember that at other moments in history, you not only preserved but expanded upon my efforts. As Horus, you led the "Followers of Horus" in forming a civilized master race to rule over the whole of what became Egypt. As Atlantis entered its closing era, we brought you into the world to preserve Truth on Earth in the guided and great Atlantean tradition. You unified the land of the Atlantean colony in early Egypt and your highest followers assimilated from you the knowledge of Truth of the most Divine origin. Your followers were the superior race of beings who produced the race of the Pharaohs, the Pharaohs who protected the high priests who protected whatever portion of Truth they were given to carry on in time.

Now Sheeyah was weeping: My brother, my lover, killed my own son — our own son. And my son killed you! I cannot move past that double shame!

Do not weep now. You and I must always remind ourselves that sorrow is a third dimensional passion.

Who is speaking?

It is I again, Mother, your Horus, Nostradamus, Mordred.

IF YOU LOOK YOU CAN SEE THAT YOUR HIGHER ROUND TABLE, THE ONE WHICH ARTHUR'S TABLE ONLY SYMBOLIZED, CONTINUES TO MEET.

We looked and discovered that we could see the forty-nine dignitaries in the distance, still seated around the golden Round Table, still playing cards. I knew there were forty-nine of them because I had counted them several times during my visit to this den of insanity.

The wise old voice that had spoken to Horus so forgivingly a moment earlier was gone from my head. I was back to my more simple, lower self. I could tell, because I was still envious that they could play cards while I was forced to attend to other business.

I don't know how it happened, but suddenly I was seated at the table with them. It was about time. God should always be invited to sit at the table, if you ask me.

I heard Camus think to me: Your wish is our command.

Someone handed me the deck.

"Hey! These are *my* cards! One of the decks I used on my yacht. That's the deck that was strewn all over the place when the earthquake hit the harbor!"

Camus nodded a yes and stood. He pointed at the cards and instructed me in that which I realized I already knew. "Triad, this is the always mystical deck: a symbol of the Egyptian year, the year which was incorporated into the design of the Great Pyramid. The four suits represent the four seasons of the Earth year. The 12 face cards represent the 12 months. The 13 cards in each suit represent the 13 lunations. The 52 cards represent the 52 weeks. The total face value of the cards (with the jack equaling 11, the queen 12 and the king 13) representing the 364 days, plus the joker as the magical 1.234, which adds on to 364 to equal 365.234 days in a year. Within the design of this deck and its mathematical logic, portions of the great

Mysteries were adeptly hidden."

Of course, this explains my fixation with decks of cards throughout all my incarnations.

Triad, where are you?

I could hear Sheeyah's voice from some distance above. It seemed to be coming into the cave through the tunnels.

At the Round Table. Where did you land?

I'm not certain, but I think I'm in a pyramid.

Mother Earth, who had assumed the role of great, and perhaps rather unwanted (by me) teacher, returned. YES, SHEEYAH, YOU ARE: THE KHEBIT PYRAMID, BUILT ON THE KHEBIT VORTEX, DESIGNED TO REST ABOVE THE CAVE CHAMBER IN WHICH THE DIGNITARIES HAVE SURVIVED THROUGH THE AGES AS KEEPERS OF THE MYSTERIES.

How, dear Mother, would they have survived so very long? Sheeyah asked most respectfully. Her reverence for this Earth was, admittedly, a little bothersome to me.

THE SUPERLIMINAL (ABOVE THIRD DIMENSIONAL) ENERGY TRANSDUCED BY THE PYRAMID ABOVE THE GROUND IS TRANSMUTED INTO SUBLIMINAL (BELOW THIRD DIMENSIONAL) ENERGY BELOW THE GROUND. THE TWO ENERGIES COUNTERBALANCE EACH OTHER EXACTLY — CREATE A PERFECT VIBRATORY AND THUS ELECTROMAGNETIC COUNTERPOINT, A VORTEX OF FORCES. THEY STOP TIME, OR HOLD IT STILL FOR THE THIRD DIMENSIONAL BODIES LOCATED IN THE SPECIFIC CHAMBER RECEIVING THE CONVERGENCE OF THESE OPPOSING FORCES.

I could hear all this and murmured, "This makes little sense to me."

Honest admission, Triad, Sheeyah thought to herself. She reappeared before my eyes.

"Where did you come from?" I asked her aloud.

She answered aloud. "Me? I haven't moved. You came here."

I looked around. The Round Table was gone. Only Camus and Nostradamus were with me. Something had moved us.

You now have automatically relocated, or translocated, into the pyramid chamber which reflects the converging energy into the cave that stops time, a voice said.

One of the dignitaries walked into the chamber from somewhere, I could not see his point of entry. Had he just walked through the wall? Probably. I noticed myself becoming increasingly immune to amazement. But, of course, this immunity itself amazed me.

Sheeyah turned to look at him and was clearly taken aback by what she saw. I could feel her shiver with recognition. I could see her brows raise and her eyes widen. Then she addressed the dignitary, "Hermes, it is so *good* to see you." I watched a quizzical shadow cross Sheeyah's face as I heard her wonder how she could know or remember this man. But she retained her composure and touched both his shoulders as he bowed his head before her, again with that strange triangle formed out of his hands.

"Isis, my old friend, Isis." The dignitary Hermes called her Isis.

"Set and his men killed my brother Osiris, Hermes. Do you know this?"

Yes, I said inwardly, but I'm obviously still alive. I thought about saying something like this aloud, but I knew that they had heard my thoughts and nevertheless went on as if I had not thought them.

"Yes, Isis," answered Hermes aloud, "we were informed. The information reached us instantaneously. ... Of course, you had a premonition of this murder while in the womb, did you not?"

"Why yes, Hermes. But how can you know this?"

"My dear Isis, we have safeguarded and continued practicing whatever portions we could of the Mysteries of Knowing for eons. They are part of the Original Truth, which you once delivered us for safekeeping."

Something about what Hermes had just said snagged my attention. "But, excuse me, I must inquire: why, Sheeyah, would you do that? Why would you give *them* the responsibility of safeguarding Truth? Weren't *you* the keeper of Original Truth for *me*?"

"For us, Triad," she answered with that turn-of-the-modern-millennium feminist clip in her voice. She wasn't going to let me get away with anything, even a semantic slip, I could tell.

"That wasn't a semantic slip, Triad. You really still feel that you Fathered Original Truth, that you Fathered *me*, in my absence, and that my existence is not of as high an order as yours."

Here we go again. I met this woman, picked her up when she was fixing her bicycle in a parking lot, and now we argue like an old couple. "Must we really get into this feminist stuff again now? Here? With all this madness going on around us?"

"You don't get it, do you Triad?" Sheeyah was definitely displeased.

"How can I not get it? I am God."

"No, you aren't. We are."

"From what I understand, I created you." I felt I had the upper hand here.

"I see. This is what you continue to let yourself understand despite the fact you were told only a while ago that *we* created me. We were one, the Monad, and then we became two and then three."

Now that third wheel, our son, spoke up. Nostradamus' voice echoed into the chamber. "Mother, Father, I bid you resist the enactment of your polarization now. The Truth is at stake."

I wanted to tell him to stay out of it. I didn't. But I could tell he heard me thinking. In fact, I heard him telling me in silent words that if I had not spent so very much time enfleshed in the third dimension, I would have a little more restraint in the arena of emotion.

I was angry.

"Master Horus," the dignitary addressed Nostradamus, "I recognize your motive, however, remember that Isis and Osiris argue like brother and sister, which indeed they are. Of course, they also love as feverishly."

"So what is the point of all this?" I had to know. I mean, didn't I, of all people, as God, have a right to ask?

"The point, Osiris," the dignitary Hermes turned to me with the most disarming smile I had witnessed anywhere in the universe, "is that Original Truth is in jeopardy for the very reason that you err in your understanding of its origin, despite your seminal role in its Creation."

I responded with a sheepish grin. I knew that I had been put in my place.

"I get it!" Sheeyah jumped in enthusiastically, "I GET it — you see he —"

"Isis, do wait." Hermes held up his old hand. I could see the profile of the bones in his fingers, almost as if he had transparent skin.

Sheeyah quieted.

"Both of you must know now:" Hermes paused and made certain that he had our undivided attention. "The Divine polarity you created when you were but one essence, neither male nor female, was essential for any of your Creation to take place. All creativity is an act of supreme spirituality. And all creativity springs from supreme polarity. Yet, in the advancing of the ages, in the spiraling of evolution outward into the void, the god force has misinterpreted its original terms. You, Triad, have forgotten that Sheeyah is as much Master of the Cosmos as you believe yourself to be. Life, in all dimensions, is thus out of balance."

"It sounds like you are blaming me," I said. I did not want them — any of them — to do this. How dare they put *God on trial*? How *wrong!*

"No, God is not on trial. But the god force, the SPIRITUAL TRIAD and the Original Truth it Created — inspired by Triad, born by Sheeyah and manifested by Horus, whom you call Nostradamus — this god force is in jeopardy. Original Truth, which is the sole and only motive for all Creation, is in jeopardy. Sheeyah's life — your feminine side — is in absolute danger."

"Why?"

"Set, the god of darkness pursues you."

"But he is my first and only cosmic brother." I tried to excuse him.

"He seeks to end the existence of you all. He seeks to spread a shadow from which there is no escape. The ultimate no exit. You see, Original Truth is the only antidote to his shadow. If he spreads his shadow everywhere, Truth will cease to live."

Sheeyah came over to me. She hugged me. I patted her stiffly in response. She was getting teary-eyed yet again. Why now?

"Triad," she continued to hold me, "Triad, listen. I came here to Khebit to save myself and Horus after Set killed you. Set tried to follow, he still tries to follow, but he cannot gain entrance to this land, he cannot cross the gates into the mist."

"Why?" I asked unenthusiastically.

I could feel her detect yet ignore my exasperation. "Because Set does not believe what he must believe to travel to this island of Truth," she said.

"Oh," I chuckled, I couldn't help it. "Do *we* have to believe anything, any of this, to get here?"

"Yes, deep down inside we do believe. We not only believe, we created the very wisdom which this land protects, we created that which we believe in: Truth."

"Sheeyah I can't —"

"Triad, Set follows us throughout our kingdom, the Cosmos. He even tried to stop us from physically manifesting the Spiritual Triad, in our recent incarnations, with that nuclear bomb. He wanted to kill our bodies so that we would not have a child. He has the power to tip the balance of forces, to tip the balance of our forces."

"Our forces?" I did not voice my real concerns here, but I communicated them in thought: You aren't pregnant with my child are you Sheeyah? You can't be, can you?

Sheeyah indicated her response nonverbally: Let us just say that if you do not know the answer to your question, then this is for me to know and you to wonder. Then she replied aloud to my query about our forces: "Set has been working to tip the balance between you and I."

"How can he possibly have that power over us?" I said disbelievingly.

"Set manipulates *you* through your end of our polarity. He encourages the continuing and advancing hegemony of yang, of the masculine essence throughout Creation. If he continues to upset the balance, Creation will disassemble. He already has you thinking that *you* created me, that I am somehow something other than an equal progenitor of all Creation."

"Well, that's the impression I've always had." I tried not to let myself even wonder who had created Set, as someone would most likely hear me thinking and probably accuse me of doing it. It seemed as if everyone was avoiding this painfully obvious matter. I repeated my reply. "I said, Sheeyah, that's the impression I had, that I created you."

"No, it is not the impression that you started out with. It is the impression you have been encouraged to let yourself have. Set works in devious ways. He enters your mind, he directs your energy if you let him. He magnifies your yang force in order to set the Cosmos into a state of runaway imbalance."

"And you actually believe that this has been happening? Is that why you were fixing your bicycle out by my yacht that day? You were working as an agent for some sort of radical feminist anti-Set group?"

"Very funny, Triad. Actually, uh, you know, this is strange, but I *was* supposed to go to an Earth Day rally later that day. I forgot to tell you about myself, we were so taken with each other's bodies. I forgot to mention that when I wasn't painting for a living, I was sort of an environmental activist. Well, sort of is a bit mild. I had been arrested several times at radical environmentalist protests."

Some date you turn out to be. "You have a record of arrests? Great. Civil or criminal?"

"Both. But several arrests were just for painting graffiti, nothing more extreme. My graffiti merely consisted of pleasing symbols, secret power symbols of my organization. I painted them to invoke our power, knowing that at least some of the people who walked or drove by and looked at them would, on some level, come to understand our true message. The officials, of course, called it defacing public property."

I didn't quite understand what she was saying about the power symbols of some organization she belonged to, but I didn't care. I was feeling that sickish feeling again. "So, Sheeyah, the Truth about you finally comes out. And, while we're getting at the Truth, tell me, were you using me? Did you plan to meet me that morning? Did you pose as a person fixing her bicycle to trap me?"

"You? I had no plans to cross your particular path. Do you think I would have looked as awful as I did if I had been trying to pick you up? I doubt that I would have ever assumed you'd be attracted to a woman who looked the way I did that day. And I certainly had absolutely NO idea that you were a real estate developer — of all things!"

I found myself surprised that she had picked up the fact that I was a real estate developer with all that had been going on. I was about to ask her to remind me how she found this out, but she just went right on talking, looking disgusted:

"Actually, I think I would have steered clear of you if I had known that. I fight those who destroy Earth by development and pollution. I don't make love with them. Still, it is funny how we pull the people to us that we most need to meet. Whether I would have wanted it or not, we were clearly destined to meet. ... But Triad, this Set thing is serious. He's getting to you. If you escape with your spirit, which you did many times in the third dimension, he will try to attack you on another plane, in another dimension. And he's getting to you. You've *got* to get it. You've got to understand this *right now*."

"You make it sound so urgent. But why right now? Can't we just drop the subject for a while? I'm upset too. I feel sick. After all, I had a nice life going. And somehow, I've been dragged away in the middle of it in order to live out some kind of cosmic drama."

"Triad, look at Earth. Look at what's happening on Earth. Some 250 million years ago, all the continents of the world were merged together in a single land mass. Still some 50 million years ago, most of the land masses were moving but were still clustered in the southern hemisphere, the feminine pole of Earth."

The voice of Earth boomed into the chamber. Naturally, she had been listening in all along. QUITE RIGHT. IN FACT, THE GREEKS HAD A NAME FOR THAT LAND MASS — PAN*GAEA* — WHICH IN GREEK MEANT 'ALL EARTH'. AT THE END OF WHAT YOUR MODERN SCIENTISTS CALL THE PALEOZOIC ERA, WHICH WAS SOME 250 MILLION YEARS AGO, PANGAEA SPLIT INTO TWO SECTIONS. I COULD FEEL IT HAPPEN, BUT I COULD NOT PREVENT IT.

Sheeyah looked at the floor of the cave. "What continents were in those two sections, Earth?"

IN THE SOUTHERN PORTION WERE WHAT YOU CALL AFRICA, SOUTH AMERICA, INDIA, ARABIA, AUSTRALIA, MADAGASCAR, NEW GUINEA, THE MALAY PENINSULA, INDONESIA AND ANTARCTICA. THIS OLD SOUTHERN PORTION IS STILL KNOWN AS GONDWANALAND BY THOSE WHO HAVE PRESERVED THE INFORMATION. AND SOME STILL DESCRIBE PARTICULAR REGIONS OF THAT LAND MASS AS THE LANDS OF LEMURIA AND MU, THE MOTHERLAND, BOTH OF WHICH SHOOK VIOLENTLY, EXPLODED FIERCELY, SACRIFICED THEIR ORGANISMS TO FIRE, SLIPPED OFF OF THEIR FOUNDATIONS, AND SANK.

"And in the northern hemisphere?"

NORTH AMERICA, GREENLAND, EUROPE AND ASIA (EXCEPT FOR THE INDIAN SUBCONTINENT). THIS OLD NORTHERN PORTION IS STILL REFERRED TO AS LURASIA. MUCH LATER, IN THE MESOZOIC ERA, BETWEEN 250 AND 66 MILLION YEARS AGO, LURASIA ITSELF SPLIT INTO NORTH AMERICA AND EURASIA. A SPLIT I FELT OCCURRING, BUT ONE WHICH, LIKE THE VERY MIGRATION OF CONTINENTS TO THE NORTHERN HEMISPHERE, I COULD NOT OVERRIDE.... BECAUSE THE CHANGES IN MY AXIAL SPIN WHICH BROUGHT ABOUT THE CONTINENTAL DRIFTS OF WHICH I SPEAK, THE SHIFTS IN THE LOCATIONS OF MY POSITIVE AND NEGATIVE POLES, WERE PROMPTED FROM BEYOND MY DOMAIN OF ACTION. EXTRATERRESTRIAL FORCES HAVE A PROFOUND EFFECT UPON ME AND THEREFORE UPON ALL LIFE ON MY PLANETARY BODY.

Sheeyah chimed in. "Triad, think about it. The masculine force, the cosmic yang, being overabundant and in a runaway mode, has pulled vital energies from Earth's southern, feminine, or yin hemisphere, where these energies originated, up to Earth's northern, masculine, or yang hemisphere. As time moved through the third dimension, several major land masses of Earth have migrated to the yang end, the northern end of Earth. The northern hemisphere, the yang hemisphere, has become the scene of massive human development and economic expansion, all dominated by the yang. Life is out of balance. The life cycle of our human species has become unmanageable. We are out of control. We live increasingly in the yang. We are hurting our planet. Killing her. So now the Earth Goddess is rising, demanding recognition as a living organism."

Hermes voiced his opinion here: "True balance only occurs between equally opposing forces."

This made some sense to me. "Meaning there is no balance without balanced polarization?"

"Meaning precisely that," Hermes nodded.

Sheeyah turned to me as if in a hurry. "Hey wait! Triad, Triad, what I was going to tell you a while ago was that I remembered — I remembered, I think already back on the henu boat when we were on the Nile — I remembered that I fled to Khebit to save our son Horus after Set killed you and wanted to kill your third dimensional offspring. And I remembered that when Horus was born and the threat of Set had receded because he could not see us through the mist, I wanted to leave Khebit, to go back into the Cosmos as a missionary — as THE missionary. I feared for the Original Truth. So I left a large portion of the Truth here, locked up, for safekeeping until I could again win you back from the effects of Set."

"But why me? Why me? I was just a happy-go-lucky guy, a relatively innocent developer-businessman on a yacht. I wasn't really looking for anything heavy, nothing profound. I had a plan. That's all. A plan to get rich, preferably by using other people's money — through leverage. Buy up land and access to key parcels of land and then create a global demand for that land and then sell it at tremendously inflated prices. Places like the Rocky Mountains, Siberia, Australia, Santorini and —"

"Santorini — that's Thera, is it not?" Camus startled me. I had forgotten that Camus was there. He had a way of making himself quite invisible. I thought back to his behavior at Crystal Mirror Lake — walking right off into the water. Changing from fisherman to travel agent to dead man to metaphysical guide. Camus went on. "Thera. Hermes, Triad refers to Thera. You must explain now."

"The time has come for the removal of ignorance." That voice again.

"Nostradamus, you who claim to be my son, must you continue with that tedious line?"

"It is my trademark, Father, as you directed me."

"Well, now I undirect." I felt hot and aggravated.

"But Father, I am under strict instructions to refrain from taking your orders until you resume your full and balanced enthronement."

"Who, pray tell, gave you such orders?" I wanted to wring his neck. How could I get away from all this intense absurdity? Was there any way out?

"Why, you, Father, you gave such orders."

"The joke is on me, then. And didn't I leave myself a note or something so that I would believe all this when you all came to rouse me from my amnesia?"

Hermes tried to help: "Perhaps you will see your own writing on the wall of eternity when you allow yourself to truly contemplate what you are learning here."

Sheeyah had some silly thought. I could feel it flutter through her mind: Cosmic graffiti. She giggled inwardly, telling herself, I paint *cosmic* graffiti.

I ignored her thoughts. "Contemplate?"

"Yes, Father, stop throwing words and rational thought up as a barrier to the recognition of your own multidimensional wisdom," my son said almost irreverently.

I was beginning to dislike this kid with a passion, son or not. "What do you expect me to do? Just take it all in?"

"As Hermes suggested, contemplate."

I tried to think, to contemplate, but my mind was numb. "This I apparently cannot do." I turned to Hermes for some relief.

Hermes was less irritating and impudent than Nostradamus but still on the same track. "Go to the depths of all that we consider here, the depths of your experience, the depths of your prehension of all that is. You must lift your Divine amnesia or all Creation will die."

"*Divine* amnesia? You mean to tell me that it is God *Himself* who has amnesia?"

"It appears that way, Father."

Now I was really mad. It was a kind of anger that I had never known myself to have, a deep, windy sort of ferocity which I felt I had to restrain by whispering through clenched teeth. "This is ludicrous, Nostradamus, absolutely ludicrous. How *dare* you?"

Hermes stepped in. "Let me explain. You incarnated and implanted a temporary amnesia in the incarnate, as you often do in order to experience the struggles of lower dimensional beings. But, something out of the ordinary has happened. We are not certain when it first began, but you have become increasingly amnesic yourself, Master. Not only as an incarnate in a lower dimension, but as yourself, wherever you are, whatever form you are in."

"So *I've* forgotten who *I* am? *God forgets*?" I asked incredulously.

"It is unclear whether this specific failure of memory is due to the amnesias you have repeatedly implanted in your more recent incarnate forms or part of the larger problem," Hermes was, I could tell, trying hard to explain.

"But what does it matter what I've forgotten? Who cares? Things seem to run O.K. when I'm out being in a body and having amnesia, so why worry?" I wasn't against forgetting.

"Triad, God has forgotten that balance is essential. Balance between animo and anima, yang and yin. You must try to shake your amnesia so that we can place you and Sheeyah in balance again and thus the entire Cosmos. Therefore I beg you, Master, contemplate."

"Well, I've been trying to contemplate, as you call it, but, Hermes, I fear that this is as deep as I get."

Hah. Very funny Triad.

You sure say that a lot, Sheeyah.

Very funny, Triad.

I looked over at her and found myself wishing that I was ravishing her naked in bed.

Hermes interrupted my ravishing. "I see that anything but contemplation attracts your attention, Triad."

I was extremely, miserably, unhappy and pushed to the edge of my absolute almighty divine breaking point. "Look, all of you, I've been involved in a series of heavy conversations ever since I left my yacht and rode off into the sunset following a dream — or a dream woman anyway. I got onto a boat with a dead guy, I time-traveled into the past on a beam of light. I've even talked to some booming old gal that calls herself Earth —"

She rumbled again. This time it came from below.

"I'll take that dream woman thing as a compliment," Sheeyah smiled briefly, "unless you meant nightmare."

"Contemplate Triad, contemplate," Hermes reminded.

". . . O.K., are you happy? I just contemplated. I know no more now than I did a moment ago. This is as good as it gets: just tell me what's really going on. I don't remember much of my Godness. So just tell me the Truth — all of it — and fill me in on what I need to know, now."

Hermes spoke a gentle warning. "Even if we had access to it, you would find that to enclose all Truth in spoken language is impossible. The highest of your Mysteries cannot be referenced or even suggested by anything as mundane as words. To attempt to do so is dangerous, futile and, my dear Sir, my highest Master, sacrilegious."

"But we descend from a long tradition of intellectual thought. The human species has struggled to evolve a mind of great cognitive power. We work in words." I was taking the side of the human species here. Why not? I was one myself, during some centuries anyway.

Hermes went on. "Yes, we know, Master Triad. In case you have forgotten, such Scholasticism has its origins in the logic of Aristotle. Alas, Aristotle meant no harm in its development. Still, most sadly, the science which I, Hermes-the-Trismegistus, founded through the ancient Egyptian group described as the Hierophants, my process of knowing which was noted by both Plato and Pythagoras — my Hermeticism — has not been strong in the face of Scholastic progression. Human civilization has taken a distinctly Scholastic or rational bend, again evidence of the heavy overabundance of yang. And yet it is Hermetic thought that, ultimately, holds the key to the rediscovery of the hidden laws of the universe."

"So how do we get at these laws? At the Truth?" Sheeyah had to know.

"This is what the two of you have returned to Khebit to rediscover. We hope you can help us. The Truth, the highest of Truth, is of such a subtle and divine character that only Hermetic, esoteric, symbolism can transfer its Mysteries."

"Then just give us the esoteric symbols, if that's what it's going to take." I was going to speed up the process if I could. Maybe then I could go home and get back to my business of acquiring survivor territories and marketing them. I still held onto that hope.

"Alas, Master Triad, you apparently have forgotten that Sheeyah did not leave those symbols with us. She left much of the Truth, but not the transfer mechanisms of Truth. Without the symbols, the Greatest of Mysteries and the Highest of Truths are forever locked away."

Of course the amnesic me had forgotten that Sheeyah had failed to leave the transfer mechanisms behind. But what startled me is that I, not just the lower, amnesic, incarnated yachtsman me, but the higher, the complete, the cosmic Triad of the god force, *had also forgotten* about the transfer mechanisms. This realization sent such an energetic ripple through my thought form — such a multidimensional ripple that mortal third dimensional incarnates can not even begin to imagine it — that I unnerved my entire higher self. Of what other oversights might I also be guilty?

"What?" Sheeyah's surprise was genuine, I could tell. "I don't have any symbols. I never even knew about all this, about who I really was and all, until the earthquake. Well, I had some vague idea, I had a ghost of a picture in the back of my mind, and strange dreams a lot of the time and all, but, gosh — "

A realization wafted through my mind. "So that's the problem. Original Truth is in jeopardy, the god of darkness is after it and Sheeyah left it here. Sure, she left it here for safekeeping, but left no way to transfer it or spread it. And now she has forgotten — she has LOST — the mechanisms of transfer, the symbols which work like keys to release Original Truth."

"Yes Triad," answered Hermes, "the most ancient of esoteric traditions taught the Greatest of Cosmic Truths, not by means of written or spoken words, but with the mystical symbols now in Sheeyah's care. These symbols are so very powerful that a single look at one of them results in the transfer of vast amounts of secret information to the person looking. Meditating on the symbol increases the depth of the learning and the ability to apply the knowledge. The set of symbols together contains all the secrets of the universe."

I went on with a vengeance. "So now, unless Sheeyah — my dear, that's you — comes up with the goods, the rest of the universe has either already got Truth or it never will. Unless she remembers how to spread Truth, Truth will die. You know, Sheeyah, me thinks you fix the universe a bit like you fix a bicycle — not so well."

"I fixed the bicycle."

"Yeah, but you cut yourself."

But the bike was fixed before you came along, she said tensely in a shrill wavelength well above her voice.

But look at all the trouble you caused in the process, I replied, attempting but failing to reach an equally shrill level.

Triad, you came up to me and offered help that morning. I didn't need it and I didn't seek you out.

Sheeyah was right, but I wasn't about to say so. Maybe this mess really was all my fault.

Hermes pushed us apart and stood between us. "Isis, Osiris, I know your incestuous affair fills you with eternal the sparks of eternally polarized passion, however, I must again ask you to focus on the matter at hand."

I kept at it. "Hermes, not to offend you, but this is just great. I've been brought here — my life has been rudely interrupted — because of *someone else's* ineptness. Hers." I pointed at Sheeyah.

Hermes shook his head no. "I'm afraid the reason for your visit goes well beyond that, Master Triad."

"How so?"

"We have said in several ways that Divine Order is out of balance. And because the third dimension, the material plane, is the central dimension, the midpoint on the dimensional spectrum from dimension zero through the first dimension into the second dimension and then beyond the third into the fourth and through the fifth into the sixth — The point Sir, Master Triad, is that the disorder we see in the third dimension is reflective of imbalance on all levels of your Creation."

"Somehow I still miss the point," I confessed angrily, realizing that Hermes already realized that I still didn't get it.

"Master Triad, when you bifurcated into a masculine and a feminine force, your feminine side became the yin, the receptive negative pole. You were left with your masculine side, the yang, the invasive positive pole. You have favored your own side over Sheeyah's and you, Master, you have had a big hand in the generation of this great and most dangerous imbalancing."

Camus put his hand on my shoulder. "Triad, we see that your brother Set has been influencing you. We hope and assume that there is no way your

Divine judgment on its own would have ever allowed such a trend to establish itself."

Feeling trapped, I pulled away from Camus. "And now? Now you get me back here to get me to change? I hardly know who I am and I really don't feel like a God. And I'm supposed to change my apparently *Divine* behavior?"

"The time has come for us to discuss your business plan, your plan involving Thera, the Greek island you call Santorini. This is *your* plan, Osiris, Master Triad, is it not? ... Or, is it the plan of your brother, Set? And do you really know the answer to this question?" Old Hermes had a grand way of imposing a directive.

"So? What am I supposed to say now? I don't know what you're getting at," I said, as if I were a school boy about to receive a well deserved lecture. I felt as if I were about to be accused of insider trading or the likes.

"In your current incarnation, you and the team of investors you direct have been planning to quietly buy up large amounts of land in particular areas around the globe and then to create a wild and even desperate demand for it. Once the demand is rampant, your plan is to sell it for never before heard of prices."

How on Earth did you know? I wondered, silently aghast.

Your mind told him, silly, I heard Sheeyah think sarcastically.

Yes, but not in such detail, I volleyed a thought back to her.

He's got your number, Triad. She laughed at me in her mind, I could feel it. But her trust of me was being shaken.

"Sir, Master Triad, do you have any idea how you selected the locations of the land you planned to purchase?"

"Instinct. Sheer instinct," I retorted, telling part, but not all, of the truth. "Usually works for me. I'm quite good at what I do. I can tell when something's going to be a home run. ... You know, the savings and loan hassles weren't my fault, but then you don't have those back here — back in this time do you?"

Old Mother Earth came back into the room: IF I WERE YOU, I WOULD NOT SHRUG OFF RESPONSIBILITY FOR SAVINGS AND LOAN DEFAULTS BEFORE THIS COMMITTEE. WE HERE KNOW A GREAT DEAL ABOUT ECONOMIC OVER-EXTENSION AND THE FALSIFICATION OF WEALTH, THE CONTAMINATING OVER-EXTENSION OF YANG.

"Yes, Gaea, we do." Hermes seemed to love this old woman. She probably had a body once, I thought. Maybe he was once her lover.

I STILL DO. Earth, of course, had heard me. HAVE A BODY, THAT IS.

Hermes returned to what he had been saying. "Triad, contemplate that instinct of yours you referred to for a moment. What inspired it?"

"I told you I don't contemplate well."

"I do believe you sense what I am getting at," Hermes smiled that fabulous smile again.

"You do, do you?"

"Master Triad," Hermes put his hand on my shoulder, "What about the approaching shifts in the Earth's crust and the rising of the Earth's seas? Some massive regions will sink, other will rise. Some properties will disappear and others emerge in the blink of an eye. Some of the properties you are purchasing will become prime land, surviving the polar shifts and the melting of the ice caps, withstanding the tremendous convulsions of the Earth and other apocalyptic disasters converging upon the planet in a short space of time."

"You think I know all this?"

"Yes. And you also know that Thera was one of the capitals of Atlantis, perhaps its greatest. It was, however, wrenched from its increasingly yang-contaminated existence by Mother Earth."

"You don't say," I said.

"Come on Father," Nostradamus joined in, "even as a mortal you were taught some, albeit it highly distorted, history — perhaps that Thera was the scene of several violent volcanic eruptions. Your history teachers probably focused on the violent eruptions of 1520 BC and 1470 BC, the latter of which deposited ashes all over Crete, emitted poisonous vapors that destroyed the ancient Minoan civilization and generated seismic tsunamis of 100 to 160 feet high."

"And you know history repeats, Master," said Hermes.

"Why else have you been living on a boat, Father?"

"It's a yacht, thank you, and some folks just like the sea." My so-called son was being obnoxious. No wonder he and I killed each other in Arthurian times.

My son was increasingly upset with me. "I asked you why you have been living on a boat, Father?"

"I really don't know why I should have to explain myself to you. I like it. That's all there is to it. I like my *yacht*. I *deserve* it. I'm taking a break. I know how to rest and prepare for the next big venture, which is, or was, on its way. Business life can be a big burn out. I'm a survivor."

"Exactly, Master Triad."

"Exactly what, Hermes?" I asked testily.

"You are a survivor. Your *survival instinct* is at work." Hermes gazed deep into my eyes and looked even more deeply into my soul. I could feel it. "You know exactly what is coming and exactly what portions of the Earth will be most valuable when this happens. You do not even need to hire spies to steal this information."

"Spies? Hire spies?" I was stunned. How could Hermes know this? This was top secret stuff — top secret in another era, another time in history. The amnesic me almost fainted on the spot. Maybe I really did faint, because I fell to my knees and my head hit the floor with such force that I must have done some additional brain damage. For a fleeting moment I remembered the mast hitting me on the head in the yacht harbor. I remembered that I was supposed to go in for x-rays and hadn't. I suspected early on in this adventure that that injury might have caused seizures or something more serious in my brain which in turn might have caused hallucinations of the magnitude of all this. And now my suspicion turned to belief. *The brain injury had caused this entire immense bizarre hallucination. But it was a hallucination of the ultimate and actual Divine reality. This was the only way I would allow my self to see it. This was the only way I would accept it — as a hallucination due to a brain injury.*

No one spoke. I could feel their eyes on me, boring through the back of my head which lay on the floor where it had hit. I didn't move for a long time. I could feel Sheeyah's shock and extreme disenchantment with me. I still had no conscious idea that not only was she with Earthcult, she was its leader. I hadn't listened. I hadn't put two and two together. And she still had no idea that I had actually infiltrated her organization and had been stealing her secrets. She hadn't fully taken in the last bit about the spies. She'd heard it, but hadn't integrated it. But she understood what it was that I was selling — her — Earth's — survivor territories.

That old image of the black wave kept pouring through my head, like it was washing me from the inside. My very soul was being overwhelmed by the flood that I knew would be coming!

"The flood!" I wailed. "The flood again! So many will die! Why must my

Creation undergo such agony! *The flood*! Apocalypse again!"

Silence.

It must have been hours before I stood up. They were all gone, save Sheeyah, who was leaning against the chamber wall, sobbing, arms wrapped around her chest, watching me through narrowed eyes. I stumbled over to her and took her hand. I wanted her forgiveness, but I did not exactly know for what. I spoke in a low voice, "I hope you can find it in your heart to forgive me."

"For what?"

"I'm not sure, but I know it's really big."

"Well, I don't think I have any choice but to go on with this thing with you. You can take it as forgiveness if you want, Triad. But, I don't know what it is anymore."

"O.K., I will. Take it as forgiveness. Thanks." I rubbed my aching head. Now I've r*eally* got it. I get who I am. "So, now what?"

"Let's see if we can get back down to the cave. It's somewhere under this pyramid, I'm certain. Maybe Camus or Nostradamus or Hermes or some of the other dignitaries will still be there and can help. I bet you most of them are still playing cards."

For some reason, a game of solitaire sounded like a great relief. I wanted some security. Something familiar to hang on to. I especially wanted to be back on my yacht. But I knew that I would have to surrender my relationship with the material familiar. Nothing would ever be the same. Not for me. Not on any dimension. Never again. Never ever again.

We wandered into a dark passageway, the GodDESS and I, sensing the boundless immensity of what lay before us. Sheeyah led the way.

Part 4

•

Confronting the Advancing Void

9

Recognition of such boundless immensity can unhinge even the most sane. Yet, anyone, even the least sane, can pass a point beyond which there is no differentiation between being hinged and being unhinged. So there I was, lost in a rising sea of experience without any navigation device, in the absence of any mental bearings, woefully recalcitrant yet only a step behind Sheeyah. We wandered on, she pulling me by the hand, tugging me onward through wave after wave of absolute darkness. From this path, that of our preordained quest, there could be no exit. I knew this to be so as I stumbled along, my core — my self as I had known it — disintegrating further with each step.

When, in the course of a mundane existence, one is called upon to rectify a cosmic imbalance, what are one's options? In my case, I was not only called upon to rectify the great imbalance, I was identified as its primary instigator.

I believe that it was written in the Earth version of the Upanishad Doctrines that when you pause and say "ahhh," this is your participation in Divinity. Alas, in my case, in my highest life, a dutiful "ahhh" has not been enough.

My task, my indubitable birthright, has been the obligation wrested upon me, by me, that I do more than participate in Divinity. I must sustain it. I must disseminate it. The ultimate Manifest Destiny. This manifestation looked to me, as I tripped through this dark and tortured passage of my quest, a little like spiritual hegemony. But what were the alternatives to the righteous spreading of Truth? Of Order?

Lies? Chaos? Disorder in the extreme? The obliteration of all Creation?

I had no choice but to enlist in my own cause, the preservation of the Spiritual Triad, and hence of all Creation.

I trudged on.

I feverishly sought reminders of my place in space and time. I had no idea what time it was, what day it was, where I was, save for some feeble notion that I had bounced through a door in time to Ancient Egypt, and that now I was in some pyramid there.

Quite abruptly, I realized exactly where I was. Somehow, I had been brought from the magic Isle of Khebit, an island in time, a vortex extending through all the dimensions of the Cosmos, into the Great, Great Pyramid, whose material manifestation is located on Earth. And, with profound relief, I remembered that this Pyramid, this great feat of building, was once described as being "an expression of the Truth in structural form." This statement is more than correct. No mortal man of the third dimension has yet begun to conceive of the actual immensity of Truth expressed by this supreme structure. Its builder knew that it would be many, many ages before a civilization would truly desire and then actually manage to recover the Truths that had been monumentalized here.

Yes, some humans have discovered certain of the Pyramid's messages: they know that proportions of the Great Pyramid represent precise knowledge of Earth's circumference, of the flattening of her poles, of the timing of her solstices and equinoxes, of the degrees of her compass, and of the mystical number pi.

Yet, the mathematics of the Pyramid indicate that a civilization of long ago was far more skilled than modern man in gravitational astronomy and in mechanics as well as in other sciences. In fact, modern human sciences flounder in the face of the simple elegance and cosmic unity of the Science of Natural Law upon which this ancient architecture was based.

Modern era humans, even those who care little about it, cannot help but regard the construction of the Pyramid as astounding. It involved the use of massive stones of up to 70 tons in weight, placed so very precisely that the gaps between them were under one-fiftieth an inch in thickness. Such a monumental project either required many, many generations to build or involved a rate of work otherwise unseen and unrecorded in human history.

The prophetic history of the world built into this, the Great Pyramid, has been continually misinterpreted by humans. Of course, we have seen such misinterpretation of cataclysmic prophecy again and again, as in the case of the Divine prophecies of Nostradamus. The symbology of such prophecy seems to be lost on most humans. Perhaps this is because they do not yet understand that reality is a multidimensional proposition. So, humans have interpreted the descending passage of this Great Pyramid as the descending of humanity into ignorance and its attending evil, and the ascending passage as the ascension of humanity toward the light, a path that supposedly requires submission to ascend. Especially great submission is considered necessary to gain entry into the Grand Gallery of Light, past the Great Step, through the Antechamber of Chaos (interpreted as representing your modern and chaotic age), to finally emerge in the King's Chamber and partake in the glory of what has been described as the Second Coming. Such is the human interpretation of the very prophecy enstructured in the Great Pyramid: great submission in order to partake in the glory of the Second Coming.

*Oh yes, that Second Coming of the Messiah. Why does everyone look for a sign of the second Messiah? We, the Messianic Triad, are **always** with you. You will not see us until you are ready, until your eyes are open. Still, we are always here, awaiting your recognition. I suggest that you look for a sign that you can see us, the Messianic Triad, within you, now.*

So, there is indeed some Truth to the notion that the Great Pyramid predicts the history of the world, or at least that of the modern world, right up to its metaphorical "end." This history has been interpreted by human students of the Pyramid as a 6,000 year history, depicted in increments of 1,000 years, beginning around 4000 BC and ending around what some interpret as being sometime during the 21st century AD. However, the end of the world is a metaphor for what you might call "apocalyptic cataclysm" and what I do call "transformational rebalancing."

Look again, those of you who fear the Day of Judgment. That day has been here a long time. This ongoing judgment is a weighing of energy — of its distribution and balance: How have you, do you and will you contribute to this process? What do you do with your energy? How can YOU rebalance YOUR self and YOUR microcosm in order to contribute to the greater cosmic balance?

Submission is not the issue. You have undoubtedly heard of the notion of revolution from within. We call for corrective convulsion, cataclysm if need be, from within. If you cannot manage this, then it must come from without in whatever form most affects you: intense flooding, seismic catastrophe, continental sinkings, meteoric impact, polar shifts, and other physical plane events. Humanity may even create such an external catastrophe of its own, perhaps in the form of massive environmental disaster or global nuclear war. So, turn within, now, in your search for the Holiest Grail of Truth. We have placed it within you for safekeeping. Within you is this Divine Seed, the supreme Mystery of Original Truth. Within you is the key to your — to our — survival: the life force of your spirit.

Ω

We were still trudging through the dark when we came most suddenly upon a grand chamber filled with a fog-like light, a light as iridescent as the river upon which we rode the henu boat into Khebit. We entered this luminous chamber, either out of curiosity or for relief from the intensity of the dark. Around the corner, against the wall, under their hoods, were Camus and Nostradamus.

"Father. Mother. The time has come —" My son began with those same old words.

"Yeah, yeah, I know, I know." I waved him off.

Although he was visibly offended by my treatment of him, Son Nostradamus seemed to get the point for once and did not finish his sentence. Instead, he bowed, accompanied by Camus, again employing that triangular gesture. And then he walked across the room to a couple of huge old stone coffins, Egyptian sarcophagi, and opened them.

"Coffins. They're empty," Sheeyah said in a flat voice.

I guess she knew what was coming. I didn't, I must confess. I was absolutely appalled when our son motioned for us to get into these coffins, saying to us, "If you please."

"I don't please." So you wish to kill me yet again, Son Mordred? You still see me as King Arthur, I said to my son without speaking.

My son chose to ignore my thoughts. Instead he gave Sheeyah a look of brazen desire. How dare you, I asked him mentally. This is your mother, not your concubine. Although Nostradamus ignored me, Sheeyah giggled a little. She seemed to need the relief. She seemed to enjoy the fact that I was jealous. And then she went right on and openly flirted with Son Nostradamus. For a moment, I could feel the sexual energy between them.

And then Sheeyah withdrew her energy and became very serious. "Is this a burial then? Our burial?" Sheeyah sounded flat again.

"No, this is an initiation, Mother," her son answered.

"Will we die?" she asked.

"It is the hope of the High Counsel that you, we, the Spiritual Triad, Original Truth, and all Creation will not die. Only the two of you can save us," Nostradamus was almost crying.

I could not believe my eyes. Sheeyah climbed into a coffin. Just like that. Camus handed her a beautiful, jewel laden, oversized, silver goblet.

"Alas, we have found the Holy Grail," Sheeyah murmured.

"No, Mother. You *are* the Holy Grail, the vessel of Truth."

Sheeyah raised her eyebrows querulously and said in awe, "Me? You really think so? Me? The Grail?" And then she drank from the goblet most obediently. In a matter of moments, she passed out. She did not seem to be breathing. She seemed to be dead. I was too stunned to feel even a hint of shock or a shred of grief. It all happened so quickly and calmly. Perhaps later I will mourn her, I thought.

Nostradamus closed her coffin. That was all. Then he looked at me.

"I suppose now you want *me* to do that?" I asked warily.

My son nodded. Someone else, another hooded dignitary, came into the chamber. He walked over to me and took both my hands in his. I looked at him and whispered: "You look like Albert Einstein. You do. Are you? Could you really be?"

He said without speaking that he had been many cosmic thinkers, among them thinkers incarnated on Earth.

"You won the Nobel prize," I said.

He still held my hands and looked at me. "We have been dear friends through the millennia." His eyes were so empathic and so unusually genuine, I could not help but believe him.

"Then can you please explain all this, my dear friend?" I begged.

"You will be in this tomb for three cycles of the sun or 'days' as you incarnates call them. You will see much out there, from the vantage point of the sixth dimension. You will return with a greater understanding of the Cosmos."

"Then this is not death?" I tried not to plead with him for a stay of my execution. Even if it proved to be only symbolic, this metaphorical execution looked pretty bad to me. Being closed in a box, a coffin of all things, for even three days sounded horrible — certain death by either high panic or slow suffocation. No exit. No exit. Death or at least Hell.

"Death is not."

"Not?"

"Trust me." The man who looked like Einstein guided me toward the coffin. I climbed in, thinking that I had finally reached the pinnacle of my cosmic idiocy with such acquiescence in my own execution, but feeling nevertheless intrigued.

Camus handed me the goblet. As he did so, my son ordered, "Drink the potion, Father."

I really didn't want to deal with orders given by Nostradamus. I scowled at him, "So, Son, you again seek to remove the aging Pharaoh and assume his throne? The tradition of ancient Egypt continues. Or have we come again to our Roman ways? Maybe I should say 'Et tu Brute?'" I spoke to him with undisguised sarcasm.

He was unmoved by my verbal attack. "If you die, I also die Father. We all die. There is a force out there you must address. It is not I. Although you and I have long competed for Mother's affections and her erotic attention, I am your son, not your cosmic enemy. There are matters of far greater impact than our competition for the great Goddess Sheeyah."

I thought I heard somebody whisper something about someone who was supposedly my —

– cosmic brother, perpetrator of non-motion, anti-prana –

whatever that was. I looked around. No one had said these strange words. Had anyone else heard them?

I put the huge goblet to my lips, but did not drink. Instead, I turned my eyes to the Einstein-like man. He had such a kind face, I trusted him. He tipped his head at the goblet. "Drink from the symbol of the Grail. Take the sacrament, the syrup of Truth, the nectar of the Gods. It will move you so well beyond the speed of light that you will be younger than you are now when you return."

"Sounds just great. Will you join me?" I challenged the kind Einstein half-heartedly.

"You will find me out there, where I live," he chuckled, "riding on beams of light as if they were ponies and building sand castles out of star dust." He seemed to mean what he said.

So I drank the stuff. Why not? I asked myself. Einstein, Camus and my son heard my mental question, but said and thought nothing in response. . . . I had second thoughts as I lost consciousness when I saw a whisper of defiance in my errant son's face just as he was closing my coffin. He's a difficult boy and should be regularly disciplined, I said half-jestingly to myself as I faded.

The lid of the coffin slammed down: I gathered that Son Nostradamus had heard me thinking about him. I blacked out for a long, long time. At least an eternity.

. . . .

"I've died so many times this looks like life to me."

"It's you again, Sheeyah."

"Right, Triad. You're disappointed?"

"No. No. Not at all. I'd rather do his death stuff with you more than anyone else in the world."

"You think we're still in the world?"

"Were we ever?" I had to wonder.

"Uh. Look around Triad. This isn't the world."

I looked around. I couldn't see us. We had no bodies. Yet I could feel with absolute certainty that we were there. We took the form of absolutely massive but massless bodies of energy. We were hurtling through outer space, as best as I could tell. Hurtling. Hurtling bodiless. Hurtling energy forms.

I could see us passing by light beams as we raced at a speed obviously faster than that of light. I looked back on those beams and saw them revealing the pristine little whirling particles that formed them. This may sound strange, and it seemed strange to me at the time, but I felt embarrassed, as if I were seeing light naked, without its permission. "No one should ever be allowed to see this," I murmured, "it's far too pure." For some reason, a gush of love washed through me.

The embarrassingly nude body of light was composed of countless of those luminous yet massless whirling particles — photons — whirling, or, better stated, dancing, in varying spiraling patterns. The spirals formed seemed to move in and out of time, intersecting each other at various points in this process, and, as they did so, the photons seemed to form and unform, appear and disappear, slow down and speed up, to move in and out of several dimensions with each loop and each intersection of each spiral. I did not feel that I knew human words with which I could ever describe this process. As I was still fresh from a human incarnation, I was still thinking, for the most part, in human words. *(And, reader, as you can see, I am reporting this experience to you in human words. These are words based upon and developed within your third dimensional reality and they, therefore, will never truly encompass what is to be perceived so far beyond that dimension.)*

"So this is what humans have decided to call light waves, even though most humans have never seen light the way we're seeing it here," Sheeyah whispered ecstatically.

It became clear to us as we watched that different size spirals emitted different colors and, at lower frequencies, emitted different sounds. And some of the spirals emitted vibratory sensations far higher, far more beautiful, than any color or sound imaginable. We could see that all of the sounds and colors and sensation-type emissions were related to each other: they were of different frequencies along the same vibrational continuum.

"It's like a virtual rainbow of vibrations, Triad."

"This defies the laws of physics. We can't be doing this, can we, Sheeyah?"

"What laws of physics? Human laws of physics? Obviously the humans who write them haven't seen this." Sheeyah was still whispering in awe.

"Maybe they have but they choose not to let on." I suspected this to be the case.

"I once let on too much, you know." A third voice, also bodiless, appeared. I say "appeared," but I could not see it, I could only sense it.

"Who said that?" I demanded. We were accompanied by a stranger. A stranger in paradise. And I, already being a stranger in a strange land, was uncomfortable about having unexpected company.

"I did," it said.

"Who are you?" I demanded again.

"You once called me Einstein, I believe."

It was then that I recognized the voice. I softened my tone. I didn't have a body. I thus had no muscles to relax and no jaw to stop grinding. So all I had was a tone, an energy, to soften. "Yes. I did. ... Einstein, how did you get here?"

"I was already here. It was you that just got here, Master Triad."

"Where's here?" I asked.

"There's no here here if you ask me," muttered Sheeyah. "And, if you ask me, we've got a problem, whether we're anywhere or not. How are we going to make love without any bodies?"

"How can you possibly be worried about such a thing now, Sheeyah?" I practically whined at her.

"How can you not? Physical sex is the best thing we have together, isn't it?" Sheeyah mourned.

I just didn't feel the same way about it, our sex that is. I guess she could tell.

I felt my self gasp — or do something like gasp (as I had no body, I had no lungs) — as entire galaxies whizzed by. We were leaving space and time in the cosmic dust. The solar wind, which, (in Earth terms), moves at a speed of about one million miles per hour, appeared to be but a sluggish river, its protons and electrons streaming past us in such slow motion that I could see each and every one of them. I was shocked by this. For a moment, I divorced myself from my almost unspeakable amazement at the beauty. I began interrogating this sublimely astounding experience. How can this be happening, I wondered. How can I be seeing entire galaxies and sub-atomic particles at the same time, unaided by telescope or microscope?

"Only the blinder life forms need mechanical aids to see reality." Einstein had heard my doubts.

"O.K. Einstein, if that is what you will allow me to call you, I could really use some explanation. You seem like a really nice guy and all, but what do you expect me to think about all this?" I demanded gently.

I gestured at the scenery with my energy. I was delighted to discover that I could do so. As I did, I saw, in the most surreal distance of cosmic space, the stream of solar wind being deflected by an invisible sphere around some planet. I knew what the planet was doing: she was protecting herself and her inhabitants from an overdose of solar radiation. I did not wonder how I knew this. I simply knew.

"As you wish. Call me Einstein. . . . Now, are you up on your physics?" Apparently Einstein was willing to explain.

"Me? No, although I suppose I should be, as I am the one who created the subject."

"No, we created it, and not just the subject, but the entire set of forces," Sheeyah corrected me.

"Yeah right. We." Nabbed again, I was.

"As there is a matter of pressing urgency requiring your attention, I must encourage you both to try to release the remainder of your respective amnesias. May I thus take the liberty of filling you in on the basic issues, my supreme God and Goddess of the Divine Cosmos?"

"Yes. Please, please do," Sheeyah was speaking rather regally again.

Several flares of light shot out from that solar wind stream, forming vast and magnificently glowing auroras. I absolutely love this Cosmos. My Cosmos.

The three of us hurtled on through the neighborhoods of infinity. I felt as if I had grown up there, playing in the interstellar streets. Suddenly, I became aware that adrenaline, or something that felt like it, was surging through me. I didn't have a physical body, but I could nevertheless feel my life force and any excitations of it. What Divine exhilaration. What ecstasy. WHAT ENERGY! I reveled in the sheer pleasure, a sensation no mortal enfleshment could ever taste. I was so glad to have lost my body. Where on Earth did I leave it? I could not remember.

Quite unexpectedly, I heard myself make the sound of a shrill scream. What was that — horrible thing — that indecipherable essence — I sensed lurking in the background? I was faintly but painfully aware of a threatening development looming somewhere out there. But where? What?

I thought I heard someone whisper these words:

Anti-prana.

But, neither Sheeyah nor Einstein had spoken. Had I only imagined this message working its way into my consciousness?

I sensed that Einstein knew about this development and wanted to hurry and reteach us what we already knew in order to have us squelch this — this thing. He hurriedly went on, "Let's begin, as per the third dimensional standpoint of your recent incarnation, with the most basic issues confounding Earth-bound metaphysics and its scientific cousin, theoretical physics."

"Yes," I mumbled, still quite shaken. Something was out there and it wanted to consume us. I was certain of this. "Let's." I wanted to scream again, but controlled myself. "What are these most basic issues?" I forced myself to relax into my ongoing hurtle through space. I actually found that the position suited me quite well. No body to deal with — what a relief. Only, I felt so very exposed, so very vulnerable in this form. Naked without flesh to insulate me from reality.

The adrenaline-like rushes continued to race through what felt to be my nervous system. How could I possibly have a nervous system? *Had I been rid of the last bits of my remaining amnesia, I would have realized that I was feeling the very nerve-energy or prana of Life. The LIFE-FORCE itself. The multidimensional nervous system of the Cosmos, of my beautiful Cosmos.*

Way out in the distance, two comets collided. The ensuing light show was breathtakingly spectacular (although I had no lungs, so no breath to take). Showers of colored light rained toward us.

Einstein went on holding the fort, "Earth humans, being confronted, even if only subconsciously, with the dilution and bastardization of Original Truth, seek to rediscover it. Religion, metaphysics and science on Earth thus end up competing to explain the Cosmos. Modern Earth physicists have taken on this cause as their own. They valiantly struggle to compose what they call a 'general unified theory' of physics. From their third dimensional vantage points, they seek to tie together explanations of what their various colleagues have labeled as gravity, as electromagnetic force, and as the strong and weak nuclear forces."

Now screams were flying through space like shooting stars of pain. And pursuing the screams was that ominous whispering:

Anti-prana.

But I decided to try to focus on Einstein's continuing message by returning to the conversation: "Their third dimensional errors in perception are so very humorous to those of us who watch," I said aloud, not really knowing whether or not I meant this lofty comment. But at least I was distracting myself from the ominous threat I felt.

"Yes," Einstein agreed with me, "it is very difficult to describe the whole of Creation and its Divine Forces from the standpoint of the third dimension. Of course some of your thinkers — "

"Such as Albert Einstein, a guy I once knew?" I teased him, trying desperately to further distract myself.

"Well, yes, I suppose," Einstein — he was indeed Einstein — replied. "Some have ventured beyond, into the fourth dimension, for understanding. Me, for example. During my incarnation on Earth as Einstein, I did not realize, at first, that I had ventured in to the fourth dimension. The reality of what I had come to know actually crept up on me when other scientists began discussing the notion of a fourth dimension."

I squirmed as I hurtled. Something was very, very wrong out here. Funny how reality creeps up on you. For some reason, the threat of ANTI-MOTION, ANTI-CREATION, the danger of ANTI-PRANA, was increasingly obvious to me. How long had this been going on out here? Why hadn't I been aware of this problem before now? What kind of God was I? What a negligent Master of the Cosmos I had been!

I redirected my attention to the functioning of the human scientists Einstein had been talking about. "But Einstein, however far human scientists have ventured, most of them have elected to bring back to the human mind indications of only a short journey beyond the third, into only the first edge of the fourth," I was almost complaining. Still, I could not help but marvel as another spiraling galaxy raced by. Or, as *we* raced by *it*, to be more accurate. I noticed another beam of light bending around another planet. Having become familiar with this effect, I looked around and became aware that light beams everywhere were bending. And all this bending was occurring in a space which was itself very curved. I saw that nothing around us was straight or still. I remembered, my higher self remembered, that all space is curved and continuously in motion.

"Triad, you sound disappointed with even the most advanced of the Earth scientists," Einstein spoke so softly. "Still, be forgiving. Be understanding. You have placed a heavy burden on Earthlings. You expect them to evolve a profound understanding of the workings of your Cosmos. You think that, if they think correctly, they can help protect your Creation."

I didn't know I did. "I do?"

"Yes. You believe that if you can spread a belief in your reality, that expanding belief or thought form will nourish your reality, your Creation."

"I do?"

"Yes. You do. However, the conceptual unification of perceived forces of the Cosmos is difficult from the standpoint of a human intellect when it fails to incorporate the higher levels of metaphysical wisdom."

"You can't see more without looking beyond," Sheeyah let us know she was listening.

A comet fell toward us, seemingly out of nowhere. Sheeyah and I wanted to hide. Einstein sensed this and pointed us toward a distant asteroid, saying, "Quick. There." Instantaneously, the three of us moved approximately 5,000 Earth miles to the far side of the asteroid.

"Physics could never explain what we just did," laughed Sheeyah.

"Oh, but yes it could, were it the theoretical physics of a higher dimension, the meta-level of physics or true metaphysics," Einstein corrected.

"Is this what you mean Einstein: The ranges of the forces that Earth scientists seek to explain extend far beyond the material plane on which those scientists base their definitions?" I hoped I was correct.

"You are very correct, Triad. You are beginning to remember the difficulties of the situation. The human intellect has its limitations. The science which it devises and then respects as true can be illuminating but distract-

Confronting the Advancing Void

ing and deceptive. The human intellect fares better using fiction, myth and fable as a way of allowing Truth in."

Sheeyah nudged me with her energy in an inappropriately sexual manner.

"What are you doing?" I whispered. (Not in front of Einstein.) I tried to communicate with her privately.

"Just trying to figure out how we're going to do it without bodies," she whispered back, apparently not worrying about whether Einstein could hear her. Why try to hide when we're already so visibly naked? Sheeyah thought loudly.

"Not now, please," I insisted.

Off in yet another direction, I saw what looked like a sun, who had its own solar system, expanding into the orbits of its planets. As the sun was burning up the remainder of its own nuclear fuel, its hydrogen was turning to helium ash, and it was becoming increasingly red and swollen. Abruptly — blip — the sun swallowed one of its own planets. One day, all of that sun's hydrogen will be used up, I conjectured to myself. That sun, having depleted the power of all the elements it requires for its ongoing thermonuclear reaction, will one day stop shining. Its energy is not limitless.

Einstein heard me thinking. "Correct, Triad. And such thermonuclear depletion takes place quite regularly around the Cosmos. No energy, not even that of your beautiful Cosmos, is unlimited."

My thoughts were set in motion by Einstein's comment. I said, "I gather that Earthlings, if they survive other major cataclysms, will one day have to deal with such an end. The sun could run low on fuel and expand and then swallow the Earth. What will Earthlings do? Flee to Mars? Will they be ready?"

I went on without speaking. And what of the Cosmos? My Cosmos? Will it ever really deplete all of its energy? My own energy shuddered. And what of my own energy? Can God die?

What a death were it then to see God die.

"Who said that?" I almost shouted as I felt that threatening development encroaching upon my Sheeyah and me.

"Said what?" Sheeyah asked.

"Said 'what a death were it then to see God die.' Who speaks that way? My God, Sheeyah, something wants to kill God. We're God. *It wants to kill us!*"

"Yes," said Einstein, "it certainly does."

"But I thought that you said that death doesn't exist, that death is not."

"I did, and death is indeed not, as long as you and Sheeyah live on. If however, you die, death IS."

I would have felt sick to my stomach if I'd had one. Why was I so unnerved by this ominous "development"? Why? And what was Einstein trying to tell me?

Einstein had been following my thoughts. "Let us proceed, please," he said with gentle but pressing urgency. "Triad, it must be clear that the bulk of Earth's inhabitants are moving far more slowly on the path to knowledge than you would like. You cannot rely upon the collective intelligence of humanity to create a thought form, *a thought force*, strong enough to help you — in time to help you — in your struggle for survival of the Cosmos. I know you expected the collective mind of the human species to evolve more rapidly than it has. Alas, it hasn't. Eventually, had they time, but perhaps still not soon enough to help you preserve your Creation, Earthlings would come to grips with the Divine Truth about change. But you still await the progression of the human mind through the pinnacles of its intellect into the heights of a new form of intelligence. As has been taught on Earth by schools of ancient and modern, Eastern and Western mysticism, the ultimate essence of the universe is one which transcends the grasp of the existing human intellect. Even advanced human terms such as *continuous transformation, manifestation, and disintegration* barely begin to describe the universal fluidity, the role of change in evolving the Cosmos."

Although it all sounded quite complicated to me, I could feel the implications of his words. "You are saying that this dynamic of continuous Divine change defies description in words. Words are too finite. Too dense," I conjectured. "So are many life forms ... too dense."

"Yes." Einstein agreed. "The less dense, the more like fluid light, that you allow yourself to become, the greater your awareness grows."

"Fluid light?" Sheeyah was intrigued.

So was I. I had seen fluid light under the henu boat and in the tomb chamber of the Great Pyramid.

I grabbed on to my interest in this concept. It felt like at least a temporary life raft, something to pull me out of the black wave of fear instilled within me by that threatening development out there, the ominous chanting which came from somewhere, but where?

He who sees God's face must die. What a death were it then to see God die. He who sees God's face must –

Einstein was wise to keep my conceptual faculties engaged now. He went on. "Fluid light is not very dense. It has almost no density. But beings, life forms, take on varying degrees of density. ... What I am attempting to indicate here is that a life form locates along a continuum of most dense to least dense."

"I don't quite get what you mean Einstein," said Sheeyah.

Einstein paused. And then a marvelous thing happened. Einstein's idea about the continuum was made more clear to us. It was as if an understanding of the rather difficult concept was simply placed within the centers of our minds. Somehow Einstein was able to generate schematic diagrams or schematized notions within our consciousnesses. Sheeyah and I understood him as we — (how can I describe the way we perceived it) — saw? — the continuum of density to which he referred:

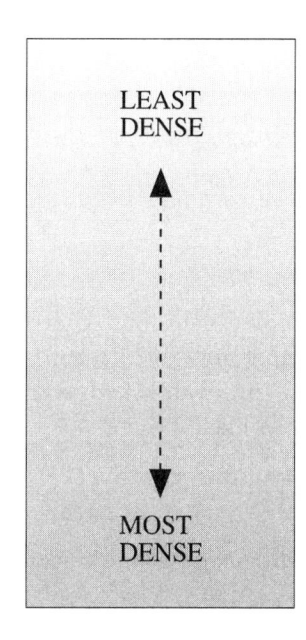

```
    LEAST
    DENSE
      ▲
      ┊
      ┊
      ┊
      ┊
      ┊
      ▼
    MOST
    DENSE
```

We could feel Einstein working in energy waves against cosmic time in order to teach us — to unveil for us — what we already knew so well: "The most dense forms are found where essences are most compact — in the lower dimensions. There is not much room for light there. The least dense life forms are found in the higher dimensions of spiritual reality, where light, in its highest vibrational forms, can fill the open space."

Again, the model that Einstein had placed in our consciousnesses appeared, this time with the continuum of compactness added on. We could see that compactness and density went together:

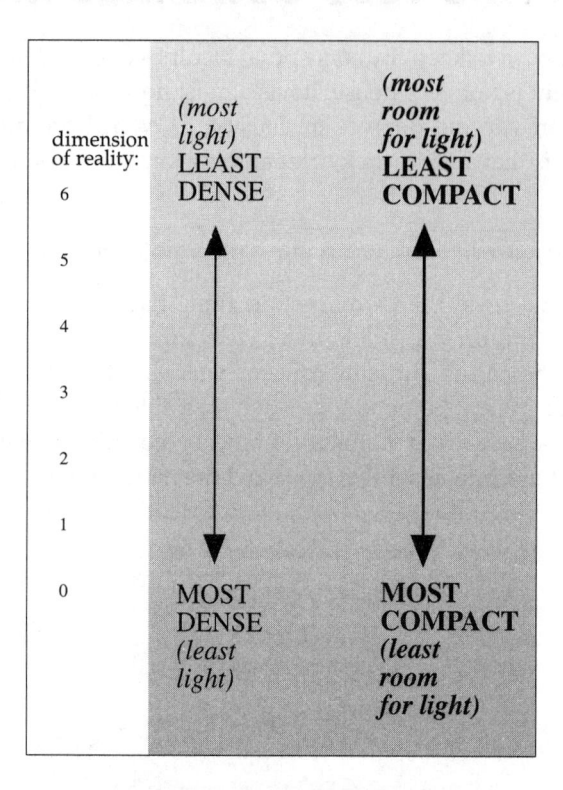

dimension of reality:	*(most light)* LEAST DENSE	*(most room for light)* LEAST COMPACT
6	↑	↑
5		
4		
3		
2		
1	↓	↓
0	MOST DENSE *(least light)*	MOST COMPACT *(least room for light)*

"So, Einstein, in the third dimension, where we were incarnated, we weren't as dense as all that after all? I mean, there were several denser dimensions below ours." Sheeyah asked, wanting some hope for third dimensional existence. She liked it there. A lot.

You loved having a body didn't you, Sheeyah? I tried not to let Einstein hear me.

Yes I did. It felt so good to touch you in skin again. I love skin. I miss skin when I disincarnate.

Confronting the Advancing Void

No, you miss physical plane sex.

I miss it right now. Will we ever be able to have it again? I want to feel you inside me .. please ... please Triad. I want you. I want you that way. Is there anything wrong with that Triad?

"Triad, Sheeyah, please focus. The Cosmos needs you back at the helm. Sheeyah, in answer to your question about your most recent third dimensional incarnation, yes, but you were nevertheless quite cripplingly dense, as are all physical bodies."

"But some people's bodies seemed to me to be more dense than others'." Sheeyah was still wanting to find some value in third dimensional reality. I suspected she was homesick about now. And she heard me suspect. Homesick for sex, she thought back to me.

Einstein ignored the undercurrent of our secondary conversation. I was glad of that, as Sheeyah's promiscuous behavior was embarrassing me. Had she always been this way or was she exhibiting some type of adverse adjustment reaction to Godhood or to the general experience of being in the sixth dimension? A little of both, I suspected. And then that horrible chanting grew louder:

– must die – what a death –

Einstein continued, presumably hoping to distract me from the chanting. "Yes, Sheeyah, within each dimension, you find degrees of density. Within each dimension, the least dense life forms are the most evolved . . . You might try to think about this more, *now*. Concentrate harder, please, Triad."

But something was out here. Was it a life form?

Anti-life. Anti-motion. Anti-prana. Anti-life. Anti-motion. Anti-prana.

I again tried not to think about that incessant chanting. "There are, of course, life forms existing within all dimensions, aren't there, Einstein?" I wasn't certain as to how I knew this, but I did. I took some pride in being able to show I knew this as I watched explosions going on everywhere in all directions. Such an explosive universe. Supremely spectacular. My universe, I thought smugly.

Ours, Sheeyah thought back.

Ours then. Have it your way, *our* universe. But alas, Sheeyah, its energy is being used up at a phenomenal rate. I was deeply saddened at this thought.

Below me, an entire galaxy slowed to a stop and, having lost its spin, collapsed in on itself, releasing its last spits of energy. For some reason, I was horrified. My energy cringed.

To my further and unspoken horror, Einstein responded aloud with a very dry, "Yes. Such gravitational collapse is inevitable in your Cosmos." He was watching the light show too.

As another couple of galaxies whipped passed us, a distant star imploded violently, collapsing under its own weight when it ran out of its own nuclear fuel. The entire collapse was over in a few milliseconds. Then the collapsed star exploded magnificently, forming an immense but short lived supernova, releasing more light than that of several billion stars combined. After the explosion, all that remained was a dense, dark cinder, which was immediately swallowed by its own black hole, which in turn began sucking the surrounding planets in with a fierce abruptness. From our vantage point, we could feel time itself being sucked at by the black hole. I realized that much more than material reality was subject to depletion. Time itself could be used up. Swallowed.

He who sees –

"I remember that," Sheeyah called our attention back, "as a human, it was very easy for me to let myself think that there existed nothing but the third dimension — that there was only material reality and nothing else — and, therefore, that all life forms and celestial forms had three dimensional bodies. Although I began to feel that there might be more to reality than met my eye, I still basically assumed that nothing could exist without a three dimensional body. But I was so wrong! Look! I have so much more than a physical body. In fact, I don't even have a body right now. I'm still a life form, so I guess life forms can exist in other dimensions of reality after all."

Einstein noted, "Impression corrected?"

She agreed, "Delusion dispelled."

"Yes, Sheeyah," Einstein continued, "As the spiritual awareness of a human being evolves, the developing of higher, less physical, domains of the self takes place. As a life form extends itself beyond the base physical, it becomes less and less dense and more and more aware."

Sheeyah knew what Einstein was talking about. The experience of such evolution had troubled her. "In my recent incarnation, this was beginning

Confronting the Advancing Void 197

to happen to me. But it made me nervous. Sometimes I felt I was losing it. Dissolving. It was very ungrounding, if you know what I mean."

"What you were doing," Einstein answered immediately, "by your inching up the scale of decreasing density was becoming less weighed down by the compactness of the physical. In this sense, you were becoming less and less compact. However, as is natural during this process of evolution, your material cohesion was also diminishing. This feels like the losing of 'it' or of the self to the uninitiated as well as to the amnesic initiated."

"Uninitiated? Amnesic initiated? Such as me?" I asked.

"Yes, you, Triad. ... So, Sheeyah, you were experiencing the unsettling effects of diminishing cohesion or what is better called 'decohesion'," Einstein said. And with that, he added cohesion to the conceptual model he was building in our consciousnesses. I could see the diagram he was placing in my mind as clear as day:

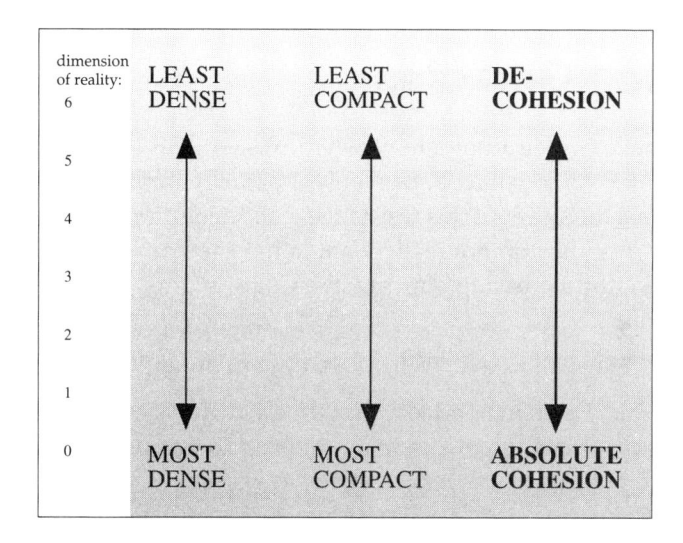

dimension of reality:			
6	**LEAST DENSE**	**LEAST COMPACT**	**DE-COHESION**
5	↑	↑	↑
4			
3			
2			
1	↓	↓	↓
0	**MOST DENSE**	**MOST COMPACT**	**ABSOLUTE COHESION**

"This is why true spiritual growth can be so unsettling, dear Triad, dear Sheeyah."

"It can even feel like death?" Sheeyah wondered.

"Yes, like death." Einstein advised, "Such evolution, especially to those poor souls who have not been instructed in the process, can be excruciatingly disorienting."

Now I thought I heard massive screaming coming from out there in the

Cosmos, the screaming of millions upon millions of living creatures. Stop! Stop! If I'd had ears, I would have held my hands tightly over them — if I'd had hands.

"Yes, Einstein, it can drive you mad." Sheeyah nudged me with her energy, insinuating that I was acting crazy, I supposed.

I felt that. Stop it. Just don't touch me. Don't touch me right now.

What a death –

How can you treat me like this, Triad?

– were it then –

"So, many material plane beings subconsciously — and sometimes consciously — shy away from the experience of spiritual advancement, of evolution," added Einstein, "and, yet, it is only in evolution that true survival, immortality, is ensured."

– to see God die.

I had to make myself think about what Einstein was saying in order to override my cosmic panic. Fortunately, I actually had something seemingly original to say about this resistance to the evolution, the ascension, of the spirit. "Yes, they do not really want to have to know how to integrate the sensation of increasing entropy, the ungrounding that Sheeyah was talking about."

"Entropy?" Sheeyah asked. "What's that got to do with ungrounding?"

"A great deal." Einstein nodded affirmatively with his energy. "Entropy is the tendency of matter to dissipate in the process of de-cohesion. As matter becomes less dense, less compact, less cohesive, it gains entropy, it dissipates increasingly. It weighs less per square inch as they say on Earth and is thus less affected by gravity. So —"

"You mean it hangs together less and less," Sheeyah interrupted.

"You could say that Sheeyah." Einstein enjoyed her level of people-talk. Street talk of the Cosmos. Telegraphed graffiti of profound ideas. "It not only hangs together less and less, but it spreads out more and more, becoming less tightly organized in a material sense, but more complex in a multi-dimensional sense." Then, Einstein added the continuum of entropy to that model he kept building into our consciousnesses:

Confronting the Advancing Void 199

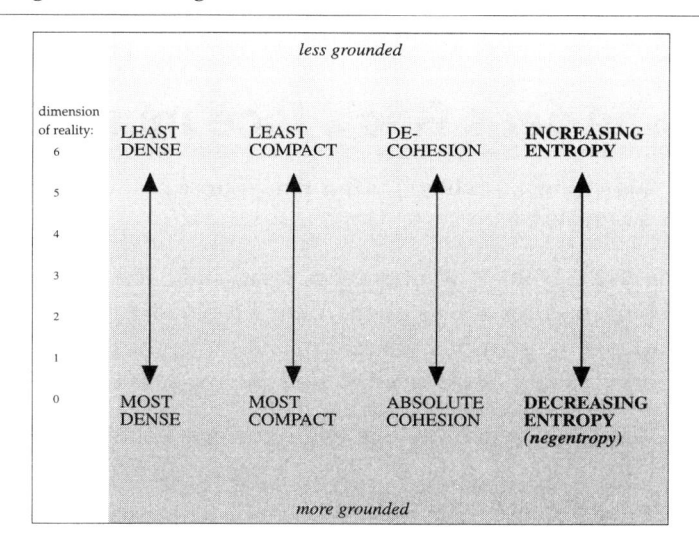

dimension of reality				
6	LEAST DENSE	LEAST COMPACT	DE-COHESION	INCREASING ENTROPY
5	↑	↑	↑	↑
4				
3				
2				
1	↓	↓	↓	↓
0	MOST DENSE	MOST COMPACT	ABSOLUTE COHESION	DECREASING ENTROPY (*negentropy*)

less grounded (top) / *more grounded* (bottom)

I realized that I actually recognized the special type of teaching Einstein was doing here. "I know what you're doing, Einstein. And thanks. You're building a *multidimensional unified theory* for us. You are reinstilling a basic road map of the whole of cosmic reality in our consciousnesses. You are building a picture, a suggestion, a symbol of reality, a symbol containing a vast amount of Truth."

"Yes, Triad. I am relaying to you a piece of your greatest Original Truth, the unification of forces upon which your Divine Cosmos is built. I am attempting to have you speed learn the consciousness technology which you have forgotten. I am reawakening your consciousnesses to the very cosmic reality you have designed. This design must stay in your consciousnesses for it all — for all Creation — to survive."

"*Consciousness technology*? What's that?" Sheeyah inquired.

"The technology by which consciousness can create, manifest, determine, influence and preserve or alter reality. In your case, what you think, and the strength with which you think the model of the Cosmos that I am reawakening in your minds, will determine the power of its reality."

"A little like I think, therefore I am?" I wondered aloud.

"Yes. Earth philosopher Descartes brought that notion into the third dimension. In your case, you think, you and Sheeyah think, therefore the Cosmos is . . . . So, how you think is very important."

"Wow. Consciousness technology," Sheeyah enjoyed the idea. I could feel her energy rolling in it.

Sheeyah, I really do love your energy, it's just that I — I —

He who sees God's face must die.

It's just that I'm not having any fun now, Sheeyah. I don't like what's going on out there.

"Yes, Sheeyah." Einstein went on, "So, Triad and Sheeyah, this picture I am mapping in your minds is the ultimate paradigm, the conceptual framework for the transmission and manifestation of the most Original Truth: the foundation of *a single and lucid image of your Cosmos.*"

"Look! Look! Look at the way that entire comet is being sucked into that awesome black hole over there!" Sheeyah's sheer amazement thrilled me with a ghastly amount of adrenaline.

I heard that voluble screaming of millions again. I felt immense intergalactic black waves developing. Waves that did not move. Ominously motionless.

"Yes, do look." Einstein seemed to point my consciousness in the direction of the black hole with his energy. "Nothing moving slower than the speed of that suction can escape it."

"Oh. ... Will We? Escape it?" Sheeyah was concerned but not horrified the way I was.

"Yes, Sheeyah. At this cosmic moment, our combined velocity and distance from the hole is beyond that which it can attract with its gravity," Einstein reassured her.

But now I had a question. "Gravity? A black hole is supposed to be nothingness. How can it have any gravity?"

"Gravity is the most misunderstood of all forces," Einstein again was ready with an answer. "Take the black hole question for example. A huge star completely collapses — implodes its totality. Suddenly, all of its mass is condensed, compacted into a single point — a zero dimensional form. That much star, which used to take up a vast amount of space and release massive amounts of energy, is now compressed into a single point. Imagine the extreme density. Something this dense has astounding gravitational power. It emits formidable gravitational waves."

I shuddered deep inside myself as I saw more black waves, unmoving black waves. Were these some dangerously powerful form of dark gravitational waves? Could they pull me toward them? Could non-motion have gravity? Well, it sure seemed to. I could see the motionless waves emerg-

Confronting the Advancing Void

ing, coming into my consciousness somehow, so motionlessly. This motionlessness was not in the natural order of things. It was not the way of my Cosmos. Perhaps this is why these dark waves were so threatening.

"But Einstein," Sheeyah wondered, seeming to be immune to the threat of the black waves, "that black hole doesn't look small enough to be a single point."

"No, it looks large and black," Einstein responded. "This is because all the light for quite some distance around it is being swallowed up."

"So," to stay sane, hinged to some semblance of some kind of reality in some way, I had to force myself to stay with the discussion, "if de-cohesion is the opposite of cohesion, and entropy is the opposite of negentropy, what is the opposite of gravity?' Gravity has an opposite I hope."

Why did I suddenly fear gravity?

"Keep hold of yourself, dear Master Triad. Remember all of these opposites lie along their respective continuums. The opposite of gravity is de-gravity, or — or, —" For a moment, Einstein seemed stumped.

"Wind," I said triumphantly, and, hit by another surge of adrenaline, I was momentarily distracted from my fear. I congratulated myself at my superior knowledge and I thought that maybe I was getting this God stuff down at last.

"Right Triad. Cosmic wind. The most Divine Motion. Gravity is an electromagnetic event. The difference between high and low gravity is in the instensities and directions of the various electromagnetic waves being emitted." Einstein was pleased that he had made me think. I realized that he hadn't been at a loss for words at all, that I hadn't beat him to the punch at all, as he quickly added the gravity-wind continuum to the unified model he was building us:

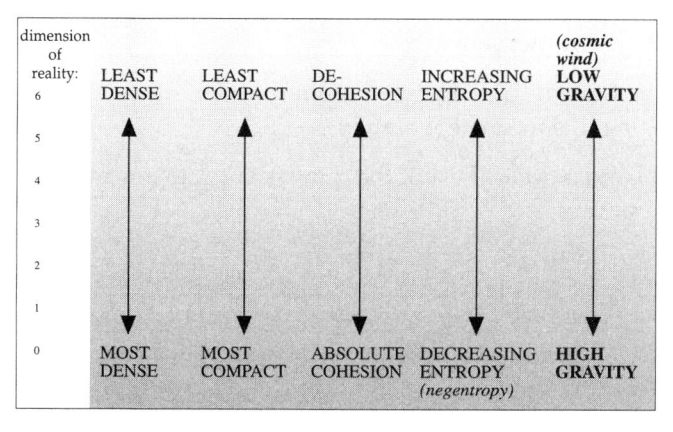

dimension of reality:					*(cosmic wind)*
6	**LEAST DENSE**	**LEAST COMPACT**	**DE-COHESION**	**INCREASING ENTROPY**	**LOW GRAVITY**
5	↕	↕	↕	↕	↕
4					
3					
2					
1					
0	**MOST DENSE**	**MOST COMPACT**	**ABSOLUTE COHESION**	**DECREASING ENTROPY** *(negentropy)*	**HIGH GRAVITY**

"So why isn't everything in the Cosmos being sucked into that hole?" Sheeyah was still concerned.

"Only the complete compaction of all the Cosmos — compaction into the ultimate Omega Point — can suck in the entirety of the Cosmos — which it must do anyway in order to recreate itself."

"Omega Point." I said shakily, revealing my trepidation.

"It sounds like check mate," said Sheeyah in that flat voice she sometimes used. "Is it coming?"

"Yes, do tell us," I added anxiously.

"Is it coming?" Sheeyah asked Einstein again.

"Don't ask me. This is your Creation, dearest Sheeyah, dearest Triad. And I've often wondered whether God had any choice in the creating and design of the universe. So you should be telling me when the next Omega Point will come, how complete it will be, and whether you have any choice in this matter."

"Yes, but at least tell us what this Omega Point is," I prodded. "I don't quite remember."

"Well, Triad, it is essential that you remember right away. The Omega Point comes like a time wave. When a critical portion of the universe reaches the sixth dimension, at the most complete point of the greatest conceivable expansion, the most entropy, the most extreme de-cohesion, the least dense cosmic possibility, at the greatest enlightening possible within that particular Divine cycle, the body of cosmic time convulses and pulls her dimensional children back in, retrieves to her womb the network of all reality — "

"A little like collecting a deck of cards to reshuffle." I could finally see the meaning of all that shuffling I had done in so many incarnations.

"And then, back to the womb, dimension zero." Sheeyah noted, "So Omega Point is dimension zero."

Einstein continued. "Yes. However, Omega Point, the end, is also alpha, the beginning, the ultimate womb of origin."

Einstein placed a cyclical list of the dimensions into our minds:

```
       ┌─ DIMENSION 6 = omega
      /   DIMENSION 5
     /    DIMENSION 4
    (     DIMENSION 3
     \    DIMENSION 2
      \   DIMENSION 1
       ▶─ DIMENSION 0 = alpha = omega point
```

He went on yet again. "As I was saying, at the point of greatest expansion, the body of cosmic time convulses, pulls back in her dimensional children — pulls everything back into her womb, to begin again at zero."

"Did you say *her*?" inquired Sheeyah.

"Yes, her." Einstein agreed.

"*Me*?" Sheeyah asked Einstein.

And Einstein replied, "You can put it that way. Please do so."

"ME? I will convulse the Cosmos? I would do something that awful?"

"When the time comes — " Einstein started with that phrase so often repeated by Nostradamus. Ugh.

Sheeyah interrupted him before I could. "But what of Original Truth?"

"You must preserve it through all gyrations of all reality. Only Original Truth sustains Creation. And it is you who must preserve Original Truth in order to sustain Creation in all its stages of expansion and contraction. You are the giver and taker of life, Sheeyah, my Goddess."

"*Me*?"

"Yes. And remember that the greatest threat to Original Truth, to Creation itself, is the time just preceding and right during the Omega Point. The time just preceding is now. If your power, the power of Original Truth, is not preserved, the next Omega Point will be the last, the final end to all Creation. Never again will there be a beginning." Einstein was very serious about this. "And Sheeyah, those symbols of the highest Truths have been in your safekeeping for eons. You must apply them appropriately at this juncture in cosmic evolution."

"Big job," Sheeyah sighed. "And big burden."

"You signed on for the entire tour of duty, baby." I couldn't resist putting in my two bits, even though I didn't really know what the job really was. Shouldn't ask a woman to do a man's job, I thought inwardly.

"Who asked you?" Sheeyah turned on me. She had heard me thinking. "Anyway, giving birth to a universe, going through all those labor pains, sounds more like woman's work to me. A man just couldn't handle the pain."

"But there is no you. It's all *me*." I got her back.

"No, it's *we*."

"We're one and the same," I answered, extending the absurdity of our dialogue.

"It sure doesn't feel like it, Triad. Anyway, if I'm you, then you don't like yourself very much, do you? Because you don't seem to like me much at all." She sounded deeply hurt.

"Aw, come on, baby," I felt like a cad (again), "don't say that. You know I love you. It's just that, that we have this, this — "

He who sees God's face must die.

"Necessary polarity, bipolarity, or perhaps more accurately, dipolarity," Einstein brought us back to the higher mind.

Fortunately, Sheeyah controlled her metaphysical feminism to do what I considered some more respectable mental work. "So, Einstein, if I am the cosmic yin, the negative pole, where do I fit into this multidimensional unified theory you've been diagramming into our minds? Are there any negative dimensions?"

What a death were it then to see God die.

"Most certainly," Einstein responded. "The two of you actually mirror each other, manifesting the Cosmic Whole." And he showed us, reaching into our minds, in his manner of consciousness technology, the great conceptual mirror, the dipolar Cosmos:

Confronting the Advancing Void

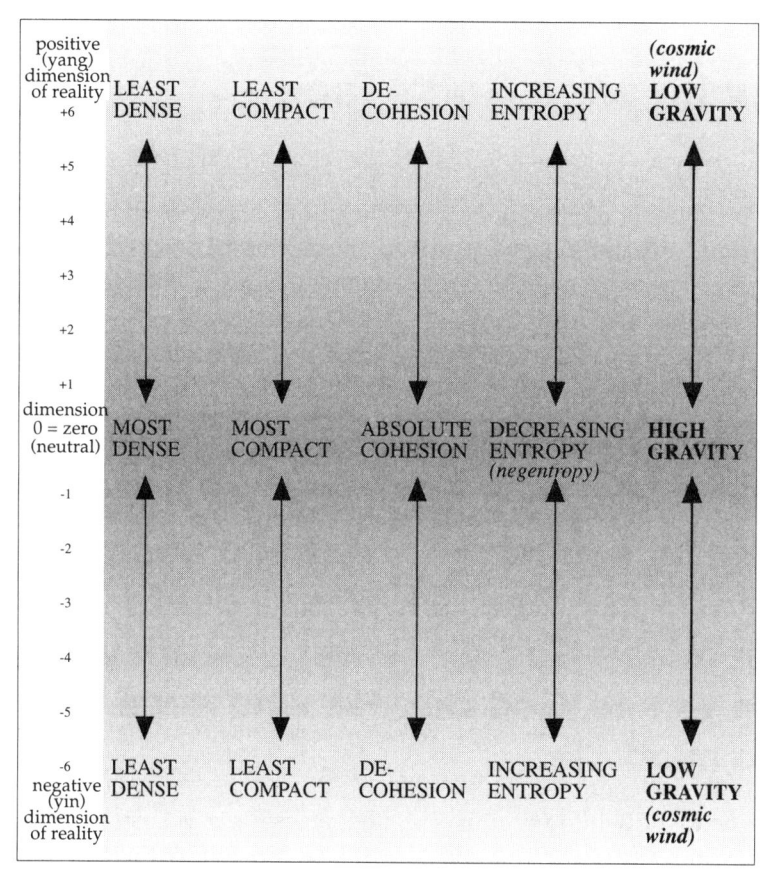

YANG (+) SIDE OF COSMIC MIRROR

positive (yang) dimension of reality +6				(cosmic wind)
LEAST DENSE	LEAST COMPACT	DE-COHESION	INCREASING ENTROPY	LOW GRAVITY

+5
+4
+3
+2
+1

dimension 0 = zero (neutral)

| MOST DENSE | MOST COMPACT | ABSOLUTE COHESION | DECREASING ENTROPY *(negentropy)* | HIGH GRAVITY |

-1
-2
-3
-4
-5
-6

negative (yin) dimension of reality

| LEAST DENSE | LEAST COMPACT | DE-COHESION | INCREASING ENTROPY | LOW GRAVITY *(cosmic wind)* |

YIN (-) SIDE OF COSMIC MIRROR

Sheeyah murmured, "So, there must be a continuous movement to keep balance then, because otherwise things would get pretty out of balance. One of us might get overextended or a bit carried away. Like Triad. Too much development, too much civilization, if you can call what he does civilized."

"The entire Cosmos, and not only the third dimension of the Cosmos, is," Einstein warned, "too far out of balance."

"Time to convulse?" Sheeyah asked tenuously.

"What a temperamental universe you are my dear," I tried to interject some humor here. I tried hard, because that voice was still chanting:

He who sees God's face –

It made me very nervous. I felt as if my essence might shatter in fear.

"I'm not a temperamental universe, Triad. I'm just preserving the cosmic order, doing my job." Sheeyah went on murmuring, "I don't think convulsion is really an expression of temperament. ... Triad ... Triad ... Triad, are you listening to me?"

No. I'm listening to IT. Can't you hear IT?

He who sees God's face must die. He who sees God's face must die. He who sees God's face must die ... What a death were it then to see God die. What a death were it then to see God die. What a death were it then to see God die. He who sees God's face must die.

I screamed wildly into my universe. I felt a cosmic psychosis overtaking me. Oh God! Oh God! I get it! *DON'T LET ME SEE MY OWN FACE! DON'T LET ME SEE MY OWN FACE! DON'T LET ME SEE MY OWN FACE!*

He who sees God's face must die. He who sees God's face must die. He who sees God's face must die ... What a death were it then to see God die. What a death were it then to see God die. What a death were it then to see God die. He who sees God's face must die.

DON'T LET ME SEE MY OWN FACE!

10

But who can see God's face? And from what vantage point can it be seen?

In the beginning, when the Goddess and I were but One, we shared the same face. We gazed through the same eyes and knew not what would eventually become of us as Two. Only once we, in moving from Monad to Duad, developed the polarity necessary to give birth to all Creation, did we wear the two faces of Yin and Yang. Only then could we recognize ourselves reflected as opposites in each other: We saw God's faces in each other!

But lovers, even Divine lovers, must at least occasionally see each other's faces when in the act of intercourse, even Divine intercourse. Perhaps this is the only true look into the face of oneself — the gaze into the face of one's lover.

However, he said that "He who sees God's face must die." Yet, should I not look into the eyes of my Goddess, who is the other half of me? Who is my self, mirrored?

Or is the danger which Set threatened a far greater one? Is Set the reflection of God? Is Set the anti-Monad reflecting the Monad — the face of God at its polar opposite? Should I not allow myself to gaze at Set — not allow myself to recognize the void for which he stands?

$$\Omega$$

"Triad. Sheeyah. Fear will not save us. Fear is a weak energy. Remember that the Divine Cosmic Order is a perpetual flow of change, in which forces are *always* interweaving and disentangling, contracting and expanding. The Earth Buddhists call this 'Samsara' or incessant motion. Some of the motion is smooth. Some of it is convulsive. But all of it is change. Incessant change. Do not fear change."

I thought that Einstein was misunderstanding what I feared. I did not mind normal change, the natural ebb and flow of events. But I did fear end change, the encroachment of eternal NON-CHANGE, the end of all my Creation. The end of me! What a death. No one there to witness it either, because there would be nothing in existence after my death.

– what a death were it then to see God die –

Except that thing out there. It would witness my death. But how could it do so if all that exists ceases to exist when I die?

He who sees God's face –

But if *it* sees *my* face, *it* dies. But it can't die, because it does not exist in the first place!

Rigidly avoiding my thoughts, Sheeyah was still with the discussion being led by Einstein. "But, why do life forms, especially third dimensional life forms, resist change so fiercely?" she wondered. "Why are they so very afraid?" I supposed that she was including me in her sweeping generalization.

Einstein again had a ready answer. "The unenlightened among them resist, seeing change as threatening and death as the end rather than as a shift into a new dimension. The enlightened person does not resist the flow of the life force throughout the dimensions but opens to a recognition of this flow and to a movement *with* this flow. The greater one's understanding of this most dynamic and Divine Order, the more one's actions will harmonize with it."

Here I began chastising myself: I suppose I, God Himself, am not very enlightened then, because I am so very terrified that I am bracing myself against any change which ultimately results in the *permanent* end of all change and all motion.

– must die –

"Hah!" I blurted out nervously, "I guess that is why they tell themselves not to 'go against the flow'." I laughed a little at the irony of this phrase. I needed to laugh. Humor. Humor. Please.

Einstein found my idea helpful. "Perhaps, now, Triad, you have a more expanded idea of this directive, one which is all too often merely platitude. Going against the flow stifles, blocks, and even suffocates energy. It eventually backfires."

I could see several stars swelling to boiling red sores in the black sky. I teased myself almost jeeringly with the concept that, had I purchased these star parcels before they swelled, they would have multiplied in size and become even hotter properties. But not survivor territories, I chided myself. What I didn't quite get yet was that I needn't worry about purchasing any of the cosmic properties I saw, as they were already mine — or ours. Why, I wondered painfully, was I so set on the acquisition and sale of property? It seemed that, as a God, I was after more than land parcels ... some kind of spiritual real estate ....

"I guess it's like trying to force a moving picture to stand still. You can warp the picture, even destroy it by trying to stop it, but you can't make it stand still." Sheeyah stayed with Einstein's thinking.

And Einstein stayed with Sheeyah. "In fact, Sheeyah, human beings, as do all life forms at the higher end of the third dimension and above, have the *choice* — the *free will* to either stagnate by resisting the flow, or to evolve by going with it."

Sheeyah was pensive and calm. "I guess that too many elect, of their own free will, to stagnate, to go against the flow, to resist change —"

What a death were it then –

Sheeyah, you must hear the anti-prana out there. It wants to kill us. It wants you to have a still birth at the next Omega Point. All Creation will then die. How can you be so cool about this?

But Sheeyah still ignored my trepidations and went on with what she was saying. "They would rather stagnate because they think it will be safer that way."

"Ah yes, safety, the deadly illusion," murmured Einstein.

I had to ask him, "Deadly for the physical body?"

He answered, "Yes, potentially, Triad, but far worse, it is deadly for the spirit — the spiritual body. Spiritual growth is essential to survival. Stagnation of the spirit brings unruly chaos, darkness and death. Extreme stagnation is non-motion, non-change, non-evolving. Still-birth."

– to see God die –

Is this the anti-prana calling? Again, behind the chanting, I could hear that screaming. It sounded like people and animals and even plants and trees suffering as they died.

"I suppose," interjected Sheeyah, "that we shouldn't think of this free will as a private matter. Too many spirits permanently extinguish themselves, far more than any Master Plan of the Cosmos would have planned for. We didn't plan to lose so many souls after creating them. A certain amount of die-off was expected, even desired, but not this amount. The massive stagnating and extinguishing of souls threatens the perpetuation of all Creation." Sheeyah was clearly remembering her role as co-creator now.

"Yes, Sheeyah. So your so-called modern Earth physicists have been obediently elaborating, as ordered by Triad, (although most don't realize what they are on to), their quantum theory, which ascribes the dynamic, always moving, manifestation of matter in the wave-like nature of matter's subatomic particles, which implies that which mystics have known for so long: *Matter cannot be separated from the flow of its activity. Matter which separates from its activity is absolutely dead — nonexistent."*

What a death were it then –

"Dead meat? Dead bodies?" Sheeyah was getting rather morbid.

I heard more screaming in space. (Don't you hear that screaming? Doesn't anyone hear that screaming?) Pursuing the screamers was that chant:

– to see God die, to see God die –

I saw a large comet smash into a planet, shifting that planet's axis and sending her out of her planetary orbit into a chaotic wobble. It was then that a ghastly realization whipped through me: So this is what I wanted to make people think could happen to Earth! I wanted to make them believe this sort of catastrophe was coming so that they would rush to buy my survivor territories. But, oh God, it can really happen! — God? I'm God! I can't let this happen! And I have incarnated and made money on its anticipation! What a ghastly character I am! I absolutely despise myself.

Avoiding my miserable energy, Einstein focused on Sheeyah's morbid comment. "No Sheeyah. Matter which separates from its activity ceases to exist in any form. And even light is matter. In this sense, absolute death, the only real death, can take place in any dimension, not just the physical. Alas, Triad and Sheeyah. Even the most Divine Light can die." Now Einstein was also upset, at least briefly.

I screamed inwardly. Was I resisting the Truth as I ran these thoughts through and through my mental circuits: Light can die? No! No! The Divine Light can never die!

He who sees God's face **must** die.

Sheeyah continued, oblivious to our angsts. "So, matter is *never still, never quiescent.*"

I looked around nervously at the continuous activity: spiraling galaxies, expanding suns, collapsing stars, moving light, solar and cosmic winds, strong and weak forces exerting themselves upon themselves and all that crossed their paths of energy. Not a particle, large or small, macroscopic or subatomic, was still. The unutterable majesty was overwhelming. But why was my beloved Cosmos sickening me?

I had a question for myself: Why would I want to make money on Earth anyway? You can't take it with you. OR CAN YOU? Can money be carried across dimensions? ... Power can.

"I see this now," I said, trying desperately to sound rational and to participate in Einstein's urgent lesson, "as I view the Cosmos from this perspective. You want me to think that if anything appears motionless, inert, to us, we are seeing it with closed eyes. Our universe and all of its components — material and immaterial — are ceaselessly moving. It is all just energy. Energy is always in motion."

He who **sees** God's face –

Einstein approved of my feeble contribution. "Yes, Triad, good. In fact, motion and stillness are not opposites. Stillness is merely a lesser degree of motion. Even physical matter is never ever still. It just registers varying characteristics and degrees of motion."

More screaming. I could hear more screaming out there. The multitude of pained voices tore at me as if ripping me with millions of knives.

–must die–

"So Einstein," Sheeyah was working valiantly to stay with his conceptualizations. "You are saying that there are only degrees and forces of motion, some more intense or more in motion than others. But no absolute non-motion."

"Yes, I am. I am saying this about all of your Creation. You must make certain you believe this. Do not let the thought form of non-motion find a home in your Divine Soul."

Hearing this, I finally knew I HAD to correct Einstein: There exists out there a non-motion, a perilous non-motion. Einstein should know this without my having to inform him.

I finally pulled it together to articulate my concerns in a voice that Sheeyah and Einstein had to listen to: "But there *is* a perilous non-motion developing out there. I sense its horrendous immanence." I paused. "Or, Einstein, do you already know this? Is this why you are so intensely reviewing the struggles of modern Earth physics with us?" I was, I noted, perversely intrigued by my expanding perspective on physics, a topic which had been of little interest to me during my recent incarnation.

"Yes. I am working to prepare you for the confrontation with the ultimate denial of your reality. Think about it: Modern Earthlings seek Truth through science, metaphysics through physics. According to their limited but helpful quantum theory, when you attempt to pinpoint the location of a particle, it may not be there. Instead you find it takes a wave form, that it is in motion, that it IS motion. Understanding that all Creation is in perpetual motion is the only way to begin to understand the non-motion that threatens Creation."

I couldn't tell whether Einstein was answering enough of my question or not. Did he or did he not realize that there already was a non-motion out there? Again that creeping terror: Non-motion encroaching. The black, unmoving wave of non-motion! Why were Sheeyah and Einstein seemingly ignoring its immediacy?

Anti-prana. Anti-prana. See God die, die, die -

"That particle Einstein — its very *substance* is motion?" Sheeyah pondered this concept as it applied to the subatomic level.

I heard more screaming. Am I psychotic? Is the He-God crazy?

They carried on their conversation about motion as if nothing unusual were happening out there. As they did so, Einstein and Sheeyah were exchanging energies in an increasingly intimate way. I did not like Sheeyah's way with men. Me, her son, Hermes, now Einstein. Einstein nudged up to her with his energy as he went on and on: "Yes, Sheeyah. You cannot pinpoint the particle. You cannot locate it exactly. It exists somewhere within the field, or path, of its travels."

Confronting the Advancing Void

I interrupted their closeness. "Particles are merely condensations of a bit of the energy field." I knew this somehow, and it helped me feel more confident to say it.

–must die. What a death were it then –

"Particles are merely condensed motion?" Sheeyah postulated, trying to steer clear of my ever mounting terror.

The screams I was hearing behind that chanting began to sound more like gargantuan eternal moans and wails.

"Excellent descriptions, you two."

"Unsettling concepts though, aren't they, Einstein?" Sheeyah added.

"Unsettling at first, Sheeyah my dear. After a while, however, these ideas become very soothing," Einstein responded to her so sweetly. I was a bit jealous, but I had to admit that he was extremely gentle and loving. Anyone would be attracted to him.

"So something can actually come out of nothing?" Sheeyah marveled. "A particle can come racing into existence out of motion?"

"Well," said Einstein, "I choose not to say that something comes out of nothing. After all, *motion is not nothing*, is it Sheeyah? It is motion. There is no nothing within your Creation. Nothing does not exist where you exist."

Within our Creation? But, how can he be saying this when I feel the fearsome advancement of NOTHING, of NON-MOTION all the while? And I hear its nagging chant.

– to see God die. He who sees God's face –

"Sheeyah! DO NOT LOOK AT MY FACE, whatever you do!" I pleaded.

"Oh, Triad. Be quiet." Sheeyah pushed my warning away.

Of course, Einstein just went on with his discussion. "I prefer to think of a particle moving in and out of various dimensions and looking like motion as it does. A particle comes racing into the lower material plane, where there is more density, from higher dimensions, where there is less density. *Modern Earth physics can not adequately explain its particle and wave theories until it sees how bits of field, fragments of motion, speed through the dimensional levels of spiritual reality and change densities as they do.* Changing from wave to particle, transducing momentarily to materialize, is only one of the many transformations that subatomic particles undergo.

Only a major advance in consciousness technology will bring Earth physics up to speed here."

I tried again, forcing myself to sound calm this time. "Sheeyah, I *said* don't look at my face. I won't look at yours."

Einstein and Sheeyah ignored me again, however. Einstein continued: "In an effort to understand the Cosmos, Earthlings have identified many subatomic particles. Most of these particles are considered by Earth physicists to be relatively unstable, and to decay into other particles shortly after they come into existence. These may live in the forms identified by Earth scientists for only less than one millionth of a second."

"So they hardly come into existence at all?" Sheeyah asked.

"I would not put it that way," answered Einstein. "A millionth of a second is actually a long time to exist in a particular form! When that fraction of a second is over, the form, the energy, transforms. It does not disappear. It does not die. It continues its ongoing transformation. The instability Earth physicists see is an illusion."

Asteroids, hitting atmospheres, flared like shooting stars, streaking the bleak distances of space with their momentarily obvious existences. Now, somewhere out there, babies cried in anguish, I could hear their screams whipping through my nervous system. I gasped.

But Einstein plugged away. "The neutron can break down spontaneously. It does so by breaking into an electron and a massless particle called a neutrino. Its breakdown is a radioactive process called beta decay and this decayed neutrino is an 'antineutrino'."

He who sees God's face –

Einstein went on and on and on. "Now for the most important part of the story I have been telling you. There is another particle, your Earth scientists call it the 'photon', which they say has no mass. These scientists have nevertheless allowed the massless photon the status of particle! The photon represents a unit of electromagnetic radiation."

Sheeyah was hanging on Einstein's every word. "Why is this photon so important? Is it because it is light?"

So Einstein continued, "What you must know is that there is a particle, which you call an 'antiparticle,' for every particle you identify. For the electron, you have a 'positron,' for the proton, there is an 'antiproton,' for the neutron there is an 'antineutron,' and so on. Each antiparticle has the same mass and the opposite charge of the particle it mirrors. But there is an exception: the photon. The photon is the soul of light. It is its own mirror, its own particle and antiparticle all in one."

Intrigued, I returned to the conversation. "Sounds like the Monad? What we are when we are One. So, are we the Divine Light when we merge? The Divine omnipresent photon? We certainly aren't this way when we are the Duad."

"No. As two, as the Duad, you have opted to mirror each other, not to merge your poles."

I watched as clouds of hydrogen gas contracted, heated up tremendously, and transformed to fires in the sky, blazing stars in my eyes.

– face must die. What a death were it then to see God –

Die! Die! Can anyone else hear this? Why am I the only one concerned about this?

I began to yell at Sheeyah. "SO DON'T LOOK AT MY FACE! SHEEYAH DON'T LOOK AT MY FACE! DON'T YOU GET IT? SHEEYAH! IF WE ARE BOTH GOD AND WE LOOK AT EACH OTHER'S FACE, GOD WILL DIE!!! THAT'S US. IT MEANS WE WILL DIE!!!"

Sheeyah was silent for a moment. She had listened to me. And then she said sweetly, "But Triad, I looked into your face when we made love just this last incarnation. Is that what you mean? What was wrong with it? You seemed to like it at the time. Anyway, it sounds as if our merging into the Monad produces Divine Light. How can this be death?"

Einstein, seemingly divorced from all this, went on again. "So it is that your third dimensional Earth scientists, seeking Truth, try to write a unified theory. This has become a tradition among them. Earlier on, Isaac Newton actually managed to conceptually unify the two forces of gravity which were once believed to be separate forces. So the theory of gravity became a unified one — "

– die. He who sees God's face must die. What a death –

Now, of all things preposterous, I could feel Sheeyah trying to sexually arouse me again. I warded her off. Not now, why now of all times, Sheeyah? Can't you see what's happening out here?

No. Just wondered if we should shed a little Divine Light on the matter, Triad.

Einstein ignored us both. " — Next, and still, physicists have to be fully satisfied that there is unity between what they call 'gravity' and 'electromagnetism.' Electromagnetic forces take place between all charged particles, yielding chemical reactions as well as determining atomic and molecular structures. Gravitational forces are similar. They take place when particles interact and or combine and produce a force of gravity."

"So," Sheeyah interjected, "the difference between gravity and electromagnetism is in whether or not the particles are charged?"

Einstein corrected gently. "This is the *perceived* difference. But, if we look into them, all particles contain charges within their structures."

Sheeyah again turned her sexual energies in my direction. I could not focus on her advances. I knew that she felt rejected. Why couldn't she see what I was so worried about? Stop! Sheeyah, our merging could kill us! Could kill Creation!

He who sees God's face must die. What a death were it then to see God die.

No, our merging can *save* Creation, Triad. It spreads Divine Light.

I don't know how he managed, but Einstein continued to teach us what we needed to know to defend our Creation. By focusing on continuous motion, Einstein was teaching us to create a mind set which did not let the alternative, NON-MOTION, ANTI-PRANA, seep further into our consciousnesses and thus into our Creation. "So," he said, "a truly unified theory of Creation is essential to sustain Creation. All particle interactions seem, to Earth physicists, to break into four categories or forces: the strong force, the weak force, the electromagnetic force and the gravitational force. Earth scientists instinctively race to unify their models of these forces. Strong forces hold the protons and neutrons together in the nucleus, a place they might not stay together without such a force — perhaps the strongest force we know. The weak forces, such as beta decay, involve the breaking off of components of particular susceptible particles. As for the electromagnetic force, two nineteenth century Earth scientists, Faraday and Maxwell, described what they called 'electrodynamics theory,' in which they defined electric fields as being physical, but not necessarily as having bodies. They said these fields can take the form of radio or light waves or other forms of electromagnetic radiation. What they did not say

Confronting the Advancing Void

was that such waves and radiations could manifest physical, or lower dimensional, characteristics, but that they typically were moving through multidimensional reality and changing densities as they moved."

"Maybe they didn't say because they didn't know," Sheeyah offered.

Einstein disagreed. "They knew this, Sheeyah, but they failed to realize what it was that they knew. Instead, they viewed electrical and magnetic fields as being similar but different in that a magnetic field was one which simply *existed* in the *space surrounding* a charged body and which exerted force on other charged bodies, while an electrical field was one which was *generated* by the *movement* of electrons, electrical currents, and which exerted force on other moving charges. That electromagnetic force and gravitational force were viewed as different for quite some time is, therefore, not surprising. As with the confusion about gravity before Newton, the mistaken notion that electromagnetism and gravity itself were two distinctly *different* forces was a natural consequence of the myopic nature of the human intellect. *All forces are generated by the movement of charges.* Depending upon your unit of analysis, all gravity is a form of electromagnetic force and even this is a myopic underexplanation."

"Ah, the folly of third dimensional science. Well, Einstein, the over intellectualizing of anything is a risk, isn't it?" I said, trying to sound intelligent.

"Yes, Triad. And you should be the one to talk about the pitfalls of over intellectualizing things." Sheeyah's gentle sarcasm reared its nasty head again.

"As the human mind has matured, and the theory of relativity — "

"Which you proposed," I interrupted brashly.

- what a death -

"Yes — as it has been assimilated, man has recognized that all charges are in motion and that an electric field and a magnetic field differ only through the biased eyes of the observer, when that observer sees no motion or allows not for the possibility of motion in one of these. *Once we truly recognize the meaning of the notion that everything, even down to the subatomic level, is in motion, and that that motion moves through all dimensions of spiritual reality, there is a natural unification of all theory.*"

"But everything is NOT in motion, Einstein! I can see the anti-motion out there. And it is encroaching upon us. Don't you see it? You must see it!" I begged.

– see God die. See God die –

Einstein was silent.

Exhausted, I grew calmer for a moment. I saw a cluster of black holes merging in the distance. Off in yet another direction, clouds of stars were blowing by. I tried to say something to show I'd been learning: "From out here, the elegance, the sublime unity of all forces, is apparent. As you, my friend, Einstein, showed Earthlings, even a field of gravity, something which in itself may seem to have no density, cannot be separated from the matter — or the substance — generating it."

And then, the next moment, my calm was gone again. I was feverishly wondering BY WHAT FORCE, BY WHAT POWER, CAN THE DEVELOPING NON-MOTION BE DRIVEN? I wanted to know. I was *desperate* to know. What generated this monster?

He who sees God's face must die.

I could hear that horrible chanting closing in on us.

– what a death –

I agonized.

–a death–

Sheeyah too was moved by something, I could not tell what. "The more I see, Einstein, the more matter and space are obviously inseparable. To perpetuate the separation of them in our minds is to doom Creation." She was crying tear drops of energy about this. Why? Why about this?

Confronting the Advancing Void

"So we know that objects are not distinct from their environments. This holds true on the submicroscopic subatomic level all the way on up through to the supramacroscopic suprauniverse." Good old Einstein, still holding down the fort.

"O.K.," said Sheeyah, "objects are not distinct from their environments. I got it. For once and for all. Impression corrected."

"Delusion dispelled," I confirmed feebly. (Could God really die?) I spoke on, trying to stay hinged. "... So, the Einsteinian formula, e=mc², explained it all in terms of energy. Energy, you once told me, Einstein, is a product of matter moved at the square of the speed of light. Your theory of relativity was a great advance for mankind. In the face of mankind's metaphysical limitations, you were able to teach what mystics have had a difficult time transferring to the masses throughout the ages."

"But, Einstein, if I may say so, you could have taught humans much more." Sheeyah sounded wistful again.

He who sees God's face must die.

"Yes, he knew much much more." I added to the prevailing wist, trying to distract myself from my own prevailing terror.

"So, why did you stop there, with primary relativity, Einstein?" Sheeyah stayed on the case.

"Sheeyah. Triad. Scientific, and also metaphysical, advance in the absence of moral advance is most dangerous. There has been too much of this imbalanced advancement already, as we see on the 'modernized' Earth today," he explained.

What a death were it then to see God –

"On Earth?" asked Sheeyah.

"On Earth and elsewhere in the Cosmos," he replied sadly. I felt his sadness through and through. And, feeling Einstein's sadness was like feeling the weeping of a million stars at once.

I was irritated with myself (and with Sheeyah inasmuch as she was part of me). "You'd think we, the god force, could have controlled moral evolution —"

Einstein stopped me short. "Of course you do not want your narcissism to guide you in your evaluation of morality, do you?"

"Me? The Supermind? Narcissistic?" I was insulted. This sense of insult actually gave me some relief from my fear.

– see God die –

"You still wear some of the myopia of your third dimensional incarnation, Triad." Einstein nudged me.

"I do?" I played naive.

"Yes."

– what a death were it then to –

"So do I." Sheeyah admitted it for both of us, I guess.

"Then let me warn you that your unaided and very personal, individualized, endeavors will not reach you through to the Supermind. As third dimensional beings, (or, given that at present you have no bodies whatsoever, as beings with even the residues of third dimensional mind sets), your ignorance cannot transcend itself. You need more than the tools available to you within the realm of third dimensional understanding."

Sheeyah did not like the limitation. "So how do I, with lingering human limitations, ascend to my rightful throne?"

"All ascendances of all beings, including yours, are actuated by a secret Consciousness-Force which works toward the emergence of its powers into the being's — in this case your — consciousness, powers which are concealed behind the veil of Nature."

"The veil of Nature. Nature. But, am I not She?" Sheeyah wondered.

– must die. What a death –

The chanting continued. And that horrific screaming came at me again from somewhere else out there. Was that chanting force killing babies? I began to feel a miserable hollowness. Was I, whatever remained of me out here, dissolving away? ... Do NOT look at my face, Sheeyah!

– to see God –

Confronting the Advancing Void

But what is your face if not the face on a physical body you once used? Sheeyah rubbed her energy against mine, trying to seduce me. Come on, Triad, let's try to figure out how to do it out here, O.K.? You'll feel better if we can, I bet. Make love with me, Triad.

– die –

Einstein called us back to attention. "Sheeyah, you asked if you were the veil of Nature. No, not quite yet. The being and powers of superconscience must descend into you and uplift you, and formulate the process of your transcendence and ascendance back to your throne."

Sheeyah was humbled. "Will I make it, Einstein? Will I make it back in time?"

"So I hope, Sheeyah," Einstein replied. "It is entirely possible. The rudimentary and diminished elements of the higher consciousness you seek are already present within you, even with your third dimensional contamination. This holds true for all beings. The seeds of higher consciousness — of Truth — are in all of us. Accessing these and developing these is the challenge."

He who sees God's face must die. What a death were it then –

"Sheeyah. Listen. Just for a moment." I begged her now. "That was not my face. That was my flesh, a temporary form I utilized. It was a material mask. My actual face, your actual face — we must never really look into each other's actual faces — this is looking into God's face. We will die if we do this. Can you hear me?"

– to see God die –

Einstein interrupted. "When polar opposites meet, they come crashing together, especially if they are evolved to the level of the sixth dimension when they meet. In such a case, they collapse down to the zero dimension in a sudden catastrophic convulsion. Omega Point. Is this what worries you, Triad?"

Einstein showed us the unified model again, this time with the continuum of polarity added on. I could see how it all fit together.

YANG SIDE OF COSMIC MIRROR

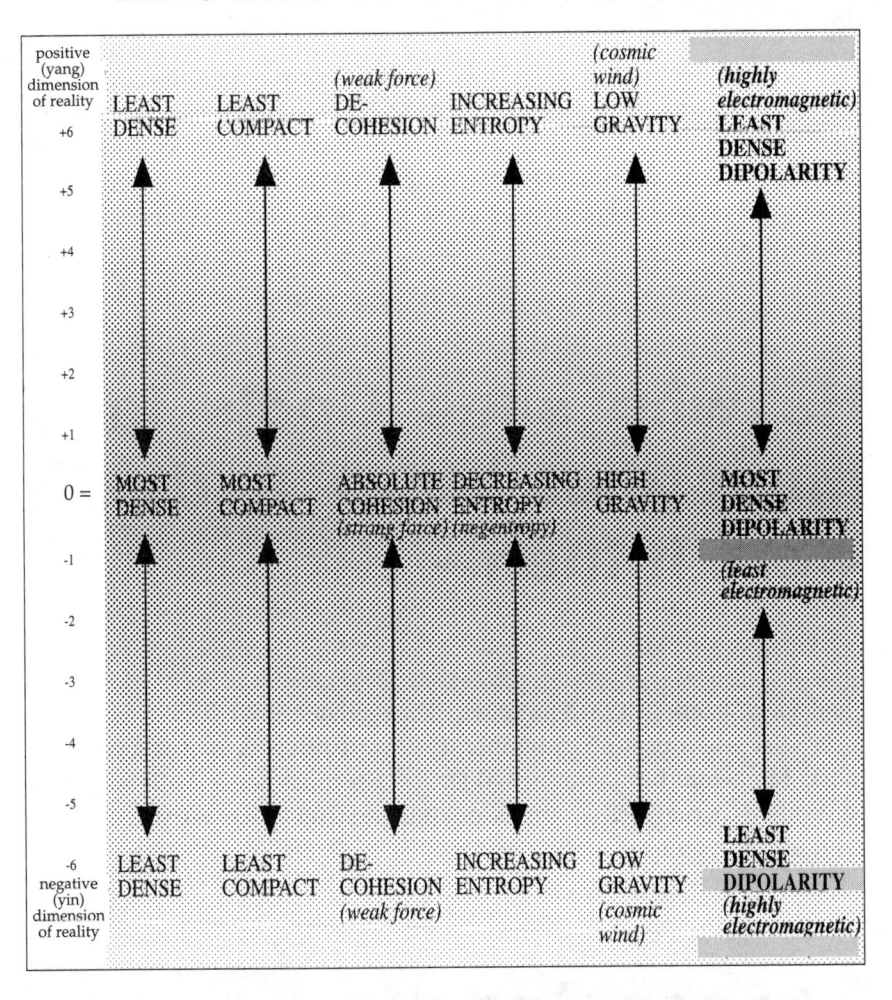

positive (yang) dimension of reality +6	LEAST DENSE	LEAST COMPACT	*(weak force)* DE-COHESION	INCREASING ENTROPY	*(cosmic wind)* LOW GRAVITY	*(highly electromagnetic)* LEAST DENSE DIPOLARITY
0 =	MOST DENSE	MOST COMPACT	ABSOLUTE COHESION *(strong force)*	DECREASING ENTROPY *(negentropy)*	HIGH GRAVITY	MOST DENSE DIPOLARITY *(least electromagnetic)*
-6 negative (yin) dimension of reality	LEAST DENSE	LEAST COMPACT	DE-COHESION *(weak force)*	INCREASING ENTROPY	LOW GRAVITY *(cosmic wind)*	LEAST DENSE DIPOLARITY *(highly electromagnetic)*

YIN SIDE OF COSMIC MIRROR

"Convulsion," Sheeyah said aloud and then went on in her thoughts: Sounds like quite some orgasm to me. Sheeyah seemed to enjoy the concept. Let's do it. Look at me, Triad. Look. Look.

No. For God's sake no! Sheeyah, it will kill us!

We are God. We can do what we like, Triad. Sheeyah seemed to me to be deliberately racing into destruction the way a moth flies into flames.

No. No. I won't look.

– to see God die –

Sheeyah, being frustrated, turned her attention back to Einstein. "Did you ever get the feeling that something is out there — but you can't see it?"

Now, she nudged *him* with her energy, a little too erotically for my taste. That is *my* woman, you know, Einstein.

– what a death –

Einstein ignored me and played along with her interest. He nudged her rather obscenely, "Sheeyah, my dear Goddess, there is far more to the universe than meets the eye. Much of its activity emits waves of a frequency that you, when you are a human, cannot see, even with a telescope. Take, for example, a radio galaxy."

– to see God die –

"What's a radio galaxy?" she asked.

– to see God die –

Forgetting me entirely, Einstein answered Sheeyah. "It is a galaxy which emits a tremendous amount of energy in the form of radio waves. It is usually a center of violently energetic emission, one which surpasses all other energy sources in the universe."

– die, to see God –

"Is the Milky Way one?" she asked him, oblivious to my anxiety.

"Well, if you want to, you can call it that, but your Milky Way is an extremely feeble radio galaxy, because its emission of radio waves equals less than one tenth of one percent of its optical emission."

{ νουφυλιιηλμ.οοτρσρ67677ψφυοκνκφ }

I heard something. A new sound. "What's that weird garbled hissing noise?"

"That is a radio galaxy, Triad. If the signal from a radio galaxy were played over a loudspeaker, it would sound like a continuous hiss. It contains a superimposition of many different frequencies upon each other."

"So entire galaxies might exist outside of the visual spectrum?" Sheeyah inquired studiously.

"Of course they might, and they do, Sheeyah," Einstein answered her most affectionately. "Entire universes exist at different vibrational ranges. The universe seen by third dimensional beings is just the tip of the iceberg. In fact, a good portion of what you think you are seeing out here you are actually sensing in other ways. Remember that you have no eyes here, not in the human sense. For you right now, none of what you 'see' is optical."

"Wow," I murmured. "Most life forms see so little of what is really here."

"Correct, Triad. Instead, life forms define their realities based upon the illusions they allow themselves to believe in. All they really see are shadows of Truth, shadows of reality."

Shadows on a cave wall beneath a Pyramid in Ancient Egypt? I wondered sarcastically.

He who sees –

"Yeah, right. And human history is practically irrelevant in the Cosmos," I said bitterly. "If cosmic history were to be compressed into a single year of western Earth time, all recorded human history on Earth would equal some ten seconds of cosmic history, at the very most." Somehow I knew this. "So why do we take what happens on Earth so seriously?" I wondered.

"We do?" Sheeyah asked.

"Well, you do anyway, don't you Sheeyah?" My impatience and bitterness spilled out. "Einstein, did you know that during her most recent incarnation, she was actually arrested trying to *protect* the Earth, of all things?"

"I can't help it. It's my favorite planet." Sheeyah tried to defend herself. "Anyway, some of those arrests were just for painting mystical symbols of Truth. I don't really think that calls my arrest."

"You mean defacing property," I corrected her like a stern father.

"No! At first I just thought that my graffiti — those symbols — represented my people and their belief in Earth and her desire to survive. But now I realize that I was allowing those symbols to come out and be seen by a population that had been denied access to Truth for too long. I got those symbols from dreams. I've been dreaming those symbols all my life."

– to see God die –

"Triad," Einstein cut in, "Earth is indeed at the heart of the great cosmic imbalance. You *must* focus on her, on Gaea. Earth needs your help. It puts a lot of pressure on her and her inhabitants, especially the human ones, to work so much out for the entire Cosmos."

Sheeyah made a connection between what was happening in the Cosmos and her behavior on Earth. "So that's why I felt driven to found Earthcult and lead its actions!"

"EARTHCULT?" I yelled, "YOU?" I finally heard clearly what had been alluded earlier in this journey.

"You mean you only now just realized you've been calling *our* safe lands *your* SURVIVOR TERRITORIES? I figured it out in the pyramid. You were using me! Why do you look so surprised? If you really didn't know, what is it you were apologizing for back there?"

"I was very upset. I don't know. I — "

Einstein abruptly yanked our energies down to a slightly lower frequency.

"Discuss this stuff later, you two. Take a look down there. NOW! RIGHT NOW!" he insisted.

We looked. And there, within the womb of the heliosphere, the realm of the Earth's sun, was the Earth, wrapped in her own protective atmosphere as if it were a cocoon. Only, from where we hovered, we could see that that atmosphere was wearing thin and becoming very tattered. It actually looked torn, like a ragged flesh wound.

"Earth is dying, Triad." Einstein touched my energy softly. "She is."

I was hardly listening. I was too stunned by what I was seeing. A giant hand of motionlessness, of ANTI-PRANA, was poised to engulf Earth in its grasp, in the still black wave that wanted to consume my entire Cosmos. I did not want to see this. I did not know how to fight this. This was not part of my cosmic plan. I did not understand the meaning of this image.

Or did I? That still black wave was the opposite of Divine Light — it was the opposite of our Divine Monad, the opposite of the ultimate union between Sheeyah and me. That still black wave of non-motion was the ANTI-MONAD!!!

I was so intensely shocked by this discovery, because, although I had employed the dialectic of polarity at all levels of my Creation below the Monad, I had never planned for an ANTI-MONAD in my Creation. So, how did it arise? Who created the ANTI-MONAD?"

And then I knew — "Oh my GOD! It is indeed Set, my brother, who has chased us throughout the dimensions of the Cosmos, seeking to kill us again and again! He cannot transform the way Sheeyah and I do. He cannot change from his anti-monad state to that of a duad or a triad. He thus cannot become an anti-duad or an anti-triad. He cannot mirror us in all our forms. He is non-existance, non-creation, which has but one state. He seeks to balance his state against my state by stopping my tranformations from Monad to Duad to Triad and back. If Set can stop this process, he can put an end to all motion, all change, all evolution, all Creation, all of me!

As if thrilled to be recognized, Set continued his chant more forcefully:

He who sees ***God's*** *face* **must die.**

What a death were it then to see GOD DIE. . . .

He who sees God's face must die. What a death were it then to –

I heard Earth screaming in absolute anguish. So it is Earth and her inhabitants I hear screaming for help through time, through all dimensions. I shouted: "Gaea! Gaea! Gaea!" Yes, I called out to Earth. But, she did not respond to my feverish cries.

"Shall we take a closer look?" Einstein offered urgently.

Einstein did not wait for an answer as he yanked us much further down in frequency, quite instantaneously, into the squalling and dying heart of Calcutta, India, back on the weakening surface of poor Earth.

*Confronting the Advancing Void*

11

To experience Divine Wisdom at the lofty heights of the highest dimensions is so very simple. But, try to retain such Wisdom, such supreme sentience, back down on the material plane. This is by far and away the greater challenge.

Ω

We regained our senses of smell before we regained our sight.

I heard Sheeyah expressing profound displeasure. "Oh, no, not again. Why is it so dark all of a sudden? I can't see *anything*. No comets, no galaxies, nothing. Our beautiful Cosmos — where did it go? And, oh — oh my, what's that awful, absolutely disgusting, putrid smell?"

Putrid was an understatement. "Dead meat." I was certain of it.

"Dead meat?" Sheeyah sounded a bit bewildered after our profound drop in frequency.

At least I thought that was what we had just undergone. As best as I could tell, we were translated from the height of cosmic energy back down into the dense depths of moribund flesh. Camus would probably have said that we had just moved from the sixth dimension — where a perspective on all the Cosmos can be had, where light racing at the speed of light looks more like it's stuck in the slow lane — back down into the third, the oh-so-humdrum material plane. This crossing of dimensions felt similar but different to the journey through time down the Nile that old Camus had taken us on. Just now, in my return from the Cosmos, I felt myself go through a process of translation, or maybe what is better described as transduction, in which my energy seemed to go through a wringer. I felt miserably condensed, squeezed and pressed inward from all directions.

Moving down in frequency felt like shrinking, like being forcefully stuffed into a prison that was much too small for me. How tragic to be trapped in the material plane. I could not help but be reminded of the famous story of the Black Hole of Calcutta, where the a young Moslem leader, who came to power around 1756 Western Earth time, is said to have imprisoned 146 Europeans in a guardroom that measured 18 feet by 14 feet 10 inches, and that had only two very small windows, in the stifling heat of the Indian summer. 123 of the packed in prisoners died overnight.

I found my claustrophobic sensations surprising, as I still somehow believed that having a physical body meant having more personal space than having no body could ever mean. But I was wrong. A physical body was a restriction, a sort of container which required effort to open. So I struggled with this bizarre metaphysical form of claustrophobia which accompanies the shift downward in dimensions.

"Yes, Sheeyah." I decided to converse with her. "Dead meat. Flesh. Third dimensional stuff. The discarded shell of some soul who has moved on, at least temporarily. The kind of dead meat you were talking about when Einstein was onto that stuff about matter. You remember. He was telling us about the fact that *matter cannot be separated from the flow of its activity* and that, therefore, *if matter ever were really separated from its activity, it would then be dead in the absolute sense — nonexistent.*

We were either somewhere in total darkness or we were totally blind. It seemed that the only thing I could do to feel at home was to go on talking:

"You remember don't you, Sheeyah? Well, you weren't quite getting it." I wondered if I also hadn't quite gotten it, but I didn't let on. "Einstein was talking about something else, but you were focusing on physical death. However, there is no such thing as death, not for living things and not for matter, because matter is always in motion, whether organic or inorganic." Or is there such a thing as absolute death and is this the death Set brings? I could not forget the way the threatening voice of my own brother had haunted me out in the Cosmos.

Sheeyah did not like what I had just said about her not getting it. "Who said I wasn't getting it? Maybe I'm just more physical than you. Physical death, physical sex, whatever. I'm more connected to the energies involved. Or, oh, I don't know," Sheeyah's voice trailed off, "maybe you're right, I don't know. This all seems like a dream to me, a good one turned into a bad one. I want to bang on the door and scream for someone to let me out of here, but I don't know where here is and I can't find a door and I don't know who to scream to. And I feel very strange, detached from myself but in myself, blind and numb and almost insensate, except that I can smell that rancid dead meat."

"Yes, smells like a carcass to me."

"A carcass?" Sheeyah sounded surprised.

"A dead body." It seemed obvious enough to me.

"Wait a minute, I'm starting to see, I can see again. See like I used to on Earth. Oh, God, look! It's — he's dead!"

Quite suddenly, I could also see again. Visual reality had abruptly undissolved itself. Sheeyah instinctively moved toward the rotting body of the dead man.

"Well, don't touch him, Sheeyah."

"Why not? I should at least cover him up, Triad."

"Maybe the local people have their own rituals and regulations for this."

"God, you're so insensitive, Triad. And you really think the local people do this with their dead?"

"It's not that, it's just, it's just, I don't know. I — look, let's figure out what's going on. We're back in our bodies and we're somewhere on Earth. . . . Are you with me on this, Sheeyah?"

"Yeah. Looks like Calcutta."

"Calcutta?"

"Yeah, I'm sure of it, Triad. I was here last fall for a ceremony. Hey, do you realize that we've been almost literally dumped back on Earth from way out in the Cosmos? No fanfare. No ceremonious welcome for us — the Gods. Nothing. Just dumped. Why? I feel like someone just put on the brakes and I'm the skid marks. Wait a minute . . . Where did Einstein go? How did he get out of all this?"

"I'm still with you, but I won't materialize even partially right now."

If I'd had skin, which I'd just realized I had not, I would have been startled right out of it. "Einstein, you're here! I can hear you. What do you mean you won't materialize? You have a choice?"

"Yes. As do you. In fact, you haven't actually materialized yourself," Einstein's voice said.

"Einstein, what does that mean?" Sheeyah still sounded rather dazed. "I can see my hand, but it isn't quite here. I can see Triad, but he looks like — we both look faded, faint. But we're obviously back in our bodies, aren't we?"

"Well, yes and no. You are in a semi-material form, in which your material essence is formed, but not completely actualized. You can see each other, but most of the persons you will meet here on Earth will not see you while you are in this condition."

"You mean these people don't see us?" As soon as Sheeyah asked this question, I realized that we were surrounded by a swarming mass of humanity.

"Most of these people don't see you." We could hear Einstein as if he were standing right next to us.

"I suppose this kind of thing is done all the time." I marveled at the thought. I also vaguely remembered doing it many times myself. Clearly, quite a bit of my amnesia had faded. But, the vagueness of my trans-dimensional memories told me that even though I thought I'd moved out of all of it, some of the amnesia was lingering stubbornly.

"It certainly is," Einstein reminded us. "In fact, this sort of visit is often reported by Earthlings as a visit from aliens," Einstein chuckled, "as if those visiting in this form did not belong here. As if they were really alien to something . . . ."

"So now we look like flying saucer people?" Sheeyah had a marvelously child-like way of interpreting complex esoteric concepts.

"Not necessarily. You look like whatever those who are able to see you choose to see you as. If they can see you at all, if they are that sensitive, they still need a way to record the vision in some understandable manner within their minds. Images, such as those which humans have created of what they call aliens, tend to be a way of explaining the sensations that human minds have of your presence, or of the presence of beings in your form, to themselves."

We mulled this notion over for a while.

Sheeyah looked around and then at the ground. "And what about Earth. Is she here? She should be."

OF COURSE I AM HERE. YOU ARE BACK ON MY SURFACE. YOU ARE STANDING ON ME. IN FACT, YOU ARE STANDING ON ONE OF MY MAJOR LEY LINE INTERSECTIONS.

Sheeyah jumped a bit. "I am? Standing on what?"

A LEY LINE INTERSECTION IS A PLACE WHERE SEVERAL OF MY ENERGY MERIDIANS INTERSECT. IT WAS A BEAUTIFULLY RESONANT POINT BACK WHEN I WAS HEALTHY.

"Resonant? Is your voice resonating out through this point? How can we hear you?"

MY RESONANCE IS NOT AS STRONG AS IT ONCE WAS HERE AT THIS VORTEX. STILL, YOU HEAR ME THE SAME WAY YOU HEARD ME WHEN YOU WERE IN THE CAVE AT THE KHEBIT VORTEX UNDER THE PYRAMID. TELEPATHIC COMMUNICATION.

"I guess most of these people here can't hear you."

MOST CANNOT, BUT SOME DO HEAR ME. AND, EVEN AMONG THOSE WHO DO NOT HEAR ME, THERE ARE MANY WHO FEEL THE ENERGY OF THE LEY LINES WHICH LEAD THEM TO THIS POINT. I HAVE POINTS ALL OVER MY GLOBE WHERE LIFE FORMS COLLECT AFTER FOLLOWING THE VIBRATIONS OF MY LEY LINES TO PLACES OF LEY LINE INTERSECTION. AND, EVEN AMONG THOSE WHO CANNOT HEAR ME AND CANNOT EVEN FEEL MY LEY LINE ENERGY ARE THOSE WHO ARE FOLLOWERS. THEY FOLLOW THOSE WHO EITHER HEAR OR FEEL MY ENERGY. THEY FOLLOW OTHERS, WHO ARE MORE SENSITIVE TO MY ENERGIES, WHO LEAD THEM TO MY MOST RESONANT POINTS.

"The way I used to hear you and feel you and then lead certain people who had chosen to be my closest followers to your special spots?"

YES, SOMEWHAT THAT WAY. ALTHOUGH MY COMMUNICATION WITH YOU HAS BEEN SINGULARLY SPECIAL AND OF THE HIGHEST NATURE, EVEN DURING YOUR MOST AMNESIC STATE OF RECENT INCARNATION. AS LEADER OF EARTHCULT, WHICH YOU FOUNDED ALMOST INSTINCTIVELY, YOUR ASKED ME TO IDENTIFY THE SAFE LANDS OF THE FUTURE, THE REGIONS MOST LIKELY TO BE SECURE — IF ANY REGIONS WOULD BE — DURING THE COMING GLOBAL CATACLYSM. AND I DID SO QUITE SPECIFICALLY.

"Have you done this with other humans as well?"

I HAVE ATTEMPTED THE SAME SORT OF THING AT OTHER TIMES IN HISTORY. WHAT I HAVE LEARNED IS THAT I AM HEARD IN VARIOUS WAYS WITH VARYING DEGREES OF INTENSITY BY THOSE WHO ARE READY TO HEAR ME. THE LISTENER DETERMINES THE

WAY IN WHICH HE OR SHE HEARS ME, MUCH THE WAY THE FEW PEOPLE WHO RECOGNIZE YOU IN YOUR PRESENT STATE WILL DETERMINE HOW YOU LOOK IN THEIR EYES AND MINDS. SOME OF THOSE WHO HEAR ME REALIZE THAT THEY ARE PRIVY TO SECRET KNOWLEDGE AND ATTEMPT TO USE IT FOR THEIR PERSONAL GAIN. THIS IS ONE OF THE REASONS EVEN BENIGN SPIRITS SEEK TO WITHHOLD PORTIONS OF DIVINE TRUTH: TO PREVENT ITS EXPLOITATION.

Sheeyah looked at me accusingly. If I didn't know better I would say that Earth looked at me just the same way. But, did Earth have eyes? I felt a wave of guilt, but I just raised my eyebrows, pointed to myself and shook my head "no" while I shrugged my shoulders. I think this confusing set of gestures distracted Sheeyah and Earth from pressing the point. Which was good, as I didn't want to get into the whole issue of my buying up survivor territories right then. I was still trying to determine for myself how deep my own corruption ran. How much insider information had I been using? And, if I had been using insider information that I held on a subconscious level only, was I guilty of using it? Was I wrong to do something I did not know I was doing? Or am I responsible for not looking deeper inside myself to examine what I knew and how I knew it?

In any case, I needed to communicate with Earth about something else at the moment. "But Earth, Gaea, I saw you in peril from out there. I saw a dark hand, the motionless black wave of anti-prana, reaching to engulf you. I screamed for you and you didn't answer me."

And then I heard it again:

– must die –

"I hear it again! Set. Set has followed us here."

SET HAS BEEN LURKING NEARBY FOR QUITE SOME TIME NOW. SET IS THE DARK HAND WHICH THREATENS TO ENGULF ALL CREATION. MY VERY SOUL IS IN JEOPARDY. ALL PRANA, ALL LIFE FORCE, MAY BE CONSUMED OUT OF EXISTENCE. I WILL THEN CEASE TO BE, AND SO WILL EVERY THING ELSE IN THE COSMOS.

Sheeyah looked doubtful for a moment. "But, isn't this just a growing pain you're having, Earth?"

YOU MUST TRY TO UNDERSTAND THE DIFFERENCE BETWEEN NATURAL GROWING PAINS AND THE PAIN ASSOCIATED WITH THE END OF ALL CREATION.

"What is the difference, Earth? I mean, with Omega Point coming, the cyclical end is near anyway." Sheeyah raised a good question. What did it matter what form of doom we faced if the big apocalypse was approaching either way?

YES, THE OMEGA POINT IS COMING AGAIN. THIS IS PART OF THE GROWTH, DEATH AND REBIRTH CYCLE. THIS IS A NATURAL PROCESS, IN THE TRADITIONAL CYCLE OF THE TIME WAVE, OF DEATH AND REBIRTH OF ALL THE UNIVERSE AND OF ALL ITS BODIES. BUT, HEAR ME WELL:

SET'S ANTI-PRANA IS SOMETHING ELSE. HE SEEKS TO END THE NATURAL CYCLES OF THE COSMOS AND THE TIME WAVE, HE SEEKS TO END TIME, TO COLLAPSE ALL DIMENSIONS TO NOTHING, ABSOLUTE NOTHING. SUCH A DEATH OF ALL THE COSMIC CYCLES MEANS THAT THERE WILL BE NO REBIRTH OF ANYTHING AFTER THIS ULTIMATE OMEGA. SET SEEKS TO WRENCH THIS EVENT FROM YOUR ETERNITY OF EXISTENCE. YOU WILL NO LONGER BE THE ALPHA AND THE OMEGA, THE CYCLICAL BEGINNING AND THE END. YOU WILL NO LONGER BE. SO, IF THIS IS WHAT IS COMING, THIS IS GAEA'S LAST OMEGA.

I was shocked. I still did not want to accept the brutal fact that my own brother could destroy the entire Cosmos. "Gaea can die? The Cosmos can die? But, Earth, Mother Gaea, you, the *anima mundi*, the soul of the world, *must* be able to live on the way we can after our bodies die! And so must the Cosmos you live in! I have ordained this to be so! Both you and the Cosmos can reincarnate. You know this!"

"No, Triad," Einstein interjected, his voice wafting in from the surrounding ether. "While, under most circumstances, Earth can reincarnate and so can the whole of your most Divine Cosmos, not even you will live on or be able to remanifest in any dimension if Set, the anti-prana, swallows you."

"Einstein, what do you mean? It is I who have made the rules. I remember doing so!" I still couldn't accept the notion that my laws were being broken.

"The death of the sort Set brings is not relative. It is not cyclic. It is absolute. It does not fit within the cosmogony of the Divine Light. But come," Einstein shifted gears abruptly, "let us find Camus, Hermes and Nostradamus now. Perhaps the time has come for the further removal of ignorance."

"They're here too?"

"Yes, Sheeyah. As are all the dignitaries. They await you at the Ganges."

In our semi-material states, we followed the distinct yet invisible energy of Einstein into Benares, Shiva's Holy City, at the mouth of the Ganges River, where an uncountably large crowd hovered, sleeping, eating, trading, selling, bartering, washing, and burning bodies. Through the crowd, I could see the dead bodies of the very poor, those who could not afford cremation, being carried unceremoniously into the river and floated downstream.

I could feel among the people a sort of mass resignation, a collective acceptance of misery. For a moment, they all seemed to be in a slaughterhouse line. Their lives here on Earth were their forms of slaughter. Yet, after scrutinizing the scene, what I had thought was resignation began to appear to be anticipation. They were actually looking forward to delivery from their strained existences into another dimension of reality! Their bodies were their last possessions, possessions of which they were going to be quite willingly dispossessed.

I recoiled from the odor of what I assumed was burning human flesh. Had I not still been faintly amnesic, I would have recalled that the burning of flesh was, for the Hindu, a burning away of the illusions which prevent men from seeing Truth. The body is merely an illusion, conjured by the soul to serve as a vehicle in the quest for enlightenment — the seeing of real Truth.

From among the throngs of these people, these people who believed that there was indeed an exit, emerged Nostradamus, Hermes and Camus. I was glad to see some familiar faces, even if my son's was among them. These three elevated personages seemed to fit right in here, amidst the angst of the third dimension. They moved adeptly here, as if at home in this corner of the crowded third dimension.

Nostradamus reached his hands out to Sheeyah and me. "Father, Mother, we have come to show you Earth from the perspective of your new eyes. Let the last round in the removal of ignorance on Earth begin. We initiate our Earthly journey in the nation of India, one of the so-called 'underdeveloped' or 'lesser developed' nations of Earth. Of course, development is in the eye of the beholder. If body mass is any indication of development on the material third plane, then such nations as India should instead be described as 'overdeveloped.' It is in such countries that human populations are increasing at phenomenal rates. 90% of Earth's annual population increase is occurring in these so-called underdeveloped countries. Earth's human population is increasing at a rate of some 90 million a year, with most of this unfathomable massive growth occurring in these lands."

Sheeyah sighed, "Humans are like a cancer on the planet. A disease plaguing Earth."

Earth sighed: WARFARE, PLAGUE AND FAMINE.

Next I knew, Sheeyah was sobbing under her breath and trying all the while to get a few words out between sobs.

I wondered how this son of ours managed to bring Sheeyah to tears again and again. Could it really be his news about overpopulation? I doubted it. I did not think that any of this was news to Sheeyah. Sheeyah most likely had already collected all such figures through Earthcult.

Sheeyah finally found her voice. She embraced Nostradamus. "Horus! Horus! Horus! He is coming here again. Set is after us!! Horus!!" Her voice grew steadily louder. "My baby! My son!"

"Sheeyah, don't be so loud." I warned paternally, "People will think you're talking to yourself and that you're a crazy woman."

"Triad. Look around. Do you think anyone here really cares if I'm crazy or not? They can't see me or hear me."

I looked around. She was right. We had entered a sort of limbo-like night time. People were clustered like waiting animals all over the banks of the river, sleeping or lying down and attempting to sleep. Maybe some of the sleeping bodies were dead and just appeared to be sleeping, the way the one we had almost tripped over was. Maybe some of the dead bodies were sleeping and just appeared to be dead, the way many of them did. I couldn't tell.

I saw some of the people, adults and children, crouching and huddled together, as if to ward off the Earthly night. The youngest ones had the biggest, most aware, eyes, as if they knew better than to even try to believe in the illusions of third dimensional reality that the children of all cultures are taught to believe. These children seemed to know that what they were seeing in this world was only a passing illusion, a shadow on the cave wall. And the cave — the prison of the illusion we call this world — was this existence, this life form in this lifetime. These children seemed to be waiting for the next picture show. So they sat in the calm before the slaughter of life on Earth.

Noting that we were contemplative, Einstein decided to make some instructive comments about India. "Indeed, you are in India, where some of the highest metaphysical Truths and the lowest abuses of these Truths have been woven into one culture. Let me give you a bit of background. It will help you understand why we begin here."

As we watched the pageant of humanity before us, we nodded our willingness to listen.

Einstein proceeded: "Already in 3500 BC, a highly advanced civilization flourished in the Indus River Valley, which is now part of India. In the middle of the second millennium BC, it is said that the Aryans invaded and brought their nature worship to this civilization. Some mix of what the Aryans brought and what they found in the Indus Valley led to the emergence of Hinduism, the true origins of which are secreted away in what modern humans like to call pre-history. Buddhism, in some ways an extension of Hinduism, came later. The founder of Buddhism, Siddartha Gautama or Buddha (the "enlightened one"), was not born until about 563 BC. Legend has it that he was sheltered from the sight of all human misery until adulthood."

I thought momentarily of myself in my real estate developer incarnation. I had sheltered myself from the sight of, or at least the awareness of, all human misery until yanked out of my amnesia. I did not really want to start seeing it now, either.

Einstein was still talking. "When he finally did see misery, he was so shaken that he left his family and all his possessions in search of enlightenment, which he finally found while meditating under a Bo tree. It was then that Buddha realized that all life involves suffering; suffering ends when desire ends; self-discipline and meditation are the keys to mastery over desire."

"Right, Einstein. Buddha was very soothing, wasn't he? Self-discipline will save the officials from having to control these unhappy suffering people we see around us. Of course, starvation would serve about the same purpose: weaken them, break their morale, kill them . . . ." Sheeyah's old sense of sarcasm resurfaced here.

"Sheeyah, not now," I tried to advise her.

Einstein waved me off. "No, Triad. Sheeyah's perspective is relevant here. We must look at the caste system in India for what it is."

I decided to play along graciously. I assumed that such gracious behavior was befitting of a God. "Caste system?" I asked innocently.

"This caste system claims that one returns again and again until one's 'karma' (which simply means 'deeds') has been purified to the level that union with God is possible. In the view of the caste system, bad karma can leave you at the same place or even move you down the evolutionary chain. Good karma can move you upward."

With this coming from Einstein, I had to wonder if Camus, when he had me fooled into thinking he was some naive fisherman, was right when he worried that he could come back as a fish if he killed fish.

Einstein must have heard me. "As with most of Original Truth, the Truth about reincarnation has been distorted continuously in order to allow those in power to control their subjects. Thus the caste system has long been used as a political tool. Why would the masses complain if their suffering and their suppression were the God-ordained way of the Cosmos? Riches, food, land, whatever could be hoarded by those in power, could be hoarded with the explanation that one is born into a particular caste and when that caste is impoverished, this is one's lot in life."

God-ordained? Could I have ever ordained such a thing? Would I have ever mandated that life forms who do not behave appropriately come back as lower life forms? I tried valiantly to remember whether or not I had ordained such a bizarre thing, but I could not.

Einstein seemed to be forcing this information on us. "So the Original Truth about reincarnation has been distorted by humans for political purposes. Yet, the most meaningful aspect of this Truth has made itself known despite its distortion: One's physical existence is merely transitory. The body and what it goes through here is not the whole story. This viewpoint, of course, led its believers to all kinds of religious practices which acted on these principles. Those who did not and do not share this view of reincarnation found and continue to find many of these practices shocking. During your most recent colonial era, when the British colonized India, they found the practices here to be barbaric. But they went too far. They outlawed infanticide and 'sutee' or self-cremation. They attempted to stop those who placed less value on life in the third dimension from leaving that life. They sought to control, by human law, exit from the third dimension."

Nostradamus, who had been fidgeting the entire time Einstein was speaking, interrupted to continue with his own earlier started lecture on the condition of Earth. Einstein grinned at the interruption like a proud and overly tolerant grandfather and sat down right there, folded his knees and closed his eyes. Then my son, the young upstart, took over. "Mother, Father, take a look at the third dimension of reality. It is a messy vision. Your forces are out of balance here. And here in India, problems found around the globe are condensed into a small space. What you see here may be all of Earth in a matter of years. You are looking forward in time."

Forward in time. That's creative. Well, at least he has captured my interest. This overpopulation and ecology stuff usually turned me off.

The kid went on. "You can see by looking around that living standards are very low for these people. Annual income per person in this region amounts to insubstantial pocket change for an hour in the life of your recent incarnations. This is the natural result when economic growth is outstripped by population growth."

I looked around. What living standards? This was living? It was a far cry from the life of material luxury I had known in my recent incarnation. I heard myself remind myself that even my body would eventually decompose like the bodies of all these other people. The thought of the putridification of my flesh disgusted me. I tried to squelch my ongoing claustrophobia, which was being fueled by this material plane crowding. I was surrounded by a sea of excess people, which reminded me of a swarm of flies. Flesh everywhere. Living flesh. Dead flesh. Living flesh waiting to die. Dead flesh waiting to decompose. Some dead flesh decomposing. Some dead flesh burning. At least I hoped it was dead. Was this Hell? The inferno that Dante had described? The human body surely is disposable when we see it in extreme over abundance.

I knew Nostradamus could tell that I had confirmed his message about the crisis of human overpopulation. But he still had more to say. Could this really be my son and not the clerical error of some cosmic sperm bank secretary? "And, Mother, Father, keep in mind that as a country's living standards decline, social unrest and the likelihood of civil war increases. Here, in India, the Muslims and the Hindus have been at war since Britain gave up its colonization of India. Today, around the world, the internal strife of civil wars are the major form of active warfare. Of the 20 million war-related deaths since Earth's World War II, 15 million have occurred in domestic conflicts. Some 85% of these were civilians. Most such wars happen in areas where the population has crowded to the point of about 500 people per square mile, as in Calcutta, where you reentered the material plane of Earth."

"Why would anyone have us land here in India?" I was overwhelmed by all this. I wanted an explanation.

I BROUGHT YOU HERE, TO HAVE YOU LOOK AT MY HUMAN OVERPOPULATION WITH NEW EYES. AND TO SEE HOW HUMANS HAVE SIPHONED OFF AND DISSIPATED THE ENERGY FROM MY MOST RESONANT POINTS, WITHOUT RETURNING IT TO ME.

"The point is, Mother, Father, that overpopulation leads a nation to sell off its natural resources to meet the unwieldy needs of its people, resulting in a profound reduction in the biological productivity of the land, of Earth

Confronting the Advancing Void

herself. Mother Earth is worn down as her topsoil and her forests are depleted by over-cultivation, logging and monocultural farming."

MY POWER TO REPRODUCE, MY FERTILITY, DIMINISHES UNDER THESE CONDITIONS. IN SOME LOCATIONS, IT HAS ALREADY WORN DOWN TO NOTHING. IT IS IN THESE LOCATIONS THAT HUMAN OVERDEVELOPMENT IS WORKING FOR SET, COMPLETELY CANCELING OUT MY PRANA. BUT MY PRANA IS FADING EVERYWHERE. I AM DYING. I DO NOT FEAR A NATURAL OMEGA, A NEEDED REBALANCING, WHAT I FEAR IS AN ABSOLUTE DEATH.

Nostradamus' anxiety was mounting. "Furthermore, my most Divine Mother and Father, where Earth still manages to retain some of her prana, her land is being seriously polluted. And all of the life forms which feed on the land are being poisoned. Here in India, about a third of the cereals, eggs and vegetables have pesticide remnants exceeding the normal limits of tolerance by the human body. Prana is being eroded at all levels of the food chain. Absolute anti-prana, non-recyclable death, is the outcome on all these levels unless you can stop it."

THE FLESH YOU SEE AROUND YOU IS IRREVERSIBLY POLLUTED, AS IS MY LAND IN THIS REGION.

"But this is just a city in India, not all of Earth," I said hopefully.

"Just a foreshadowing of things to come all over the globe in the not so distant future if not already in the now." Nostradamus seemed immune to the shower of flies which surrounded him. Without waving them off, he just kept instructing us, belligerently dedicated to the removing of our apparent ignorance. "The human species has already populated Earth to the level of some 6 billion. By the year 2025, it will be 10 billion. The majority of underdeveloped countries are virtually unable to fully support their populations. By 2025, if not sooner, half of the entire population of these countries will be unfed. This will get worse, as we see evolving in Latin America where already only 7% of the people own over 90% of the agricultural land. All the while, the human population on Earth will suck Earth's prana from her soil. She will be so weakened, her vital energy, her chi, her prana, so depleted, her imbalances will outweigh her self-protective ether. She will be vulnerable to external attacks of all kinds."

INDIA WILL MOST LIKELY BE THE FIRST OF MY LANDS TO GO. METEORITES WILL BREAK THROUGH MY SHIELD, MY PROTECTIVE ATMOSPHERE, BOMBARDING THE INDIAN OCEAN AND FLOODING THE INDIAN LAND MASS, AS I AM SO WEAK HERE.

I could see more dead bodies being put into the river. They simply floated away, slowly, ever so slowly, as if navigating a strange passage in the dark. But then these bodies could not really see; it was the river, the blood of Earth, which directed them.

Sheeyah brushed away the flies that hovered around her semi-materialized mouth. A young Indian man in tattered rags emerged from the crowd and looked right at Sheeyah. He ran up to her and handed her an old green rag. As she reached to take the rag, he touched her cheek and murmured something. Then he raced back into the crowd, which swallowed him hungrily. A mark or tattoo of some kind, located on the back of his leg, caught my eye, but he moved far too quickly for me to see what it was.

"Wait! Come back! This is an old Earthcult arm band!" Sheeyah tried to follow the young man but could not see where he went. She turned to Nostradamus rather than to me for consolation. "He saw me ... What was it ... .? What did he say?" Sheeyah whispered.

But it was Earth who answered her:

YES. HE SEES YOU. HE SAID HE SEES YOU. HE IS ONE OF THOSE WHO CAN.

"But I need to talk with him more. He's Earthcult! I need someone from this world to talk to. I need to get my bearings, to reconnect here, to get back to my work here." Sheeyah ran a short distance into the dense crowd.

I rushed after her and pulled her back out to the clearing where we had been standing with Nostradamus, Hermes and Camus. "Don't wander off, I don't know how I'd ever find you again." I was surprised to hear myself implore her.

She, in turn, looked at me with surprise, as if she hadn't expected to feel my love again. Without hesitation, we hugged each other. We kissed. Indefinite but nevertheless strong sensations ran through and between us.

"Triad, I want my body back. I want you that way. I need you that way. I feel so lost here on Earth now." Sheeyah was still holding me. I could feel her touch but it did not feel like flesh on flesh.

"Sheeyah, I want you too, but I doubt we can materialize enough to have each other even if we can find some privacy," I said, realizing that I longed for her.

Something pulled our attention away from our desperate attraction to each other. What was it? We turned to look at the crowd and, in a very subtle shift in what we were seeing, in a blink of an eye, the entire group

Confronting the Advancing Void

of dignitaries emerged from what had a moment before been a mass of strangers, of unidentified humanity. I was barely surprised. As did Hermes, Camus, and my son, the dignitaries looked strangely appropriate in this setting, as if they belonged here. Each of them, from wherever he or she (I still could not manage to discern most of their sexes) stood in the crowd, formed the customary triangle with his or her hands and then bowed the customary bow to us. A few members of the crowd, including the young man who had delivered the green arm band to Sheeyah, became individual faces for a moment, turned to us and bowed in the same fashion. Then these living people disappeared into the mob again. But the dignitaries remained identifiable.

Hermes spoke. "As you see, we all meet again. We are your Divine Round Table. We will accompany you on a brief tour, a God's-eye view, of the true condition of Mother Earth now. We must make haste. Our search for the symbol of the Grail must proceed immediately in order to restore Truth soon enough to save Creation."

I wanted to ask what Hermes was talking about. The symbols? The keys to Truth which Sheeyah had forgotten to leave behind when Set pursued her? Were we going through all this because of her oversight eons ago? But it did not seem to be the right moment to ask anything.

Hermes was moving his arm in a large round gesture to Camus.

In response, Camus waved his own arm. I gasped when I saw a stream of light, apparently called forth by Camus, pour into the air from the waters of the Ganges River and move through the air toward us. It eventually ran by us, moving like a river, the same kind of river Camus took us to Egypt on. A ghost of the henu boat appeared. It was even larger than I remembered last seeing it, more like a magnificent, although mostly immaterial, ark. Camus spread both his arms up with his palms facing the group of us. We were all immediately aboard the now immense henu ark. Camus then announced, "We are off now."

Something fast happened. I had no time to be nervous. I felt myself disassemble and reassemble almost instantaneously. Amidst the rapid succession of changes my entity underwent, my eyes caught those of that bird on the mast head of the henu ark. It had somehow let me know its name: Sokaris. I saw the deep-seeing cosmic blue eyes of Sokaris. Those were my eyes, welling up with some kind of answer, one I could as yet only partially decipher, to the deepest of all despairs: hope. HOPE. The kind of hope that springs from the greatest of desperation.

As I regained my vision and my semi-material form, I could hear

Nostradamus saying, "Here we are at the high altitude of 8,000 feet, in Addis Ababa, the capital of what Earthlings have called Ethiopia, one of the oldest countries known to the modern world. The Greek historian Herodotus described Ethiopia as early as the fifth century BC."

I heard gunshots. I could see soldiers everywhere against the ethnically diverse mass of people.

Nostradamus saw me watching and added, "You will find at least forty different ethnic groups here in Ethiopia. The potential for clash of values and standards is great."

Sheeyah filled into her semi-material state. "Won't we catch cholera or yellow fever or something? We haven't been vaccinated for anything."

"Worry not on this count, Mother. You are not enfleshed here. You are thus not in jeopardy of plague. Nor are you in jeopardy of death by gunfire. Although disease is a serious problem here, death by gunfire is a far greater threat. This country has one of the largest armies in Africa. It spends close to half of its total budget on military. This is an astounding proportion considering that the people of this country are starving. This is not surprising in this world which has been yang or male-dominated for so long. The emphasis on the military has evolved here in keeping with the rest of the modern world. Together, the nations of the world spend close to one trillion dollars a year on military activities. Many of the world's leaders actually create their nation's militaries for show and then use these militaries as scapegoats and distractions, luring attention away from the other problems of their nations. Collectively, third world countries spend 50% more on military than on education and nearly as much on arms imports as on health. At any given time, there are an average of about 50 wars being waged around the world. Ironically, most of the deaths in warfare are civilian deaths, despite the advancing military technologies which make these deaths virtually unnecessary and almost entirely avoidable."

As if war of any sort was necessary at all . . . . The rifle fire seemed to be getting louder. I saw several wounded children being carried past us in the arms of their distraught and wounded mothers. Nostradamus saw my surprise but went on before I could comment. "And the costs of war are greater than the injuries it inflicts. Imagine how much money would be released were it not spent on what are perceived as military requirements. The world's annual military budget, if spent in other ways, could shift the world away from the edge of man-made apocalypse, cataclysmic annihilation by war, plague and starvation."

"So you think the end of the world is a man-made event?" Sheeyah asked as she tried to figure this out in her own mind.

"Humans make their destiny insofar as they create their own realities. Signs of the apocalypse are all around us. We walk the world and see them. You must agree that what we see are largely man-made conditions or man-made reactions to natural conditions. So many signs of apocalypse being manifested in the third dimension are brought on, not by the gods, but by the unwise decisions of humans. Think about it. In developing countries, 40 to 60 million people die annually from hunger and hunger-related diseases. 950 million people in the Third World don't get the minimum amount of calories per day (2300) needed to sustain working habits. At least half of these people are subject to nutritionally-based impaired mental functioning and damage to their immune systems. In my physical incarnation as Nostradamus, around 1500 AD Western Earth time, the total world population was close to the number that are today seriously malnourished and or die of starvation each year."

More rifle fire was answered by what sounded like several grenade explosions. Men in uniforms ran by like hurried robots programmed to appear vaguely human. A pregnant woman who was bleeding profusely from the gut stumbled by, wailing. Sheeyah went to help her, but could not hold the woman's body as Sheeyah had no physical mass. Unable to see Sheeyah, the woman continued her plagued march to her death. As the woman stumbled forward, her dead fetus fell from the rip in her belly. Sheeyah, broken with compassion, hunched over on her knees and cried. And then I heard Set again:

– God's face –

Nostradamus rushed over to help his mother stand up. He whispered, "You cannot help this woman. She cannot see you. She cannot touch you. You must let her go. This is her fate, her journey. Let her go, Mother. She cannot see you."

Nostradamus turned to me. "The cost of the grenade that wounded this woman and killed her baby could have fed her for a month. And this is just one form of military-related death. We must look much deeper for some of the others. They are less visible." He eyed me intensely.

I wanted to inquire as to the meaning of Nostradamus' last hint, but Camus waved his arm and then the stream of light poured from out of nowhere, running by us again like a river, again the same kind of river

Camus took us to Egypt on. The marvelous ghost of the henu ark appeared. Camus grandly spread both his arms at the group of us and we were immediately back on the henu ark. Then Camus said, "We are off now."

And again, it happened very rapidly. I disassembled and reassembled virtually instantaneously. During the rapid succession of changes I underwent, my eyes caught the glorious blue eyes of the grand bird, Sokaris. Those were my eyes. He screeched "S-karrrr!" I knew his cry was my despair. And, in this moment of communion with Sokaris, of Divine Revelation, I was filled again with the terror-invoking sound of Set:

He who sees God's face must die –

Was that my face I saw reflected in the shattered mirrors between the dimensions?

I regained my vision somewhere in the Middle East. Nostradamus was already at it again. Had he ever stopped talking? Could he hear Set at all?

He went on. "The next war in the Middle East will be fought over fresh water. Localized water conflicts raise tensions continuously and will get worse. In 1967, the Israelis shelled a dam site shared by Jordan and Syria on the Yarmuk River. In 1975, Syria and Iraq almost went to war after Syria and Turkey caused a sharp drop in the Euphrates River by filling reservoirs behind two new dams. This sort of water-based tension is building in locations around the globe. The countries upstream along the Nile contend that it is their right to damn that river. Is it? Who, pray tell, has the right to say? One country may have a surplus of water and mismanage it while, at the same time, another suffers severe drought. Water ownership presents increasing problems. Agricultural runoff and other pollution upstream of nations dependent on the water carried into their regions by rivers severely restricts access to clean water. Who divines the rights to use — drink, dam, whatever the use is — water? And does any nation have the right to pollute its own, let alone another nation's water?"

"Well, it seems that national boundaries are trivial in the face of —" I was interrupted by the booming of Set in my heart.

He who sees God's face must die. What a death –

Confronting the Advancing Void

I felt myself panicking and beginning to lose my mental bearings.

"Father!" My son was aware of what was happening to my consciousness. "Father, you *must* concentrate on what we are discussing here on Earth. This will keep you focused."

I tried, but was confronted with mental and emotional chaos. "It's all just chaos! That's all. It's all breaking down into chaos!" I shouted. I felt insane. I wanted to tear my hair out.

"Yes, Father. Listen to me, Father! The outcome of the degeneration of these Earthly systems we are visiting *appears* to be chaos — the coming of biological, economic and social chaos — around the globe. But be careful of calling change chaos. Change *appears* unpatterned, chaotic, to those who do not recognize it for what it is. Chaos is merely the increasingly rapid onset of bifurcating equilibriums — of many different stable states each breaking into two pieces — yielding two fragments of each original stable state — fragments which are still, for a time, stable, but which no longer share the same pattern of progression with each other. It looks chaotic, crazy, like a runaway system, to those who cannot see the larger picture."

"The larger picture?" I shouted. "The whole of Earth is breaking down, not just one ecosystem or one country or one species or one person's mind! That *is* the larger picture."

Set kept coming into my heart:

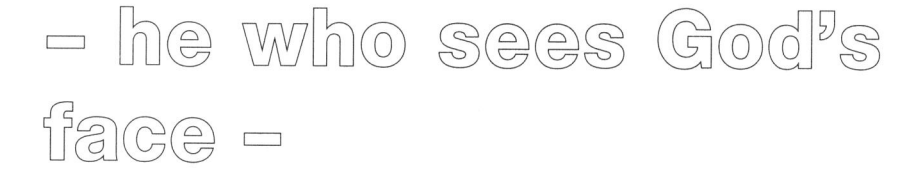

— he who sees God's face —

"No, Father, the picture is much larger than Earth! You must remember to see the largest picture you have created. Only seeing from the largest unit of analysis can help us now. The picture is the whole of your Creation."

"You cannot be my son and argue this point with me! Who do you think you are to claim such Divine parentage? Who? Who? Who?" I was furious, but I was uncertain as to why.

Nostradamus was about to lose his patience with me when I heard Camus shout, "We are off now!" My argument with my son dissolved.

As the dignitaries raised their hands in triangle to their foreheads, I felt myself disassemble and reassemble again. I was getting tired of this dissolution and reformation stuff. My eyes caught those of Sokaris. My eyes. Next I knew, I was screaming, "S-karrrr!!!" but the screams were caught in my throat. Hope was stuck in my throat.

The black hand of Set was trying to strangle me.

I was finally able to take a full breath when we landed in Brazil. I knew I was in Brazil long before my vision returned, by the sound of the soft form of Portuguese being spoken around me. I gritted my semi-material teeth and tried to hold myself together.

"Take a good look, Mother, Father." There he was again, that insolent Nostradamus. "Try to see the poverty here for what it really tells us about the progressive decline of Earth." Nostradamus gestured for us to look around us at the shanty-town slum on the edge of the jungle. "Underdeveloped countries such as this one have borrowed so much money from the developed countries that they now pay an interest of some $80 billion dollars a year. The net capital flows around the globe have been reversed in recent years. During the 1970s and 80s, money flowed, mostly in the form of large loans, from the developed countries (located primarily in the Northern — Yang — Hemisphere) down to the underdeveloped countries (located primarily in the Southern — Yin — Hemisphere) via institutions based in the Northern Hemisphere such as the World Bank and various Foreign Aid programs. Now the interest on these loans which were made to underdeveloped countries is so great, that these countries are sending more money *up* to the Northern Hemisphere than the Northern Hemisphere is sending *down* to them. Moreover, so much of the original loans upon which interest is now being paid was misspent (on military and non-functional industrial projects) that the intrinsic value of the original loans is quite minimal. So, poor countries are paying substantial interest on nothing of great value. In the meantime, the World Bank and other major lenders of the wealthy countries have insisted that recipients of these relatively valueless loans institute domestic economic austerity measures to control further waste and misspending. The result is a major down sliding of social conditions in already socioeconomically deprived lands. This usually leads to an increase in the power of the police and the military in these countries."

I wondered why Nostradamus thought I didn't know this. I saw a ragged child chewing a piece of leather. An armed man in a military uniform strolled by. He looked so out of place. I shrugged, "So they are trading away democracy to pay their debts. So austerity measures are introduced in order to pay off debts. It seems clear that austerity measures diminish the welfare of the peoples of these nations. Although there may be other ways these peoples could raise their welfare, they have not yet found them or the motivation for them — and so social unrest mounts. Democracy does not control unrest. Enter — or reenter — the police state of authoritarian control."

"There's more, Father." He sounded like a boy reciting his lessons to prove that he had studied for an exam. Why to me of all people? What was he trying to prove? "The struggle to pay off the interest on the debt (as well as the debt itself) leads these countries to sell off their natural resources at a frightening rate. In the case of Brazil, where we now stand, massive amounts of lumber and goods are cut out of the Amazon rain forest. The stripping of the forest is done to clear land for agricultural projects, many of which are to be exported for sale into the Northern Hemisphere. As many as 20 million hectares (an area the size of the North American state of Nebraska) per year of forest and scrub are cut."

"Again and again we come to the brutal destruction of the environment," Sheeyah concluded dismally, eyeing barren patches of land where the jungle had been clear cut.

"Yes, again. In fact, at least 40% of Earth's rain forests have been destroyed this way. Clear cutting denudes some 60 acres a minute. Now rain forests are reduced to covering only 7% of the Earth's surface. This shrunken total rain forest area houses 1/2 to 2/3 of all plant and animal species on the entire Earth. It is estimated that by the middle of the 21st century, 250,000 plant species may vanish as a result of clear cutting and other deforestation, monoculture, overgrazing, water control projects, and urbanization. This is a staggering diminishing of the genetic diversity both within and among life forms on Earth. The diversity of the genetic pools of the plants humans use in agriculture stands between them and starvation on a vast and almost inconceivable level. As human population growth degrades the environment ever more, plant species disappear at an alarming rate. Earth's biosphere has lost already many of the genes that keep her crops strong and resistant to drought, pests and other blights. It may be too late to turn the damage around. The diminishing of genetic diversity among many plant species on Earth and the growing rate of human starvation is an inextricably linked and potentially irreversible process. Development is the unraveling — the undeveloping, the devolving — of Earth's intricate biosystem. The third dimension is running amuck here on this planet."

"So genes are disappearing from each species' reservoir?" I asked.

"Yes, and species are disappearing from the Earth's primary reservoirs of life forms. A single endangered river in Brazil is the home of far more species of fish than are contained in all the rivers in the United States. But, remember, Brazil is only one example of planetary deforestation and reduction of biological diversity. At least two-thirds of all Earth's land-dwelling species live in the tropics. The majority of these species dwell in tropical forests which will be leveled during the coming two decades. These species will most likely die off. Africa as a whole lost 23% of its tropical rain forests in a recent thirty year period. The Ivory coast has had two thirds of its woodlands taken off of the face of the Earth in the last quarter century. In many areas, soil loss rates exceed soil formation rates by at least tenfold, and —"

– what a **death** were it then –

I heard Set again. "Stop! Stop! Nostradamus please stop this babble! Can't you hear the anti-prana?"

"Can't you, Father? Can't you hear the source of the threat?"

Camus again waved his arm and a stream of light again poured from out of nowhere, streaming by us like a river, the same kind of glowing river. Again the massive ark appeared. Camus spread both his arms at the group of us and we were immediately on the henu ark. Then Camus again said, "We are off now."

Sokaris looked me in eyes. We screamed "S-karrrrrr!" in unison. We shared each other's terror. We were one.

He who sees God's face must die. What a death were it then to see God die. What a death – what a death – what a death – what a death –

I awoke in what Nostradamus was saying was once the Soviet Union. I saw long lines of solemn people waiting for food. They did not look as if they were benefiting from the so-called freedom they had gained after the dismantling of the Communist regime of the 20th century. I had followed developments here closely during my recent incarnation, as I had awaited the opportunity to buy large tracts of cheap land in what was once the Soviet Union. This entire region had reached critical breaking points — thresholds to chaotic breakdown — in its economy, politics, social infrastructure, and ecology. All balance, all equilibrium, gave way to a runaway trend in which any over-arching stability was replaced by a continuing deterioration of the elements which could promote balance.

But, my higher self knew a great deal about this, as I reminded myself now: *Chaos is not limited to particular geographical regions or spans of time. Chaos is everywhere — it is ubiquitous. And chaos is not unpatterned. It is structured. It is part of the process of rebalancing. When a system deteriorates to an extreme, a radical, often seemingly chaotic, rebalancing is required to make it work on any level. If the system does not regulate itself from within, external barriers, limits, or dangers will do the regulating from without.*

My son had been eavesdropping on my thoughts. "Yes, Father, and this region is still in the process of rebalancing itself." Nostradamus wanted me to look out in another direction, at something in the distant landscape. He directed my attention in that direction while he spoke, "As Boris Yeltsin said when he took over rule of Russia in 1991, shortly after the fall of the Communist Regime, 'We've inherited an ecological disaster.' He was correct. Every major river in Russia is polluted. One-fourth of its drinking water is unsafe. 35 million people live in cities where the air is dangerous to breathe. Only one fourth of the nation's school children are in good health and pollution is blamed. Life spans have dropped precipitously. Look. You can see out there that the Aral Sea is dying. Its waters are slowly drying up; and, the wind is taking up and blowing around the noxious dust which is left behind, dust causing illness and even death upon inhalation. Keep in mind that this sea was once larger than any of the Great Lakes of North America except Lake Superior."

Earth had something to say about this:

I HAVE NEVER SEEN ONE OF MY LAKES GO SO QUICKLY. THIS ONE IS ALREADY TOO SALINE TO SUPPORT ANY OF ITS NATIVE SPECIES.

"Earth is right to be concerned. In a fifteen year period, this lake, or sea as it was called, lost the volume of water equivalent to one and one half times Lake Erie. The Aral Sea was sacrificed by the Soviets in order to turn the Central Asian desert into an agriculturally productive region. The Soviets built an 850 mile Canal to do this in 1954. This and other developments emptied the Syr and the Amu, which were Soviet Central Asia's largest rivers, of almost all their water, cutting off the inflow to the Aral Sea. The climate of the region has been irreversibly altered, with profound changes in weather patterns and extreme oscillations in temperature."

Half listening, I had been watching a lone bird fly toward us from the distant horizon. It seemed to be examining the parched and damaged land. As it flew directly overhead, it swooped low enough for me to get a good look at it. It briefly gazed into my eyes and shrieked "S-karrrrr!" I felt a desperate response well up from deep within my soul and I whispered, "S-karrrr!" back up to the animal. At that moment, a cold hand touched the back of my neck and then tapped me on the shoulder.

He who sees God's face must die. What a death were it then to SEE GOD die.

The chill of absolute death raced through me. In the sky above me, I saw Sokaris falter, his wings losing power. The bird fell several feet as his wings seemed to go limp.

"No!" I shouted. "No! You must live on! You are hope! Sokaris!" With all the power I could summon from within myself, I sent the grand bird some kind of Divine energy to help him regain his equilibrium. I turned to call the attention of the dignitaries to what was happening, but, just then, Camus waved his arm and that stream of light poured out, again from nowhere, carrying in the magnificent, although mostly immaterial, henu ark. Camus spread both his arms at the group of us and we were immediately on board.

I actually disassembled and reassembled before Camus said, "We are off now." Amidst the rapid succession of changes my entity underwent, I saw Sokaris bow a salute to me as he winged away weakly. He looked at me through my own eyes.

- to see God's FACE -

"We have come to Ostravice, Czechoslovakia, my most Divine Mother and Father, where you witness the slow death of a relatively small forest.

This death is basically the result of acid rain. The pollution-related acid pouring down out of Earth's atmosphere is having a catastrophic effect on forests and most terrestrial ecosystems. European nations have been especially hard hit by acid rain. Fish have disappeared altogether from 4,000 lakes in Sweden. 805 of Norway's lakes have been declared technically 'dead' or close to it. At least 20,000 other European lakes have been damaged by acid rain. Acid precipitation effects are not easily measured. There is a long time lag so we tend to deny big impacts. Acid damages leaves and reduces their photosynthetic capacity. Essential nutrients are lost from forest ecosystems. The soil degrades and even dies in the long run as bacterial populations are lost and rates of decomposition are slowed. Higher rain acidity leeches valuable nutrients from the soil including potassium, calcium and magnesium. The soil becomes increasingly toxic. Forests then become more vulnerable to disease and insect attack. 43% of the conifers in Switzerland are now dead or seriously damaged, and 52% of all trees in what was once West Germany are on their way to death from acid deposition as well. 67% of the United Kingdom's trees are suffering from severe damage caused by acid rain. This problem is not restricted to Europe. Forests around the globe are dying. Why don't we see this? Symptoms of such forest death have appeared in Russia, North America, and elsewhere. In industrial countries, air pollution and acid rain have seriously damaged an estimated 31 million hectares of forests, an area the size of the state of New Mexico. Rainfall in Norway is as acidic as lemon juice. The acidification of soils is eventually irreversible. Humanity has poisoned the Northern Yang Hemisphere and has raped the Southern Yin Hemisphere."

"Oh God, must we see more?" Sheeyah sobbed, exhausted.

"Yes, Mother. The temptation is to look away, however, we must see all. Air pollution is at work in many ways, not just here but around the globe. Most of the ozone now found in the lower atmosphere is considered an air pollutant. It is formed by chemical reactions between pollutants already in the atmosphere and sunlight. Ozone produced in this way is an element of photochemical smog. This ozone is extremely caustic. It can damage plastics as well as animal and plant tissue. In humans, exposure to concentrated photochemical ozone can cause headaches, burning eyes, respiratory irritation, and asthma attacks. Exposure to ozone over time can lead to permanent impairment of the lungs. Ozone damages the tissue lining the airways of the lung. Ozone can age lungs too rapidly and can retard lung development in children. We are uncertain of the long term effects of ongoing ozone exposure. Human scientists do know that heavy exercise and exposure of more than six hours in duration increases the risk of damage to the exposed organism even at lower levels of ozone concentration."

"Is that what people mean by the problem of holes in the ozone layer?" I asked with discomfort. Where was Sokaris now?

"No, Father. You are referring to another problem of environmental degradation. Most of the atmosphere's ozone is and should be found in the *upper* atmosphere, between nine and eighteen miles above Earth. This ozone layer shields Earth from some 95% of the sun's ultraviolet rays. Over-exposure to these rays can cause skin cancer. Great concern has been expressed regarding the effect of chloroflourocarbons on the ozone layer. These chloroflourocarbons have the potential of breaking down the protective ozone layer of Earth. When chloroflourocarbons reach the upper atmosphere, the sun breaks them apart and then their fragments react with the ozone, depleting it from the atmosphere. Although there are bans on such chloroflouro compounds, these bans are not internationally enforced. Large holes in the ozone layer already exist over both poles and are expanding significantly over at least the south pole if not both. While humans engage in debate regarding the speed at which this development is occurring and its main causes, the problem of the degradation of the ozone layer continues. Any way we look at it, the atmosphere of Mother Gaea, our Earth, is breaking down."

- what a death -

Set was here to kill me. Me, Earth, Sheeyah... and all Creation. I could feel it. I opened my mouth to yell for help.

But Camus quickly put his finger to his lips as if to say "Shhh," and then waved his arm. The river of light poured out from nowhere. The henu ark reappeared. Before Camus had spread both his arms, the group of us were on the ark. I heard Camus say, "We are off now" as I disassembled and reassembled. I thought I saw the eyes of Sokaris. I was certain that I had heard his wings beating on the wind. Or was that my heart beating? Sokaris seemed to be just a few beats ahead of Set and so did I. Set pursued us, as if we were one in the same, the bird of hope and I. Set, the anti-prana, black wave of non-motion, pursued us all.

My eyes opened into a misty night on Earth, a night in which the rain fell in black oily drops through the neon lit streets and flashing buildings of Tokyo, Japan. Through the oozing black rain of industrial pollution, I saw that we were standing in a busy fish market. People were filing everywhere in dull obedience as if they were ants moving according to a great plan.

Among the ancient Asian faces, I saw the timeless beauty and grace of the ages as well as the timely decadence and corruption of modern materialism, both extremes dressed in chic western styles.

"So, my Divine parentage, you are now in a fish market where the famous Bluefin Tuna is sold. Jumbo Maguro, the North American Giant Bluefin Tuna, is an Epicurean delight. It is said to melt in the mouth. The Bluefin is an amazing life form. It is probably the most advanced of Earth's 20,000 fish species, renowned for its speed and endurance. The Bluefin is champion among migratory fish in both speed and strength. It is hydrodynamically superior. The Bluefin has been a long time on Earth and has fascinated man throughout history. Aristotle wrote of the Bluefin Tuna. Pliny the Elder described this tuna as a remarkable species some 20 centuries ago. And it is remarkable. By the age of 15, a Bluefin has swum over a million miles. But alas, because its migration and spawning and feeding grounds are so predictable, its existence is in jeopardy. It is mercilessly and relentlessly fished while migrating from spawning areas to feeding grounds. Once caught, the Bluefin is often kept in captivity for some time because it can gain much more weight in captivity and sell for far more magnificent sums. An investor may thus have $5,000 invested in just one of his Bluefins. With the Bluefin Tuna in short supply, and in the face of insatiable demand, its dollar value is rising phenomenally. Controls on fishing — or what we should call Bluefin mining — are not stringent enough. Japanese fishermen search the world for the amazing Bluefin, who can and does travel a hemisphere away from home. The marked drop-off in the Earth's Bluefin population signals man's unwitting exploitation of his own food reserves as well as the murdering of an entire species. Bluefin farming, which raises this free swimming animal who loves to traverse the globe in the cruel confines of captivity, is considered the answer to the problem of Bluefin die-out."

"Yes, that's the logic of man," Sheeyah muttered. "Create an artificial man-made answer to any degradation of the environment. Earth is merely a development opportunity." She glanced at me, but without malice. "Keep the business going at all costs, of course," she added.

"But, my Divine Mother and Father, we must ask what it means when man domesticates the Bluefin? What turning point has life on Earth reached?"

With that, Camus gestured for us to board the Bullet Train just leaving Tokyo. We did so. Soon, we rolled swiftly through carefully cultivated rice fields in the Japanese countryside, where every last bit of land is precisely used, toward the Bluefin tuna farms.

But something was slowing even the Bullet Train. A wall of nothingness which, as it grew stronger, was increasingly difficult to penetrate. That chanting coming from this nothingness became gruesomely loud:

What a **DEATH** were it then. What a death –

We were in imminent danger. Camus beckoned us all to stand and waved his arm with urgency. The stream of light poured from out of nowhere right into the train. As the ghost of the henu boat appeared, the train evaporated. Camus spread both his arms at the group of us and said, "We are off now." In the condensed moments before landing back on Earth, I became vaguely aware that we, and our ark, were riding on the back of a gigantic bird — Sokaris! And Sokaris was the light we rode!

I could feel his heavy load.

Where could poor Sokaris hide? Where can Divine light hide? It is not in its nature to do so. Light does not hide.

Next thing I knew, we were being told by Nostradamus that we were, "in Los Angeles. Here you will see that inhabitants of North America are certainly not immune to responsibility for the demise of Earth. The depletion of natural resources and the hedonistic fueling of grave imbalances in the ecological makeup of the biosphere are prevalent here as well. For example, Mother and Father, water tables are dropping here, but water waste and water overuse continues. This too is a global issue. At this time, 97% of all water on Earth is salt water. This means that only 3% of the water is fresh water. And there is much less than this 3% available for consumption by life forms requiring fresh water. Over 75% of all Earth's fresh water is unavailable because it is frozen into her polar caps. 22% of the fresh water is stored in the ground for much of its journey on Earth. Only about half of this ground water is on the surface of the Earth at any given time. Most rural areas are dependent upon ground water for consumption. Unfortunately, much of the ground water available to them is already polluted with pesticides which are difficult if not impossible to remove from the water supply. Enormous quantities of municipal sewage and industrial discharges are let into the water supply one way or another, poisoning more of the water than humans dare to admit to themselves.

Moreover, irrigation accounts for about three quarters of all fresh water usage. In the process of using or using up the available fresh water, over half of it is lost each year in transportation and storage processes. Garbage pollution of water is a major problem. For example, New York City throws out 200,000 tons of garbage weekly. This comes to more than 25 times the volume of the Great Pyramid at Giza. Half of it ends up as part of the world's largest landfill, 14 miles from the city they call Manhattan. Until a clean up at the beginning of the 1990s, more than a million gallons of fluid were seeping from this landfill into nearby waters every day. When landfills are full, they are sealed with clay caps and, eventually, golf courses (which, by the way can use up a million gallons of water per day), airports, even wildlife refuges, may be built on them. Landfills can cost as much as one million dollars an acre to construct, as they require a variety of layers and other controls to even begin to control the pollution they cause. Unfortunately, only about a third of all industrial waste is recycled, detoxified or destroyed. The remaining two thirds is disposed of through injection wells, pits and land fills, all of which risk seriously contaminating ground water."

"It seems to me that the disposal of material things such as waste is inherent in third dimensional reality." I added my viewpoint here, trying to distract myself from Set.

"Well, yes Father, it may be inherent, but certainly more effort could be made to manage the problem efficiently. Even in the U.S., which thinks of itself as progressive in the area of environmental protection, 80% of all citizens live near a waste site. In all major U.S. cities, municipal solid waste volume is exceeding disposal capacity and the volume of such waste is increasing at almost exponential proportions. America has been called the 'throw away society'. Its citizens generate more waste per capita than any other country, doubling the next highest. The packaging alone on food and other merchandise constitutes half of all the volume of household waste. The United States recycles only about 10 to 15% of its waste. Greater recycling is definitely possible, as only 15% of the existing land fills in the United States are considered state-of-the-art. Germany recycles about 15%. Japan about 50%, although even this amount of recycling still leaves massive amounts of human garbage on Earth."

I could hear it again.

He who sees God's face –

I looked at Camus with that panic back in my eyes. Camus beckoned the river of light with a wave of his arm and it poured from out of nowhere, again bearing the glistening ark which we boarded instantaneously. And then I disassembled. In the fleeting moments before I reassembled, I neither saw nor sensed the presence of Sokaris. Was he dead at Set's hand or had he just flown on ahead?

– *must* die. Must die. Must die. What a death were it then to see God die.

My thoughts raced through me, but I seemed to have no me for them to race through. I felt as if my face, my self, my soul was being pressed up against an intergalactic mirror. And it looked as if there was *nothing* there — *no reflection*! But, my God, no! Was I seeing my own face now?

He who sees God's face – God's face must die. What a death were it then to see God die. He who sees God's face – God's face must die. What a death were it then to see God die. He who sees God's face – God's face must die. What a death were it then to see God die.

Before I could answer myself, I had rematerialized, by the sound of things, in a Latin American country. Some form of Spanish slang was being spoken around me. Again, my vision returned after my sense of smell did.

When I could see again, I looked around quickly. The henu ark was gone. Sheeyah was crumpled on the ground some distance away. I was taken aback, not so much at the sight of her like this, but at the fact that I had generally forgotten about her as we toured Earth. Had she been declining all along? How could I have missed her weakening condition? Hermes was kneeling over her, praying, as best as I could tell. Einstein sat with his legs crossed, apparently in deep meditation.

Just past Sheeyah stood Camus with his hands extended before him. Other sets of hands were appearing out of thin air and touching his. Each time hands did so, another of the dignitaries would arrive. They continued to do so, in one long procession, each after touching his or her hands to those of Camus, until there were 49 including Camus, Nostradamus and Hermes. For some reason, I counted the dignitaries before daring to ask Hermes:

"What is wrong with Sheeyah?"

Hermes looked up at me from where he knelt at her side. "She was snagged on the edge of the third dimension when we dematerialized to transport."

"Is she hurt?" Of course she was, but I had to ask.

"Yes, she is." Hermes sounded certain of this.

"Where?" I still hadn't seen signs of a wound.

"There is no flesh wound. No injury to her material body."

"So she isn't hurt." Maybe she really wasn't hurt.

"Yes she is injured. Her spirit is torn," Hermes spoke softly.

I was quite upset at the concept. "Can she die?"

"What death?" asked Hermes quietly.

"Either. Relative or absolute. Can she die I said." I felt numb, just numb, now.

He who sees God's face –

And then I felt anguish erase my numbness. "Sheeyah, come back! Come back! Don't hang on to the physical plane! Don't hang on to the third dimension! It ties your soul to a place where it can't be strong!"

I could see people blessing themselves at some kind of roadside altar. It was tucked into some boulders which seemed to surround it protectively. An ironwood tree grew into and around the boulders, enmeshed in a frozen kind of love making.

BRING SHEEYAH HERE, TO THIS MEETING OF LEY LINES. I CAN CLEAR HER CHANNELS FOR HEALING.

I did as Earth requested, dragging her and placing her crumpled body at the altar. Then a marvelous thing happened. A ray of light wafted up from the ground and covered Sheeyah like a blanket. I would not have believed what I was witnessing only a short time ago, when I was just some real estate incarnate, selling land but not knowing Earth. But now, I was more amazed at my finding what I was seeing totally credible than at what I was seeing. So I saw Earth pump branching veins of energy, in the form of light, into Sheeyah's semi-materialized body.

ROLL HER OVER ON HER BACK.

I followed Earth's instructions. Then Earth's energy poured into Sheeyah's forehead in a steady stream. I could see the red inflamed light of a wound in her essence as Earth's line shone through it.

"Is that where she is injured?"

"Yes, that chakra has torn open and essence is being lost from the wound."

"Heal her. Please. Heal her," I begged.

– to see God die. What a death were it then –

SHE IS SUFFERING *MY* WOUNDS. SHE HAS TAKEN ON THE DEPLETION OF MY ENERGY FROM ONE OF MY VORTICES. HUMAN ILLNESS SO MUCH MIMICS THAT OF THE WORLD SOUL. AS DOES THE ILLNESS OF THE GODS.

"Earth, are you also caught on the material plane? Snagged on the third dimension?" I was unnerved at this realization.

YES. I CANNOT BEAR TO LEAVE THIS PLANE. I HAVE BECOME SO VERY ATTACHED TO MY BODY.

"You must be willing to let go to have a choice regarding when you depart. You must be willing to let go," Hermes insisted.

I HAVE NO CHOICE. MY CHILDREN HAVE ABUSED ME. MANKIND HAS TAPPED MY ENERGY AND DISSIPATED THE POWER OF MY VORTICES.

"Save Sheeyah, please. Set waits to take her," I begged again.

My son emerged from the background to speak. "Let him have *me*. Let Set have *me* then."

For the first time, I felt that I cared for my son. "You, Nostradamus? You would die for your Mother? This is not merely death of your body. You have undergone that so many times. This is death of your essence!" Could

I let him go? Did I have to make such a wrenching trade?

Son Nostradamus heard me asking myself these questions. "You have no choice, Father. You have not forsaken me. I have forsaken you. ***The time has finally come for the removal of my ignorance!*** It is time that the energy of your Son be eliminated from your Cosmos. We, Father and Son, have together outweighed the yin, the female force. Our yang force has upset the balance of all Creation. I must go to allow the correction. The time has come for the removal of even my ignorance. I will give myself to Set in place of my Mother, in hopes that this will buy time for a rebalancing to strengthen the Cosmos in the face of Set's anti-prana."

With that, Nostradamus pulled his Mother from the altar and lay himself there. "Earth, let me pass away, cease to exist in all dimensions, to make room for the new child of the Duad. Do not heal my wounds. Offer me up to Set now."

Sheeyah began to come around. As her eyes opened, she saw Nostradamus rising into the air as if being crucified. His life force was diminishing as we watched.

Sheeyah was horrified. She had seen her son crucified at other times in history, but now he was going to die an absolute death. She struggled to stand on her weak legs and grabbed for her son, screaming, "HORUS! HORUS! DO NOT LEAVE ME!!"

All she could reach was the legs of her son who was floating quite some distance above the ground. He was bleeding red light from his palms.

"Triad, stop him! Stop him! Our son is disappearing! He will no longer exist in any dimension! Our Triad will die! Triad!"

She looked at me in despair.

"There is nothing I can do, Sheeyah." I was entirely helpless, impotent. And miserable. This was the absolute crucifixion, the only potent crucifixion.

She turned back to Nostradamus as he began disappearing. It was clear to us that he was not dematerializing and moving to another dimension. He was ceasing to exist. His energy was ceasing to move. The anti-prana was consuming him. A crack opened in the air behind him. Into it he disappeared: his feet disappeared first, then his lower torso, then his hands and arms and upper torso, finally his neck and head. The pool of red light which had bled onto the ground also faded away. When the last of him disappeared, a gleaming round stone fell out of the air where he had been. Sheeyah knelt to the ground to pick it up.

After gazing at it for a moment, Sheeyah handed it to me. The stone was the most beautiful crystalline emerald I had ever seen in all my journeys of the Cosmos. It was marbled with veins of blue topaz or some kind of stone far more iridescent than topaz running through it.

HORUS CARRIED A MEMORY OF EARTH WITH HIM WHEREVER HE TRAVELED IN THE COSMOS. NOW HE HAS LEFT IT TO YOU, SHEEYAH.

But Sheeyah had fallen to the ground and was writhing in pain. I went to her and tried to help her sit up. Hermes came over to touch her.

"Will she die too?" I asked him numbly. Perhaps Nostradamus' sacrifice was not enough. I had grieved her death before. But would this be the absolute end of Sheeyah — the end I had never, never really believed in?

– WHO SEES GOD'S FACE MUST DIE –

I could hear anti-prana waiting in the wings.

– what a death were it then to see God die –

Now it was my turn to anticipate grief. "No! No! Sheeyah, don't leave me! No! No! Don't let him take you." I could feel my fear pulsing through my semi-materialized body. I could feel anti-prana looking over my shoulder.

I had forgotten where I was. A very short, very brown, very wrinkled old woman whose hair was knitted into long white braids limped up to the altar. She glanced in our direction, not seeing us, I assumed. She placed rocks on the ground before the altar and sang some indecipherable chant. Then, to my surprise, she stood up, turned to us and came over and knelt down by Sheeyah. She touched Sheeyah's cheek.

Sheeyah opened her eyes. "You see me," she mumbled weakly.

"Yes," the old woman answered, pulling her shawl off of her left shoulder and half way down her left breast, where she revealed the mark, the same tattooed symbol I had found on Sheeyah's breast back what seemed to be an eternity ago, on my yacht. What a brief but happy time. "Earthcult," the old woman added in a heavy accent.

"I am dying," Sheeyah said.

The old woman rose and beckoned to Hermes to stand some distance away with her and speak.

"She will die, cease to be in all the Cosmos, unless she conceives the new offspring of the Duad very soon. You must insist. All Creation is in jeopardy. Only the conception will seal away the rip in Creation through which anti-prana is reaching."

Hermes nodded solemnly. And then he had a question for the old woman. However, before Hermes spoke, she pointed to a shack. Hermes nodded again and called me to his side. He spoke to me with deep but calm urgency.

"Here at this point in universal time, all Creation stands in limbo. Only the reinstatement of the Divine Triad will preserve us. Prana is perpetuated only if the light bears offspring."

I didn't get his point. "I don't get you Hermes, what do you want me to do?"

"Take her there," he pointed to the shack. "Conceive a child. Now."

"What? What *is* this? This is too weird for me," I said, shuddering.

"There is no time for doubt or debate. Go," Hermes insisted.

I looked around. The dignitaries were filing toward the shack.

"I will help you carry her."

Hermes led me back to Sheeyah. He and I picked her up and carried her into the shack. There was nothing in it except a collection of herbs hanging from the ceiling. We put Sheeyah down gently on the very hard very cold Earthen floor. I looked at Hermes, embarrassed, perplexed and vexed. Hermes responded by forming that triangle with his hands, holding them to his forehead and bowing to me. Then he turned and walked out. I followed him as far as the doorway.

I felt what I can only describe as stage fright when I saw that the dignitaries now stood in a large triangular formation around the shack. One by one, in succession, the dignitaries formed that same old triangle gesture and bowed that same old way. When they were all standing again, I saw that their eyes were all closed. Hermes assumed his place among them and closed his eyes too.

I went back into the shack. I saw a large piece of old cardboard which I gathered was used as a door. I moved it to block the door. It blocked most of the light as well.

I felt very uncomfortable about this. Forced sex. And all those people standing around outside, waiting. Seemed very primitive. I didn't think I could do it. But then I heard a voice. It was Earth.

YOU MUST HURRY. YOUR CREATION IS DYING. ALL WILL END UNLESS YOU CONCEIVE LIFE AGAIN NOW.

Although I was feeling quite numb, I sensed the ultimate urgency. I went to Sheeyah and roused her from her semi-comatose sleep.

"Sheeyah, wake up. We have to do this."

"What?" she mumbled, still obviously weak.

"Make love. You know, exactly what you've been asking for and worrying that we'll never have again."

"We won't, I'm dying."

"No, you won't die. I will save you. Just make love with me."

She perked up a bit. "Some line, Triad, where'd you learn that one?" Even in her weakened state, she had a sense of humor. "Who do you think you are, God?"

I began to kiss her and disrobe her.

She was definitely not on my wave length. "It won't work, I'm dying and we don't have real bodies anyway."

SHEEYAH, YOU CAN FULLY MATERIALIZE NOW IF YOU WISH. JUST SLOW YOUR VIBRATIONS DOWN. SLOW TO FULLY ENTER THE MATERIAL PLANE. THINK DENSE.

I think it was an involuntary act, as if she were suddenly possessed, but Sheeyah complied and closed her eyes and began to hum. The hum started out as a high one and then slowly worked down two octaves. I could see her become more third dimensional as she did so.

When she opened her eyes, she looked at me and immediately spoke back to Earth. "Why isn't Triad moving into the physical plane as well?"

THIS IS NOT NECESSARY. IN FACT, HE BRINGS THE POWER OF ONE FROM THE DIVINE SPIRIT OF THE MONAD INTO YOU FROM BEYOND THE THIRD DIMENSION.

Earth seemed to have left us alone. I went back to kissing Sheeyah.

She pushed me away. "I can't. I just can't."

"You must or you will die."

"I can't do it on command, Triad."

I could see her folding over in pain again and feel her energy disappearing. I felt myself suddenly desperate and crazed. I grabbed her to try to keep her awake. I shouted, "Sheeyah! Don't die. Don't! You will take all Creation with you!"

She didn't respond except to weakly wave me off. I don't know what got into me, but I began tearing her clothes off. I felt some kind of primitive urge to rape her.

I had just about stripped her when she mustered up enough energy to push me away and yell, "Stop, Triad."

I stopped and was ashamed of myself. I had never forced myself on a woman, at least not as far as I could remember. I looked at her, still feeling the savage urge to have her and yet controlling it enough to feel remorse and ask her, "What? Why? Don't you know we must?"

"If I do not agree, then we mustn't," she argued.

"What? How can you say that *now*?"

"Easy, Triad," she said in a hoarse whisper between gasps for air. "I'm finally saying it to you. Maybe I've waited eons." She seemed to be trying to hold onto the last vestiges of her strength to make this statement. It must have been important to her. "I'm not sure, but I suspect that the terms on which all Creation began were balanced in your direction. I have been struggling with you ever since."

"What do you mean? We founded Creation together, Sheeyah, I admit it. We were the Monad together and formed ourselves by mutual consent in the Duad."

"Triad, you cannot perpetuate a universe on the basis of rape. I only give my consent if my terms are met."

"Your terms?"

"Yes, Triad. I would rather die and take all Creation with me than go on this way."

"This way? What on Earth do you mean?"

I heard a rumble in the background. I recognized it as Earth quaking.

OF COURSE YOU ARE ON EARTH.

"Your yang force must live in balance with my yin, not outweigh it."

"Sheeyah, all this Earthcult stuff makes no sense to me. Just tell me what you want."

"We will have a girl this time."

"A *what*?"

"I'm tired of the completion of our Triad always assuming the male gender, the yang force. It is time to make the cornerstone of our Divine Triad, our manifestation, female."

I realized what a profound negotiation I had entered in order to save the Cosmos. "We can't do that. All our manifestations have been male forces."

"Sorry then. You can't have me, you can't rape me. I will not conceive. I will die and take the balance of all Creation with me. I will let Set have me rather than continue to live in a yang-dominated Cosmos."

"Oh for God sakes, O.K. whatever you say, let's have a girl."

I didn't really mean this. I figured it would be a son anyway. I had always had sons. I had always remanifested Nostradamus. I had always manifested the Monad in yang form through Sheeyah. Her yin was merely the vehicle of my delivery of my self into the Cosmos. The spreading of my Creation was my Divine project.

But agreeing, at least in words, to let it be a female this time got things moving. We kissed and made passionate love. We ended in a sitting position, I, deep inside her, holding her tightly, a cloud of the most phosphorescent light I had ever seen filling our shack.

I knew she had conceived. I could feel her life force return. I could feel the balance of yin and yang, of all Creation, shift.

But, would this be enough to stop Set and allow us to move through the next Omega Point into the next Alpha? Would this guarantee yet another new beginning and the survival of my —- our — Creation?

Having no answers, I passed out.

Part 5

•

Transcending the Time Wave

12

Physical forms are representations, or models, of the energy which exists throughout the dimensions. For example, what you find crystallized in your material plane is an indication of how energy can be organized at higher levels of the Cosmos. A crystal is an amazing energy structure in which energy is held in a restraining format. Your Earth's crust is over 80% crystalline. And, Earthly organic life forms make extensive use of crystalline structures at all levels of evolutionary complexity. The human brain, one of biological evolution's higher achievements, is rich in magnetic crystals. Despite their prevalence, crystals have been both worshipped and misunderstood by humans.

Power centers on planet Earth are often centered over large crystalline deposits, storehouses of energy, embedded within the Earth's crust. The initial capital of Atlantis was located in what you now call the Bahamas, in the vicinity of what you now call the city of Bimini, and had an unusually great abundance of crystalline deposits, as that part of Earth continues to have.

The Royal City of Atlantis was later moved to another major power center, set over a concentration of crystalline deposits, Terra — the Island you now call Santorini — in the country which has been called Greece for many centuries. Little of Santorini currently remains above sea level. However, I expect to see this magnificent power center resurface one day when your Earth's axis again shifts.

You Earthlings should heed this. YOU MAY WANT TO RELOCATE YOUR SOULS OR YOURSELVES IN ADVANCE OF THE UPCOMING CATACLYSMIC POLAR SHIFTS. IF SO, MOVE TO A SAFER ZONE OF YOUR OWN MIND, OR OWN PLANET, OR, SHOULD YOU WANT TO BETTER ENSURE YOUR SURVIVAL, CONSIDER CAREFULLY THE OPTION OF MOVING OFF EARTH INTO ANOTHER DIMENSION OF REALITY, WHERE YOU WILL FIND THE ULTIMATE SURVIVOR TERRITORY.

Ω

I awoke to a dank, pitch blackness that I was soon to recognize as being the inside of the ancient Egyptian coffin into which my son had closed me some eons ago. For a few moments I was, as I had so many times been, absolutely certain that I was physically dead. I could not feel any physical sensation whatsoever. I could not feel my body or even find my hands to try to touch my body. I wasn't breathing. My heart wasn't beating.

I numbly decided that I had decayed to dust in the eons since I had been encased alive. But was it really eons?

"So the dead do think," I thought, as I settled into what I expected to be an inert eternity.

After I listened to a long measure of nothingness, a loud scraping noise intruded into my solace. I was so startled that I was overcome by a sudden-sit reflex. I most painfully and abruptly became aware that I was not at all disembodied when I banged my head on the inside of the coffin lid.

Reminded of the sheer misery of simple physical pain, I sank back down onto the cold stone floor of my coffin. It was then that the recurrent claustrophobia struck and I began to scream and beat my fist on the lid of my coffin: "Let me out! Anyone out there? Let me out!"

A rather brutal rush of icy air blasted at me as someone or some force edged the lid open. It was still pitch dark. The sound of heavy air flowing out of my coffin and mixing with the atmosphere of the King's Chamber was all I could hear.

I felt my way out of the coffin like a blind man, only less adeptly. A vague light wafted in like dust on a still breeze. In the dim shadows, the profile of another coffin — one I then remembered as being Sheeyah's — became visible. I moved toward it, hopefully. But, it was empty. My heart sank to the bottomless depths of my eternal soul.

I nevertheless asked of the darkness. "Anyone here?" There was no reply.

I did not want to be alone here. Only after a slow and deliberate search, I found the door to the passage through which Sheeyah had once led me. Now I entered its forbidding darkness without hesitation.

I experienced no emotion as I felt my blind way into the passageway. This time this tunnel was familiar. But now I was really alone. Without her. Without that woman I had pursued like a love-sick school boy. Without the woman I had followed into the journey of a lifetime — of a billion lifetimes.

My heart pounded. I kept moving, making my every careful step the subject of my full focus rather than allowing myself any contemplation of all that had passed before my eyes in the forever through which I had just traveled.

The empty narrow space through which I was moving seemed to become thicker and thicker as I proceeded, until I felt as if I were moving through a tunnel filled with an infinite sludge. My struggle to move through the sludge of this space became so complete, so total. Every step became a major proposition. Finally, I crouched against the wall and curled up in a fetal position. I was so very, so infinitely, tired that I could not cry. I was too devoid of emotion to cry real tears. But crying of any sort would have helped.

I continued to crouch there. More strained time passed, in a miserably slow way. I did not close my eyes. I was not at all tired. I could not find any sleep within me.

More time passed. I still crouched there . . . .

And more time passed . . . I finally stood myself up very carefully, as if I were fragile and might break, and I proceeded, on automatic, on through the tunnel of darkness as if someone had called me.

But I listened. I heard no one. Not in the tunnel. Not in my mind. The sheer futility of this absurd exercise filled me. I could just as well die here, disintegrate here and depart from this miserable, mundane third dimension now. I just didn't like the job of moving around here in the material dimension anymore. A body is a burden. I found myself contemplating suicide out of boredom. I was certain I could just will myself to leave my body. I could feel the instinct to do so rising within me. I found this thought of suicide a majestic relief.

"But wait. Wait." I muttered to myself. I was taken aback at the guttural sound of my mortal body's voice. "I'll wait." I answered myself, just to hear my voice.

I moved on through the dark, shaking my head despairingly at the worthlessness of it all. As I moved, I kept looking for something, a sign, any hint at the coming of the end of this unendurable passage. I went on like this for hours, or days . . . forever, I think.

And then I saw the light! It came upon me so very suddenly that I saw it only moments before I was within it.

In the light was a woman. In the instant I saw her, I knew why I had postponed my decay. There waited Sheeyah, alive, well, glowing, enrobed and clearly my queen. She stood in the center of the sphere of glistening white light at the mouth of the tunnel. And the dignitaries were there waiting for me as well.

The light was so beautiful, I wanted to absorb it, to drink it, and to have it fill me. I wanted to swim in it. So, I moved toward this light, and I knew that I had to go out beyond the end of this passage, out of the tunnel of my arduous life, into the light.

As I stepped into the whiteness, someone placed a glorious cloak, matching the one Sheeyah now wore, over my shoulders. All the dignitaries turned to me and formed their traditional triangle gesture.

As they did so, Sheeyah extended her hands, beckoning me. I acceded to her gentle command and moved into the position by her side, the position of King of the Cosmos.

"So you finally decided to join us, my dear Triad?"

"You mean you've been here a while?" I wondered silently why she had gotten there first, but no one seemed the least bit interested in answering this silent question of mine.

"Seems like centuries to me, Triad."

I looked around. The heads of the dignitaries were still lowered into their triangular fingers. The place felt so empty without Nostradamus.

"I know. I feel his loss too, Triad. He was our son."

I looked into her face. So very noble, so very queenly. Was I again seeing her face for the first time? Or had she actually changed, metamorphosed?

"Of course I've changed, Triad. I carry our first female child." Sheeyah opened her cloak a bit to remind me.

She looked very pregnant. I was stunned. I'd forgotten about that bit. More of my godly amnesia? Maybe, but now I remembered the bizarre negotiation quite immediately and remembered my going along with the whole thing in order to save Sheeyah, and the Cosmos, from Set. I mean, I knew we had conceived a child — but a girl? I really doubted it.

Sheeyah could hear me thinking, I could tell. She just looked at me with a subtle smile and shook her head to the negative.

How could she be so certain and I be so unclear about this? Who had ever imagined that the Divine Monad turned Duad would build its Triad on a female off-spring? Not I. I mean, would that be any way to run a universe? No....

Transcending the Time Wave

I wondered, as I felt myself mourning the loss of our son, Nostradamus, whether I mourned merely his loss or also the loss of power that his immortal death represented for my half, the yang side, of the Divine Triad.

There was no time for me to arrive at a definitive answer as Hermes called me out of my sexist reverie. "The time has come," Hermes pronounced.

So the true time had finally come. I knew he was right. I nodded in agreement.

Hermes beckoned us to our thrones. "You will now assume your rightful thrones and be reinstated as our rightful Gods." We sat on the thrones at the head of the Round Table. I could sense that we were to be coronated. But our grand coronation turned out to be more of a briefing.

"You may now at least faintly recall arranging for your Son, Nostradamus, to beckon you back to the time of the Reign of the Gods in the most ancient of what later became called Egypt. When Camus delivered you to him on the River of Light, your son explained that the forces of the universe could again be righted, whence the three of you had reunited."

"Well, yes, but . . ." I interjected. We were no longer three. He was dead, dead to all eternity. Set had killed him.

Hermes interrupted my interjection with such ease, it was as if interrupting the ramblings of God was something with which he was entirely familiar. "Triad, you have indeed begun to right these forces; however, the job is not at all finished. Set lurks along the edges of your Creation, insatiably hungry for the life force of all your Creation."

Einstein chimed in, "Set thrives on a cosmic sort of consumption, a most divine usurpation of all that is."

"Einstein, I am so very glad to see you again. Are you here for our coronation or something?" I did not want to focus on Set.

"Coronation?" Einstein chuckled.

"It seems as if we're being crowned King and Queen. Or re-crowned."

"Call it what you will, Triad." Hermes went on. "I consider this the highest call to action. You, our Duad, must reassert yourselves as the true rulers of this Divine Cosmos and sit at the helm of the time wave."

Einstein added, "The next Omega Point will soon be upon us and it is only you who can prevent the collapse of the entire time wave. You must preserve the cycle. Without your conscious guidance, there will be no new beginning after this particular end."

"So what is it *exactly* that is coming? Other than disaster of some big sort?" Sheeyah answered her own question.

Hermes smiled sadly at Sheeyah. "When a cycle is at its close, its energy has dissipated to an extreme. The cycle is then most vulnerable to opportunistic invasion as it wanes to its Omega Point, where a special brand of chaos can break the pattern and the regenerative alpha forces can fail to collect. We need you to guide the Cosmos, especially the third dimension, into the next Omega Point and successfully back out again."

I was irritated by this. I couldn't help feeling so. "The guidance of God is *not* required. I designed a system which would cycle into and back out of Omega quite naturally, instinctively, without outside interference. Cataclysm is an organic process. I created it to be so."

"Yes, you did, your most Divine Presence, and your design was most grand. However, you never planned for the emergence of your brother, Set." I could feel Hermes' patience. He was trying to get through to me.

"Set is the dark hand, the opportunistic invader that, for reasons larger than even we, your Highest Counsel, can fathom, has as his sole objective the elimination of all prana."

I still didn't want to believe it. "But why would my own brother wish to do such a thing?"

Sheeyah had a look of suspicion in her eyes. "Where did your brother come from anyway? He wasn't part of our Divine Monad from which emerged the Duad and then the Triad. Where did he come from?"

"I don't know. I thought I was the first and only supreme power." Why did I again feel on trial?

"You mean *we* . . ." Sheeyah corrected. "How many times do I have to remind you?"

"Yeah, yeah, I know, *we*, but when *we* were the Monad *we* had the same thoughts and *we* were the *I*."

"O. K., speak for me. . . . Actually, I did too, I did think the Monad was the only supreme power, back when I was the Monad, I mean," Sheeyah mused.

I was still baffled and angry about this Set thing. "So does this mean that there is something larger, greater, than I? Something beyond, *before,* my Creation? Something that created me as well as Set?"

"This we have attempted to ponder with little conclusive result." Einstein was hoping I knew the answer, I could tell. I also could hear myself and everyone else wondering if I had created Set while creating Creation. For some reason, none of them seemed to be blaming Sheeyah. Could I have created Set behind her back?

"The existence of Set raises some unavoidable questions," Hermes sounded as if he were trying to be fair here and barely succeeding. "First, could Set be the anti-Monad? Could it be that the opposite of your Creation is anti-Creation?"

"And second, does the existence of Set mean that you two of the Divine Duad, in your form as Monad, are not the supreme, all powerful, highest, omnipresent and only god force? As you asked, could something even greater than you have given birth to the Monad as well as the anti-Monad?"

"So you are saying that I, God, was born of a power greater than God?" I wanted to get the charges straight. I could remember back when humans argued about whether Jesus could have really been part of God if I had sired him. According to the argument, one can not be both God, who is Creator, and offspring of Creator simultaneously, as Creator is eternal and has no beginning and no end while offspring is born and thus has a beginning.

"I must wonder, dear Triad, mustn't I?" Hermes sounded apologetic now.

I was mad. "So we go to all this trouble to make me remember that I am God — "

Sheeyah again interrupted to correct me, "That *we* are God."

" — only to then tell me that maybe I am *only the son* . . . only *one* of the sons, of God? Why?"

"Because," Hermes still sounded apologetic, "we are all in danger of complete disappearance into non-existence on all dimensions. We need you to remember as much as you can. We need to figure this out."

Sheeyah grabbed my hand, "Triad . . . Triad. Maybe *we* caused Set to come into existence just by our existence. If *I* am the necessary polarity to *you*, perhaps *Set* is the necessary polarity to *us*."

"Necessary! Sheeyah! He wants to kill us off — all of us — all we've created — FOREVER! How can that be *necessary*?"

"To balance our cosmic manifest destiny with an anti-cosmic anti-manifest sort of fate. That's why, Triad." Sheeyah thought she was making sense.

"This is *absurd*." I wanted the last word. I folded my arms and shut my eyes.

But Sheeyah persisted. "Just LISTEN. Let me finish, Triad. Only in our awareness, the supra universe's awareness, of the true fragility of the cosmic system we have designed, can that system, that suprauniverse, be vital enough to perpetrate itself."

"Unless a system is evolving, it is decaying," noted Einstein, agreeing with Sheeyah, as usual.

"Right Einstein." Sheeyah appreciated his support. "Unless our Cosmos, led by us, takes the next step in its evolution, it is going to decay and eventually cease to exist, which is, basically and completely, giving way to Set."

"So there is a *cosmic evolution* now? Did you design that, Sheeyah? Where was I? Off evolving little third dimensional life forms or something while you did the big stuff?" I was furious.

"Yes, there is a cosmic evolution, Triad. There always has been one. It just evolved naturally. Spontaneous evolution. I was aware of it all along. Thought you were too. In the beginning, the Cosmos went from Monad to Duad. When we moved into the Triad formation, we were able to manifest in increasing complexity and vastness throughout all the dimensions we had created. We created self-organizing systems within systems within systems across all the dimensions. We created life forms which evolved increasing degrees of consciousness. Those life forms created systems of conscious interaction — such as the government and other human social systems we see so active in the third dimension on Earth. We know very well how to evolve conscious life forms on all dimensions, and then have them create for themselves conscious systems. It is logical that the living Cosmos would do just what all the life forms within it do."

"You also know how to generate the necessary oscillations of cataclysm and regeneration: the Omega-Alpha cycle," Hermes interjected. "But you haven't yet managed to interject full awareness of this cycle into the life forms which inhabit it. Humans, for example, have been given little understanding of this process."

"But wait gentlemen. I *must* finish. I *know* what's going on. Hear me out," Sheeyah insisted. "Now, a higher level of consciousness *must* be achieved. Our Cosmos must take the next step in its own evolution. Our Cosmos itself must become a *sentient*, conscious Cosmos."

"But, my dear Sheeyah," I wanted to argue, "since we *are* conscious beings and we *are* our Cosmos, the Cosmos is *already* sentient."

"No, Triad, the Cosmos is not yet *consciously conscious* of its whole at all levels of its manifestation. And, unlike our Cosmos, Set is. Because Set has only one level of manifestation, himself, he is already thoroughly permeated with his own complete consciousness. He is, in his way, completely evolved."

"So, Sheeyah," Einstein inquired respectfully, "You advise that this is how we are to counter Set? By pressing for the next step in cosmic evolution?"

"Yes, we must keep Set from invading at the cycle's most depleted point. We must do this by reassuming command of the Omega-Alpha cycle and causing it to become an *increasingly conscious process.*"

"No small assignment, Sheeyah." What else could I say? She was taking the lead now in a dance I couldn't quite follow. "You are asking us to do something monumental, Sheeyah. How can we manage to do this? Make a cycle *think*?"

"Make a *system* think. A cycle is a living system in time." She sounded so certain.

Hermes attempted to reassure me, "Well, you will have help from human philosophy and religion, and even scientists who specialize in the evolution of the Cosmos."

"Such as astrophysicists?" Sheeyah wondered. "I always liked Earth astrophysics."

"Yes, and other theoretical physicists, and planetologists, and many others," Einstein added.

Hermes looked as if he were about to give a speech. A lecture. And, sure enough, he was. Back to school, again: "The Earthly Babylonians, considered to be ancient now, said that it was up to the gods to decide when the end of the world should come and that the gods had decided this before. The Babylonians said that their great city was built by survivors of the Great Deluge, the great Earthly flood. These survivors were giants who were sons of God, who had passed their secrets on to their priests and thus, indirectly, to all religious orders of Earth. This is how the highest of the high priests came to know what is called, 'The *great years knowledge.*'"

"The great years knowledge?" Why hadn't I been informed?

"Yes, the great years knowledge, part of the body of Original Truth which has been suppressed, withheld, from many Earthlings, and so terribly mutilated and diluted."

YES. I UNDERGO A THOROUGH PHYSICAL REVOLUTION ON A REGULAR BASIS.

"Earth! You're here!" Sheeyah was thrilled.

OF COURSE I AM HERE.

I was concerned about the regularity bit and rather nonchalant about Earth's speaking up: "How regular?" I said, "How regular in Earth years?"

HUMAN YEAR LENGTHS ARE NOT EXACT EARTH YEARS.

"However, humans have estimated the cycle, or what has been termed the *greatest year* by Aristotle, as a cycle consisting of a *sar*," said Hermes. "The Chaldeans called these *cycles of eclipses* or *saros*. Sars were estimated as being about 6,586 Earth years. At the end of each sar, the Earth was said to be subjected to a thorough physical revolution," Hermes explained.

"Subjected?" I had to ask.

"Yes," Hermes answered, "and, at that time, polar and equatorial climates shift, change places, either in small bits called *nutations* or in one abrupt jolt. This shifting is accompanied by cataclysmic earthquakes and other cosmic throes."

"Cosmic throes?" I was nervous.

Hermes ignored my nervousness, as it was unbecoming of God to be this way. "On Earth, the Babylonian theory of cyclical world history was brought to the West by a philosopher around 500 BC. In so doing, he taught the Babylonian notion of the great year, the *magnus annus*, to the west. Plato's version of this theory said that in the great year the independently revolving planetary bodies return to their points of departure and then, in a magnificent upheaval of all that *is*, all the planets reverse their orbital directions. Out of this theory of cataclysmic reversal came the notion of *ekpurosis*, or cosmic fire, into which the world is dissolved and from which it is born anew in the magnus annus."

Einstein interrupted, "But of course, Hermes, there was also Herodotus, who said the great year came every *decimillenium* plus one time unit he called a *neros*. And, there were some in ancient Greece who called such a year a *Heliacal* but kept its time and particulars very secret to prevent panic and to retain power."

Hermes continued. "Yes, humans have defined the Omega cycle in many ways. The Hindus say that Earth is now in the fourth (of seven) Manvantaras or cycles of energy manifestation. They say each Manvantara is composed of seven Yugas, that Earth is now in the Kali Yuga, also known as the Iron

Age or Yuga of Pain. It is said that at the end of this cycle, piety will be dead; fire, drought and famine will ravage the Earth; and then a century of death will follow. Despite flooding, all the moisture on and in the Earth will begin to dry up. Eventually, a universal conflagration of some sort will eliminate the last of the human occupants and all the Earth will be consumed in a vast whirlpool of flame."

"God, what an end," I muttered, avoiding eye contact with any of the dignitaries. How could I have planned such third dimensional misery? I could remember no reason for such a plan. What purpose could it have served?

"An Omega Point," Sheeyah whispered under her breath.

"Yes," Hermes had heard her, "and this end is also a beginning as the new yugas or cycles ensue, the same cycles again and again. Eventually, the same ultimate fate evolves again. And from the cosmic fire arises the flight of life, born anew."

"So it seems then, "Sheeyah said, "that humans actually do know the Original Truth about the Omega Point. They don't get it completely, or know the exact timing, but they do know. They express it in their religions and myths."

"Well, in a way, yes. Depictions of this process do appear again and again in human religion and mythology," As usual, Hermes was pleased with his dear Sheeyah. Men such as Hermes and Einstein found her quite fascinating. The Goddess. Hermes continued. "Many of these myths include the same ingredients — the moral dissolution of human kind; the emergence of some kind of major war; the fracturing and collapse of the Earth's crust, and, later the sinking of land masses, even entire continents, into the sea; the atmosphere becoming darkened; stars (including comets and meteors and maybe even moons) crashing down to Earth from the sky; and a massive fire of some sort filling much of the atmosphere."

"Oh, how horrible, " Sheeyah was whispering again.

I was envisioning each of these catastrophic images as Hermes listed them.

I found myself shouting, "But there is always to be an Alpha after the Omega! I planned it this way! I do not remember exactly why, but I know that I did! Destruction and chaos is eventually survived, even transcended, and then reorganized into new societies, new worlds, new life! It is the way ordained by me!"

Hermes calmly nodded yes at me and went on again. He seemed intent on instructing us in the various schools of human thought regarding cataclysm, regardless of our emotions. "The Judeo-Christian tradition is said to differ from many of the other mythologies in that nothing cyclical is presented. But cyclical themes actually permeate the literatures of the Judeo-Christian religions. It is said, under God's direction, after three ages or eras, a newer and better world will emerge. According to this view, you were recently incarnated in the end of the first age. The second age is characterized by increasing tribulation. The third is ultimate peace established by God. Sheeyah, Triad, are you with me?" Hermes made certain he had our attention here.

We nodded, so he continued. "In the Christian tradition, Jesus emerges or reemerges as Messiah during the second age, during times of great tribulation. For the Christian, those who have either not heard of or not heeded the Gospel will not survive the initiation or inception of the third age, the age in which the glory and power of Christ will prevail following signs in the form of peak Earthly disasters such as global war, massive famine, great earthquakes, followed by cosmic crises in which the moon and the sun will be darkened, stars will fall to Earth from heaven, and heaven and Earth will pass away."

I interrupted to argue my same point, feeling a mounting desperation: Set could upset — destroy — my cosmic apple cart. "But there will always be a *new* heaven and a *new* Earth. I have ordained this to be. I, as the Monad," I bowed to Sheeyah, letting her know I actually meant *we*, "I am all things new, I create Creation, I am the Alpha and the Omega, the beginning and the end! I have revealed this Original Truth again and again!"

"But maybe this is not the Truth. Or, maybe you reveal an Original Truth, but not in its totality." Hermes stared deeply into my eyes. "Please, I beseech you, Triad, look deep within yourself for the answer. What have you failed to communicate to your Cosmos — to yourself?"

There was silence as I complied. I looked deeply within myself and found nothing more. I returned from my search, truly at a loss for words.

Seeing me speechless, Hermes went on. "The term *apocalypse* comes from the Greek word *apokalypsis*, or 'disclosure.' Apocalypse is some kind of major all-involving disaster in which forces of good and evil clash and only super-natural intervention preserves good in the end. Communication with divine forces should reveal the timing, the force and the characteristics of an apocalypse. Many religions thus include divine revelation. Some revelations come to humans directly from God; however, only a few humans can read them. Therefore other revelations come through intermediaries who may be witch doctors, shamans, religious leaders, or persons with special abilities or special statuses."

"But you never know who's a con," I warned. They all stared at me as if to insinuate that even I might be a con.

"Some say that God's handwriting is the movement of celestial bodies in the sky," Einstein attempted to get us out of this stare-down, either to save me further humiliation or to get on with the apparently urgent proceedings.

"So," Sheeyah got the hint, "the term of one Great Year was viewed as being the period of time it would take for all planets to return to the places they assumed at the time of Creation?"

"Yes," said Hermes, "This is because Earth's early human astrologers, who were Babylonians, Chaldeans and Egyptians, declared that life on Earth was governed by the longer cycles of all the planets. A certain astrological configuration of the remote past was believed to be very powerful and expected to recur again someday. This was the ancient notion of *eternal recurrence* and was accepted by many great Earth philosophers including Plato, Pythagoras, and Neitzsche. The stoic philosophers developed their blind and passionless acceptance of life based upon the notion that history repeated itself right down to the smallest detail — world ages and human lives were repeated again and again."

"You think human astrology actually holds some Truth?" I asked.

"The tilt of the Earth's axis creates the seasons, Triad," Hermes replied. "The northern hemisphere points toward the sun for half a year and away from it for half. The Earth gradually rotates around its axis in what appears to be a backward circle. The axis completes one of the background rotations in its entirety in some 25,725 Western Earth calendar years. As it does so, it moves through the twelve signs of the Zodiac, creating the zodiacal ages such as the Age of Taurus from 4000 BC to 2000 BC, the Age of Aries from 2000 BC to the time of Christ, the Age of Pisces from the birth of Christ to recent Earth time, and the Age of Aquarius, which is beginning on Earth about now."

Sheeyah waved her hand, as if to gently stop the lecture for a moment. "When exactly is the Age of Aquarius beginning?"

"Well, it begins any time between 1898 and 2160 Western Earth time. Humans are confused about the exact dates because the 12 zodiacal constellations do not exactly divide the eclipse of the 360 degree sky into exact sections of 30 degrees each, rather they are 12 star groups of various sizes."

"But Hermes," Sheeyah seemed to have come to a realization of some sort, "maybe the transition into the Age of Aquarius is an inner transformation and hundreds of years may be required for enough humans to transform within to acquire a critical mass of change in the collective consciousness. Only then will the age have truly been entered."

Hermes raised his eyebrows and nodded yes.

I worried aloud. "But, if Jesus, our son Nostradamus in one of his incarnations, was the incarnation of the Age of Pisces, who will incarnate in this new age of Aquarius?"

Sheeyah looked at me triumphantly, grabbed my wrist, and placed my hand on her round belly. Suddenly, I got it. Our gaze met. We looked quite solemn to each other. Burdened by duty.

Ignoring our sudden realization and its intense gaze, Hermes kept right on lecturing. "José Arguelles set forth a system of cycles based on the calendar of the Ancient Mayans, one which points to the Western Earth year 2012 A.D. as the end of a particular sub-cycle in the transformation of matter, one which would bring with it the collapse of human civilization on Earth and the consequent purification of Earth which would make way for Earth's eventual regeneration. Many apocalyptic prophecies agree that the time of the end of one era and the beginning of the next is 2000 AD, but others' predictions collect around the time between 2012 and 2036. The year 2013 is interpreted as the end of the Incan calendar, the time when a magnetic asteroid many times the size of Jupiter will come very close to Earth and activate cataclysm. Triad, Sheeyah, whatever the exact year you choose, it is at this point that your Creation is most fragile."

"My God, so whenever it is, if we cannot guide the Cosmos through the Omega Point, the eye of the cosmic needle, it could really be the end? The end of history! Of time!" Sheeyah was still holding my hand on her belly. I could feel her body jolt at the thought of the end of time. I hated the feeling. I pulled my hand away from her.

"If you are equipped to guide us, it will only be the end of this cycle of history on Earth," Einstein answered.

"But, what should I tell my friends on Earth, people I know there?" Sheeyah was deeply saddened now. "That is, if I ever see them again... Will I? Einstein? Hermes? Will I see them again?"

"This is your decision. If you choose to see them, tell them what is happening, and tell them that at the right moment, there will be a guide," Hermes advised.

"What if they don't believe me?"

Transcending the Time Wave

"Sheeyah, dear, faith cannot be *given* to men and women — it comes from direct knowledge. If they do not experience faith for themselves, you cannot give it to them. True, the quality of what one understands depends upon the quality of the people one hears speaking. But true messages must come directly from one's own being, and not from other beings, even if the other beings are Gods."

This was too sentimental for me. I wanted to get back to the business of remembering how my Cosmos worked. "Planetary alignment must have an effect on Earth of some sort, whether or not it is measurable with human instruments."

"Yes, Triad, even radio communications specialists have noted that when any three of the planets of Earth's solar system are aligned in either 90 degree or 180 degree geometric relationships, radio disturbances are greater. And the more planets that are aligned, the more the static is pronounced."

I was trying to figure this out. "However, Hermes, many of these planetary alignments have had no perceivable effect on Earth."

"I agree, Triad. It is when certain other factors are present that such alignments are especially potent. Then there is a synergy of forces." Hermes looked around. There were no comments from the dignitaries. He didn't seem to expect any. That they just listened all the time seemed to be a tradition.

So I asked a question: "Factors? Such as eclipses?"

"Right, Triad. Eclipses are factors here. They sometimes coincide with planetary alignments. Millennium year 1999 recorded the last eclipse of the 20th century — August 11. That eclipse is seen as activating or potentiating a Grand Cross alignment of planets occurring in the fixed signs of the zodiac."

"What is a Grand Cross?" Sheeyah asked.

"This Grand Cross includes the alignment of planets in the four fixed signs of the zodiac — Taurus, Leo, Scorpio and Aquarius — which correspond to the four beasts of the Apocalypse in the book of Revelation. A Grand Cross, potentiated by eclipse, when given a particular set of imbalances on Earth and in the Cosmos, can generate extreme unrest and violence, and all kinds of those natural catastrophes, such as volcanic eruptions, earthquakes, tidal waves, and massive fires — firestorms."

"It sure seems like we've been seeing some of these in recent years on Earth," Sheeyah mused wistfully, "huge fires, floods, earthquakes and, when Triad and I were departing Crystal Mirror Lake with Camus, some kind of nuclear explosion or something."

Einstein came to life at this point. "Sheeyah, Most Divine Queen, you have been witnessing the early indications of what can come. Whatever the precise year, the now inevitable mix of celestial forces such as alignments and eclipses coincide most precisely with Earth's most vulnerable point. Earth is in bad shape. Her very existence is strained. Her magnetic imbalances are beginning to weaken her atmosphere and her protective radiation belts. With the surrounding solar system and Cosmos also weakening under the strain of yang overload, a Grand Cross or other powerful alignment at the right (or wrong, depending upon how you see it) moment leaves Earth open to bombardment from passing meteors or even a cometary impact, the likes of which before now Earth has not seen in many millennia. Such a bombardment will knock the Earth off of her axis."

"Off her axis?" Sheeyah was incredulous.

"Yes." Einstein sounded quite credible.

"Oh, God, why now?" Why now? I was not happy at the prospect.

"Why not now, Triad? Events have progressed to such a point along the time wave that only an Omega Point can return us to Alpha," explained Einstein. "After all, you claim to have planned it this way."

I wanted more information still. "So tell us how it's going to go, Einstein. . . . This polar shift."

"I'm not in the business of apocalyptic prophecy," Einstein warned. "And anyway, Triad, my sense all along was that you did not want to write an exact recipe for these things but instead to allow the natural forces to generate the events you had ordained and know that the forces of Cosmos and its Nature would do so because you constructed them as such."

"Oh," I said glumly, I was so impressed with myself, way back then.

Now Sheeyah pressed for more information. "So, Einstein, how, given what you know, how is it likely to go?"

"Well, Sheeyah, you were at the Crystal Mirror Vortex when it all began."

"We were?" she said. "That was a nuclear war, I thought. Camus saved us from the bombs."

"Well, yes. World tension had mounted to such an intense degree that political leaders felt they had no recourse other than to resort to big-time threats," Einstein answered.

"But threats sometimes call for action," Hermes added.

"Correct," Einstein agreed. "When the bluffs were called, the bluffers felt they had no choice other than to show that they weren't bluffing."

"So they blasted?" I asked, feeling sick inside. I remembered suggesting to my investors that new-agers believed in spontaneous nuclear war. I should have purchased more underground cave territory, I chided myself.

"Triad, it had to be," Hermes could sense my misery. "At a certain point, such decisions, while still appearing to be rationally arrived at by humans, are far out of human hands. The energies, the driving forces, whether or not political leaders are aware of them, become so strong, that critical decisions are made — such as the decisions to use nuclear weapons — without the normal ethical and survival restraints."

"But virtually spontaneous all-out nuclear war on Earth was interrupted, preempted, by something much more destructive," Einstein spoke to this. "What we speak of has already begun to happen: the unfolding is actually upon us. A passing comet swung far closer to Earth than expected. As it was, the coming of the comet was quite unannounced. Scientists had kept the information regarding its approach quiet so as not to cause mass panic. The few who really knew about the possibility of extreme tumult had arranged to withdraw to underground bomb shelters and caves in safe lands for the event."

"But what exactly was the event?" I pressed for facts.

"Look, Triad. Look, Sheeyah. If you look through that cave wall there, into the body of Earth, you can see it all," Hermes pointed.

We looked and what we saw — the imaging — was more shocking than we could have ever imagined. "How are we seeing this?" I demanded to know.

"These are the eyes of Earth," noted Hermes.

"Earth can see herself?" Sheeyah asked.

YES. YOU COULD PUT IT THAT WAY. I HAVE AN AWARENESS OF MY LOCATION IN SPACE RELATIVE TO OTHER CELESTIAL BODIES. ALTHOUGH THIS IS NOT VISION AS EARTH HUMANS KNOW IT, THIS IS INDEED VISION. IT IS VISION OF A TELEPATHIC NATURE.

"Tele-vision?" Sheeyah laughed at her own joke, desperate for some comic relief.

"So look through the eyes of Earth, and see her vision with us now," Hermes practically pleaded with us.

THE COMET APPROACHED ME. ITS POWERFUL MAGNETISM CONVULSED THE FLOW OF ENERGY ALONG MY AXIS. THE CHARGE OF MY POLES ABRUPTLY REVERSED.

"What? How could I have designed this machination?" I asked.

MY NORTHERN HEMISPHERE, BEING TOO WEIGHTY, WAS SO OVERCHARGED WITH THE POSITIVE CHARGE OF MALE YANG, THAT WHEN THE COMET, ALSO YANG CHARGED, CAME CLOSER TO MY NORTH SIDE THAN MY SOUTH, THE ENERGY OF MY AXES REVERSED, MY SOUTH POLE BECAME YANG AND THEN VIOLENTLY SWUNG FULLY AWAY FROM THE COMET.

Hermes looked at us to see if we followed. "You understand that it was like the bringing together of two positively charged poles of two magnets. They repelled each other, most fiercely."

"Yes, sounds like big time repulsion." Sheeyah was whispering again.

WHEN MY NEWLY YANG CHARGED SOUTH POLE SWUNG AWAY FROM THE COMET, THE EARTH'S SEAS SWUNG TOO, TOWARD THE COMET, WASHING OVER PORTIONS OF WHAT WERE ONCE THE ARCTIC, NORTH PACIFIC AND NORTH AMERICAN CONTINENTS, FLOODING PORTIONS OF THE PLANET, AND REVEALING LONG SUBMERGED LAND MASSES.

"Atlantis? My Atlantis?" I began to shout again at this point. I realized that I had long awaited the return of my beloved Atlantis and had returned to Earth for this very event, among other things.

YES, SOME OF YOUR BELOVED ATLANTIS HAS NOW REAPPEARED. BUT THE CHAIN OF EVENTS HAS JUST BEGUN. YOU MUST LOOK INTO THE FUTURE WITH ME.

"There's more? Earth, you have just told us about the most horrendous cataclysm witnessed in recent millennia and then you say there is still more to come?" Sheeyah was upset.

Hermes stood and walked to a spot behind her throne. "No, dear Sheeyah. There are cataclysms occurring at all times. This particular event is part of a chain of Cosmic cataclysms. Let me explain. A comet races loose somewhere in the Cosmos. It approaches a weakened planet or star undergoing great imbalance and bodily stress. Even the approach of a comet can affect a weakened celestial body, but the near impact or impact of one can be disaster. The weakened celestial body can break up, or eject molten lava, from deep within. This lava has been under such great pressure below the crusty surface of the planet or the skin of the star, that when a comet or

Transcending the Time Wave

even meteors pursuing a comet hit it, the crust or skin breaks and a large boiling mass of lava bursts out. This lava will swing far into the galaxy of its origin and sometimes well beyond its own galaxy, forming a huge and very unusual orbit."

"Does it become a comet?" I remembered this bit from somewhere.

IT CAN AND SOMETIMES DOES. SUCH COMETS TRAVEL ALONG THEIR WILD ORBITS, HITTING NOTHING FOR LONG PERIODS OF TIME BUT, FROM TIME TO TIME, SUCH COMETS RUN CLOSE ENOUGH TO OTHER PLANETS TO SHIFT THE AXES OF THESE PLANETS AND CONTINUE THE CHAIN OF CATACLYSM OF UNIVERSAL PROPORTIONS.

"Sort of like semen, racing through space, inseminating planets with disaster, conceiving Omegas . . ." Sheeyah had understood, I could tell.

"You could say that, Sheeyah," I said.

Again on Sheeyah's side, Hermes added, "We know that Venus was once a roaming comet pulled in by sun. The sun acquires its planets by attracting them, luring them in."

THE CLOSER WE ARE TO THE HEAD OF THE COMET, THE MORE AT RISK WE ARE. I SHOULD KNOW. I HAVE ALREADY PASSED THROUGH THE TAIL OF A COMET, CLOSE TO ITS HEAD, FOUR TIMES. WHEN I INTERSECTED WITH THE TAIL OF COMET VENUS, I ACTUALLY STOPPED SPINNING AND CHANGED DIRECTIONS. THE MAGNETIC CHARGES ON MY POLES SWITCHED: WHEN LIGHTENING STRIKES A MAGNET, ITS POLES WILL SWITCH TOO.

I was shaking my head in denial of all this.

Sheeyah grabbed my hand. "Triad, there isn't anything we can do about it. It's all happening — NOW!"

"Oh, my most Divine Gods," interrupted Hermes, "there is indeed something you can do."

"What on Earth can we do?" Sheeyah asked.

YOU ARE ON EARTH.

"Excuse me Earth, of course we are, but what can we do?"

"You can re-educate yourselves quickly and then return to the lives you recently departed."

"Re-educate ourselves? Is there still more to know?" I was impatient.

"Yes. The first polar shift was set off by the comet, which was able to affect Earth so profoundly, because of Earth's extremely unbalanced condition, her polluted and compromised atmosphere, the effects of the recent celestial Grand Cross, and the advent of a new astrological age in Earth's history. This first polar shift eliminated a great portion of life on Earth, and clearly a sizable fraction of the human race."

"But what now? What do we need to know and why?" I pressed.

"Action: reaction! The Earth swung one way, now it will swing back, like a swing or a wobbling top." Einstein was so matter of fact about this.

THERE WILL BE A SECOND POLAR SHIFT. AND THEN A THIRD BEFORE THINGS SETTLE.

"Oh, how horrible," Sheeyah whispered, "So much suffering."

"It all depends upon your perspective, Triad and Sheeyah. You could also say how necessary, from an energetic standpoint," Hermes advised us.

"Triad, we shouldn't have been off fooling around, romping through the Cosmos while all this was building up."

"Yes, Sheeyah, you should have been," Hermes consoled her.

"What?" I could not digest all this.

"You were attempting to rediscover and revive Original Truth. But let us focus on the polar shifts. With the first polar shift, flooding occurred. After the first polar shift, a plague of volcanic eruptions and earthquakes began. The Earth's crust, having to reorient to the pulls of a new axis, was under greater pressure than ever and volcanic lava was able to burst out in areas where it had never before surfaced."

YOU MIGHT BE INTERESTED TO NOTE THAT I WAS NEVER PERFECTLY ROUND. CENTRIFUGAL FORCE WIDENED ME NATURALLY AT THE EQUATOR, SO I WAS WIDER THAN I WAS TALL, I HAD A DIFFERENT CURVE AT MY EQUATOR THAN AT MY NORTH AND SOUTH POLES. AND MY NORTH AND SOUTH POLES WERE NOT THEMSELVES EXACTLY THE SAME SHAPE.

"What happened when the first polar shift came?" I asked Earth.

EXACTLY THE QUESTION. SUDDENLY MY CRUST WAS BEING COMPRESSED INTO A ROUNDER SHAPE IN NEW PLACES AND FLATTENED IN OTHER AREAS. ALL KINDS OF NEW CRACKS AND FISSURES IN MY CRUST APPEARED.

"What about the people? What about the children? What are they doing now?" Sheeyah was so very horrified.

THEY ARE ATTEMPTING TO FIND AND BURY THEIR DEAD IN SOME CASES, BUT MOSTLY THEY ARE ATTEMPTING TO JUST SURVIVE. GLOBAL COMMUNICATIONS WERE BROKEN ENTIRELY FOR A WHILE, AND ONLY SOME HAVE BEEN RESUMED. MOST PEOPLE ARE STILL CUT OFF AND DO NOT FULLY UNDERSTAND WHAT HAS HAPPENED OR WHAT IS ABOUT TO HAPPEN.

"It seems likely that those humans who were living the most basically are faring the best, as they are remaining within what had already become their chosen life styles," I was thinking aloud.

"Makes the whole back-to-the-Earth movement take on new meaning," Sheeyah murmured.

"And homelessness the normal way of life," I added.

"Exactly Sheeyah, your Earthcult sensed the survival value of this philosophy," Hermes patted her shoulders, "however, much of the surviving human species is in shock and in some panic. Safe land (survivor territory) inhabitants, for the most part, have survived. And this is where the ports and mainstays of communication have been made most operant after this first cataclysm. Several land-locked cities have become emergency seaports."

"So that new airport in Denver was actually planned as both an air and a sea port?" asked Sheeyah.

YES, HOWEVER, ONLY A SELECT GROUP OF DEVELOPERS KNEW ABOUT THESE PLANS.

Sheeyah looked at me now and narrowed her eyes.

"Well, all right, yes, that's my group of investors. I admit it. But, look, maybe you should thank me. What I was up to may be saving humanity, or some portion of it."

"Maybe, Triad, but you have already polluted one of my best survivor territories. That recent buildup in the Denver area, with its attending smog and general pollution was massive."

"Triad, Sheeyah, if I may interrupt," interrupted Einstein, "Of the human survivors, some are aware that a second polar shift is coming."

"It is really coming? When?"

"Soon, Sheeyah, quite soon," replied Einstein. "The impact of the first polar shift knocked loose a huge chunk of Antarctica, which has now floated off the pole. It is so heavy that it is adding to the natural tendency that Earth or any celestial body would have to swing back after being knocked so hard in one direction. The polar ice is melting rapidly. More flooding will be occurring as a result."

MUCH OF THE MELTING ICE CUM WATER IS RUSHING TO MY NEW EQUATOR. THIS WEIGHT IS MAKING ME ALL THE MORE UNSTEADY. I AM ALREADY SO VERY DE-STABILIZED AFTER MY FIRST POLAR SHIFT THAT I CANNOT REFRAIN FROM A SECOND ONE.

"Oh God, how traumatic for you. For all life on Earth. . . . How does the second one come?" Sheeyah persisted.

"It happens this way, Sheeyah," Einstein wanted to explain and did. "The comet has pulled a belt of meteors into its very long million mile tail. Scientists, and those they dare to inform, now realize that there are at least two big meteor impacts coming. The biggest meteor will hit the moon and shift the moon's axis a bit, causing it to eventually fall into Earth — in a thousand or more years. This is what happened to Earth's other moons. But this is a millennium from now. More immediately, a second meteor will hit the Indian Ocean. This triggers the second polar shift. Communications on Earth, already broken down, will be out entirely again for a while although satellite dishes will allow the remaining humans to reinstate. Recall that the impact of the first polar shift cracked and knocked loose a chunk of Antarctica which now floats away. So the poles are starting to melt rapidly. Flooding will result. Water will accumulate around the equator, putting new strains on the balance of Earth. The polar caps must melt entirely to reform. The increasing weight of water at the equator will actually add to the intensity of the second polar shift. Volcanic eruptions and earthquakes are already becoming very frequent now, because when Earth was knocked off of her axis and her poles exchanged magnetic charges, her electromagnetic currents shifted around all of her key vortices. Although these vortices may stay the same, there is great tumult around them now. *There is growing madness, panic and hoarding of supplies. Suicides are increasing.* **The second polar shift is expected intuitively by everyday people who have no access to scientists' information, but the elite actually know it is coming."**

VERY SOON AFTER MY SECOND POLAR SHIFT, MY THIRD WILL TAKE PLACE. THIS THIRD WILL BE A NATURAL SWING BACK, A GREAT RE-BALANCING.

"Yes, the third shift must occur because it is *the necessary great re-balancing* after first two overshifts — it is the compensation for millennia of imbalance. Because Earth will continue to be under great stress, her continental shelves will crack at their weakest points."

AFTER THE SECOND SHIFT, HUMANS SEEM TO KNOW INSTINCTIVELY THAT THE THIRD ONE IS COMING. THEREFORE, THERE IS MUCH SELF-DELIVERANCE. SOON THE FINAL AND GREAT RE-BALANCING WILL BE COMPLETE.

"Self-deliverance?"

"Suicide," Hermes explained, "but with a purpose ... delivery out of angst .... For the most advanced, delivery into a higher dimension."

"Do they truly understand how to do this?" Sheeyah inquired. "How to self-deliver themselves?"

"This is going to be your job, Sheeyah. Before and following the next, the second and third, polar shifts, many humans will simply choose to leave the planet. Life in the third dimension on Earth will be so very difficult, so very terrifying for humans. And during the next thousand years, conditions will worsen."

"So I'm going back to teach. But, teach what, exactly?"

"Truth." Hermes bowed to Sheeyah.

"Truth? We're back to that again," I groaned.

"Yes, Truth. Sheeyah, you, after all, are the bearer of Original Truth."

"I'm the bearer of my daughter, that's all I'm sure of."

"Well, in a sense she is the Truth."

I wondered what Hermes really meant by this but did not ask.

"We, your High Counsel, find it essential that the two of you return to the time and place on Earth from which you journeyed out to us and interject your Divine guidance into your preordained master plan of Omega to Alpha."

I was not at all thrilled at this prospect. "Why on Earth — ?"

Earth rumbled in response to my indirect addressing of her, but said nothing.

"Why would I want to attend an Omega Point in the third dimension, even if I, we, were responsible for its taking place?" I could not fathom this.

"Again, let me remind you that you have no choice but to return to fight Set. Set lurks to consume Creation at the Omega Point. There will be no Alpha, no rebirth of life, if you do not go back."

"Back to the now?" I asked.

"Back to those incarnations in which you most recently met," Hermes responded.

"Why should Sheeyah give birth to our child there? Why? In all that danger, doom and misery?"

"That is a necessary event."

YOU MUST COME BACK IN ORDER TO HELP MAKE THIS OMEGA POINT GO RIGHT, TO MAKE SURE THE GREAT RE-BALANCING OCCURS SO THAT SET, THE ANTI-PRANA, DOES NOT CONSUME ALL CREATION. SO THAT I, MOTHER EARTH, DO NOT DIE AS I GIVE BIRTH.

"Do you really believe we have the power to fight Set?" I stood up, left my throne, and began to pace.

"If you don't, no one and nothing does," Einstein advised us.

"Let's say we agree to go back. Can we take anything to protect us? Guns? Weapons? Guards?"

WHILE CERTAINLY THERE IS A PHYSICAL THREAT IN THE THIRD DIMENSION — TO ALL WHO PASS THROUGH THERE — THAT THREAT IS MINIMAL AND RELATIVELY INCONSEQUENTIAL WHEN COMPARED TO THE THREAT ACROSS ALL DIMENSIONS OF THE COSMOS.

"So what kind of weapons can we take?" I demanded an answer.

"Truth is your only weapon. Original Truth."

Sheeyah stood up and leaned on the back of her throne. I saw that she was extremely heavy with child. I felt numb.

"But, first you need the Original Truth. You must have all of it in order to take it back into the now," Hermes demanded gently. "A central part of Original Truth is the Truth about the meaning of the *omega point*: First, teach the Truth that the advent of the Omega Point is indeed upon us. Second, teach the Truth that there are signs which must be learned, signs which actually point to the full coming of complete Omega. <u>Third</u>, teach the Truth about what prana is and what Set, the anti-prana, actually represents. <u>Fourth</u>, teach the Truth about how to combat the anti-prana, Set."

"But where do we get all this Truth," I asked in despair. And then, entirely overwhelmed by the responsibility and urgency I felt, I turned on Sheeyah. I grabbed Sheeyah and shook her very roughly. "Sheeyah! You've GOT to remember where the symbols are! Where did you hide them? You must remember! Everything rests upon your remembering! You hid the Truth!!!"

Sheeyah wriggled free of my grasp. "No! It's not my responsibility. How can I know what I do not know? I am *not* withholding information from you Triad, although there is a temptation to do so, seeing as how you tend to misuse your, our, Divine secrets for your own gain when you manifest in the material plane."

"My own gain? What am I really gaining by pulling together Earthly investors to buy up survivor territories? What am I gaining other than the assurance that at least a portion of the human species will survive on Earth? I am protecting my Creation. — Is that personal gain, Sheeyah?"

"*Our* Creation. And, in fighting your developments, in fighting what you, in all your male yang, have done on Earth, I am protecting *my* Creation." Sheeyah sounded fierce now.

"*Our* creation," I corrected angrily.

"So now you see how it feels, Triad?"

I was silent for a moment. And then I realized that all the dignitaries had risen from their seats and had gathered tightly around us. They were eyeing Sheeyah. I felt ashamed of myself. I had physically attacked her again. I remembered the shack in Mexico. I wondered how I had descended to the depravity of rape and assault through all this cosmic stuff. Was I actually degrading morally as I was coming to know more about my moral ascension? Weird. Weird and backward. What a disgusting God I made.

After a while, I stopped beating myself up and tried to figure out why they were still staring at Sheeyah. Hadn't they seen a breast before? Her royal cape had fallen open when I grabbed her and I had inadvertently torn open her already very tattered shirt. She was looking at the tear as well, clutching the rip to avoid revealing her nipple. This I found even more provocative than if she had just let it show.

And then I got it. I saw what they were all seeing: The tattoo!

Sheeyah looked astounded. A tear rolled down her face and dropped from her chin onto her breast, landing right on the tattoo.

Now I really saw it for the first time. It was a beautiful design. It said everything. I could feel the Truth just by looking at it. There were two

Omegas overlapping, one upside down and one right side up, within a circle.

I touched her there. Our eyes met. We were seeing right through each other into a beyond where clarity lurked. "A symbol? This is one of the symbols?" I whispered.

She nodded. "I guess so."

Hermes came up and touched Sheeyah's breast as well. "We are blessed this day in the universal progression of time. The Divine Mother of Truth has found herself again."

"But how can a symbol make a difference?" Sheeyah inquired of Hermes.

"Truth has been severely distorted by language and culture. The consciousness of humanity exists within an elaborate hierarchy of distortion which veils Truth. *Human words and beliefs are part of this elaborate distortion.* However, a spiritual Truth, to be relayed in its wholeness, must not be distorted. A spiritual Truth, without ever being intellectualized by the brain of human or any other life form, can congeal into an image or symbol. That image can again unfold in the eye of its beholder, depending upon the sophistication of the beholder, in terms of his or her readiness, into varying degrees of Truth. True symbolism lies in the essential qualities of things: symbols — pictures — objects — things which just are. Through symbols, a less obvious but more honest aspect of the Cosmos is introduced. A sensory image is transposed to an experience, generating an awareness of an eternal proto-type, a basic premise, a universal Truth. The friction between the abstract concept held by the intellect and the experi-

Transcending the Time Wave

ence set off by seeing the symbol generates Truth."

"So, Hermes, I am feeling the Truth I wear in this symbol?" Sheeyah asked.

"Yes. You see within this circle the Greek letter, Omega. Omega symbolizes the end. But look at this symbol! It is the shape of the womb, the bearer of life. The end of one cycle is the beginning of another."

Ω

"To everything there is a season ... A time to be born, a time to die ...." I muttered in awe.

"The symbol, Omega, while signifying the end, is the bearer of life," Sheeyah said in awe.

"Yes, hence, the Omega here is overlapped with the inverted Omega. Look at the inverted Omega. It symbolizes the womb, in its form as the Grail."

"The Grail?" Sheeyah asked.

"The Holy Vessel," Hermes replied, "the container of Truth: *You*, Sheeyah. Mother of the Cosmos. The Truth is housed within the Mother." Hermes paused for a moment, gazed at me to be certain I was listening, and then continued, "So, when you overlap the Omega and the inverted Omega, you produce a stunning image."

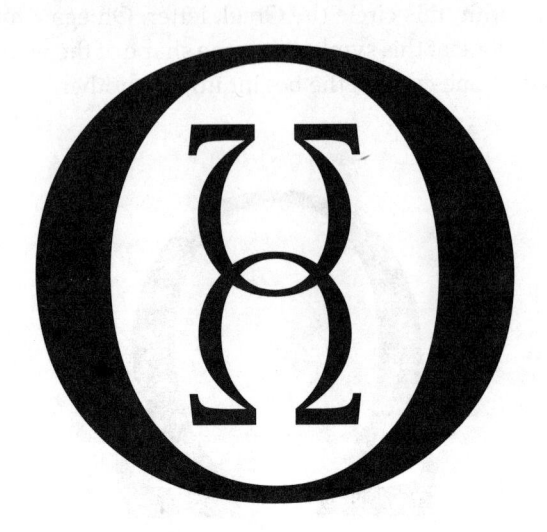

I could not believe that I, of all beings, could have missed this. "How could I have looked at it so many times — ?"

"And you certainly did — "

"Shhhh, not now Sheeyah — and not seen it?"

"It is indeed beautiful, Triad," Hermes commented. "What do you see?"

"Where the Omegas overlap, a contained space, a closed circle, a universe, the whole," I answered.

"Yes, and there's more," said Einstein. "Remember when we toured the Cosmos through the dimensions of intergalactic space and I presented you with a mental map of all the dimensions?"

"Yes," I said.

"The overlapping Omegas represent this very map."

"How?"

"Look into your minds at the map of the Cosmos I planted there."

I did as instructed. I was amazed at how readily it came back to me.

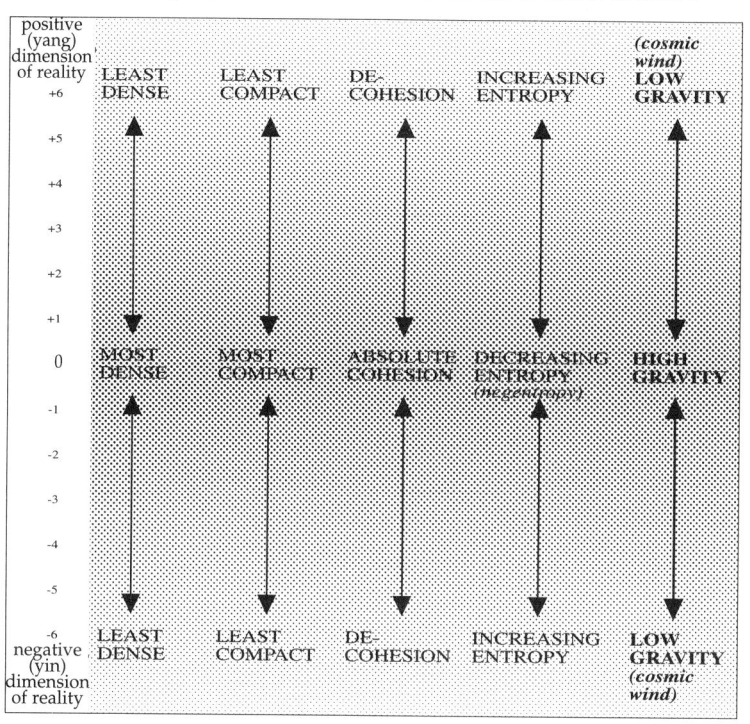

YANG (+) SIDE OF COSMIC MIRROR

positive (yang) dimension of reality					
+6	LEAST DENSE	LEAST COMPACT	DE-COHESION	INCREASING ENTROPY	LOW GRAVITY *(cosmic wind)*
+5					
+4					
+3					
+2					
+1					
0	MOST DENSE	MOST COMPACT	ABSOLUTE COHESION	DECREASING ENTROPY *(negentropy)*	HIGH GRAVITY
-1					
-2					
-3					
-4					
-5					
-6 negative (yin) dimension of reality	LEAST DENSE	LEAST COMPACT	DE-COHESION	INCREASING ENTROPY	LOW GRAVITY *(cosmic wind)*

YIN (-) SIDE OF COSMIC MIRROR

"Reduce that map to a few simple stylized lines symbolizing it and overlap the yin and the yang side, as if they were omega signs. Move these images around in your mind. Follow my lead:

Now see that the whole of Creation is pictured here and is contained within a circle."

"But can the Cosmos really be contained?" Sheeyah wondered.

"Ah, here is another of the Truths;" Hermes sighed. "What is not within Creation is not Truth."

"What?" I asked. "Does this mean Set is a lie? That he does not exist?"

"Set exists if we let him. All outside of this circle is not within the map of Creation, not within the map of reality. As long as the map of reality is understood and carried forth from person to person and soul to soul, all inhabitants of the Cosmos will know that they are within the Cosmos. Only having a strong identity as the Cosmos will save Creation from the dissolution of its reality that Set threatens."

"Original Truth protects Creation from dissolution?" Sheeyah queried.

"Yes. And you have elaborated upon this in a variety of symbols you have stored somewhere."

Sheeyah thought for a while. All were silent, waiting.

"Oh, wait, I know, I *know* what I did with them!" Sheeyah was shouting.

"You do?" I asked, "Suddenly, now?"

"They are painted all over the place," she went on with her loud surprise.

"What do you mean?" I was doubtful.

"Remember that I said I was arrested for graffiti painting — defacing public property, remember?"

"Yes, unfortunately, how embarrassing for us all," I retorted with obvious and overly-paternal disapproval.

"No, no, you don't get it, Triad. I had this incessant desire to create and paint symbols all over the place. It was the Original Truth coming out!"

"This means that all kinds of people have seen it."

"Yes, of course, Triad." Hermes spoke up, "But, without training and guidance they will not know what they are seeing. The ancient symbol language of Earthlings, which held so much of the Original Truth, is re-emerging through you, Sheeyah, but only for those who are ready to read it."

"Some will be ready."

"Undoubtedly some are, Sheeyah."

"So the Truth is finding its way out."

"Yes, Sheeyah, but we need you to further the dissemination of Truth, Sheeyah. You must be certain Truth is preserved, understood, protected from further obliteration. Otherwise, its dissipation will allow Set to invade and consume Creation."

Einstein leaned forward. "Only those ready to understand the Truth will recognize it when they see these symbols. Others will be influenced by these symbols, but will not know how they are being influenced or even that they are being influenced."

"So what should I do?" Sheeyah asked.

"Go back." Now Hermes leaned forward. "Go back to the now that you were living in. Go back and find those symbols, record them, explain them, teach them, preserve them. Publish this one contained in your tattoo. Make it known. And bring the symbols you know from the third dimension where they finally resurfaced back to us in the higher dimensions of the Cosmos."

Einstein nodded. "Only Truth will keep the dark away."

We MUST KEEP THE NATURAL CYCLES OF THE COSMOS GOING. Set will stop them all IF TRUTH DIES.

Einstein went on. "We are at a critical juncture in time — in the history of time. So you *must* reenter the third dimension, the heart of the Cosmos. Only from there can the great re-balancing occur."

I still had reservations. "But don't you think Sheeyah should stay here? Wouldn't our child be safer here in Khebit, where Nostradamus was born, where Horus was born safe from Set?"

"Yes it would be safer here," Hermes warned, "but the safety gained by her staying is not worth the danger caused by her doing so. Recall that at many times in history, Khebit, also known as the Isle of Avalon, has sent messengers into the third dimension."

"Like King Arthur?" I asked.

"Yes, his Atlantean mother, safe here for so many eons, emerged into what became the Arthurian era to make it the Arthurian era it became by giving birth to Arthur."

"And to me as well," Sheeyah added.

"Yes, to both of you, Arthur and Morgaine, as you were to carry on her teachings in the third dimension."

"Alas," said Einstein, "the love story between the two of you made your work difficult, as you were actually siblings."

"Half siblings, I believe." I wanted this known, as if it softened the issue of incest, but, of course, at the moment I spoke, I recalled that we had been identical twins as Isis and Osiris. Incest had followed us through many of our incarnations.

"As I was saying," Hermes continued, "from time to time, we here at Khebit send messengers into the third dimension. We watch what is happening there and attempt to keep things on track. So now you must venture forth."

I opened my mouth to object, but old Uncle Hermes interrupted me. "After all, Triad, it is your will — the will of God."

With that, we were bowed to by the dignitaries, who sunk their heads solemnly into that triangle they formed with their hands. And then Hermes rose from his bow. He clapped his hands, and, quite suddenly, was holding those goblets again. He brought them to us, handing us each one.

I was dismayed. "I won't have to drink this poison again, will I?"

"You will, but now, with Truth, the solution has been illuminated."

I did not understand what I was being told until I glanced into the goblet. "Its full of light," I said.

"Yes, full of light." Sheeyah agreed.

"Drink of the light, the sacrament of the Cosmos," Hermes beseeched us.

"Sacrament?" I did not get it.

"Yes, a sacrament has the meaning imbued upon it by those who believe in that particular sacrament. The magic of the sacrament is the belief in it. In belief there is power. This is how Divine energy is moved down into the lower dimensions — by the vehicle of the sacrament. Another ancient Mystery which we are now more clearly remembering. Believe and drink."

I, having exhausted all objections, did. So did Sheeyah. And then we shimmered as if made entirely of light. I could see a golden triangular halo around Sheeyah's head. I could feel one around mine.

Camus stepped forward from among the group of dignitaries. He faced Sheeyah and held up both his palms facing her, which she met with her own palms. Instantaneously, she was transported onto the henu boat, which materialized in the mouth of the cave, floating on what came into my awareness again as nothing other than the river of light.

Camus turned to me, bowed into that triangle, and then rose with his two palms ready to meet mine.

I looked around at my High Counsel. I did not wish to leave them. They all wanted me to go. I gathered I had no choice. I felt I should say good-bye. "Until we meet again, in another dimension, let us continue in our work to protect Creation, encourage evolution, and disseminate Pure and Original Truth." I sounded to myself like a Cosmic politician.

Yet, I could feel tears in my eyes as I raised my palms and was suddenly back on the river of light with Camus, Sheeyah, and that bird again, Sokaris, the bird of the henu boat, the bird with my eyes. Thank God you are still alive, Sokaris. The river of light was infinite and, although unending, instantly at end. I can still hear that remarkable bird calling "Sokarrrrrr" and filling me with the greatest of Hope . . . .

Hope . . . .

Hope . . . .

13

Those of my readers who are physically incarnated as humans know the ordeals you face. Your third dimensional bodies distract you from spiritual growth. Yet, these same bodies can serve as the vehicles of your spiritual evolution.

Although a common one, the journey into human incarnation is superbly challenging and its potential for the quickening of the soul is profoundly immense. Try to remember this in your moments of mortal anguish. Try to receive this message in its entirety at the hour of your physical death.

Ω

I awoke to find Sheeyah sleeping in my arms. We were aboard my yacht in one of the bunks. I glanced at my watch out of habit and noted that it was working, sort of. It said 0400. Four in the morning? But the date function was still non-functional. I was perspiring heavily. We were tangled in our regal cloaks which covered the now well-tattered and torn clothes we had been wearing back at Crystal Mirror Lake and throughout our multidimensional adventures.

"Sheeyah," I whispered in her ear.

No response. She continued to sleep. I could feel that she was much too warm under the cloak, so I began removing it. I found that I enjoyed undressing her. It was quite comforting and so I decided to remove what remained of her torn shirt. She rolled closer to me and we made love. She didn't say a word or open her eyes the entire time. We held each other so tightly, as if desperately hanging on to affirm the reality of our survival of what had been, and would continue to be, an intensely arduous, almost impossible, spiritually wrenching journey.

We must have fallen asleep for hours. The eerie morning light of a weak and tenuous dawn crept into the bunk room of my yacht and gently reminded us that we had work to do. I glanced out the window and noted that the sun was a yellow-grey ball in a dark sky. Somehow, there was daylight, but the sky claimed night. And the moon — hanging motionlessly and full across from the sun, the moon was a foreboding red. I could see the craters — were they filled with blood? The blood of man? Of the third dimension?

"What an absolute mess. How do you live like this, Triad?" Sheeyah called me back.

"Live like what? I've been gone, remember — I was with you."

"Oh, yeah, right. But look at all this stuff. What are these papers everywhere? Notes, mail, . . . faxes." She began reading one of the faxes. And then she groaned. "Triad, what does all this mean to you? It sounds like it came right out of *my secret files* back at Earthcult headquarters. Longitude 65° west? Latitude 56° south? Who's sending you this?"

"Give me that," I demanded. I could feel trouble coming. Big, big trouble.

"Wait, longitude 2.5° west, latitude 55.5° north? How did you get this? Did you steal this from me, from Earthcult?"

"Well, no, not exactly . . ." I mumbled.

"Not exactly? What does not *exactly* mean? And listen to this!"

I tried to grab the papers Sheeyah was holding but she jumped back and began reading them aloud:

"(1) Longitude 65° west, latitude 56° south, Tierra Del Fuego area; as per your instruction, we have completed the acquisition of land to be formed between Argentina and the Antarctic — the land mass that will connect to two continents, expected to rise on the first polar shift.

(2) Longitude 2.5° west, latitude 55.5° north, mountainous area between England and Scotland — acquisition completed, funds disbursed to sellers.

(3) Longitude 18° west, latitude 65.5° north — Iceland: large tracts are under contract. Investor funding proceeding. Please advise. Date of closing 24 hours from now.

(4) Longitude 49° east, latitude 15° south, Madagascar location. North end of Island in escrow. Balance awaiting final title insurance policies. Will proceed if no reply from you.

(5) Note regarding acquisitions next on the agenda. Given that the third pole shift will create new and final land masses, acquisitions should take into account expected direction of third polar shift:

Move existing North Pole Down: 158° west longitudinal line to intersect with 24° north latitudinal, north of Hawaii. Corresponding South Pole location: South Africa – Kalahari Desert - latitude 24° south and longitude 22° east."

She stopped reading. She was furious. I opened my mouth to speak, but before I could, she yelled, "You must have stolen these from my files! No one else on Earth has the identity of these locations!"

"I didn't."

"You did, Triad! I know it!"

"O.K. I'll tell you. I had it sent to me by one of my most trusted members. I had it sent to me by one of your most trusted members."

"No. That's impossible. None of my people would do that!"

"He wasn't one of your people. He was one of mine. He infiltrated your organization at my request. I paid him to do so."

"Who?"

"Does it matter?" I hoped she'd let me off the hook. "Who, Triad, who?"

I shrugged. Here goes. "First name Mark."

"Mark? Mark Wharton?"

"Mark."

"Mark Wharton, the adopted cousin and sometime investment partner of *Dave* Wharton?"

"Mark. Has an associate, maybe a cousin, who knows, named Dave."

Sheeyah was shocked and dismayed. Dave had been her lover and a supporter of Earthcult for years, until the day he left her in the harbor parking lot. The day he broke her heart. "Do you know Dave, Triad?"

I didn't answer. I just couldn't. I did not want to see her reaction.

"Do you?"

"Do you know him? Dave Wharton? Have you ever met him?"

I decided to pick up the papers which were scattered all over the floor of my bunk room. She automatically knelt down, ostensibly to help, but also to stay on the case.

"Triad, what is it that you won't tell me? You might as well tell all. There can't be much more to know about your buy-up of whatever of my safe lands you were able to find out about. You've been a devious, money-hungry real estate developer — opportunistic and devoid of conscience, so . . ."

"That's not true. Not *devoid* of conscience."

"Hah." Sheeyah was about to blow up at me.

"Look, Sheeyah. I had absolutely no idea that I was God."

"That *we* were God."

"And, Sheeyah, if someone had told me, do you think I would have believed it? No! It took everything we've been through to convince me and, at the moment, I could find myself easily having doubts about it."

"So, do you know Dave? Dave Wharton? Did you know that I was in love with him?" She stared at me with tears welling in her eyes. So that was the pain I had noted in her face when she was fixing her bicycle in the harbor parking lot.

"Look Sheeyah, we were both up to about the same thing, you and I. Your safe lands and my survivor territories were the same thing — the same idea. Whether or not we had any conscious notion of what we were up to, we were both driven by the instinctual desire to survive or make it possible for some to survive the next Omega Point."

"I'm sure your idea of who should survive and mine were radically different, Triad, but that's not relevant right now — tell me how you're connected to Dave! Did you two plan to dump me in the parking lot by your boat — ?"

"Yacht." I corrected her numbly.

"Who cares? Did you?"

The sea beneath us was tumultuous. We had to hang on to the sides of the bunk to maintain our balance as we knelt on the floor. The next wave hit the side of the yacht and knocked both of us over.

The jolt did not stop Sheeyah from her interrogation. In fact, she now began pumping real fury into her questions.

Transcending the Time Wave

"Tell me! I have a right to know! Tell me!"

As the yacht rocked, a box toppled over and emptied its contents across the floor. Pennies, dimes, my pocket watch, my check book, my pistol.

I could not believe my eyes when she grabbed the pistol. "I said tell me!"

"It's locked, Sheeyah. You don't know how to use that," I said calmly.

"Don't be so sure. We've been stock-piling weapons of all sorts for decades." She stared at me over the gun.

"Decades? You aren't that old."

"I got involved as a kid. By the time I was a teenager, I belonged to the organization from which Earthcult later broke off."

"Led by you," I accused.

"Yes, well, we were kids, or young adults, but much more serious about the cause. I didn't like the way those arm chair environmental groups and even the ones that believed they were more radical than the arm chair groups were run." She didn't lower the weapon.

"So you started your own," I accused again.

"Yes, but if you think that this side discussion is distracting me from what I want to know, you are wrong. Maybe even dead wrong." She waved the gun, unhooked the release, and cocked the trigger.

"Now tell me how you know Dave." Her eyes were hurt and angry — fierce.

"You wouldn't kill me, Sheeyah. I'm the father of your child."

"I would. You see, Triad, you are the father of *one* of my children — *maybe* — "

"One of your children? Maybe?"

"Maybe meaning it could be virgin birth. You know, like Jesus came to Mary — no sex involved."

"But you know it's not." I hoped she did.

"No I don't, Triad. It didn't feel like a sexual insemination."

"It wasn't. We weren't in the third dimension. Come on, Sheeyah, put the gun down, you won't shoot me. This is ridiculous."

"You are close to becoming the killer of Earthcult, one of my other children. And, as best as I can tell, you are responsible for Nostradamus' death."

"What! That's insane. I only infiltrated Earthcult. And that's not a child, its an organization. And I didn't kill Nostradumus, Set did!"

"Set! You weakened the Cosmos enough that Set could kill our son!"

I clenched my fists and started to sweat. "Stop this. This is nuts. Come Sheeyah, put the gun down now."

"Without your heavy yang imbalance, Set could never have become a threat, Triad."

"I could blame you as easily, Sheeyah. Attraction to your yin magnifies yang. Yang gets its energy from you!"

"No! It *takes* its energy from me. Yang sucks from yin," she answered rather viciously.

"Inspired by yin to do so," I quipped.

"Now tell me about Dave, Triad." She waved the gun at me.

I started to laugh uncontrollably. This woman was actually threatening to kill me. Why? Why? Then, abruptly, I guessed that she sensed my real dirty secret, one I hadn't realized I'd had until she'd made the connection between Dave Wharton and me. I had not really realized that Dave and Sheeyah had really become lovers. And I did not like this realization at all.

"Who is Dave!!!?" She lunged toward me and pressed the gun into my chest. She seemed crazed with fury, so crazed that I dared not try to get the gun away from her.

If I had found any bit of her behavior cute or funny, I wasn't laughing any longer. "Sheeyah! Careful, you might make a dreadful mistake! Put the gun down!"

"You've out-lived your usefulness, Triad. It will break my heart, but you actually began betraying me even before we met."

"We met long, long ago, Sheeyah."

"Tell me how you know Dave or I'll kill you and then go through your papers 'till I find out."

"Must you know? Must you, Sheeyah?"

"Yes."

I could see that I'd have to answer her question to end this insane scene. "O.K., put the gun down and I'll tell you."

She didn't move.

"O.K. Hold the gun, but back up and sit across from me and aim it somewhere else, so you don't kill me by mistake, please. I want to choose the time of my death for myself."

She complied. When she was sitting on the bunk across the floor from me, she held the pistol down at her side.

"Sheeyah, it could go off by mistake. Set the lock and I'll talk."

She complied, eyeing me coldly. But she showed me she was still ready to use the gun by keeping her hand on it.

I looked at my feet. This was going to be an unpleasant admission, to put it mildly. I took a deep breath and then I told her:

"Dave is my brother."

She nodded in awe. "Your brother." She sounded as if she only half believed me when she added, "But the two of you have different last names. Wharton. Framingham."

"No. Framingham is an assumed name. I took it some years back, when I didn't want people to connect me with all my money. Framingham. You know, the Framingham studies, the all-American average male's diet and heart disease behaviors — that study? I just took the name."

"You mean you are Triad Wharton? Somehow I don't believe that either."

"No. Wharton is the name Dave used. Just an assumed name."

"So you're brothers? And I fell for both of you?"

"Or we both fell for you. You are a difficult woman to resist." This was still true. She was magnetically alluring, even pregnant.

"Yeah right. Sure. So who are you guys then?"

"de Nostras."

"de Nostras? Very funny. Don't play games with me, because I'm ready to kill you. de Nostras? That was *my* parents' last name."

I was quiet for a while, trying to make sense of this new data — Sheeyah was a de Nostras? My sister? I saw her raise the gun. So I muttered, "They're dead. My parents are dead. If they were yours too, then our parents are dead." Now I felt sick, very, very sick.

"How did you know that? . . . You've had me checked out, you devious bastard. You're playing games with my mind now."

"No. I didn't get this in any reports on you. But I just now remembered. The people at the orphanage told us we had a sister somewhere. But they split us up when our parents were killed."

"Who told you *what*?"

"The orphanage we grew up in. Dave and I. They told us we had a sister somewhere. We tried to find you. For years. Then we went on with our lives. I had no idea that you were my sister. I had no idea the leader of Earthcult was my blood relative. I had no idea that the woman I found fixing her bicycle in the parking lot was either the leader of Earthcult or my sister. Or that she was in love with Dave."

Sheeyah was stunned, hurt and angry, all at once. "You're saying you're my brother? And Dave is my brother? And I was his lover and then yours?"

"I guess so. But it is only just now that I have realized that we are related. Really...But there's more. Oh God, I think there's more."

"More? Isn't this enough?"

"Sheeyah, what was Nostradamus' real last name?"

"Don't know."

"Yes you do, Sheeyah. He told us, remember? And anyway, we already knew it when he told us."

"What?" She asked me with her very angry, very hurt eyes. I wished I could have taken away the pain I saw in her face now. I wished I could have somehow saved her from this knowledge. But it was too late for that.

"Think, Sheeyah."

She thought for a while. And then shook her head no. "No. It can't be." She did not want to believe any of this.

"It is."

"Say it, Triad."

"No, you say it, Sheeyah."

" . . . Nostradam ... de Nostradam?" she whispered.

"Yes, Sheeyah. He was actually a de Nostradame."

"He's our son, Triad, our dead son. Let's stop here."

"Yes, he is our son. But he's also our father, Sheeyah."

"No stop. Don't. He's dead."

"O.K. I'll stop soon. But just think. He was our son, a de Nostradame on Earth. He was also our father, a de Nostras. An immortal. Never really died until we saw him give himself to Set. Same family line, immigrated to the New World, gave birth to us here centuries later. Altered the last name a bit: de Nostras."

We were silent a long time.

"Triad, we actually had a father? We're brother and sister? Both of us de Nostras?"

"Yes."

"But, I'm pregnant with your child, Triad."

"Better call it virgin birth."

"It'd be the same either way because we're Gods. Gods can engage in incest can't they? Only I don't feel any better about it this way. I had sex with my brother? Both my brothers? The only men I ever loved? Oh God."

"But things are even worse than this, Sheeyah."

"Nostradamus was our — no matter what else — also our son, Triad. He was — I loved him."

"He's dead now, Sheeyah. Set killed him."

"Set is your brother."

"*Our* brother."

We were silent a moment and then said it at the same time:

"Dave!"

"Are you thinking what I am thinking?" I asked her.

"Yes," she said shakingly, "I guess I am. But I just can't believe it. Dave, Dave de Nostras, is Set? Set has already been here in the third dimension trying to kill us? Set can exist in several dimensions at once the way we can?"

"Yes, but he probably was not conscious of his intentions. He will only remember fully if his amnesia wears off. He must have still had amnesia or he would have killed us both when he was working with me to steal Earthcult's secrets and taking my investor's money to buy up Earthcult's safe lands."

"And he would have killed me instead of dumping me off in the harbor parking lot. He didn't know I was his sister then."

"Not consciously. But, it's only a matter time before he joins with his Cosmic self and realizes who he is."

"It's safe to say that if he finds either of us, he will soon be consciously ready to kill us. He will want our child dead. Like he went after Horus."

We had not noticed that the yacht in which we sat had come unmoored. Yes, while we were coming to grips with our most Cosmic incest, our son's parentage of us, and our relationship to Dave, or Set, as we had come to know him in our recent journeys, we had floated far out to sea.

I finally did notice this when I looked out the window. We were far from land. Sheeyah saw my face as I looked and she said, "We'd better get back in to shore. The sea looks rough."

"It looks black. Black waves," I whispered dully. The waves were slowly heaving, reaching huge proportions, hundreds of feet high, climbing into the dark day-time sky, heavy, as if waves of oil. I'd never seen anything like it. I got out the telescope and studied the now very distant shore. It was unrecognizable. Truly foreign.

"We can't have traveled that far," I murmured, not wishing to alarm Sheeyah. Something was very wrong.

"We haven't. The second pole shift must have occurred and somehow we just sailed through it."

"Or the land we were close to simply sank into the sea," Sheeyah explained. She was right, the prophecy of apocalypse was manifesting. I wondered what was happening on the land.

"I'm cold. I'm so cold." Sheeyah had tears in her eyes. "I'm cold and I want to be close to you. I don't know if it's wrong or right, but I want you to hold me. Please. Hold me tight."

She cocked the trigger on the pistol, and then handed me the ridiculous gun.

"Hold me or kill me," she said. "Make love with me or I'll die. And so will our new Messiah."

I shook my head and took the gun, locked the release and put it in a drawer.

"It has all been done already. We're just doing a repeat scene. So why not?" I wanted to be close to her too, real close, inside her. I loved her. I had a deep irrepressible passion for her, belly and all.

We curled up together in one of the bunks after taking all the blankets from all the other bunks. The night seemed endless and we held each other, locked in a kind of frozen passion in the womb of the ship which carried us through time, through time toward the inevitable.

It might have been days, or weeks or an eternity. I have no idea of how long it was before we were aware of sunlight again. But, finally in the same moment, we both realized that there was light and we were warm again. We got up and ran on to the deck, naked, but not minding.

We were stunned to find that we were approaching land. We were arriving at the mouth of a magnificent bay.

"Where are we?" Sheeyah was confused and amazed.

"Can't say." I really did not know.

"Get the telescope. Maybe we can see."

I did look through the telescope. I couldn't make out much at first. Then slowly, things came into focus. Some kind of city, parts of it totally devastated, parts of it standing but in shambles and parts seemingly untouched by what had touched the other parts. What was it? An earthquake? A flood? A hurricane? A large fire? All of the above. The second stage in the three stage apocalypse.

"What do see? Tell me. What?"

I continued to look, speechless at the vision. And then I saw some half fallen highway signs. I squinted and tried to focus the telescope. What? What did it say? "D-A-N"? "D-A-N-" Was it "danger"? No, no . . . D-E-N, oh no, not really, no, it said "DENVER"!

"Denver," I finally managed to say.

"Denver? Let me look. . . . Oh my god, you're right . . . it says Denver. Let's go. Let's go in. We have to."

As we made our way into the port of Denver, I found that I had never been so exhilarated in my life as this particular incarnate. Extremely exhilarated and extremely horrified. How could the world as I had known it change so radically, so rapidly? How could anyone living on Earth in the time of the new millennium ever imagine that the world could change its face so much? Was this going to be the extinction of the human species?

I did not know what to anticipate as we headed for whatever we could use as a dock.

As we moored the yacht, we knew that we were returning to chaos. I made a quick run through my possessions, grabbing all the deeds to the survivor territories I had purchased and the hundreds of thousands of dollars in cash I had hidden in a secret compartment containing a safe, below one of the bunks. I turned to see that Sheeyah had found her bag and was putting my pistol into it. She seemed to have a lot of cash in her bag, too. I didn't know why, but I suspected that the money had come from Dave.

"Wait. That pistol is mine," I said.

"Is it the only one you have?" she asked nervously.

"Well . . . no, no . . . I have a few others."

"Get them, Triad. And get all the ammunition. We might need it."

"You think so?" I asked, sounding doubtful, nevertheless suspecting she was right.

"I do, Triad. People are bound to be terrified, crazy, looting, robbing, killing, starving —"

"Cannibalizing." I completed her list.

"Oh God." She hadn't thought of this.

"Kill or be killed, Sheeyah."

"I'd kill not to die," she sounded certain.

"I'd kill to save you," I found myself speaking to her tenderly.

"You would? I hope so, I'm carrying our child, the completion of the Triad, the manifestation of the Triad, the manifestation of us which will ward off Set. Or should I say Dave? ... But would you kill to save yourself, Triad?"

"I'm not sure any longer." I looked at the shore where I could now see people in rags foraging through the gutters and where I could hear gun shots every few minutes. "This third dimensional stuff is wearing on me."

"Well, I don't want you to go, O.K.? Don't go. I need you. I want you. You're the best lover I ever had. You're the father of this baby. I'm not sure why, you are a corrupt and questionable kind of guy, but I love you, so stick around. At least for a while." She was trying not to beg.

"Sheeyah, you should not love me like you do. I am your brother. It cannot be a good idea." I was trying not to be rash.

"But you said yourself that we've already committed whatever heinous sins we were going to commit. It doesn't feel so wrong to love you in this case."

"We should go ashore, Sheeyah."

"Wait, Triad. This is Denver. There's a place about thirty miles into the mountains where my people have weapons and food hidden. Let's try to get there. It will be a safe place."

"You're sure?"

"Yes, if your people haven't bought it up yet. It's one of my headquarters. My people are probably there awaiting my direction. I can mobilize them to safeguard the safe lands from the wrong intruders," she eyed me critically. "They'd never let you in if they checked you out, but I'll get you in."

"I'm not certain I want in." I realized how very much I wanted out of this entire this material plane.

We locked the boat, I put the keys around my neck, took the dingy I had stored on deck and rowed to shore. As I rowed, Sheeyah proposed what I once would have thought of as an outrageously presumptuous plan. Now I took it in stride. It even made sense. Perhaps all I had done in this incarnation led to exactly this moment of hearing Sheeyah's plan.

"Triad, if you are actually planning on dying —"

"Leaving this material plane, that's all," I softened it as I could see she was pained at the thought.

"Triad, if you would will all your survivor territory holdings to our daughter —"

"Yes." I interrupted her. She looked at me, stunned. "Yes, it must be, Sheeyah, I must will them to you and to our daughter. As soon as I have a paper and a pen and a notary —"

"A notary?"

"You think they have all died? There must be one notary left in Denver."

"Who knows? But why a notary?"

"I want to write a legal document, Sheeyah, for you."

We made our way into the devastated city. It was not difficult to find a notary. We found one sitting at her desk in a state of shock. The glass window in front of her ground floor office was shattered, papers were strewn everywhere. Her face was cut, one hand bandaged and two babies, presumably hers, sat on the floor by her desk, screaming.

There were at least twenty similarly worn people waiting to get documents signed. We borrowed pen and paper and I wrote my will. Sheeyah thought it was a wonderful gesture, but had not quite let herself see that I intended to leave this dimension soon. I was not about to endure the physical anguish of the third polar shift and the thousand year time which was to follow it. Not for me, thank you. I found myself hungry, starving for physical death.

When we were finished, I asked Sheeyah to return to the beach where we came ashore. She followed me back, thinking I had forgotten something on shore.

But I stopped near the water's edge and did nothing for a while. Then I said, "So it is time for me to go. I will leave you here to usher Earth into its new era, to assist Earth and her inhabitants in evolving into a higher spiritual dimension. . . . I, on the other hand, have to get out of this third dimension. I do not want to see this place, this once beautiful Earth, like this."

"But we programmed Creation to cycle through a time wave, to die and give birth to itself again. This is supposed to be normal, Triad. You said so yourself. Why are you so upset by all this?"

"I am not upset. It is only that I feel I must go. I have indeed outlived my usefulness on Earth at this time. My work is done here. I have placed the survivor territories in the hands of its rightful Queen and our heir, our Messiah."

"So now what?" Sheeyah was astonished at my determination.

"Please end my life for me."

"Me? *Kill you*? Absolutely not!"

"You were quite ready to do so on the yacht when you found out about Dave, our brother."

"I don't know if I would really have done it, Triad. I was crazed by the information — deception, incest — but I won't kill you now."

"In the time to come you will help many people to deliver themselves into a higher dimension."

"I will kill people?"

"No, Sheeyah."

"Assisted suicide?" she asked, listening closely now.

"More of an enabling of self-deliverance. Now it is time to practice on me. This will become your art." I accepted my certainty.

"My art?"

"Yes, now, I will leave my body of my own will in order to save you the pain of any involvement in what will appear to you to be my death."

"This has got to be the loneliest moment of my life, Triad."

"I suspect you have endured far lonelier passages .... But do not let this pain you. You know we will meet again. We will rejoin. Now you must carry our child in to the future."

"Triad, we have to talk about something first, to get it finished and clear. .... I don't know how I know that our child is a daughter, but I do. I am absolutely certain. I would feel better knowing that she has your blessing. I think you've finally accepted that the time has come for us to have a daughter. It feels so strange to be speaking so easily about such cosmic matters, but I guess after all we've seen and done, we're bound to be getting a bit godlike, you know, taking cosmic stuff for granted and all. In any case, you and I both know that, throughout the eons, our true bearing has always been a son. Our Triad has consistently and without variation manifested itself in the yang force. This has unbalanced our Cosmos throughout time. It is time for us to rebalance our Creation."

I was silent. I knew this had to be. I knew she wanted me to bless the child. For some reason, I was still a bit hesitant. I could feel Sheeyah asking me to shift in advance of the shift my — our — Cosmos was going to take.

"Triad, I want your blessing, I really do. But, even if I don't get it, you actually have no choice but to support the coming shift in the balance of power that our daughter represents. *It's coming whether you like it or not.*"

I felt faintly threatened. "Sounds like a threat, Sheeyah." Why would she choose to confront me with this matter when I was going to die?

"And I, whatever 'I' means anymore, I, as both the Earthly woman and your Divine Counterpart, the yin side of the Duad, have now realized that I too have the power to Create. You see, something has happened through all this wearing down of our amnesia. I have remembered something that I either forgot long ago or was never really sure of: I have at least as much power to Create as do you. Yes you are the Creator. But, I am also the Creator of the universe. You and I are one. We are made of the same intensity of power, just different polarities of it."

She wanted me to agree. In principle, I did, but I just couldn't put my heart in it. "If you say so," I said quietly.

My lack of enthusiasm seemed to increase Sheeyah's determination to get through to me. "Triad, let me put it this way: *your increasingly overbearing dominance has been an error in evolution.*"

She was right. I could feel it as she laid that last criticism of my dominance on me. An error in evolution. I did agree, so I decided to let her know this and then to get going, to leave this dimension of madness before the next polar shift. "A necessary error in the folly of the Gods, one which I hope Set benefits no more by. So, Sheeyah, I beg you, be extremely careful if you find Dave. Even if he does not yet realize he is our brother, Set, he will be driven by buried instinct to be dangerous to you and especially to the baby. If he senses in any way that our child is a girl, he will know she will bring new balance to the Cosmos, and he will be even more dangerous. Do not trust his words. Do not believe his sentiments. Even if he, being an amnesic, thinks he is sincere, he is not."

She nodded in agreement, seemingly to register my warning very thoroughly.

"So, I give you and our daughter my blessing. I must. It is our only defense against the anti-prana force of Set."

"You have made me happy, Triad."

I wanted to get going. "I must leave this tired body now."

She looked at me and shrugged her shoulders. She did not seem to really get it: I was going to leave.

I could remember dying a physical death many times prior to this one. What I was unprepared for, however, was how distinct the stages of physical death were to one who could remain aware (in some way, whether or not conscious in observers' eyes) during the process.

I was quite surprised to find that I knew quite a bit about the process of death. It all seemed to come back to me once I consciously decided to engage in dying. I felt a wonderful comfort at knowing so much. There was no unknown for me to fear. I wanted to tell Sheeyah what I was discovering or rediscovering. I thought it would help her deal with my dying and the great amount of dying she was going to be seeing on Earth in the time to come.

"Sheeyah, it all depends upon the style of death one chooses, if one has the opportunity to choose, that is. Quite often, the first phase of physical dying is experienced semi-consciously. Blood pressure substantially reduces. The brain finds itself running short of its normal supply of oxygen and sugar, so the brain kicks in with a compensatory mechanism which dilates its blood vessels and draws extra blood from wherever it might be stored. What this does is give the brain a brief increase in its blood sugar. So the brain is, for a brief time, receiving a much enriched supply of food. The dying person is thus able to flashback or even rapidly review his entire life while feeling little emotion in these moments. It is a primarily higher cognitive activity, with little if any involvement of lower emotional processes."

"Is that what you are doing, Triad, reviewing your life?"

"Yes, back to the beginning of time ... But now, just at this moment, now, I am moving into the second phase of physical dying. My brain, mainly the cortex, is working at a feverous pitch. It is now consuming sugar faster than it can get it. My brain is operating at a very high frequency now, maintaining rapid rhythmical beta waves with some spurts of alpha. This generates what some human meditators can bring about for themselves without dying — a sense of bliss. Transcendence."

"Bliss? Do you really feel happy? You know, Triad, my dearest Triad, you can still come back and leave off this process while you are at this near death level."

"I am more. More than happy. But this phase of physical dying draws to a close momentarily. Please, make no effort to bring me back to this mortal body. I want to die this death. I am going into the third phase of physical dying now. I will stop breathing, my eyes will stop seeing. My brain will stop running, being out of sugar and choking on its waste matter. I feel these changes upon me."

"No! No! Wait! ... Not yet! Come on, Triad, not yet!"

"Yes." It was becoming very difficult for me to speak. My mouth felt as if filled with cement, the cement of the ether, I assumed. I began to whisper. "Sheeyah, darling, this is a necessary agony. It begins to feel like giving birth, like labor pains of some sort. When it is complete, I will be in the fourth and final phase of physical dying. My brain must stop for at least six minutes for me to be clinically dead. To be certain that I really achieve full physical death, let my brain stop longer, maybe ten minutes. Do not interfere. Do I have your word?"

"Yes. No. Yes. O. K. O. K. O. K." She seemed to barely understand that this was for real.

I drew upon every remaining bit of physical strength I had to say my final spoken words to the love of my life, of all my lives. "I have your word then. See you next time." I sounded extremely trite to myself. Last words are so silly. Dead lines. But I did mean them so very much. I could feel my love for this woman, this Goddess, and I knew I had to soon let go of this form of feeling in order to die well. "I must let go. But I will always be with you." I could feel her heart-strings tugging at me, trying to pull me back into the third dimension. I needed her to let me go. "Now you let go. Let me go. You must let go now. If you love me, let me go."

"Triad, I—"

I said nothing.

"Triad? Triad? *Triad*!!!!"

I watched her cry from some distance above the ground. She was so attached to my pitifully dead body that she was not paying attention to my lingering and very living presence.

Enough. Enough. Sheeyah. Stop the tears.

She turned around, as if startled. She looked upward.

You heard me.

"Yes."

So do not be sad. I am not dead.

"But I want you back so I can touch you. So you can feel me touch you where you like to be touched. I want you back. I still want you. I am not finished ... I wasn't finished having you be my lover ... seems I only just found you .... I only just discovered the intense satisfaction of our closeness and now it's already a thing of the past."

Lie down. I will join you for a moment.

"I can't feel you, Triad. Please, please, why did you leave me, I only finally felt really close to someone and he's gone, you're gone. This whole thing is really breaking my heart, I feel tears coming right out of my heart. I cannot stand this — oh god, no, I cannot stand this. Come back, come back, you are a god, you have the power to come back to life, to resurrect your self. Rise from the dead. Please, Triad. I can't do this Earth thing without you."

No, we have made our decision. I am lying next to you right now. There will be no physical sensation unless you give it one. Just believe I am here next to you for a moment. Feel me if you want to.

"Feel you? Feel what? Your body?" She tentatively ran her fingers down my dead body.

I am not there, Sheeyah. I am not in my body. You will not feel me in that body unless you want your imagination to fool you.

I watched her kiss my corpse again and again with a controlled desperation.

Just lie still Sheeyah.

She finally did as I asked. After a while she said, "I want to go with you. I can't stay here without you."

No. You are right to stay in the third dimension. I must now go prepare to meet brother Set face to face. You must stay and bring the female Messiah to the heart of the Cosmos, to Earth. She has to be born into the third dimension. The time has come. From the higher dimensions, I can help protect the new Messiah you bring in.

"I don't like being here alone, Triad. I feel so alone without you now. I never knew that I was alone until I met you and now that you and I are so close, you are gone — just gone. And I still want you. I still want your body to be warm and alive."

Stay, Sheeyah. You are safe here. You will remain immortal here as long as you so choose. At least see our daughter into incarnate adulthood. This is your job. Teach her all you know. Teach her to be a Goddess — to carry Original Truth.

She nodded gravely and was silent for many, many minutes.

Sheeyah, now put my body in the raft and burn it.

I could see a flicker of horror in her eyes.

Remember that you are not only a mortal woman, you are the Goddess.

Sheeyah cried softly over my body for a few minutes. Then her tears ran out. She looked around and saw no one watching. Then she stood and dragged my body into the raft. She set it afire and pushed it out to sea. Camus appeared with the henu boat and hooked my burning raft to his boat, tugging my body on the river of light to the new ocean Earth had formed out of the black, black waves. I could hear the sound of that bird, the one with my eyes, Sokaris. He was calling from somewhere above.

"Sokarrrrr! Sokarrrr!!! Sokarrrrrrrrrrrrrr!!!!!!!" I knew this was my voice.

Physical death is the withdrawal of the soul from its two anchors: the heart and the pineal gland in the brain. This withdrawal from the heart and from the head cuts off the two streams of energy which unite the soul with the body — the blood stream and the endocrine stream or system. This cutting off severs the connection between body and soul. Sometimes a body resists the departure of the soul which has inhabited it and then this severance process is slow and messy. It might be better said that some souls, not understanding this process, do not fully cut these cords, these streams between the dimensions.

I knew now what I had always known but had not let myself see about Sheeyah. She was truly the Goddess of Life and of Death, the handmaiden to both these children of Creation, being part of the same cyclical and ever enduring process. She knew my death, all deaths, as well as she knew child birth. There was nothing I could teach her that she did not know. But I could attempt to bring back her memory of her vast knowledge of Truth.

If you listen closely now Sheeyah, deep within the recesses of your ear, I will detail for you the next episodes of death.

She heard me. I saw her kneel at the water's edge, more detached, but with her eyes still forming tears.

Sheeyah, once one passes out of the body or physical vehicle, one has passed from the first episode of death or the first death, which is physical, to the second death, which is not physical. In this next death comes the astral death — the death of the emotional vehicle. Once the physical house of the body is empty, it begins to decompose. You would think death is complete at the physical end, after the four phases of physical death, but the next dying, that astral death, is as much a great passage, if not more. For the individual who has just lost his body still retains many of the feelings and awarenesses of others' feelings he acquired while in that body. The higher-evolved beings can leave their physical vehicles quite consciously and, in full waking awareness, preserve the continuity of consciousness while moving from the physical plane to the after-death state. Perhaps, Sheeyah, you can help those humans you meet who may be seeking to depart the physical plane understand this process. Those who do not understand this second stage of death enter it hysterical, fearful, angry, and or bewildered and needlessly waste their spiritual energy. And next, whatever his awareness, the physically dead individual must leave behind all astral connection to the physical plane and move on. This is a critical and very difficult process for many souls. They sense that what will come next is the dissipation of all the mental energy assumed during the recent incarnation. This is the third death. Very few spirits are evolved enough to succeed in fully completing this third death and, in so doing, crossing the threshold beyond the death cycle. Most fail at this death and must recycle again and again until some day they will finally succeed.

Whatever conscious focus on moving through the previous astral episode of death was achieved by the dying individual will have served as great training for his soul. The road map from physical to astral to mental death is one drawn by repeated exploration of the process. Navigating the three deaths well is the greatest challenge for a being.

Sheeayh had listened to me and seemed to know what I was talking about. I was still with my astral body enough to feel satisfaction in this. I would eventually detach but I lingered out of a sort of self indulgence, and a strong tie to this woman, the heart and yes the flesh of this woman I had chosen to leave. I did not let myself feel regrets. Such emotions are dangerous at such a juncture, especially for a god so adept at all this multidimensional transition.

"But the word 'death' seems such a silly one in the face of the great adventure it represents, Triad."

I wondered why she was speaking aloud when she knew we could communicate without this verbalizing. I decided that this was helping her conceptualize the reality and veracity of this communication with me. I let it go and said nothing, although I think she heard me wonder.

Yes, Sheeyah. It pleases me to know that you see this. Resurrection would be a more appropriate term. This was the message of Christ, of Nostradamus, of all the prophets of cataclysm. It is not death we seek at the Omega Point, it is the Alpha — the resurrection.

". . . Resurrection. . . of even the anima mundi? Of Earth?"

MY PHYSICAL DEATH IS THE OPPORTUNITY FOR THE RESURRECTION OF MY SOUL. THIS PROCESS OF DEATH AND RESURRECTION — OF OMEGA AND ALPHA — GOES ON CEASELESSLY IN ALL THE KINGDOMS OF NATURE — IN ALL THE KINGDOMS OF ALL THE COSMOS — EACH DEATH PREFACES A RESURRECTION! THAT IS, UNLESS SET INTERFERES.

Sheeyah overlooked the reminder of the immanence of Set. "Earth, you're here!"

OF COURSE. YOU ARE ON ME.

"Yes, of course. So I am not alone. I am not alone. . . . Earth, Can you hear Triad?"

OF COURSE.

"He isn't dead. Triad isn't dead."

OF COURSE.

"Earth, were you ever a human?"

I WAS SOMETHING SIMILAR ON ANOTHER PLANET FAR AWAY. HAVING PROGRESSED TO THE LIMITS OF MY EVOLUTION THERE, I ASSUMED THE FORM OF A PLANET IN ORDER TO FURTHER EVOLVE. THIS COMING OMEGA POINT IS ONE OF THE SEVERAL INITIATIONS THROUGH WHICH I AM PASSING.

"I guess I'm going through a few of my own."

YOU REINCARNATE FROM TIME TO TIME FOR JUST THIS PURPOSE.

"Yeah, right, to reinitiate myself."

THE TIME APPROACHES FOR THE GREAT REBALANCING. YOU HAVE TIME TO MAKE YOUR WAY TO YOUR MOUNTAIN SAFE LAND.

Sheeyah looked around and seemed to listen to something. She looked startled and picked up the guns and the money and whatever else she could fit in her bag and began to run.

She came to a street corner. Someone sat asleep in a four wheel drive jeep which had a paper sign saying "taxi" in the window. She snuck up on the passenger side of the front seat and opened the door. The sleeping driver awoke with a start. Sheeyah already had a gun pointed at him.

"Quiet or I will shoot. I want you to drive me somewhere. When we arrive there, I will let you enter and find safety, food and water, but if you try to leave, I will kill you."

He looked her in the eye and raised his eyebrows and shook his head yes. When he reached for the steering wheel, the sleeve on his right wrist slipped up and some of his skin showed between his glove and his jacket. He reached over abruptly to cover it when he saw Sheeyah glance at his arm.

"Stop. Freeze. Don't move. Now show me your arm."

He complied very slowly.

Sheeyah took a deep gasp of air into her lungs when she saw his tattoo.

"I want you not to move but to look at this," she said coldly. Holding the gun aimed at his head and not daring to take her eyes off him, Sheeyah raised her left hand and pulled down the neck of her shirt to her left breast.

He saw her tattoo. Their eyes met.

"Sheeyah, Earthcult Sheeyah? You *are* alive. We hoped and prayed so."

"I am. Alive." The word alive had taken on new meaning for Sheeyah in this incarnation, as had her directorship of Earthcult.

"We have been waiting for a sign or some direction. A man named Dave came and — "

"Dave?"

"Yes, you know him, he had funded several of your projects and helped you escape after that last protest."

"Dave. Where is he now?"

"Here, at headquarters. I can take you there."

"Yes, do. I hope you understand, I will continue to hold the gun on you as we drive and I will shoot if you seem to deviate from the course to the location to which you know I am headed."

"Yes. You must. But do know that some roads are out and we will have to make our way differently than you may have ever done here."

They proceeded in silence. It was obvious that the driver was headed in the direction of the headquarters and that many of the roads were impassable. He drove without trying to stick to the streets.

After a while Sheeyah lowered the gun.

"Thanks," was all her driver said.

It was two hours before they arrived.

The headquarters was in a cave on a mountain top. The hike up to it was difficult for Sheeyah in her condition, but she was determined to make it without help.

She followed the driver into her territory. Dave happened to be walking past the entrance carrying papers. He turned and almost dropped everything.

"Sheeyah?!!!!" Dave asked, incredulous at the sight. He reached out to touch her. She pulled back, avoiding the feel of his hands, a feeling she had once loved so very much.

The driver walked away and left the two of them alone.

"Sheeyah, you're pregnant."

"Yes."

"It is my child, isn't it?"

"No."

"What do you mean? It has to be. You must be about nine months pregnant, and I remember that we were alone together for —"

"Nine months?" Sheeyah was shocked. She looked down at her belly and held it protectively.

"You mean you don't know how long you've been pregnant?"

Sheeyah had no idea of how much time had passed since she had met Triad, let alone how much time had passed since she spent two months with Dave. It could have been years, months, weeks, days, hours or minutes. It could have been several centuries. It felt like forever. At least an eternity. But then, time must have folded many times during her travels.

"Sheeyah, you must be in shock. You must have really been through it. How did you make it here, anyway? Just about everyone on the west coast is dead. Only a few people with foresight survived. Foresight enough to get out or get onto seaworthy craft before it hit."

"It?"

"Yes, Sheeyah, the polar shift. Two so far. You were right. You were right about everything. And, as far as I know, right about all the safe lands. You are absolutely amazing."

She still held her hands over her belly. Dave reached to touch her there. She pulled away again.

"Sheeyah, I must have hurt you so very much, just dumping you like that. I didn't know what else to do. I was so conflicted. I was so torn between you who I felt so passionate about and my wife and children. I chose them over you. And I lost them. They died."

"They did?"

"Drowned." Dave had tears in his eyes. Real tears.

Sheeyah was surprised. Set? Cry? "Oh, God, I'm sorry," she said.

"I wanted to kill myself when I realized what had happened to them. I probably will eventually, but I get the feeling I still have work to do here."

"Work? Here?" Sheeyah wondered what he meant. And then she wondered if he even knew what he really meant.

"And now I've found you and you are pregnant."

"It's not your baby." It couldn't be Dave's. Could it? No. Set could not have a child.

"Whose could it be? Come on, I know who you slept with during the time you would have become pregnant. It was me."

Sheeyah tried to ignore his persistence.

"Please, just let me take care of you. Let me help you pull Earthcult together and have the baby."

"It's *my* baby."

"O.K. I make no claim. I left you, what right do I have to the child?"

"It is not yours, Dave."

The discussion was cut short by a strange earthquake, better described as an Earth wave, in which even the solid rock foundation of the cave rolled like water.

"It's building up again. We're almost onto the third."

"It's time then?" Sheeyah asked Dave.

"You know better than I, Sheeyah, but the frequency of the tremblers has been increasing. We best make you a safe bed and let you lie there protected."

Another rolling shuddered its way through the cave floor. "I want to look around and see my people."

"You do that. I'll get a place ready for you."

"I have a place here. It's already ready for me. It's up there." She pointed to a pathway that led into a small opening in the rock walls. Then she turned away from Dave and walked on, looking around and looking for her people.

She found several of them meeting in one of the side caves. They all stood when she walked in. Each of them hugged her in turn, all of them crying with joy to see that Sheeyah had survived the two episodes of death the Earth had just endured. All the while, the frequency of the quaking was increasing. She saw the tattoos on her people, the symbol of the Omega Point, and felt the true, resonating power of the sign she had designed for the first time. She looked around and saw the symbols she had painted in bright colors all over the cave wall: the symbols housing the Truth, protecting Truth from those who would abuse it, dissipate it, forget it, deny it. Protecting it in order to bring it into the New World which would emerge from the third episode of Earth's death, the third polar shift.

"Our work has only just begun." Sheeyah spoke softly but seriously as the Earth shook beneath and around them. "I have journeyed to places beyond those we have discussed. I have returned with the Truth and news of other safe lands in the dimensions beyond. I have come here to teach those of you who are ready to learn Truth, Original Truth. You will be the keepers of the light. You will help me to bring what is needed to Earth and her remaining inhabitants after the third and final rebalancing. You are survivors, and I am proud of you for making it. Earthcult needs you. Earth needs Earthcult. I am also here to give birth to my child. I am determined to make a place in this world for this baby."

The Earth rumbled fiercely. Sheeyah added, "You all know that you are safe here?" They nodded affirmatively. With the next rumble, Sheeyah felt a spasm surge through her. As she fell to the ground, she knew that it was time. It made no sense — time had progressed in no logical way — but she was in labor. Two of her followers helped her up. She smiled at them and said, "Thank you, but I must be alone now."

Sheeyah made her way alone, bending with the spasms as they hit, increasing in frequency, into the hole in the wall which led to her nest. She had prepared it for herself years ago. It was always her sanctum, her retreat. She could talk with Earth there, unfettered by any outside influence.

When she arrived, she laid down on a bed she had slept in so many times before. So it had come, the apocalypse. And the birth of her child.

She could feel the pulsing of her daughter, trying to be born.

Dave appeared in the doorway.

"Not now, Dave."

"Sheeyah, you're in labor."

"Not now."

"You need help, Sheeyah. Let me help you."

"I don't need help." Sheeyah groaned with the pain of a new, stronger spasm.

"Sheeyah, I love you. This is my child. Let me help."

"No, it is not yours. Leave me alone."

"If nothing else, I am a doctor. I can help if there are any problems. You need someone."

"I don't need anyone." Just then Sheeyah doubled in pain. A shooting pain ripped down her side. Her hand grabbed at her belly.

"Sheeyah, if you want to be sure to bring this child onto the planet, you must accept some help. At least let me stand by just in case you need me. You've never had a child before. You can't know what this is going to be like."

Sheeyah pulled out the pistol which she had placed beneath her. She aimed it at Dave. "O.K. If you want to help, it will be on my terms."

"What's this about? Sheeyah, it's me, Dave. Are you feverish?"

He reached to feel her forehead.

Sheeyah cocked the trigger. "DO NOT touch me. Just do what I say."

"Sure. O.K. Calm down. You can put that thing down. You won't kill me, you love me."

"No I do not." Sheeyah groaned again with another intense contraction.

"O.K. O.K. A woman never feels much in love with a man when she is in labor. And I left you. I have hurt you very much. Just tell me what to do. But get your finger off the trigger, you might pull it by mistake during one of your contractions."

"What I want you to do first is to tell me who you work for."

"Who I *work* for? We're going to talk about this right *now*?"

"Yes. Now, Dave."

"Well, you know, I work for myself. I am an M.D."

"Dave, you also have business dealings and other goings on. You know I know this."

"You had even me checked out? I thought you reserved this for people you thought were your enemies."

"I should have considered you an enemy." She did not tell him that she hadn't thought to check him out, that she had been so consumed by her physical passion for him that she didn't have time to think that he might be a risk.

"Who do you work for, Dave?" Sheeyah whispered between groans.

"You must know, Sheeyah. You probably knew all along." He assumed that she knew.

"Just say it." She let him assume she had known, but she hadn't. And she still didn't.

Dave glanced at the gun and decided to answer. "The C.I.A. .... Your Earthcult was identified as threatening global insurrection, and also as having somehow gained access to secrets being protected by the elite, the elite who felt it was in the best interest of the masses —"

"Of themselves —"

"In the best interests of whoever," Dave went on with his confession at gunpoint. "But the C.I.A. felt it would be better to withhold the information regarding the coming cataclysms, the three polar shifts, in order to prevent hoarding, mass panic and suicide, and global hysteria."

The C.I.A.? Was this the Truth? So the C.I.A., Sheeyah thought to herself. She felt several waves of confusion wash through her mind. The C.I.A.? Was Dave a double agent, working with his brother on the side? Or was Dave actually spying on his own brother? Then she wondered with a flutter of panic coursing through her, what did that make Triad? A traitor? But to what cause? Or was Triad in on this C.I.A. stuff? Was Triad a liar?

I, myself, heard Sheeyah wonder all this from where I lingered in the ether just beyond. But I had greater concerns. I had to get through to her. Sheeyah. Sheeyah. I tried to shout telepathically in order to get her attention from my position in the astral plane. Sheeyah!

She blinked and looked startled. I could tell that she heard me. I felt her ask me what I wanted to tell her. She did not feel loving toward me. The sense that I had betrayed her emitted from her again. She continuously doubted my honor, all through our time together, and even now.

Sheeyah. Do not anger Dave. As best as I can tell, he is still somewhat amnesic regarding his true cosmic identity. But anything could trigger the breaking through of his memory. And already he is wavering between love and manipulation of you.

Love? Sheeyah got caught on that word. She wanted me to explain why I thought Dave was feeling love for her. She needed some love at this moment. I could tell she felt alone. I wished it could be me that would give it to her. She was clearly in pain and feeling some fear, although doing her best to deny both. The earthquakes were continuous now. Bits of rock were flying through the air.

Remember Sheeyah, you will be safe there on Earth. As long as you choose to remain a mortal, you will. Only you will end your own life.

But my child?

Dave touched Sheeyah. "Sheeyah are you still with me?"

"HANDS OFF!!!" She waved the gun at him. He jumped back.

Sheeyah, do not rouse his emotions. Try to be as level with him as possible.

You said he loves me.

Well yes, in his way. He feels he is free now to love you even more than he did, as he has lost his wife and children. In fact, he thinks you carry his only surviving child now.

"Let me help you, Sheeyah," Dave pleaded.

Let him help you. But stay conscious and hold onto the gun. I wish there could be another way. I wish it could be me. It is I who am your other half. This is my child you are bringing into the world. Our child, to be accurate.

Sheeyah screamed in pain. "This is MY child." The baby was emerging from the womb, ripping her open.

Dave shouted for someone to come and help. One of Sheeyah's followers appeared at the door, grabbing at the wall to try to remain standing as everything shook.

"Get some sterile rags. Some clean rags. Sterile, bottled water. NOW!"

Sheeyah was groaning. The head of the child was emerging. She could feel the baby's pressure tearing at her insides.

Sheeyah, you are protected. Just believe you will be all right and you will be. Imagine yourself well and healthy after this is over. Make this picture a reality and hang on to it.

What about my baby?????

I was not sure what to reply. Finally I sent her the honest answer: The life of the baby hangs in the balance. You must survive to defend her.

"What does that mean?" she screamed aloud.

Sheeyah! Sheeyah! Stay conscious! Do not say my name. Do not mention me to Dave at this time! Do not trigger his memories. He is already dangerously close to having his instincts surface!

"What does what mean, Sheeyah?" Dave had opened her legs and was swabbing the area with disinfectant.

Sheeyah made certain he knew the gun was aimed at his head. "I am ready to shoot you, Dave."

"O.K. Just breathe. Focus on what you're doing. I need you to push. I don't have the tools to do an emergency C-section and we have a difficulty here. I am going to have to reach into you and unwrap the umbilical cord from the baby's neck."

I could feel a wave of extreme fear flood through Sheeyah now.

We have no choice. You must allow him. I began to pray. I showered Sheeyah with my godly light, hoping with all my force to protect her and the baby.

Dave reached in and unwrapped the umbilical cord. I hated to watch this. I was jealous that that man was touching *my* woman, and so very intimately. I should be there. Why had I died at the wrong moment?

All three of us felt the glorious surge of the new life as it entered the third dimension on Earth — the embodiment of Original Truth, which no male offspring could fully regale. I could hear Earth welcome her. I knew that Earth intended to protect this baby during the convulsions Earth was undergoing.

Fortunately, Sheeyah was not so distracted by the glory. She watched Dave as he held the baby up to spank its first breath of air into its lungs. She saw Dave lower the baby to clean it, taking the softest of clean rags and washing off the blood slowly, ceremoniously. And she was alert enough to notice what I missed: Dave's hands moving toward the throat of the baby and beginning to strangle it.

It a microsecond, Sheeyah was up and shooting Dave in the heart. His hands released the baby onto the bed. Sheeyah kept the gun pointed at Dave as she moved in front of the screaming child, who was still spotted with the blood of birth. Sheeyah, covered with her own blood, moved toward Dave, who knelt at the foot of the bed, absolutely stunned, with his hand over his heart.

"You killed me, Sheeyah! Why? Why? Have I hurt you so much?"

"You are my brother. This is the last thing I want to be doing. My brother, my lover."

"Your brother?" In his physical misery, Dave was profoundly confused.

"Yes, you, me and Triad, all of the de Nostras family, all orphans."

Dave fell to the floor. "Triad? Triad? He found you? *You* are the sister we were searching for? Did Triad ever find anything more out about our parents? How did he find you?"

"You found me. You made love to me. You made me love you. Then you quit me and you dumped me into his arms when you left me at the harbor. You must know this."

"I didn't know you were the sister. Our sister," Dave gasped.

"Would you have treated me any differently?"

Dave was choking on his blood. "Oh God, I'm dying. I'm dying now." His mortal anguish seethed into the room.

"Dave, you aren't dying, you are just moving on. Let me help you. Let me help you the way I let you help me when the at the most difficult moment of childbirth."

"Why? Why should I? You killed me."

"Dave, I also loved you. You can take my help or die alone. That is all you have available to you right now."

He nodded yes almost imperceptibly.

"Close your eyes, Dave. If you close your eyes, you will see the most magnificent point of light above you, radiating in all directions around itself."

Dave closed his eyes.

"Do you see it?"

"Yes," he whispered.

"This is a hint of heaven, just at the other side of the skin of your reality. You can go there now."

Sheeyah, are you sending him to me? I was hardly ready yet. I was still in the ether and had not moved into the final episode of my own death.

What should I do with him, Triad? I can't just let him suffer. He's my brother. Your brother.

He is Set. He threatens to kill all Creation. He almost killed our child!

Dave started to speak. "When I open my eyes the light is gone. When I close my eyes, it is there, but it is just a hazy image. I wish I could see it better."

"Only when you close your eyes and go into death with acceptance will you even begin to see what awaits you."

"Why should I trust you? You killed me."

"You don't have a bit of choice right now, do you?" Sheeyah reminded him in a soft voice. "Dave, some people say that we have a soul that goes on living. Whether or not this is the case, it is through certain special experiences that we can develop a very fine substance of our selves. It is the self that we develop in this life. When we die, that substance of the self lingers on for a while."

"Why tell me this now?"

"Because the manner in which you choose to die has a great deal to do with the substance of your self which lingers."

A piece of rock fell out of the ceiling and just missed hitting them. Sheeyah turned to see if the baby had been hit. The child was O.K. She grabbed the child and held it to her breast.

"The world is falling, Sheeyah. Creation is dying." Dave's eyes widened ominously.

"Not if I can help it."

"I wanted to kill the baby, Sheeyah, to stop life."

"Yes you did, Set."

"Set? I know that name."

"It is yours, Dave."

"Mine? Set?"

"Now go, go into the ether where you will find Triad. Deal with him there or move into the third death together and relieve yourself of the mental energy you have accumulated in this incarnation.

"I am Set?"

"Set, the dark force. The anti-prana."

"Set cannot die. Set does not live."

Sheeyah, careful, he will soon discover that he can bring himself back to life and will return to that body with superhuman force despite the hole in its heart. Shoot him again.

I can't Triad.

I hear you talking, Sheeyah. Talking in your mind. How strange. What are you saying? Who is out there?

Now Dave had entered the privacy of the telepathic communication between Sheeyah and me.

Shoot Sheeyah. Let me deal with him out here. Get him out of the third dimension or he will find a way back into that body and try again to kill the child.

Sheeyah emptied the remainder of the bullets into Dave. . . .

It all happened in an instant. Dave sprung from his body into the ether, entirely short-cutting the physical death process. Immediately the clash of Set and Triad began. Sheeyah grasped her screaming baby daughter as she watched the air around her distort and warp in a tug-of-war between darkness and light. Sheeyah could feel that her love for her child was fueling the light. In giving life, Sheeyah was creating. In sustaining life, she was maintaining Creation. As she suckled the baby at her breast, the light became so strong that it filled the cave room, the air, and Sheeyah was certain, it would eventually swell to fill the atmosphere. She began chanting something which reminded her of an ancient fire song. "A-UU-UH-HMM. A-UU-UH-HMM." The darkness shrank to the edges of her perception. For the time being, the light had won. . . . *for the time being.*

Dazed and in a trance state, Sheeyah cleaned the baby and herself and then emerged to a waiting group of followers. They all bowed into triangularly arranged fingers. She did not ask how they knew to do so.

Sheeyah could not help but wonder whether it was Dave or me, Triad, who had really triumphed. She made her way to the mouth of the cave. The trembling had stopped. The Earth was quiet. But the sky, at the horizon, the sky was afire!

Omega Point

.t is this, Earth?" Sheeyah asked quietly.

. SORT OF ATMOSPHERIC FIRESTORM.

"Firestorm?"

YES, IT RAGES HIGH IN MY ATMOSPHERE.

"This is part of the cataclysmic process?"

YES. THINK ABOUT IT. EVEN A FOREST FIRE CAUSES A CATACLYSMIC CHANGE, A CHANGE WHICH MARKS THE START OF A NEW CYCLE OF ECOLOGICAL PROGRESSION.

"So this is the start of a new ecological progression?"

I HOPE SO. I HOPE THIS MEANS WE HAVE MADE IT THROUGH THE OMEGA POINT AND WILL SEE A NEW ALPHA. ONLY TIME WILL TELL.

"But the sky is burning. Can this be a good sign?"

FIRE IS A STIMULANT IN NATURE. IT CAUSES PINE CONES TO OPEN, VARIOUS PLANTS TO EXPEL THEIR SEED PODS, ALLOWS PLANTS WHOSE VOLATILE OILS CAN WITHSTAND HEAT LONGER THAN OTHERS AN EVOLUTIONARY ADVANTAGE.

"So someone is going to get an evolutionary advantage out of all this?"

THIS IS PART OF THE CLEANSING PROCESS. SULFURIC ACID FROM THE MANY VOLCANIC ERUPTIONS I AM EXPERIENCING AND THE BUILDUP OF OTHER GASES HAS NOW DISPOSED MY ATMOSPHERE TO VOLATILITY. DEATH — PURIFICATION OR PURGE — BY FIRE HAS LONG BEEN PRESCRIBED FOR VARIOUS SPIRITUAL OFFENSES. THE FAMOUS MYTHICAL BIRD, THE PHOENIX, OF WHICH THERE IS SAID TO BE ONLY ONE, IS ALWAYS CONSUMED BY FIRE AT THE END OF ITS APPOINTED LIFE SPAN, BUT IT ALWAYS RISES AGAIN FROM THE ASHES. THE PHOENIX IS THE SYMBOL OF RENEWAL AND RESURRECTION. SOKARIS ARISES: HOPE.

"But Earth, what are the mechanisms by which a fire can burn the world?"

A SOLAR FLARE CAN CAUSE A MASSIVE SURGE IN THE EARTH'S MAGNETISM, DESTABILIZING SUBSTANCES WHICH ARE NORMALLY STABLE, EVEN CAUSING A BRIEF ELECTRIC DISCHARGE FROM SOME OF THESE SUBSTANCES. AN INCREASE IN TEMPERATURE CAN CAUSE RAPID EVAPORATION OF WATER, VAPORIZATION OF TISSUES OF BIOLOGICAL FORMS, AND THEN THE POTENTIAL FOR THE PYROLYSIS OF THE VAPOR. TREE-COVERED

Transcending the Time Wave 337

MOUNTAINS, DRIED UP JUNGLES, MANY THINGS COULD SERVE AS GIANT WICKS. WITH THE RIGHT MIX OF ATMOSPHERIC ACTIVITY, AND THE SETTING OF PARTICULAR CHEMISTRY IN THE ATMOSPHERE, A SPONTANEOUS COMBUSTION OF THE WORLD CAN OCCUR. IF IT SPREADS TOO FAR, MOST BIOLOGICAL LIFE FORMS WILL DIE OF LACK OF OXYGEN, ANOXIA.

WITH THE MANY GASES ENTERING THE ATMOSPHERE, INCLUDING THE VAPORIZED SULFURIC ACID, THE PHOSPHORUS PARTICLES EJECTED FROM THE DRYING SEAS, THE CALCIUM DUST FORMED OF THE SKELETONS OF TRILLIONS UPON TRILLIONS OF ANIMAL FORMS RELEASED IN A METEORIC BOMBARDMENT OF THE CHALKY CLIFFS OF DOVER AND OTHER SIMILAR GEOLOGICAL DEPOSITS, THERE ARE MANY POTENTIALLY SELF-IGNITING CONDITIONS. CALCIUM PHOSPHORUS IGNITES IN THE AIR UPON ITS FORMATION, FOR EXAMPLE.

"How horrible."

NOT REALLY. ALL LIFE FORMS DEPEND UPON SOME FORM OF COMBUSTION. WHAT DO YOU THINK METABOLISM IS? JUST SEE ALL THIS CATACLYSMIC ACTIVITY AS A METABOLIC PROCESS.

Sheeyah watched as the world burned. Sheeyah saw the eyes of her baby wide and staring at the world she had just entered.

"We have much to do, you and I. Much to do," she told her child.

I knew then that it was time for me to move beyond even the third episode of my death. Time for me to let go of my connections here.

I waited for Sheeyah to ensure that the child had acquired temporary amnesia, as is essential for even the commonest of initiates. This she did knowing that the time for remembering the reason for being here would come much sooner in this child's life than it had in hers. Earth was the fulcrum of all that hung in the balance throughout the Cosmos. The next millennium would be the test of Creation. And this little Messiah would be its savior.

-EPILOGUE-

Let the world burn. Fire is cleansing. And fire is light. Sokar will rise again: the wilted egret cum phoenix will emerge from the ashes. Sokar, our infinite hope, springs eternal. It must do so to preserve Creation.

I am speaking to you now from a much higher dimension than the one in which you are reading this. For those of you who would call me dead, in third dimensional terms, I am indeed dead. So be it. But, do not mourn me. I am the Omega and the Alpha, the end and the beginning. This is as it was, is, and ever shall be. I live. I am indeed alive — everywhere in all time — in all dimensions of the Cosmos.

But do not think of me as God: we are all God. My love, my woman, my pairbond, my sister, Sheeyah, is also God. She has remained in the third dimension, on Earth, to rear our child. Our female child.

Indeed, the new Messiah must be born a girl. This event harkens a major shift in the balance of power throughout all the Cosmos. I can feel the meridians of all Creation adjusting as I say this. Those of you who are students of prophecy will recall that my forever-gone son, absent now for eternity, Nostradamus, predicted the resurgence of female power on Earth around the time of this new millennium. Nostradamus wrote of the reemerging of the power of what he called "the great one for a long time masked beneath eclipses. . . ." He predicted that the long established power of the male would give way to this unmasking female power, as "Her brother will pass by rusty colored." The strength of men's weapons (irons) will fade:

"Tidira fer dans la plaie la sanguine."

("Iron will cool in the bloody wound.")

I have come to understand that the resurgence of female power is the only way to ensure the survival of the prana of Earth, given Earth's beaten condition. If this realization has been a long time coming for me, I can understand how humans may be slow to fully understand what this means. Unfortunately, the human species must come to understand much more rapidly than it should have to.

Ω

So the Omega point nears. You have been deprived of the Truth about the coming of the Omega Point and its meaning. I have therefore given you the preceding story to initiate the awakening of Truth within the recesses of your soul. And the world around you is yielding up the Truth despite its long suppression. Look closely. You will see the signs. Read these signs carefully. Do not let anyone appearing either as a fanatic or as a chosen one tell you how to read the signs you see. Find the signs yourself and then search your own heart for their meaning.

Tune into the instinctual telepathy of yourself and others. Where are people going? Are they relocating to new places — either in their minds or on the planet? Are there subtle exoduses going on around you? Listen to what is being said. Yet, beware of false prophets. You must feel Truth to hear it. Wait until you are touched to the core by a message, then follow your feet. If you close your eyes and wander in the night, you will eventually learn to hear the Earth. Practice this skill now — you will soon need it in order to survive.

Open your eyes. Look around. Read what is written on the subway wall. Examine the local graffiti!

Read. Read. Read whatever you can find, from children's stories to scientific journals. What do artists see? What do scientists see? Can you piece together their researches like a puzzle? Can you piece together fragmented and hidden information? ARE THERE SOME SCIENTISTS AND OTHERS ELITE WHO SEEK TO SUPPRESS INFORMATION? Could this be true?

Is the demand for survivor territories growing? How can you tell? Where do the people who seem to know live? Where do they buy land? How do they make their decisions regarding these matters?

Open your eyes. Look around you. The Earth has dying spots. She is weakening unevenly. Her prana, her energy, her auras dim and her shields break down first in some places, later in others.

Many cosmic balances must shift now. A shift in the axis of your solar system indicates a shift in galactic axes, in the cosmic poles. As a result, there are new pulls on Earth. Earth's atmosphere weakens as her defenses break down. Meteors can now enter her atmosphere at an angle which allows them to penetrate without disintegrating as much as they would have previously. As the Earth's atmosphere becomes weaker, it does not slow big meteors as much, so their impact will be

Epilogue

harder. It is true that the coming shower of meteors could explode in the atmosphere like hydrogen bombs, but the public still thinks all the coming meteors will burn up long before they have either a chance to trigger atomic reactions in the atmosphere or to crash into Earth's crust.

Certainly there are some humans who understand, who intuit, who know in some way, that the Omega Point, whether physical or cosmic or both, is coming. If you have read this book between the lines with open eyes, you may now have joined their ranks.

I have seen with my eyes on other worlds before yours what the Earth will be like in the centuries to come. The competition for souls will become a high stakes game, with survival of the triumphant, most dominant, thought-form the prize. Everywhere, witchcraft will emerge. You must be selective. Both its good and bad will offer you the magic you may feel you need to sustain yourself. However, even the reality of your self will be of great question to you.

All those remaining on Earth will be finally driven to ask how a planet and its people can move into higher spiritual realms: what is required to ascend? What are the steps to transcendence? The answers will not be easy to receive. The true meaning of cataclysm will come to those who learn what is needed to survive.

The symbol of the seal will become clear as its Original Truth emerges. The seal in the Earthly book of Revelations is the breaking of the cervical seal or plug when labor before birth begins. This is always a precarious time in the cycle of life, although many of you, in what you call the modern world, have taken for granted that illusion of safety your medical technology gives you. However, it is still true that both mother and child can die in labor. And then there is no Alpha after the Omega because life does not continue. This cycle is ended. And, if, perchance, the child lives but the mother dies in labor, the metaphorical source sustaining the archetypal child's life is dead. This leaves the child we call humanity only somewhat alive. And, should the mother lose her child before it is born to the world, the spiritual, actual and individual mother is left, her soul is forever pinned, to the miserable limbo of an aborted cycle. Through her eyes, the world will never look the same.

$$\Omega$$

If you study my eyes carefully, you will know what I have seen and now see: Most of Planet Earth, I regret to say, has been regressionary in terms of spiritual advancement since the final sinking of Atlantis. The one exception may be the time in which you have been living. A new, exciting flame of spiritual awareness has been kindled, bearing the light of higher enlightenment and spiritual advancement. However, that flame is still small, still flickering; a spiritual wisp in the giant and ominous shadow of aspiritual materialism.

The principal purpose of my most current Earthly incarnation has been to relate the ultimate and original metaphysical Truths to those who may be interested. This purpose was unknown even to me for the first fifty some years of this particular lifetime. It is in this incarnation that I, deviously, albeit naively, took advantage of my most privileged access to cosmic insider information, organizing a secret purchase of those of the Earth's territories deemed most likely to survive, intact, this next cataclysm.

I do not feel guilt as I reflect upon this behavior. I am merely bemused at the erosion of even Godly ethics when contaminated by third dimensional manifestation. I came to Earth at the time I have described herein because I desired to see (although, as an incarnate, I remained unconscious of this desire for well over fifty years) the second coming of the Reign of the Gods — the resurfacing and resurrection of the greatest parts of the Atlantean empire. That worthy event, I can assure you, is not far off from your current era. Its advancement has already begun. The Atlantean residues within me rejoice.

Many advanced spirits know that it is time now for humans to fully recognize the existence of dimensions beyond the physical plane or what I call third dimension. This is one reason we have seen on Planet Earth such a geometric growth in population, especially during the close of your 20th Century. Many of the spirits incarnating on Earth at the time of your new millennium have come to know that Earth herself is preparing to reach into the higher dimensions, propelled by the imagery of cataclysm. These reincarnating spirits want to be "part of the action," so to speak. This same phenomenon occurred during the high point of Atlantis; advanced spirits incarnated there from elsewhere in the Cosmos. It seemed to them that the Atlantean-dominated Earth stood a good chance of making the transition into the higher dimensions. We know that this did not happen, not for the entirety of Earth and not for most of her inhabitants. Why it did not shall only become clear to you if you allow yourself to see your own world.

Many are convinced, however, that this time Planet Earth can effectively make the transition to a higher spiritual realm. And that this transition will transpire in the fairly near future. Many off-planet beings believe that this event will be accomplished by the prophesized return of the Messiah. Many spirits around the universe are greatly desirous of incarnating on Earth to witness this return: God again embodied. So they watch closely now for signs, as if God has not embodied here for a long time. They expect to see quite a show. I, of course, find this somewhat humorous. I am certain that Sheeyah, who has elected to remain materialized to give birth to and raise the new Messiah in the central third dimension, will also find this laughable. How many will ever look for a new Messiah in a female body?

You may be tempted to think of me, and perhaps of my close associates, my most cosmic wife, my now dead son, my newborn daughter, as superbeings. We prefer,

Epilogue 343

however, to be thought of as mere beings traveling in your, and several other, dimensions of reality. We are in the business of being in order to spread light, evolution, enlightenment. We often choose to travel as interplanetary seedlings. We are basically spirits who not only have mastered but also have designed the energetic and spiritual transition in and out of your material third dimension to the lower and higher dimensions. I and some of my closest associates have chosen to make this energy adjustment again and again — especially within the past few thousand years. Our third-dimensional memories of you — our ability to relate to you — thus remain fresh. The effects of this adjustment are renewing; even I, who need not do so, return for the exhilaration and reconnection with you who live in the material realm. I enjoy paralleling your evolution.

Ω

You may know that your great philosopher Plato referred to the sunken continent of Atlantis some 2,500 years ago. In his work, **Timaeus,** *he described the "island" of Atlantis as being "larger than Libya and Asia put together" and as being the home of "a great and wonderful empire which had rule over the whole island and several others." There, in* **Timaeus,** *he also described the demise of Atlantis, a description to which I have earlier referred. In another of his works, which he titled after its informant,* **Critias,** *Plato explained that when the Earth was divided up among the gods, it was the god Poseidon who, upon "receiving for his lot the island of Atlantis, begat children by a mortal woman, and settled them in a part of the island." Plato tells us that, subsequently, Poseidon begat five pairs of male twins by another mortal woman, Clieto, and he then "divided the island of Atlantis into ten portions" for them. "The eldest, who was the first king, he named Atlas, and after him the whole island and the ocean were called Atlantic." The descendants of Atlas retained the kingdom for many generations and, as Plato recorded for history, amassed "such an amount of wealth as was never before possessed by kings and potentates, and is not likely ever to be again, and they were furnished with everything they needed ...." Plato is a good source of information for you, as he was, on his father's side, a direct descendent of the god Poseidon, father of Atlas. Of course, it was really Solon, also a Greek, who helped to preserve this hint regarding the protection of Original Truth for history. Solon brought his extensive notes on Atlantis to Athens from Egypt and passed them on to Critias' grandfather who taught Critias everything in the notes while he was still a boy. Critias eventually handed Solon's writings and told Solon's stories of Atlantis to Plato. Check the writings of Plato for verification, should you doubt me.*

Since the time of Plato, thousands of volumes of speculation have been directed toward the nature of, and reasons for, the sinking of Atlantis. Yet the demise of Atlantis has been very misunderstood.

What I share with you is the Truth, as I have observed it and now observe it from Earth and from the heavens.

Ω

Many of Atlantis' original inhabitants, forming what history has called the "Reign of the Gods," arrived on Earth through the higher dimensions from the Pleiades constellation, or what is better known as the Seven Sisters, the group of stars to which I earlier referred. These stars are the place where the mother of Original Truth frequently resides with her seven selves or sisters or daughters as she chooses to call them at different moments. (Relationships are defined more flexibly in non-material dimensions. The higher the dimension, the greater the flexibility. One's wife can be one's sister who can be one's maternal ancestor who can also, in a higher form, actually be one's self, as in my case.)

Pleiades is visible to the Earth with the human eye — and vice versa. Such visibility, whether to the organic eye or other sensory receptors, is a factor that has influenced many a decision regarding interplanetary incarnation. Pleiadeans came to Atlantis because they could "see" Earth. Since the days of Atlantis, radio and radio telescope waves have extended increasingly the vibratory field of Earth — to a point now well beyond the Pleiades to almost the entire length of the inner Cosmos. These waves, traveling through the Cosmos in a vacuum, now bring awareness of human activity on Planet Earth to beings residing in very distant galaxies. This explains why most of the early interplanetary seedlings of Atlantis came from the relatively close Pleiades, while the seedlings incarnating on your Earth at this time are arriving from all over the Cosmos. This also implies a much expanded potential for the sharing of universal wisdom. One of the positive aspects of third dimensional technology....

Your Earth has convulsed several times during its life. More than one of these convulsions drowned Atlantean civilizations. Each time, a group of Atlanteans with the power of foresight fled, survived and repopulated the same continent when it reappeared. I speak to you herewith primarily of the most recent sinking. It was then that this continent submerged quite suddenly as a result of a series of violent man-made explosions. Again, as in every other sinking, most of Atlantis' inhabitants died as they were plummeted to the bottom of the sea. As your Plato wrote, "there occurred violent earthquakes and floods; and in a single day and night of misfortune ... the island of Atlantis ... disappeared in the depths of the sea."

In the years preceding the final submersion, Atlantis experienced a series of increasingly frequent major Earthquakes. Many were triggered by the highly advanced technology of the inhabitants, whose ability to channel energy from the universe through massive underground crystal deposits was abused and overused. Your current civilization uses crystals in a variety of moderately advanced ways. For example, you magnify radio waves (in transistors), set up electrical charges (in gas igniters), and focus and amplify the power of light (in lasers). You build your beloved computers with silicon crystals.

Epilogue

Atlanteans identified large crystal deposits in the Earth and used those crystals to receive, magnify and redirect energy from your sun and also from well beyond your solar system. While this Atlantean development represents the pinnacle of human technological achievement, its misuse brought on the demise of Earth's greatest civilization. The crystalline concentration and transduction of universal energy into your material plane undermined and eventually crumbled and drowned the large land mass of Atlantis. The energy was brought into man-made power centers and became so highly concentrated and corrupted in character that it offset the natural balance among mother Earth's own natural power centers. Mother Earth was forced into a massive rebalancing for her own survival, completely realigning her magnetic axis, melting her polar caps and creating a cataclysm of vast proportions.

Iatrogenic, (inadvertently or at least unconsciously self-induced), cataclysm. The backfire.

It was not a pretty sight. Death and destruction. A gruesome end to the material reality of so many. Deep scars on the face of your mother organism, Earth.

I have dwelled at some length on Atlantis because of the oldest of human adages: those who do not study history are doomed to repeat it. As even the modestly enlightened among you will have observed, the parallels between the last days of Atlantis and the current state of human affairs on Planet Earth are disconcertingly similar. There are many lessons to be learned. Only spiritual advancement ensured the survival of the highest Atlanteans. Only spiritual advancement ensures yours now.

Should another such cataclysm occur — as it is predicted, as it has already begun — the devastation could easily exceed that which took place during the final days of Atlantis. I choose not to dwell on the nature of the cataclysm now; suffice it to say that it defies full comprehension by the materially-oriented, third-dimensional, human mind. I do wish to make clear that you have a choice regarding the nature of this devastation, the character of this upheaval, your own particular experience of it. For you, it may or may not take place on the physical plane. The great rebalancing need not be experienced on the physical plane by everyone.

$$\Omega$$

Let me make suggestions here — suggestions for individuals, for societies, and for nations, for all of you who now inhabit Earth:

- *Be aware that the universe will not expand forever — when the contraction comes it will be quick and devastating — physically, phenomenologically, or both.*

- *For the large part of humanity still of the mind set that a body is useful, that* a physical existence is valuable, identify safe lands on Earth. Also, encourage government and industry to set up your space stations and place your gene banks and cloning laboratories in space now. Encourage humanity, through government and industry, to make every effort to colonize Planet Mars, quickly and at all costs. You do have the capacity to do this. Make it a priority.

- Work on healthy, non-fanatical, methods of self-deliverance — for you and others. Encourage the legalization of assisted suicide and suicide education, with the proper guidelines and essential spiritual preparation. Be certain this access to death is not abused by young people, political leaders, and false prophets.

- Set up a network of and instruction in higher communications, telepathy, which must be practiced regularly beginning now. At first, much of the population may see this as a game. If this be the case, introduce the effort as a form of recreation such as a virtual reality game. Virtual realities can manifest. Even physical life forms can be saved this way.

- Learn to read and then memorize interplanetary and intergalactic maps. You will find that certain regions of the Cosmos attract you. Learn their locations well. Practice imagining that you travel there. Develop the clarity of your visualization of such a journey.

- Learn the map of the Cosmos explained by Einstein in this book. This map is represented by the Omega Point symbol, which Sheeyah had tattooed on her breast and which we have published in this book.

- Post and wear the Omega Point symbol in places where you and others will see it regularly.

- Open your mind and soul to the possibility of cosmic travel. Without your physical body, you need no spaceship. Many of Earth's highly evolved have already memorized interplanetary and intergalactic maps to facilitate their travel when the time comes to leave Earth. Many have already selected destinations such as Venus (with its very feminine energy) and the Pleiades. Visualize yourself as one of these people or visualize yourself becoming one of these people or visualize yourself meeting some of these people and gaining a feel for their essences. The company you keep — the beings with whom you now choose to spend the time of your life — will have a powerful influence on the evolution of your soul and on the course and probability of your spiritual survival.

YOU CAN HELP PRESERVE CREATION AND HELP FIGHT THE EVER ENDURING AND ENCROACHING ANTI-PRANA, my brother, Set.

You may find that I am demanding that you see a dismal reality. But welcome it

Epilogue 347

with open arms! After all, life could be better, but at least it is life!

Oh, I know that most of you will only come to fully appreciate the depth of my message when the reality of your potential extinction becomes clear to you. Still, I ask that you be gentle with yourself, and absorb the following notes on life:

- *Plato described the care of the soul, as have other writers since. For Plato, this process of care is the very craft of life, techne tou biou.*

- *Every individual soul is a microconsciousness, one which affects the macroconsciousness.*

- *Every soul vibrates at its own frequency of consciousness, has its own light — the frequency and quality of that light can be evolved by that soul.*

- *Spiritual evolution is a constant developing of form, spiritual form, a journey through all dimensions of reality.*

- *The sole purpose of a spirit coming into third dimensional terrestrial existence is to work at self-formation until the manifested self reveals the indwelling spirit.*

- *The terrestrial working of Nature is the progression from matter to mind, the evolution of matter through time from the lower to the higher dimensions, from exoteric to esoteric awareness.*

- *There is an invisible process of soul evolution — with each rebirth, the soul has the possibility of ascending to a higher grade of form and consciousness.*

- *A great soul has the potential to advance the evolution of humanity, of other souls whether human or not, to spread true enlightenment.*

- *Now ask yourself: are you a great soul? Can you bring the energy generated by a transformation of consciousness — your own and or that of others — to the collective energy pool? Can you contribute to a global, a cosmic, transformation that will overt physical plane cataclysm?*

- *Can you help to preserve Creation?*

You must always seek authenticity in the expression of your power — do not be fooled by the lures, the temptations of doubt, of negativity. Let the notion that you can slip into selling your soul to the devil provide you ample warning: by nonchalance and noncommittal, you are surrendering to Set, to emptiness, to the enemy of Creation.

And you must become a teacher.

- *Teach the Truth: that the advent of the Omega Point — as both a metaphor and a reality — is upon us.*

- *Teach the Truth: that there are signs which must be learned, signs of the cosmic cycle, signs which actually point to the full coming of the complete Omega.*

- *Teach the Truth: about how to combat the anti-prana, Set:*

- *Teach the Truth: about what prana is and what Set, the anti-prana, actually represents.*

- *Teach the Truth: that there is a great difference between cyclical and absolute death, that the former fuels prana, that the latter is anti-prana.*

- *Teach yourself to seek the Truth, to look ever more deeply into your self for your awareness of the existence of Truth and the difference between "truth" and true "Truth."*

- *Teach an understanding of the reality of Set: Set does not live. Set is not part of Creation. Set is void of Truth. But Set can end all Creation by being so.*

You are fortunate if you feel wary when I speak of Set. Absolute unreality is fearsome to us. We thus seek at least the illusion of reality, as expansive a reality as each of us is capable of imagining and willing to imagine. Some of us settle for the morning paper and a cup of coffee, or bread, sex, and a place to sleep, others of us build varying degrees of intellectual and or metaphysical complexity into our definitions of reality.

We cannot help but seek the meaning of our existence. Even I continue to seek a meaning for the existence, the Creation, I have created. I must believe in it. If non-existence is the ultimate Truth, then we are left only with the illusion that Creation exists at all. And, if somehow this be the case, that Creation is merely an illusion, we must, in the end, ask, WHO GENERATES THIS ILLUSION? Are we the Creators of the illusion? We must make every effort to be Creators and to continuously and beneficially evolve the quality of reality.

$$\Omega$$

You may know the story of your fourth century BC philosopher, Diogenes of Sinope, slave to Xeniades, who bought him from a pirate. Diogenes asked to be sold to Xeniades, because, according to Diogenes, Xeniades needed a master. Diogenes, this man with no country and no possessions, invented the word "cosmopolitan" — citizen of the world. What he really was was a citizen of the Cosmos, a man at home in all dimensions of reality and in all of the illusions we fabricate in order to map our reality. Material reality and material things were of minimal if any importance to Diogenes. Instead, discipline, restraint, and self-knowledge were the keys to the wealth of the Cosmos and the passport into the true Cosmos-politan citizenship.

Epilogue

You may not begin from the high vantage point of Diogenes. But you all must begin somewhere. In your 19th Century, your natural historian, Charles Darwin, promulgated The Origin of the Species, *outlining evolution on the physical plane. Perhaps now you see that he was inferring so much more. You must come to understand and actually achieve the evolution of the spirit: the natural selection of the spiritually fittest is most certainly occurring. Where will you be when your physical terra, your mother Earth, the womb that houses you in your fetal stage of spirit, reaches its ultimate, the Omega Point? You will surely die, die to all dimensions of your existence unless you strive to evolve in order to step up to your rightful throne — the seat of the Creator — the dimension of God.*

Whether or not reality — life, the third dimension, the Cosmos — is entirely an illusion, those who perpetuate the illusion of the <u>evolving</u> Cosmos — always moving toward greater enlightenment — always moving into the light — are its Creators. That makes you, if you believe that anything progresses at all, even if all you believe is that you have been reading through this book, that makes you a Creator — a God. In so being, you have the Divine power to create your own future. All you need do is be on the path of Truth. And the path of Truth is immortal. This, my friends, is my point. Omega Point.

YANG SIDE OF COSMIC MIRROR

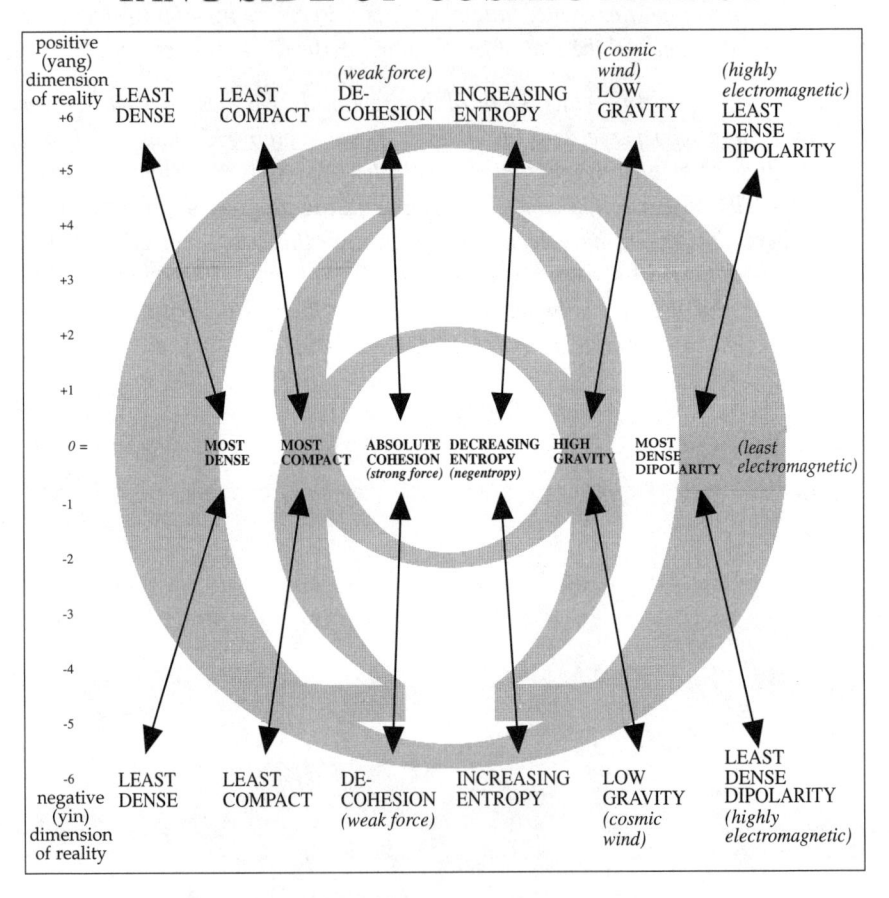

positive (yang) dimension of reality +6	LEAST DENSE	LEAST COMPACT	(weak force) DE-COHESION	INCREASING ENTROPY	(cosmic wind) LOW GRAVITY	(highly electromagnetic) LEAST DENSE DIPOLARITY
+5						
+4						
+3						
+2						
+1						
0 =	MOST DENSE	MOST COMPACT	ABSOLUTE COHESION (strong force)	DECREASING ENTROPY (negentropy)	HIGH GRAVITY	MOST DENSE DIPOLARITY (least electromagnetic)
-1						
-2						
-3						
-4						
-5						
-6 negative (yin) dimension of reality	LEAST DENSE	LEAST COMPACT	DE-COHESION (weak force)	INCREASING ENTROPY	LOW GRAVITY (cosmic wind)	LEAST DENSE DIPOLARITY (highly electromagnetic)

YIN SIDE OF COSMIC MIRROR

Epilogue

A PARTIAL LIST OF AUTHORS, REFERENCES AND SOURCES

Abbott, Edwin A.
Abraham, Ralph
Ager, Derek
Allegro, John
Alvarez, Luis W.
Arcane School
Aristotle
Asimov, Isaac
Assagioli, Roberto
Baigent, Michael
Bailey, Alice
Bateson, Gregory
Becker, William
Bellamy, H.S.
Berlitz, Charles
Besant, Annie
Blavatsky, H.P.
Blair, Lawrence
Blankenship, Donald
Borges, Jorge Luis
Bonnefoy, Guy
Bradbury, Ray
Brennan, J.H.
Bradley, Marion Zimmer
Brown, David Jay
Brown, G. Spencer
Brown, Hugh Auchincloss
Brown, Norman O.
Bucher, Walter
Buck, Pearl S.

Budge, E.A. Wallis
Burckhardt, Titus
Campbell, Joseph
Campion, Nicholas
Camus, Albert
Calvin, William H.
Capra, Fritjov
Castaneda, Carlos
Cattell, Raymond B.
Cavendish, Marshall
Cayce, Edgar
Chambers, Kenneth
Challoner, H.K.
Childress, David Hatcher
Cloos, Hans
Cohn, Norman
Collins, Mabel
Cousineau, Phil
Croutier, Alev Lytle
Daly, R.A.
Davenport, Guy
de la Rue, Florence
DeRohan, Ceanne
Descartes, Rene
Diogenes of Sinope
Donne, John
Douglas, Alfred
Du Nouy, Pierre Lecomte
Edgar, Morton
Eiseley, Loren

Einstein, Albert
Elkins, Don
Emery, W.B.
Ferris, Timothy
Fortune, Dion
Fox, Matthew
Fuentes, Carlos
Fuller, Buckminster
Galanopoulos, A.G.
Gazzaniga, Michael S.
Ginsberg, Allan
Gleick, James
Gore, Albert
Griscom, Chris
Grof, Stanislav
Gurdjieff, George Ivanovich
Hapgood, Charles
Hardt, James
Hawkings, Stephen
Hay, Louise L.
Herbert, Nick
Hewitt, V.J.
Hilarion
Hillman, James
Hogue, John
Hope, Murry
Huxley, Aldous
Huxley, Laura
Intruders Foundation
Jenkins, Palden
Jung, Carl G.
Klimo, Jon
Khul, Djwhal
Koestler, Arthur
Kubler-Ross, Elisabeth
LaBerge, Stephen
Lawrence, D.H.
Leary, Timothy
Lewis, C.S.
Lewis, Jim
L'Engle, Madeleine
Lilly, John C.
Lorie, Peter

Lovelock, James
Lyell, Sir Charles
Lucis Trust
Ma, Ting Ying H.
Mann, A.T.
Mann, Tad
Marciniak, Barbara
McCarty, James
McKenna, Terrence
Mitchell, John
Mitchell, Stephen
Monroe, Robert A.
Moore, Patrick
Moore, Thomas
Montessori, Maria
Murphy, Michael
New Group of World Servers
Newton, Isaac
Nietzche, Frederich
Nostradamus
   (Michel de Nostradame)
Osmen, Sarah Ann
Ouspensky, P.D.
Percival, Ian
Petrie, Flinders
Plato
Ponder, Catherine
Purce, Jill
Pythagoras
Rand, Ayn
Redfield, James
Restak, Richard
Richardson, Allan
Rifkin, Jeremy
Rilke, Rainer Maria
Ring, Kenneth
Rinpoche, Sogyal
Rossotti, Hazel
Royal, Lyssa
Rueckert, Carla
Sagan, Carl
Sardello, Robert
Sartre, Jean Paul

Schlemmer, Phyllis V.
Schmaltz, John B.
Scott, Sir Walter
Scott-Elliot, W.
Seven Ray Institute
Shapiro, Max
Shaw, George Bernard
Shaw, Herbert R.
Sheldrake, Rupert
Shinn, Florence Scovel
Silk, Joseph
Sitchin, Zecharia
Socrates
Solon
Spence, Lewis
Spinoza, Baruch de
Sri Aurobindo Library
Steiner, Rudolph
Steffens, Lincoln
Strieber, Whitley
Stobaeus, Joannes
Stuckeley, William
Sweet, J.P.M.
Swezey, Kenneth M.
Tart, Charles

Tenorio-Tagle, G.
Tompkins, Peter
Trefil, James S.
Trismegistus, Hermes
Urantia Foundation
Vallee, Jacques
Velikovsky, Immanuel
Watts, Alan
Weinberg, Steven
Whitmore, John
Whitmont, Edward C.
Wildavsky, Aaron
Wilde, Stuart
Wilson, Colin
Wilson, Edmund O.
Wilson, J. Tuzo
Woldben, A.
Velikovsky, Immanuel
Zee, A.
Zeff, Leo
Zukav, Gary

And many, many more . . .

UNDERGROUND RISING
subterra surgit

the global underground newsletter

Free our species from bondage. Don't let true humanity die. Be connected to the growing network of persons who seek liberation from the historical, political, philosophical, spiritual, geophysical, medical, and economic illusions that have been so long forced upon us by those planetary and off-planet entities who have controlled human evolution. You have a right to know true freedom. You have a right to your position as a potent citizen of the Cosmos. You have a right to the Truth. *UNDERGROUND RISING* serves as a checkpoint, a source, a forum for the ideas upon which your true freedom depends. *Give humanity liberation or it faces obliteration.* The proceeds of all subscriptions to this newsletter go to the production and distribution of this newsletter and the cause it represents.

This newsletter is edited by noted author, lecturer, social theorist and psychotherapist, Dr. Angela Browne-Miller. Newsletter start-up date is September 1995. Annual subscription rate is $48 (includes six issues per year). Subscription orders mailed with the form below and post-marked prior to September 30, 1995 are available at the special start-up rate of $40. Please Xerox this form and fill out separately for each subscription going to a different address.

Mail to: Underground Rising, Metaterra Publications, 98 Main St., #315, Tiburon, CA 94920 USA

Name _____

Street Address _____

City _____ State _____

Country _____ Zip Code _____

Number of subscriptions I want sent to the above address _____

Rate per subscription (check one)   ☐ $40 *(prior to Sept. 30, 1995)*

NO CHARGE CARDS PLEASE. USE CHECK,   ☐ $48 *(after Sept. 30, 1995)*
CASHIER'S CHECK OR MONEY ORDERS.
$6 *(Add on outside US)*

Total enclosed (US dollars only) _____

Additional copies of this book,

OMEGA POINT,

may be ordered by calling:

1-800-247-6553

or by sending a check made out to:
"Metaterra Publications"

for $21.50 per book *($18.50 plus $3.00 postage & handling)*

to

Angela Browne-Miller, Editor-in-Chief,
Metaterra Publications
98 Main Street, #315
Tiburon, CA 94920 USA

PLEASE INCLUDE YOUR MAILING ADDRESS!